THE
BREAD
HOUSE

A NOVEL

**DANIEL
JOHNSON**

Beit Garmu Press
Mt. Gilead, Ohio

Published by Beit Garmu Press
Mt. Gilead, Ohio

www.thebreadhouseohio.com

ISBN: 978-0-6151-5983-6

Printed in the U.S.A.

September, 2007

L' Miryam Channah v'Yiskah

And now it comes, the point of all points, which the Lord has truly revealed to me in my sleep, the point of all points for which...

—*Franz Rosenzweig*

Prologue

Blessed are you, O Lord, the shield of Abraham.

Jaffa Port, Judea.
Early morning, 29 C.E.

Aquiet trek of people and donkeys worked carefully down the mount. Behind them, the sun was rising over the wheat fields and would soon crest, brightening the whole harbor below. With every rock that tumbled from *his* sandals, his eyes took guard in all directions. *He* could see the shadows of a few mounted soldiers just north of the docks where several small boats were moored. Not far out from the beach, small white caps broke the darkness at the rock reef where another small fishing vessel was coming around into port.

The town was mostly gone. Foundations of houses and shops of a once thriving merchant community were all that remained amid endless rubble...*again.* Through time each army took its turn with the town using the same old logic of taking and having by destroying, and then building a little on top of the rubble using the rubble itself. Now only the docks saw life with a few houses at the edge for loading and off-loading where ruffians repaired nets and hulls while they drank and traded schemes of piracy beyond the reef.

The women struggled to keep steady as their donkeys jerked on the loose terrain of sand and rocks on the downward path. Their men guarded the procession on foot. Out front, Miryam felt the care of her beast in its husky breaths and heaves. The smell of its hide arose from the back of its neck as an aroma of comfort and home in rural Galilee, now far behind. With her own care, Miryam held tightly onto small Sara. A head scarf covered the little one's face except for her wonderfully dark piercing eyes.

Sara was *Abyssinian*. The child had lost her previous family to the everyday horrors of the Romans in Jerusalem. Not many Jews, especially those on the run, would mark themselves by taking up such a foreign child, even if it was one of a fallen comrade. Sara, three years old, knew enough to feel fortunate for her new family. And now Miryam herself was pregnant for the first time. Everything was new and terrible. To ease her mind to the more pleasant, she would think of what name their unborn child should have—names she would keep to herself. If a boy, it would be *Daniel*. A girl, *Hannah*. But then the dream would evaporate into a wilderness of reality, and all was frightening and difficult again. Nonetheless, *he* was beside her, guiding the rope of the donkey with the others behind…at least until the docks.

At last sandals and hooves rested flat on the sand in the brush. Patting a knife tucked under his tunic belt covered by a mantle coat, *he* looked up and down the beach noting the soldiers still far off at the northern end. While his brother Yaakov and the rest of the Levites out of *Egypt* kept the donkeys in the brush and rubble, he hoisted a large leather bag upon his shoulder and with deliberate stealth crossed the beach with the women and Sara to a modest fishing boat just moored to the dock.

The boatman, an experienced and trusted Zealot, beckoned them wildly to hurry their boarding.

With Sara at his side, *he* steadied the women one by one into the boat. The craft bore no sails, but was long and broad enough to make the first leg of the voyage to Cyprus, then to Sicily, and beyond—if one was careful and had luck.

Miryam was deliberately last among the women, and faltered as her first foot came to the boat floor. Her head sagged and she heaved a short cry.

"Ima!" cried Sara, her small black arms outstretched to Miryam.

He gently guided Miryam's other limbs into the boat and she turned to take the arms of the child bestowed upon them by events and God. She drew the child closely to her breast as the morning sun itself came to port giving contrast to black and olive skin in a wholeness framed by the golden tint of the rock and ground above the beach.

The boatman barked eyeing the soldiers at the north end of the beach. They needed to go.

"Abba!" called Sara, expecting her protector to come into the boat. But he did not.

He stood for a moment just looking at Sara and Miryam, and the women whose eyes were wet with tears. They knew what the child did not. Kneeling down, he let the leather bag slip from his shoulder and it fell down to his hand. The tassels of his garment were momentarily caught up with the strap.

Miryam set the child down to help untangle the strings, tears-falling among the tangles and upon his scarred wrists. Their hands worked together as their eyes were fixed on each other.

The large bag bulged with a smaller bag of supplies to be added to those already in the boat.

Such a meager offering, bread and eggs, he thought. He took a flat round loaf out of the small bag. Quickly he closed his eyes, breathed deeply, and gave his own blessing, *Lahma Mahar*. His eyes came back to Miryam's.

She nodded. And they both ate a small bit of the bread.

"Lahma, Sara," he encouraged nodding with wide eyes framed by his cropped black hair, side-locks, and brown face. He held out a clump to her.

The child's small dark hands eagerly took the sweet bread to her mouth.

He returned a half-loaf to the small bag and gave it to Miryam. He then forcefully ripped up the remainder in his hands and cast it on the water beside the boat.

His mind was taken up into a whirlwind of memories. They were as heavy relics toted far too long. But his mind's eye saw them strongly new—There was the vision of all the world's kingdoms from atop the Temple pinnacle in the wilderness of *Egypt*—and the eternal question: *Were they his?...or not?* He remembered those stern pulsating moments when his mind, like a huge wheel, had spun up into the heavens—weighing possible actions and non-actions. He saw that awful day at the Temple when things went terribly awry. Tables, men, beasts and doves falling to the ground and against each other—fists and swords, blood and cries, death and running—the Romans hurtling across the Temple grounds from their barracks at all the commotion, but too late to lay hold of the Galilean *bandits*. And then that awful night, when the *Question* only became larger. Indeed. *Was anything his…or, was it all God's?* After the spilling of innocent blood at the Temple, what good now was his *cup?* He imagined throwing it down the Mount of Olives into the Kidron Valley below. All was in disarray.

"*Yeshua,*" whispered Miryam, smiling sweetly. She pointed to the bread on the water. A fish was busy gulping the crumbs.

His eyes widened and he nodded. And for the first time in a long time, he smiled. Then his eyes burst with the thought of a task yet undone. Reaching under his tunic, he removed the knife from his belt. Turning it over in his hands, he grimaced and shook his head. "*Hobha,*" he murmured to himself. And in an instant, he hurled the weapon in a high flung arc through the sky and he watched it dive into the sea.

Miryam took his hands into hers and nodded approvingly.

He put his hands on Miryam's belly and they kissed. At that very moment a dove descended and partook of the last bread on the water, and flew off again into the blue sky.

In a sun glint's flash upon a wave, the boatman jerked the rope and kicked the boat from the dock.

The sudden reality of parting struck terror to the child, and Miryam pulled Sara to her breast burying her tears into the child's robust hair.

"Abba!!!" the child screamed, bread falling from her mouth, her little black arms and hands reaching, shaking in the air for the edge of the dock with the sickening, disorienting backward motion of the boat taking her the *wrong way*.

He held out his own arms to his wife and child, his eye glancing over the thin leather *tefila* straps upon his right arm. Immediately he whipped off the straps attached to a pouch bearing the *Word of God* and threw it to them. It landed safely in the boat hull. He pointed to the *tefila* still on his forehead in memory of the promise to Abraham—*that would someday be fulfilled.*

The sun was strong in the sky, like a giant wheel on fire…moving too fast—the same sun he and his kinsman Yonah and the other Levites labored under in the wilderness of *Egypt*.

The soldiers were starting to move down the beach. The holy vessel pushed further out from the shore with Miryam and Sara—still crying, her little arms still reaching out.

He called out to them in a strong voice. *"Lahma Mahar! Tzi-yun Mahar! Tziyon Mahar!"*

Miryam's head nodded vigorously as she wiped her tears holding Sara tightly. She called out to him,

Where will you go?

Through the wind and waves, she heard one word,

Pella

Yeshua ran back to the brush and rubble. He and his men led the beasts quietly and methodically back up the mount. By the time they reached the top, he could see the boat clear the reef into the wide sea.

Chapter 1

You, O Lord, are mighty forever, you revive the dead.

Montra, Ohio.
Friday, May 18, 9:11 A.M., Modern Times

"JONAH!!!...JONAH!!!...JONAH!!! Madeleine called toward the church upon the mount. She could see him in the cemetery next to the old white clapboard sanctuary. The glint of the morning sun reflected off the silver church spire adorned at its pinnacle with a sphere, the roundness of which served to spray down streaks of light on the gravestones below.

Jonah was talking to a man. Hearing the call, he looked down the mount toward the brick ranch-style parsonage where Madeleine stood on the back deck beckoning him. He hesitated and held his hand up to signal he'd be coming in a minute...*or two.*

Her hands dropped and she turned abruptly back in her awkward maternity waddle through the sliding glass door.

Upon the mount, the man gave Jonah an armful of small American flags and waved his goodbye.

"Maddie?!!!......You Okay?" Jonah dumped the flags on the kitchen table, a little winded.

"Yeah....don't worry, Jo-Jo," she reassured. "The Bishop's Office just called and I thought you might want to take it right away. But, it's okay. They said you could call them back."

"Oh, I'm sorry," said Jonah brushing graveyard dust off his jeans. "I should have come. Roy was going on and on about everything I should do for the Memorial Day service. He wants the

Confirmation Class to place the flags over the vet graves during the service...."

Madeleine flipped back her long black hair from her dark piercing eyes. "Two more flags than last year," she sighed, gazing out the kitchen window at the mount of stones. "How many more will we need next year?"

Jonah nodded. "I know. It makes me sick too." His soft brown eyes agreed with his wife. He nervously scratched his close cropped beard. "So, what did the B.O. want?"

"Oh! His Highness summons The Reverend Jonah Van Meter!" Madeleine blurted, wheeling her hand mockingly in the air. She threw on a Levi's jean jacket over her pink scoop-neck top and rich magenta long stretchy skirt. Peeking from under her top was an ancient thin leather cord around her neckline. Her duds had a faded peasant look, but were all newly purchased maternity gear from *Stein Mart* in the big city of Columbus. To top off her pregnant-rebel look she shouldered a bright fuchsia mesh bag bearing a string of political buttons from a rainbow peace sign to a big black *W* in a cross-out circle.

"Oh, great," sighed Jonah with a look of stomach-quease. "Well, I'll just call him on my cell. I've got some visits to do in Wapak...What are you doing?"

"Well, I am going to the grocery store to get refreshments for the CROP Walk volunteers—which is also on Memorial Day, you remember?...we're hiking 12 kilometers...And, we need supplies for the communion bread baking you want to do in Confirmation Class tomorrow...And, I'm taking Motzi to the vet, ...and Oh! Remember also.... Margot and Hunter are coming over for lunch tomorrow."

"Oh yeah....Okay." *Nothing like in-laws to spice up the weekend.* "Uh...," Jonah put his hands together in mock praying fashion. "...Would you consider helping us out with the bread baking tomorrow?" He gave a pleading sheepish look.

"Well, sure *Baker Man!*" Madeleine laughed. "As long as we're usin' *Grandpa's recipe!*"

"Yup, *Grandpa's recipe!*" confirmed Jonah enthusiastically.

"Done deal!" she exclaimed. "Well, first to the vet. Mr. Motzi had another mysterious convulsion this morning." Madeleine struggled to lean her protruding belly over the kitchen sink to peer out the kitchen window at the tri-color basset hound flopped spread-eagle in the grass. Motzi laid beneath a huge locust tree next to the split rail fence of the neighboring horse farm. Madeleine eyed Jal and Rupa on the other side of the fence, galloping their ring. The horses were like big brother and sister to the hound. The neighbors let Madeleine ride them whenever she liked, and Motzi would always trip along for the jaunt as well. That was before Madeleine became pregnant. Motzi was now confused and barked at anyone but Madeleine who approached *his* horses.

"He's had a rough morning, poor baby....same thing....all of a sudden, his eyes roll back and his jaw locks open..."

"...and he rocks his head back and forth crazy?" added Jonah.

"Yep, the whole *megilla*. So, I am taking my baby back and I am going to make that vet do something. I don't know if there's something in the pesticides they use in the fields around here or what, but we need an answer to what's going on."

Jonah nodded. "I agree. What's Sara up to after school?"

"She'll have basketball practice 'til about five...Don't worry. She'll be back by sundown," assured Madeleine. "Gotta go. I'm late already."

"Okay." Jonah nodded. "I will definitely also be home before sundown." He kissed Madeleine gently and patted her belly. "Take care of all our babies."

She kissed him back. Her eyes smiled from the corner wrinkles of her soft olive-tone face framed by long black hair. To Jonah, she was beauty on a biblical scale.

Jonah headed west on Rt. 235. He buttoned the top of his clerical shirt and reached for the white plastic tab he always threw on the dashboard and popped it into place. In his rearview mirror, he could capture the whole little town of Montra, Ohio. A dozen houses, and a church.

Emanuel Lutheran Church sat high on the mount in the middle of Montra. Modest in size and style, it was built in 1865 by Huguenots and other Lutherans from the Rhineland and Palatinate between Germany and France. The parish was replete with folks of French and German surnames—bearing the culture of their European roots mixed with middle class Americana. Don McGee, a rare Irish-American neighbor down the road from the church, was good for giving Jonah an objective view of the area's history. McGee told Jonah the story about the heroes of Montra, Ohio: The Korn Brothers.

The story went: The Korn Brothers were early pioneers in aviation. While history gave the Wright Brothers exorbitant glory for being *First in Flight* in 1903, many locals complained that the Korn Brothers never received their due. One of the Korns' most important achievements came in 1908 when they invented one of the first *pusher-style* monoplanes. The term *pusher* referred to a configuration where the propellers were positioned behind the wings of the plane—thus *pushing* the aircraft. The Korn Brothers went on to build other planes and achieved a limited national reputation. But sadly, their flying days were cut short. Many of the area's old folk still remembered the day when the Korn Brothers crashed on their makeshift cornfield airstrip, formerly the site of the horse farm behind Emanuel's parsonage. Milton Korn was killed and his brother Ed broke a leg which never quite healed.

In general, most locals swore up and down that the Wrights just got top billing due to how the Korn family *wasn't none for publicity*. True to the old folks' sentiment, there was not much left in Montra from the Korns' old flying days, save Milton Korn's grave on the cemetery mount of Emanuel Lutheran Church. It was all testimony to the unruly relationship between official and *on the ground* history.

Jonah enjoyed being pastor to most of the parish folk. But in every barrel there are a few rotten apples—people bent on cultural war, looking for liberals to skewer. Jonah and his family were demonstratively comfortable with old people and kids, the handicapped and various social outcasts not on the approved list of ultra-conservatives.

As Jonah and Madeleine became increasingly associated with so-called *radical* concerns, critics plotted their ouster. In the dark corners of the parish, the small band of rotten apples would gossip about the Van Meters. It had happened before—to previous pastors like Barry, his wife Michelle, and their daughters Sasha and Malia. The gossipers would whisper: *The Van Meters are just like the last ones—Pastor Barry and his loud-mouth liberal wife, Michelle—They didn't last long either.*

One day, after Jonah had just taken the Emanuel pulpit, Pastor Barry called to give Jonah a heads-up on the parish pitfalls to avoid. He advised Jonah, half-jokingly and half not: *Don't drink the water...there's something in it.* Alarmingly, Barry and Michelle also had a basset hound which had periodic convulsions similar to Motzi's. Their dog eventually died. Barry warned Jonah about various people—known and unknown. The unknown: anonymous phone threats and hate mail; shadow-people in the night who would bang on the parsonage windows and shine flashlights into the house. Once, a swastika was nailed directly to the church door with a note ordering Barry and Michelle to leave. And then the known: People like Ida Belle Metz and her husband Roy, the head of the Building & Grounds Committee.

Overall, the Metz family was a proverbial lynchpin in the congregation. Old-timers would tell of the days when Emanuel did not have a proper church name. For several generations it was simply called *The Metz Church.* The original immigrant Metz family was apparently prosperous. They erected a church on their own land from their own funds, and procured their own family chaplain from the Lutheran seminary in Columbus. As time rolled on, the church gradually grew to look like a regular congregation. It eventually took on a regular sounding church name, and hired pastors through standard denominational processes. But still, the Metz family held much sway. By wide reputation, they were a family that saw most things in black and white. Indeed, Jonah was appropriately wary. He had already suffered his share of run-ins with Roy and Ida Belle. And he had his own inflow of anonymous hate mail. Creative soul that he was, he found use for it. No one but Jonah and Madeleine knew what the ashes for the annual Ash Wednesday Service were made from. They were *not* produced from the palms of the previous year's Palm Sunday celebration, as was the Lutheran tradition. On Ash Wednesday, Jonah took special care to *accidentally* smear ashes on Ida Belle's nose as well as her forehead.

Jonah's blue and white Dodge *Caravan* turned north onto I-75 and sped quickly over ten miles of wheat fields to Wapakoneta. A loose bolt on the rear license plate reading MOT ROM produced a low class clanging added to the dings, dents and paint wear of the high mileage vehicle. *Wapak*, as the locals called it, was a small island of civilization amid the vast flat square miles of farmland. It had at least one of everything from a grocery store—to a fast food place—to even a Chinese restaurant.

Jonah's destination was the Auglaize County Home on the north end of town. The ancient nursing facility was an august shabby Victorian brick structure with a high central arched doorway and tower above. The old relic was augmented on its flanks with a few new boxier additions of no particular design. Jonah always preferred to walk in through the old arched doorway.

"Hi Rebekah! How ya doin' girl!?

"Hey, Pastor Jo! How the heck are ya?" The young dark bob-haired receptionist jumped up out of her chair and around the counter giving Jonah a big hug, softly punching him in the arm. "Did you miss me? I just got back from Cancun. Nah, Nah, Nah." She did a little dance.

"Woman, what do you have to do with me?!!! I ain't had a vacation yet this year, and you're goin' all Cancun on me!"

"Oh, you should go to Cancun, Jo-Jo. You should. I swear. O my God! It is so beautiful...you-would-not-believe-it!" She went on to tell of the beautiful beaches and weather, the music and food....and the service. "It was fabulous!" she exclaimed. "But really Jo-Jo, I must confess. We were away on business."

"*Business!*? In Cancun?!"

"Well, Cancun *on the way back*."

"On the way back from *where?*"

"Honduras!" Rebekah stated proudly. "Ike and I are trying to adopt a little boy from Honduras through Jewish Family Services."

"Oh my! Rebekah! That's WONDERFUL!"

"Well. We're holding our breath, you know...trying not to get *too* excited yet. We went down and met this precious little boy, and the family, and all the agency people....and oh, we *really are* just so excited Jo-Jo...but still cautious...you know? We really have you and Maddie to thank for inspiring us...We know how well things have gone for you with Sara coming from Bosnia and the whole *megilla*."

Jonah listened intently. He listened especially to Rebekah's further explanation that many of the Honduran adoptees were from poor refugee families caught in the Central American conflicts of the 1980s.

"I would like to learn more about these children, Rebekah...maybe our Confirmation Class can do a special project on it. I'm determined to have the kids do some kind of service project...a *mitzvot*, if you will...in addition to just memorizing the catechism...I would like them to start memorizing what religion *is for*—huh?!"

"A-mein, Rabbi Jonah!...Power to the people!"

"Well, speaking of people—how's Jed and Barbara doin' today?" Jonah beamed.

"Actually, Jed and Barbara are doing great today. Your flock awaits you in the Activity Room. I think they are arguing over how they can make *The Wheel of Fortune* better."

"What?! Jed's not *dead* yet?!" Jonah laughed in celebration of the old man whose impending demise was constantly heralded by a daughter obsessed with the chronic shrinkage of her father's estate.

"Nope, not dead yet. But you better hurry...Jed's got a schedule, you know!"

Jonah found Jed Elsass and Barbara Weiss sitting at a round table. Jed's walker was handy by his side and Barbara sat in a wheelchair that she called her *wagon*. Indeed, she had a wagon wheel drawn in white on the back of the seat.

"*Rom San?*" intoned Jonah beaming at Barbara as he patted Jed on the back.

"*Ya...M.O.T.?*" replied Barbara.

"*Ken!*" cried Jonah, both of them laughing.

Jed just shook his head muttering, "I just wish to hell I could figur' out what yer sayin'!"

"Oh, Jed! Some day we will let you in on all the secrets!" Barbara laughed all the more, her heavy gold jewelry jingling in delight about her neck and wrists.

"Fine and dandy, Barbara. But don't wait too long!" Jed mused holding his finger up in the air.

Jonah laid down his Communion box with a couple of familiar paper sacks. He always brought extra bread, which he baked himself, for them to enjoy. It was much better than the standard stale and tasteless wafers. Jonah opened his box holding a small bread plate and wine glasses. He began.

"The Grace of our Lord Jesus Christ, the love of God, and the communion of the Holy Spirit be with you."
"And also with you."

The short liturgy went through a prayer to the consecration of the bread and wine. Then, followed *The Lord's Prayer*. When Jonah came to the words *Give us this day our daily bread,* he pinched a bit of bread and ate it. Then Barbara and Jed took their turn eating bread and drinking wine. But, Jonah only ate bread. He concluded the Communion with another prayer.

"Well, Pastor...." Jed slowly got up to lean on his walker. "Thank you very much for the service and the extra goodies, but nature is calling me...if you know what I mean. *Arivaderci!* I know what *that* means!" Jed held his finger up very pleased with himself as he turned to shuffle out.

"The *REDs* have only been playing about ten minutes Jed!" Jonah called to the back of the old man heading toward the doorway.

"Uh, huh," the old man confirmed just plodding along.

Jonah chuckled. "I think he knows more than he lets on," he confided.

"Yes, he does," replied Barbara with a wry smile.

Barbara remained with Jonah and gave him a motherly pat on his hand. She had been studying his face and saw stress. In the old days they called her *Dr. Barbara* for all the ways she helped people and their farm animals, especially horses, with many folk remedies passed down through the generations of her Gypsy family. One of Barbara's sons had continued the family healing tradition by becoming a chiropractor. Taking Jonah's hand, Barbara turned it over studying the lines. She looked deeply into Jonah's eyes.

"You are very worried about Madeleine and the baby, Jonah?"

He nodded. "Yup. I try not to be. But I am. Worry is an unavoidable family tradition."

Barbara nodded. "Well, Jonah. I know you too well. There is the worry that all have. And there is worry that *only the few* have for *certain reasons.*"

"Yup." He looked far out the window to the fields on the outskirts of Wapak.

"I too sense this danger, Jonah. Be very careful, my dear. Very careful. May God be with you…with you all."

Jonah nodded as he stood up. "And with you too." He kissed her forehead. "Gotta go, dear." He wheeled her *wagon* to the hallway and they said their goodbyes.

The *Caravan* sped south on I-75 with abandon. Jonah's brain raced in thought. His face and eyes were frozen tense. The back of his neck and shoulder blades were locked in ache.

Suddenly, out of nowhere, a car—a blue *Escort,* swerved in the next lane. The *Ford* part of the car's nameplate was missing leaving only two rusty holes. The driver, a grey-haired woman with old-style cat glasses, was juggling a cell phone. Another gery-haired woman in the passenger seat was holding an outstretched road map. Jonah remembered he had to make a phone call himself.

"Lutheran Church, Ohio District. May I help you?" answered Mrs. Steele, the District Office Manager.

"Yes. This is Pastor Van Meter in Montra. I'm returning a call from the Bishop earlier today." Jonah was put on hold. He was used to it.

Mrs. Steele returned abruptly. "I'm sorry. The Bishop has gone home for the weekend, but left instruction for you to speak with Pastor Holloway, his Assistant. He is on another line right now. Hold. He won't be long."

Ya vol, Commandant Steele! I'm always holding...always. And now I have to hold for Wal-Boy.

Wallerund DuBois Holloway. It was just *Wal-Boy* before he and Jonah were in seminary together. Jonah and Wal went way back. They were third cousins. They grew up together in the same church, the same neighborhood, and the same schools. But their temperaments were opposites. Jonah was common—an *average Joe.* Wal had ambition and was fiercely competitive. He always strove to top Jonah in all of life's rites of passage. When Jonah went to seminary, Wal went to seminary. But Wal's main concern was his own place in the world—his own status—his own future at being *special.* So, while Jonah's goal was to be a simple pastor in a small parish, Wal made no secret of his aspirations to someday be a Bishop.

Wal's ambition was a long way from the neighborhood that he and Jonah grew up in on the west side of Columbus, Ohio. Largely a blue collar area, its economy was comprised mainly of three large manufacturing plants: General Motors, Westinghouse, and International Harvester. If one did not work in the factories, that left mainly small shops and restaurants. Jonah's parents, Daniel and Zara Van Meter, owned a bakery with Madeleine's folks, Lazare and Mirella Lechem.

Wal's father, Lou Holloway, was a *regular guy*—a shop foreman at the General Motors plant. And Wal's mother, Renee DuBois, was an average housewife and part-time school crossing guard. But it was Renee's father—Wal's grandfather, Max DuBois—short for *Maximilien,* who was the *prima donna.*

Max lived in the Holloway home and held considerable clout over the entire family, especially Wal. Even Wal's first and middle names: *Wallerund DuBois* came straight from the Du-

Bois genealogy under pressure from Max who often informed anyone, even complete strangers, that he was descended from *Maximilien I* in sixteenth-century France—as if anyone should care.

Much about Max DuBois was a mystery to neighbors and even to Wal's family, but a few things stood out immensely. Max was very active in the local area Masonic Lodge and its youth group DeMolay as well as the Boy Scout Troop sponsored by St. John's Lutheran church where the Dubois, Van Meter and Lechem families were all members.

Grandpa Max was indeed a man of grand ambition...toward *something*....no one could figure out just exactly *what*. What people *did* know about Max was his intense interest in history, especially *genealogy*—in which he spent many hours instructing Wal.

In the Holloway house there was one special room devoted entirely to Max's world. He called it his *War Room*. The enclosure looked like a madman's tangled library full of books and papers and charts. Indeed, the walls were plastered corner to corner with charts of names and genealogical tree lines. Flaming arrows of red magic marker streaked wildly across the walls from one name to another. Accenting the names, in clusters to and fro, were photocopies of various family coats of arms— shields of lions and *fleur de lis* in varying colors and configurations.

Neighbors who knew about the room just laughed. *Max was nuts.* He took himself very seriously, especially when he claimed to be descended from French Royalty. Indeed, Max was a *presence* in the neighborhood. No one could ever figure what the hell he was about *or even if he knew*.

But Jonah and his father Daniel knew. They knew a lot.

The Van Meter Family had a *Secret*—a secret guarded and passed down for generations and centuries. It was a secret so immense, the family needed to keep the lowest profile possible. They *needed* to be *common*.

The Secret was dangerous—dangerous enough to be killed for. Jonah's mother, Zara, was lost to the evil adversaries of the Van Meter House when he was seven years old. It pained, haunted, and terrorized Jonah to no end that his brain had blocked out most of his memory of the event. It happened on a sunny afternoon in late summer. He was walking home with his mother from the corner market. And it happened. They were attacked. And all Jonah could remember was that he *ran*...and ran...and ran. And. His dearest mother Zara was never seen again.

After losing his wife, Daniel Van Meter obsessed about protecting the rest of the family and *The Secret*. In grief, he was haunted with the Question: *Am I responsible for Zara's disappearance?* But in prudence, he was extremely wary of Max DuBois. Daniel knew that Max understood a few things about the *Van Meter Family Secret*, but not anything near the *whole story*...and it was best to keep things that way. Thus, Daniel Van Meter's standing order to Jonah was: *Guard The Secret...and stay away from Max.*

Jonah was always 100% faithful to protecting the *family secret*, but he had an additional reason for staying away from Max. The stories in the neighborhood about Max's *War Room* had an eerie convergence to a reoccurring dream that Jonah often suffered—a dream that disturbed him immensely—a dream that Jonah tried his utmost to forget—indeed, flee from.

The dream was about a *man* in a *room*. Like Max's, it was a dark room with many medieval coats of arms high upon the walls. In Jonah's dream, the *man*, dressed in noble finery, always appeared very troubled as if *he was trying to decide something very difficult.* And the man's decision seemed all the more pressured as he was circled by ghostly women in silverish-white gowns, each chanting in Latin and carrying a silver orb in her outstretched palm. The dream always ended with Jonah bolting out the door of the dark room into the light— *running*...and running...and running for dear life. And then there would be his mother Zara's face...the last of her he could remember... smiling under the sun...just walking...walking...walking home.

Jonah's dream always made him nauseous—as did Max and Wal. So, Daniel Van Meter's admonition of avoidance made a lot of sense.

In the early years, Daniel explained *the family secret* to Jonah in stages over time. Daniel was always fully honest with his son. He never underestimated the boy's capacity to take in realities, because *capacity* just ran in the family. Every revelation made sense to the boy seeming to lodge in an already prepared home in his brain. The Van Meter family had a peculiar characteristic: *Memory.* With each new generation, *Memory* only grew *stronger* because the Van Meter family kept marrying into other families bearing genealogies similar to its own. Daniel foresaw this could very well happen with Madeleine Garmu Lechem, the daughter of his business partner Lazare Lechem. A future marriage between Jonah and Madeleine would produce a child having an unparalleled capacity of memory—the memory of the *Family Secret*—a memory that could change the world…someday.

Max DuBois also understood the potential inherent in a Van Meter-Lechem marriage. He thought about it a lot. It disrupted the flow of the genealogy charts in his war room terribly. The fearful possibility produced a jangling dissonance in his already mad brain, and left him sleepless many nights. And Max hated the Van Meters and Lechems for it.

The cold war between the Max and the Van Meters came to a head one night at Jonah's Cub Scout *Arrow of Light* ceremony. The ritual was performed for Cub Scouts graduating to their *Webelow* rank and was held in the church hall.

The ceremony was a rather spooky affair—actually a rip-off of Masonic rituals. Jonah and his fellow Cub Scouts were blindfolded and slowly guided into the hall. When they were brought to a stationary point, the blindfolds were removed. The boys found themselves in a dark cavernous room standing before lighted candles stuck in a log. The scoutmasters including Max stood in the shadows behind the candles.

When Jonah's blindfold was removed and he stared into the candles, his immediate reaction was a short snot-spraying laugh. "This is crap!" he muttered lowly to his friends, his shoulders and chest heaving trying to keep his laughter from bursting out.

Max saw and heard. And Max was pissed. He stomped directly around the candles, grabbed Jonah by the ear, and like a madman, dragged the boy out the door of the church hall.

Jonah was immediately frightened and furious.

Max slammed him up against the wall in the hallway.

The two screamed at each other at the top of their lungs with many a fancy epithet before folks rushed out to disengage them. The last words that came exploding out of Jonah's raging red face—that no one understood—*except Max and Jonah*—were in a foreign language:

LAHMA MAHAR!!!

Whatever the foreign words meant to Max, they struck him like a lightning bolt. No one had ever seen the old man's eyes go that wide before…before he slumped in slow motion to the floor like a gently falling feather, clutching his chest.

Max died.

"Jo-Jo, my man!" Although the reception was poor—due to a distant metallic clanging in the background, Jonah knew the voice.

"Yeah Wal. What's up?"

"Well, what's up Jo-Jo is that we've been getting quite a few…uh—how shall we say?…*complaints* from your people out there. The Bishop would like to have a little chat with you about it. Say….Monday, at eleven."

"What *kind* of complaints?"

"We'll talk about that Monday, Jo-Jo."

There was a long pause.

"Alright. I'll be there," stated Jonah tersely, controlling his voice with iron will.

"Don't be late Jo-Jo. You know how the Bishop hates to wait. Say *Hi* to Maddie for me! Take care, now. Buh-bye."

Done. Jonah's heart pounded. Sweat washed into his shirt under his sweater vest.

Exiting the ramp off I-75, Jonah turned the *Caravan* east onto Rt. 235 noting the sun landing fast behind him. He slapped his hand briskly against the side of his face and stroked his long thin pony tail on the back of his neck, hidden under the collar of his shirt. He made a solemn covenant with himself to get a grip before arriving home. To calm himself, he hummed an old Jewish song.

Shalom Aleichem
Malachei Ha-shareit
Malechei Elyon
Mi-melech malchei ha-melachim
Ha-Kadosh Baruch Hu...

At last Jonah came to Montra. Turning right, he proceeded on the small road leading into town, then left, and right again at the church where the lane started down the mount to the red brick parsonage.

As the sun was quickly fading, Jonah did not see the slight figure of Roy Metz putting the lawn tractor away in the shed on the mount overlooking the parsonage...and its large open kitchen windows.

All the house lights including the porch were shining merrily. An old white-wood wagon wheel planted in the front flower bed greeted Jonah as full-dark settled over the land.

Jonah hit the automatic garage door button and the *Caravan* skidded into port. For a minute, he just sat there absolutely exhausted. He jerked the insert from his clerical collar with great force and threw it on the dashboard. Coming to full consciousness, he finally got out and lept to the door leading into the kitchen. He tapped the *mezuzah* on the door jam, touched his fingers to his lips, and entered.

All was grand. Madeleine and Sara were setting the table. The air was warm with the aroma of roasted chicken and freshly baked bread—immediate tonic for his soul.

"Daddy!!!" exclaimed Sara running with her arms outstretched to wrap around him. Her coal-black hair fell over her dark bare arms jutting out from her basketball jersey. His arms wrapped tightly around his daughter and he kissed the top of her head and held his hand to her lovely face and dark almond eyes. He pulled Madeleine to them.

"So, how was basketball practice? Didn't pull anything to-night did you?"

"No, it's all good. I'll be ready for the Wapak game. Guess what!"

"What?

"I got an A on my speech in English!"

"On the *anti-death penalty* thing?"

"Yup. Mrs. Krites said she didn't agree with me and all, but I still did my arguments good."

"I'm not surprised, kiddo. Some day your *Jewish-Gypsy thinkin'* will set 'em all straight! Well. Time to do *The Candle Thing.*"

On the modest round wooden kitchen table stood a pair of unlit candles in silver holders. In the center of the table was a loaf of bread on a silver plate under an old white satin cover embroidered in gold thread with a *Star of David.*

Sara swiftly struck the match and lit the candles. Her graceful dark hands smoothly encircled the candles and drew the glow of the light to her face three times. Covering the top of her eyebrows with her hands, she said the blessing:

Baruch atah Adonai elohaynu melech ha'olam asher kidshanu bemitzvotav vetzivanu l'hadlik ner shel Shabbat.

Sara removed the cover from the bread and said the blessing:

Baruch atah Adonai elohaynu melech ha'olam hamotzi lechem min ha'aretz.

Sara took a piece of the bread and ate it. So also Jonah and Madeleine, and each kissed and embraced the other saying:

Shabbat Shalom.

As they were beginning to sit down to supper, suddenly there was a great clap of thunder and a streak of lightening over the mount beyond the parsonage. Immediately a great torrent of rain fell, and Jonah suddenly felt a strong sense of peace, as if the rain and the quiet sleep of the coming night promised to revive him from the perils of the day.

Outside in the dark, at the edge of the tree line on the mount, was Roy Metz. Through the parsonage kitchen windows, he had seen what he should have not seen. He made a run for this car entirely drenched and with very wide eyes.

Chapter 2

Blessed are you, O Lord, the holy G-d.

Washington, D. C.
Friday, May 18, 11:59 P.M.

Eduardo Mendoza's shoes skidded stairwell to street, down from the M Street Car Park above. He knew that he was late. It was a short hop to the M street entrance of Chez Paul's at the base of the old building. A quick pull of the door under a French lantern brought him instantly into a grand piece of Old Georgetown. A waft of good food greeted him, suitable to rich dark mahogany walls, tall and ornately carved Victorian mirrored mantles, and the flickers of antique lighting.

It took a moment for Eduardo's eyes to focus in the dim light as he looked around. Down the bar at its end, under the Tiffany chandelier, sat a man over a glass of wine. The *Postmaster*, they called him. His real name, Bill Blanche, suited him. He was indeed blandly white, tall, and thin in a drab brown suit, his formerly blondish hair giving way to fiftyish grey and the manila of onset balding. His head raised and eyes focused to the approach of his visitor.

"Sorry, I am late," Eduardo offered with a cheesy smile, and sat on the next stool, his back turned to the tavern door.

"Not too bad Eddie…your drive okay?…We should order you up something here," the *Postmaster* rattled.

"…like a whole bottle, Billy," replied Eduardo loosening his tie.

"I'm with you, *mon frere*. Nico," the *Postmaster* summoned the barkeep. "Would you just bring us that bottle of Bordeaux we've started for you?"

The small thin man with a goatee quickly obliged and the two men took their first drinks.

"Everything okay?" asked Bill.

"Yes….I guess. Sorry I am late. I was watching CNN, you know. I do it without thinking anymore. I just think I might see Toby in a troop story or something…he's stationed in Mosul. The last email I got from him, he said he is commanding some secret detail to bury the dozens of bodies they find every morning…that they don't want the press to know about. But I talked to Toby's wife Anne yesterday. She heard from him several days ago on the cell phone and she said he sounded fairly well. He misses his boy, Toby Junior, very much. He said he likes to think about when he and the boy would go fishing with their dog…about how one time Toby Jr. caught such a big fish and how it popped up at him out of the water flapping crazy and he thought it was attacking him…and the dog jumped on the big bad fish…and that was the end of the flapping!…and how they just cooked and ate that big fish…and how Toby taught his boy to save the fish innards for bait to catch more fish later in the day. Anne told me that she cried when she heard little Toby ask his Daddy on the phone if they could go fishing again someday."

"Hmm." nodded Blanche. "I understand. I have a brother too. But, I thought your brother's name was Carlos…"

"Oh, yes. It is. But, in our family we just always called him Toby, because his middle name is Tobias. I really fear hearing his full name, Carlos Tobias Mendoza—it has the sound of an obituary, you know?"

"hmm-hmm."

"But, it is like me—my middle name is Raguel, but Toby always called me Reggae—like the music, you know?"

"hmm-hmm."

"…But my mother had her own nickname for me. She always called me *Ekbatana* because she always put this oil we had in Honduras called *Batana oil* in my hair because of my dry skin…and I would always say *Ek!* So, she would call me *Ek-batana…*"

Blanche smiled.

"I can tell you, Billy…I really miss the old days and all the little family things, you know?—the family jokes and the made-up words that only *your family* knows…So, how is *your* family, Billy—everything okay at your house?"

"Fine…fine." Blanche nodded, taking a drink of Bordeaux. "Believe me, Eddie. I know what you're going through. It's not that different from when I was in 'Nam. It's just as tough on families here… just waiting to hear *something*….or *nothing*, and not know what the hell is better."

Eduardo nodded and nervously flipped his hand through his dark well cut black hair. His eyes shot up to mid-bar. The TV suspended over the highback mirror was on ESPN with a soccer game.

"Excuse me…," Eduardo called. The barkeep quickly sauntered back down to the end of the bar. "My friend. Would it be possible to change the TV to CNN?"

"For you, my friend…*my brother*…anything…anything at all," replied Nico with an overly accommodating look. He tapped Eduardo's left hand and gave a soft pat to Eduardo's chest just above his suit coat pocket. Nico flew to his task with an exaggerated backfield in motion and quick flirting back-eye. Eduardo was momentarily blushed.

"It's your hot Latin looks, Eddie," chided Bill with a wry smile.

"Actually Billy, I think it is my incredibly fine looking threads." Eduardo tugged playfully on his coat lapels and raised his glass to toast the brief levity.

Their eyes panned to the TV. Eduardo grimaced and Bill Blanche sat stone-faced as the CNN reporter cited another *Humvee* of US boys fire-blown to a heap of charred metal and dark red stain. The silence just hung.

It was an unusually warm night for May and the tavern door was open to M Street. The slow hum of the city night drifted into the bar converging with the soft paddle of ceiling fans and a few muffled conversations in darkened corners. And the TV flickered onward from bombs and blood to pitches for investment opportunities the prudent should certainly consider.

Bill rubbed his forehead and eyes taking a long drink of Bordeaux. He sat the glass down, gazing at his worn silver ring bearing the U. S. Army eagle and shield. The ring covered a long journey—from the Army Rangers in Vietnam, to Army Intelligence, to the Defense Intelligence Agency (DIA), to a long stint as a Special Agent for U. S. Immigration & Customs Enforcement (ICE), and now: Deputy National Intelligence Director. It was all basically the same as Ranger work back in 'Nam. It was all *Recon*—being small and unnoticeable, but probing…avoiding direct conflict, but ready to strike if necessary in very muddy situations. Certainly now, the U. S. borders presented a muddy recon job. Gone were the days when border police just fielded the daily game between Mexican body or drug smugglers and American farmers or pushers. *Now,* everything and the kitchen sink was coming across the border—Arabs, Iranians, Chechnians, Asian Muslims—they were all the new backdoor tourists of America. Exactly *what* to recon was the question. Bill Blanche hoped his new association with Eduardo, a young DIA analyst, would prove helpful in the special project they were charged with. Eduardo's specialty was cyber-intelligence.

Blanche and Eduardo were specially drafted by Ashman Blackpoint, the head of a covert intelligence group. While Blanche was a Deputy National Intel Director, Blackpoint had no fixed relationship to that cumbersome bureaucracy—nor to any of its sixteen agencies. Somehow, Blackpoint had the authority to simply float…in, with, and under any agency he wished. He worked directly for the White House. Blackpoint told Bill Blanche that he selected him because his profile demonstrated a certain keen ability to synthesize information from disparate sources. Blackpoint liked that. He believed in it.

On the other hand, Eduardo had a *special* history with Ashman Blackpoint. Eduardo's father, Jose´ Karo Mendoza, a native Honduran, had worked for Blackpoint in Honduras in the 1980s. At that time, Blackpoint was an intelligence operative during the *Contra* episode. From his base in Honduras, Blackpoint facilitated the staging of CIA-backed squads which made incursions into Nicaragua to attack the leftist Sandinistas. Many innocent non-combatant civilians were caught in the carnage.

Indeed, Eduardo's father had been specially trained at a secret US military school in Georgia. Although Eduardo was born in Honduras, he grew up with this younger brother Carlos at the Georgia base. In many ways, they were typical military brats. They owed a lot to the US military. When their father died tragically in a car crash in the early 1990's, the family was very well taken care of. Blackpoint himself called Eduardo's mother and assured her that the boys would be provided for. And they were. Carlos went to West Point and Eduardo went to the University of Chicago, where Blackpoint's brother Andras Blackpoint taught courses in *Communication* and *Viral Technology.*

The word *viral* referred to emerging technologies whereby individuals *and groups* constituted themselves on a wide horizontal scale rather than the old *top-down* paradigm. The simple illustration of the *viral idea* was the wireless cell phone—one cell could connect to any other cell close enough to pick up a signal—as opposed to the old-style telephone literally wired to other phones through a central telephone company.

Bill Blanche was not very technical, but he was known in the intelligence community for having an uncanny type of *memory.* It wasn't the kind of photographic memory one would read about in pop novels. And it wasn't the *profiler*-type in TV detective shows with specially-gifted mediums who know things that only ghosts should know. No, Bill Blanche was *workin' class.* He did things *the old fashioned way*—he just figured them out. His friends called him *The Postmaster* for a reason. Once, when asked how his brain was able to sort through so much far flung and disparate information and then corral it to a useable theory, he responded by telling the story of how he worked in his small town post office during high school. Every morning before school, he would sort the mail into the boxes behind the P.O. box-wall. Over time, he would learn a lot about people from the mail they received. The amount of information one could examine on a daily basis from *just mail* was staggering—from the names of the senders—companies, religious organizations, governmental offices, law offices—late notices from utilities and mortgage lenders—all kinds of merchandise—newspapers and magazines from the *Wall Street Journal* to porn. A myriad of names, places, dates, amounts weighed and paid…over time, day by day, sifted and settled into a brain's portrait of those receiving the mail…and their connections to the world at large. It was *simple*. Bill Blanche joked that his brain did *by hand* what computerized postal sorting machines did by automation. He said that sometimes he heard the sound of *shuffling* in his head—a constant ticking of data—like cards and envelopes being shot into slots. Indeed colleagues said they could *see the shuffling* in Blanche's sharp steel-blue eyes.

No doubt, in addition to Blanche's previous border control work, his legendary capacity figured highly in his being chosen by Blackpoint for a very secret project extremely crucial to the White House. As Blackpoint needed the *project* to float—as he himself did, he was keen to handpick his lieutenants. They needed to be persons who were *not* locked to any single intelligence agency. But, Blackpoint's selectees also needed to be *discernable* and *controllable*. Blanche's diverse intelligence background and demonstrated loyalty to authority, and Eduardo's family history with Blackpoint fit the task entirely.

"Well, my friend. The *War on Terror* continues." Blanche hoisted a brief case up onto the bar. It looked normal enough—common black leather exterior, but wired to the hilt with GPS tracking and electro-shock theft deterrent. Blanche deftly coded numbers to the digital locks and the latches sprung. He spread three files out on the bar, and gave a quick glance over the entire room to the front door, taking note of the flew clumps of people in shadowed corners.

"We've got some weird incoming cross-border shit…and it comes with a murder already. Actually two….maybe more. We'll have to see," stated Blanche.

"…must be something special about the murdered people?— to call me out here tonight?" asked Eduardo.

"Yes. Of course. The White House is acutely concerned. It's on top of the stack. So here's the deal Eddie…we have this chap." He picked up the first file and opened it to several pages of in-house ICE memo text and photos.

"Who's that?" quipped Eduardo.

"THAT....is Giovanni Nogarro. He was a mid-level dirt bag who worked a long time with other dirt bag errand boys for things the Vatican needs done *quiet like*. Our intel on him shows him associated with the *Knights of Malta,* the *Vatican Secret Archives*, and a bunch of other secret Vatican crap. So anyway. Gio here, killed this fella." Bill slapped open a second file. "THIS is Bruno D'Anusteleos. He was attached to an interesting organization: *The Sovereign Order of The Temple of Sion.* It's official headquarters are in Zurich—but they're all over Europe...somewhat in the US and looking to expand beyond. They're one of several whacko groups that claim descent from the medieval *Templars*—you know that whole story?"

"Yes, yes. I've seen the books and the movies."

"Well, yeah. So...anyway. This group...It's actually a break-off of an older group...but seems to be on a roll...they seem to have a lot of money and backing from God knows where—but we need to know. So, we're in the process of developing resources for that knowledge."

"So...." replied Eduardo, "the Catholic-guy killed the Templar-guy. Right? From the movies and the *History Channel*, I know the Catholics and the Templars have been at each other for a long time....all the stuff about whether Jesus was married and had a *Bloodline* of descendants....and so then...it is all the same war, yes?"

"Maybe...it's hard to tell at this point," said Blanche.

"So, are they working on the Catholic?"

"No. The dude was in custody in Boston's city jail less than 24 hours...and somebody Jack Rubyed him."

"Shot him?"

"Poison."

"That makes sense," Eduardo quipped. "It is a specialty with those guys...if you watch the TV shows... you know...like that pope that only lasted three months...a little magic dust in the Pope's tea....a quick embalming and burial with no autopsy, and presto—new pope!"

"Yeah, yeah, yeah. I've seen the shows." Blanche nodded.

"So what the hell is the issue Billy?…got any ideas?"

"Well, it's pretty damned weird. And so, this is where your research techno-magic comes in. *These two guys*…we have our guys go over all their stuff completely of course, and bingo—we get one link between them. They both had documents. *Very similar* documents."

"What kind of documents?"

"Well that's where the weird part comes in. They both were carrying genealogical family tree documents of *the same family* in some damn little farm town in Ohio. And so, they both had one-way tickets to Dayton—the nearest major airport to where this family lives."

"*Genealogical* records? *Ohio*?!"

"Yeah. Ohio. A tiny nowhere place on the western edge of the state…you know one of those towns that have two roads that cross each other and that's it…?"

"Yes…I was born in one of those in Honduras."

"There you go…"

"So, who are the people in these genealogical records?"

"It's a couple. Their names are Jonah and Madeleine Van Meter. The records on him go back way into medieval times, and hers…her maiden name is L-e-c-h-e-m—not sure how to pronounce it, goes back about the same"

"So….like…What do you know about them?…anything?"

"Well, from just an initial search: He's a parish pastor—a Lutheran pastor…and she's his wife. And that's all we know."

"*Lutheran*! Why the hell would Catholics and Templars be chasing a Lutheran pastor and his wife out in *OHIO???*…out in the farm land…what you call it…*rural*, whatever?"

"Don't have a clue, Eddie. I've not seen *mail* like this before either. But the White House wants to know right quick—they've made anything weird in the way of religion coming across the borders a top priority. So again, this little project has especially high priority. So. Here's what I need from you. First, you need to spend some major cyber time on these people—this Van Meter family and their genealogy lists. Second, I want you to fly out to this little mudhole personally and dig like hell. Get the story....no ifs, ands, or buts. We're not fucking around here. Get it. Third, I want you to find somebody who knows what the hell they're doing with genealogy stuff...somebody we can trust...somebody who knows why genealogy and religion and Templar crap should be important enough to kill somebody..."

"You mean also kill these *Van Meter people*?"

"Maybe. I don't want *you* in the middle of that....you let the locals handle that shit...if you want to leak warnings...do what you think you have to do...I don't want these people dead...I want to know what they know."

"Well, that's pretty straightforward Billy..."

"Well, I'm just delivering the *mail*. I'm not sorting it...*yet*. But I've got another thing for you to run down. The Templar guy had something on him the Catholic didn't. He had a program for a theological symposium at a Lutheran seminary in Columbus, Ohio. He had circled a speaker: a Mr. Sabeel Khouri."

"Huh? That does not sound...*Lutheran*? Does it? I know it's not Latino!"

"Well, yeah. Actually it *is* Lutheran. The program indicates that Mr. Khouri is a *Palestinian* Lutheran businessman who lives in Jerusalem. His speech was entitled *Ending the Zionist Era.*"

"Oh, that's why the White House is so hot...it's the *Israeli-Palestinian* thing, yes?"

"Get to work Eddie."

Chapter 3

Blessed are you, O Lord, the gracious giver of knowledge.

Montra, Ohio.
Saturday, May 19, 6:16 A.M.

Jonah dreamed his old dream again. The dream he didn't want to dream. The dream about *the man who was his ancestor*...the dream about the *running:*

The man sat there. In a chair of rich ornamental tapestry, he sat sideways with the side of his head against the back of the chair and his eyes fixed to some unknown spot in the weave of the dark and kingly rug beneath his feet. Against the dark medieval mahogany walls flickered the light of candles intentionally placed at certain points for a ritual going on, quite independently, around the man in the chair. The women circled rhythmically and effortlessly in their silverish gowns bearing orbs out before them on the palms of their hands. With every rise of their soft and ghostly chant, the eyes of the man in the chair became more frantically pensive. His eyes traced the long line of *coats of arms* ringing the upper walls of the room. Each one was a little different in color or design. Some had lions. Some had *fleur de lis.* But altogether, the ensigns of dominion of one clan or the other, seemed all the same... to the *man in the chair.* His eyes twitched as he gazed hard into the dark reddish colors of the rug below. The chant of the women and the brush of their tresses silently enraged him. Sweat dripped from his forehead like drops of blood. He shook, but so fast, no one would have been able to tell if he was moving at all. *The man in the chair* was trying to *decide* something: A Question...a question that no one among his kin and kind had deliberated upon in a very long time.

Next to the chair was a small table bearing a regal silver carafe of wine and a goblet. Following habit, he poured into the goblet and raised the vessel to his nostrils. But suddenly, his head jerked sideways from the cup. His eyes glared at his own hands holding the nectar of privilege....*to dance for*? *To rule the world by*? His eyes flashed fire—they plunged deep down into his own forgotten soul. His mind's eye saw his arms and hands pulling upon his lost soul—pulling it up as clean water from a deep well—pulling it up from the *forgotten*—to the *remembered*. And. The *man in the chair* stood. His eyes pierced. His rage boiled. And he exploded. He hurled the cup and its dark splashing *blood* like a grenade into the vacuous coven of silver witches—white-washed vampires, circling mindlessly...he bolted from the room, throwing the doors behind him with a violent sound of splitting and cracking wood...like *pops* in a wood fire. Out he stormed. Out of the dark...into the light...running...running...running.

Jonah woke.

He was fully awake and fully aware of his mind's night journey. Sitting on the edge of the bed, Jonah looked out the bedroom window up towards the mount of cemetery stones. He recited the *Shema*.

Maddie slumbered, but turned on her side. The *tefila* around her graceful neck fell out from her nightshirt, its small pouch bearing an ancient promise was hanging from her heart on a thin cord. She turned several times muttering in a dreaming turmoil. Her night was still on. Jonah studied her eyes. They were tight. *Not good dreams...either*. He gazed over the contour of her body under the soft bed quilt handed down by Bubbie Lechem. It was made of alternating squares depicting moons, Stars of David, roses, menorahs, and horses. Beneath its warmth and protection lay the unknown future, indeed *the future of the world* ...the future under the past.

Within a half hour, Jonah's shoes were scraping up the lane to the church. The sun was just coming up over the cemetery mount and hit the orb on the steeple pinnacle. Jonah gazed at it. His night dream of witches and their orbs hung on. He knew that the *Question* of the *man in the chair* was becoming his own question. Truly. He had spent so much time over the years trying not to think about it....*Heaven's sake!*...he had a *higher calling...no? A baby on the way*! But staring at the orb, he knew it was all the same thing. The baby and the orb. *To us a son is given. To us a son is born.*

Jonah tore open the double doors of the church and stormed to the very center of the sanctuary. He stared at *Jesus*—standing on the altar, a statue of plaster and paint. His gaze and outstretched nail-pierced hands rayed down with the morning sunlight streaming through the stained glass windows.

"WHAT?!"

Jonah bellowed at the statue. "NOW?!!! NOW??? ME?!!!! Or MY SON!? OR HOW 'BOUT JUST MY WHOLE DAMN FAMILY!!!???...Okay! So, you've waited a long time...fine...I understand....But you know, waiting isn't all *that* hard, now is it?...You could wait another couple hundred years, couldn't you? Another fifty maybe? Okay. Where, you wanna start? Let's do like they do in the *suq...Please...Sir...Special deal for you. You like? Special price for my American friend, yes?"*

The statue stared back in silence.

Jonah descended the stairs to the church basement. It was a spare two room hall with a slight mildew smell. The larger part was a rudimentary multi-purpose room with a concrete floor. Everything had the look of stark utilitarianism. Flimsy tattered vinyl curtains on cheap ceiling tracks were utilized on Sunday morning to make classrooms for Sunday School. The walls bore posters with cartoon pictures of Bible personages and lyrics to familiar Sunday School songs...*This Little Light Of Mine* and *What A Friend We Have In Jesus.*

As soon as Jonah entered the kitchen at the back of the basement, and turned on the light, he heard the sound of kids bolting through the front doors above. Their laughter filled the narthex and rolled merrily down the steps along with their thundering feet.

There was Jessica Schenck and Shaun McGee who were an item; and then Shaun's incorrigible 7 year old little brother, Liam—if ever a prototype for a smart-mouthed Irish elf, it was Liam. There was neo-hippie Katt who wore wild colors and black '60s style cat glasses; and Tucker—a mild studious looking boy with a dry wit. And then there was Sara.

With Madeleine, they rolled loud into the kitchen and accosted Jonah.

"Pastor Jo....guess what?!" was Katt's set up.

"What?"

"Well, the class got together you know...and we all decided that we want to make Communion animal crackers...you know—lions, tigers and bears, OH MY..."

"...yeah, and elephants!—the big Asian kind!" exclaimed Sara.

"...and warthogs!" chimed Tucker.

"..and CATS!" cried Katt. "We will have Communion Cat Crackers!!! Big Furry Fat Cats!!!"

Jonah joined in. "And Communion Buffalos...how about Buffalos?...I'm always partial to nearly-extinct species."

"Yeah, Buffalos!!!" screamed little Liam.

"Well," said Jonah. "If there's any dough left after the bread we have to make for SANE people, you can make whatever creatures you want!"

"Yeaaaaaaah!!!" went the chorus.

Madeleine hoisted up the grocery bags of raw materials on the kitchen counter and started giving marching orders to each kid. Within 15 minutes she had each kid positioned around the table in the middle of the kitchen supplied with flour, yeast, eggs, water, salt, brown sugar, honey, and a packet of "secret" spices which Tucker was given special watch over. The measuring and mixing began.

As the sound of long spoons beating the sides of bowls set in, another set of clunking footsteps was heard coming down the stairs. By the sound of the shoes on the concrete floor, Jonah knew who it was. He looked up.

Ida Belle Metz stood in the doorway of the kitchen. Her fists posted on the angular hips of her house dress, she surveyed the whole operation with a piercing eye under her gray beehive hairdo.

"Hi, Ida Belle!" called Madeleine in a cheery voice. "Would you like to join us?! We're making Communion Bread for Sunday! The kids are doing a GREAT job!"

"So, I see." replied Ida Belle with an uncanny split-eye to Maddie and to the children. "Yes," she abruptly continued. "I thought I might come down and see if I could lend an *experienced* hand...." Ida Belle sided up to Katt, who stood next to Sara and Tucker. With a smug smile she bent condescendingly to Katt to inform, "I've baked quite a few loaves in my day."

Katt nodded, leaned over to Sara and whispered, "No elephant crackers today, girl!"

Sara rolled her dark eyes.

The rest of the kids, a bit annoyed by Ida Belle's sudden intrusion, just looked at each other sideways. And Jonah took a fine accounting of all the psychological undertones throughout the room.

"How we comin'?...are we getting it all mixed up?" Jonah called to the gang.

"Looks like bread making to me! Good and messy!" sang Madeleine as she whiffed away a cloud of flour from all the whirling spoons. Flour was getting all over the table and floor.

Little Liam, whose spoon was longer than his arm, huffed and puffed working his mix and said, "This sure is very, very sticky! How does it turn into bread Pastor Jo?...Does God do something to it?...like wave his giant God-hands and then poof! It's bread now?!"

Everyone laughed. Except Ida Belle.

Liam was the Sunday School clown. Jonah and Madeleine were happy to have him and his big brother Shaun as the sole happy representatives of the Irish in the area.

"Something like that Liam!" cheered Jonah. "You'll see how we make bread. We'll make it in a very old way…with the special spices that Tucker is going to put in our bowls pretty soon. And yes, God has quite a bit to do with it…you'll see."

"Ummmm! This already smells yummy enough to eat!" called Katt beating away.

Liam reported that he had already tried it.

And Ida Belle slowly mixed her bowl while her eyes panned like a security camera.

"I think I'll try some more," chirped Liam as he dipped his tiny index finger into the dough and then to his mouth in razor sharp fast little boy speed. "Yes, it is very good. Yes it is. I wonder if it is good for babies!?" He ran over to Madeleine and put his finger to her belly. "How do you like the bread baby?" Liam nodded like an elf. "He likes it!"

Almost everyone laughed. Ida Belle smiled weakly.

"How do you know it's a boy Liam?" chided Jessica.

"Oh, Liam knows everything," assured Shaun.

"Yes, I do!" nodded the little boy.

"Well, actually……" Madeleine led in an amused tone.

"WHAT???!!!" Jessica blurted. "It IS a boy?!"

"Uh…huh…" Madeleine beamed as she looked straight down stirring into her bowl. Everyone looked at Jonah and he just nodded and grinned.

For a moment, all his fears about the pregnancy and future of the boy and the *family secret* melted away. In the godly mist of flour-dust and children's laughter he felt the whole room transfigured into a shining white cloud of normalcy and hope.

"You know Mom, I still think it could be BOTH a boy and a girl!" Sara called out as she flipped a piece of dough at Tucker.

"Oh Geez, Sara! Give me break!" exclaimed Madeleine laughing.

Ida Belle Metz slammed her spoon down and frowned. Looking directly at Madeleine she said, "The word *Geez* sounds too much like *Jesus* for my liking."

There was a long silence. Only the clicking of spoons on the sidewalls of bowls stirred the air.

Ida Belle continued, "We always just said *Gee Willakers* when we got excited… when we was kids."

Sara glared at Tucker and put her whispering lips to his ear, "I hate this bitch."

Tucker's eyes lit up with a huge wince.

Madeleine nodded with eyes staring directly down into her mixing bowl. "Yes, of course Ida Belle. You're right. That's a good thing for us to remember. Thank you for reminding us."

Jonah could not believe Madeleine's capacity for restraining anger. She had iron control in a way he knew that he could only strive to emulate.

"This is SO cool!" Liam sparked away the silence. "Another boy just like me!"

"Well, let's not go THAT far, bud!" retorted Shaun.

All of a sudden Liam's eyes screwed up sideways with a question that popped out his mouth. "Pastor Jo and Maddie? How did you learn to make bread? Did God teach you?"

The two simultaneously laughed.

"We grew up in a bakery my dear," replied Madeleine with wide smiling eyes to the little boy.

"You did?! You *lived* in a bakery? Like, you slept with donuts every night an' you could eat 'em anytime you wanted?!" The boy's eyes jumped as he hopped and rubbed his tummy.

"…just about Liam! We had to get up pretty early to make donuts and sweet rolls and bagels and all kinds of bread and cakes. Pastor Jo and I used to do a lot of this same kind of mixing in the morning before we went to school…"

"You were *married* when you were kids?!!!!"

Jonah and Madeleine burst out laughing.

"No, no, Liam…don't you start getting ideas about girls at such a young age," laughed Jonah. "Maddie's parents and my parents owned the bakery together….they were good friends. Our fathers met each other during World War II when they were in the Army, in France. They met each other in a cemetery in an area called Pas-de-Calais—on the northern edge of France. The neat thing about how they met is that they were both on leave…that's like recess at school, from the Army…and they both had it in their mind to find the gravestone of a great, great, great grandfather. And guess what?"

"What?" The boy's eyes danced.

"They were both looking for the *same* stone! They both had the *same* great, great, great grandfather!"

"WOW! Hmm...," the boy pondered. So like, they were in the same family? Like cousins or somethin'?...and so like, you and Maddie are like cousins too?"

Jonah and Maddie looked at each other with weak grins.

Tucker snickered. "Yeah, that's why Sara's a little high strung and weird..."

Sara slapped Tucker on the side of the head and threatened to knee his underworld. "I'm adopted. Thank you very much!" she play-huffed.

Ida Belle's eyes, hyper alert, twitched this way and that, as if she were a spy taking notes of the proceedings of a *secret* meeting.

Madeleine nodded to the little boy. "Yes, Liam—a little bit *cousins*...they call it *distant cousins.* But just remember young man: In every house....The Momma's always in charge!"

"Oh, I know THAT!" Liam nodded quickly.

Jessica asked a more advanced question. "Do your parents still have the bakery? Where is it?....What's it called?"

"No, sad to say....," replied Madeleine. "Our folks are all gone now, and the bakery was sold...and now it's gone altogether—well, it's in our house now. But the bakery was in our old neighborhood on the west side of Columbus. The name of our bakery was *The Bread House*....because we specialized in bread...especially *THIS* bread which comes from an old family recipe that we've kept a secret in *MY* family, the Lechem family, for many, many generations. We're like *Colonel Sanders*...we won't give up the 12 secret herbs and spices to anyone!"

"*The Bread House!*" Jessica replied cheerily. "I like that! If I had a bakery, I would call it *The Bread House*."

"Yes, it is a catchy name," Madeleine smiled wryly. She gave her bowl a few last stirs and cast a side-gaze to Jonah, her dark long hair framing her perfectly oval face and bare soft shoulders under her peasant blouse. "Okay," she ordered. "Time to form the loaves…we do them, by old family tradition, in twos…" In no time she showed them the way to knead and form the dough into boat-shaped loaves.

Ida Belle followed along silently, kneading and eyeing this way and that, her eyes darting in strobes between her dark thoughts. The laughter and banter of the children made her head hurt.

"So Maddie…..?" chirped up Liam again.

"Yes……." Madeleine slowly played into him…smiling in wonder of what next he'd throw out.

"What'cha gonna name him?"

"The baby?!" Madeleine beamed as she vigorously kneaded the dough. Jonah's eyes latched to his wife's across the table. "Well. Our son's name will be Daniel Lazare Van Meter."

"Why those names?….*Lazare*! I never heard of *Lazare*…I've heard of *lazer* beams…spoooeah, spoeeah…." The boy finger-gunned the rest of the kids. Liam prattled on, "But I've heard of *Daniel* in Sunday School…in the lion's den…they thought the lions would eat him up, but they didn't!"

Madeleine laughed. "Well, Liam. We are glad you listen in Sunday School…that is an important story. But the main reason we picked those names is that *Daniel* and *Lazare* were the baby's Grandpas. *Daniel* was Pastor Jo's father, and *Lazare* was my father's name!"

Ida Belle's darting eyes landed on Madeleine's. A sick half-smile crossed Ida Belle's countenance.

"I am surprised Maddie—being in the *Christian* ministry as your family is, that you didn't consider a *New Testament* name." Ida Belle's lips pursed with satisfaction at the barb.

Jonah took up the cause. "It's an old Huguenot tradition, Ida Belle…the Huguenots always named children after grandfa-thers….and they preferred Old Testament names in order to stress the long history of the People of God….it was a kind of quiet rebellion-thing in their day to protest the corruption of the Church at that time…"

"*Huguenot*?" Ida Belle's eyes questioned large and passive aggressively.

"Yes, *Huguenot—French Protestants.* You, Ida Belle, along with most folks here, probably came from Huguenot families. The group typically came from the border areas around Alsace-Lorraine and the Palatinate between France and Germany."

"But your last name, Pastor....*Van Meter*...that does not sound French or German....I always thought names with *Vans* were Dutch," challenged Ida Belle with a correcting tone.

"Yes. That's right, Ida Belle. The Huguenots traveled up from Southern France to Northern France and then to Holland where there was greater religious tolerance. It was like a wagon train that all kinds of people who wanted freedom just jumped on. And, mixed in with the French Protestants were also a lot of Jews and Gypsies that just sort of blended in and went along for the ride. It happens a lot in history. People just do *what they have to do*...for a better life...for their children. So...the Van Meters married into one of these French Huguenot families that came up the trail into Holland...the French family was Du-Bois...from the Pas-de-Calais region. And it's also interesting—to me at least, that Pas-de-Calais was a major area for wheat farming—excellent farm land for it....with a great port right at the city of Calais. So actually, there's a lot of connections there with wheat and baking and the Van Meter and DuBois families."

"But I thought Maddie said the *secret recipe* came from *her* family," pressed Ida Belle. "What was the name of your family, Maddie?"

"Lechem...L-E-C-H-E-M."

"Hmm, *Lec...hem,"* Ida Belle tried to enunciate the foreign-sounding name out. "Never heard of *that one* before. And what background is that name, Maddie? *French* as well?

"*Jewish*, actually," replied Madeleine, softly touching the *te-fila* cord under the collar of her blouse.

"JEWISH?!" Ida Belle stopped kneading and looked directly at Madeleine's medium wide eyes and half-smirk. "How does JEWISH fit into your family?"

"...Well....like Pastor Jo said....a lot of people joined the Huguenots when they traveled north from the south of France, and then into Holland. Jews and Gypsies, or as we say in the other half of my family—*Roma*...my mother was Roma...her last name was Masic…it's an Eastern European Roma name. And of course, Sara's native country of Bosnia is the same area….Sara is Roma…and look where she is today!….captain of her basketball team in Montra, Ohio! So, if you look at my mother's family and Sara's biological family…they traveled an immense distance over time from Eastern Europe to Southern France to Holland to America…..and that's not even counting the greater travel the Roma did *before* they came from Europe…the Roma…or Gypsies…originated in INDIA!"

So, Pastor Jo?" Liam interrupted. "So like, are we making Jewish Gypsie bread?"

Jonah burst out laughing with Madeleine and Sara all combined.

"Yes, Liam!" exclaimed Jonah. "Correctamundo, buddy!— *Jewish and Gypsy and Everyone From Everywhere Bread!* You know, that's the way Jesus was thinking when he taught people…..like in the *Lord's Prayer*…You know the part where Jesus prays *Give us this day our daily bread?*…Well, he was speaking in Aramaic, which was the language the Jewish people used at that time. And actually, what we translate as *daily bread* means something a little different in Aramaic—the Aramaic words are *lahma mahar* and those words mean *bread for the morrow* like in *tomorrow*…and the next day, and the next day after that…So, what Jesus is telling people is to keep thinking about the bread that *all people* need day after day. That's why Jesus was always teaching people by eating with them. He was teaching them that God wants all people, whether they are Jewish or Greek or Gypsy or Black or Hispanic or Asian or whatever, to someday, sit around the same table and eat the same bread…So you see, for Jesus, bread was a symbol of togetherness…of all people…which makes sense because everybody loves bread of some kind, you know…every culture has some kind of story about bread….like the Gypsies….they have a tradition about carrying bread in their pockets for good luck…."

Liam shot in, "And if they get hungry at school or something, they can just sneak it out when the teacher isn't looking!…"

"Or offer the teacher a piece too, Liam!" taught Jonah.

"Yes, I always like to bribe my teacher. That is a very good idea, Pastor Jo!"

"Well, you gotta do what you gotta do, my man! Like David in the Old Testament! One day, he was so hungry...so hungry, he thought he was about to die! And so he asked the priests in the temple for the special bread they kept only for God. So they gave it to him and he ate it. And he lived! And so that's a good example of how everything we need, like bread, comes from God..."

"God had special bread in the temple???...was it like super yummy, the yummiest of all???!"

Jonah's eyes went wide. "Right you are, my man! Yes, it was a very special yummy bread with honey and special spices and it was baked in a *secret* way to make the bread very, very special...It was one of the ways the Jews reminded themselves that God was the most special of all. They baked twelve special loaves every week and kept them in the temple on a special golden table. They even baked them in special golden pans!"

"WOW!!!" awed all the kids. "Did the bread TASTE golden?" asked Liam.

"Well, yes. The traditions of the Jewish people say that in some way, the golden pans did add something special to the taste of the bread. Which, brings us to *our* pans and oven here. Let's pop these babies in the pans... and then we'll put them on the oven racks, two by two, which is also an old Jewish custom. But first...we have to do a little *good luck ritual*...we snatch off a little bit of the dough and throw it in the oven and turn the oven way up and just burn that piece totally up..."

"COOL! Why do you do that?" Liam loudly asked.

"Well, it's in memory of the old days when the Jewish priests would bake bread for God and put it in the Temple. Sometimes the priests would burn food so that it made a nice smell to honor God. But then, the Romans came along and destroyed the Jewish Temple and threw all the Jews out of their land...these were the same Romans who crucified Jesus. So, since the Jewish people today do not have their Temple anymore, they remember it by burning a little bit of bread...like their priests did in Jesus' day." Jonah took a pinch of dough and threw it on a cookie sheet and popped it in the oven. He turned the oven up to 500 degrees and the oven coils rapidly turned red hot.

Ida Belle suddenly threw down her dough in disgust, her fists on her hips. "Well, excuse me Pastor! But we are *CHRISTIANS* here! I fail to see the need for going into all this *JEWISH* material! It's interesting that Maddie has some Jewish blood in her family and all..."

"Well, Ida Belle, actually I do too," advised Jonah. "...like we said before...we have *common ancestors* in France..."

"WHATEVER! What I am talking about is: Proclaiming JESUS as LORD of ALL!!!" Ida Belle thrust her arm as a rocket lifting her finger to the heavens. "And let me tell you, we should be talking about JESUS, and ONLY JESUS morning, noon, and night! We certainly should NOT be talking about *JEWS* more than *Jesus!* I think that wonderful movie about Jesus dying on the cross, that came out a few years ago, showed VERY WELL what the *JEWS* are all about! It was the JEWS that KILLED Jesus!" she herrrumphed with a concluding defiant nod.

Every man, woman, and child was speechless.

Madeleine clutched the *tefila* pouch at her heart under her blouse.

Jonah looked directly into Ida Belle's red hot eyes and leaned to the oven to turn off the heat. He carefully took the hot charred morsel of bread out with a spatula and gently laid it on the table. Looking around into the faces gathered, he said, "Another reason I find this little tradition meaningful is to remember the 6 million Jews, the half-million Gypsies and thousands of others the Nazis deemed not fit to live in this world who were shot, beaten to death, worked to death, gassed and....then burnt in piles...and when that didn't work well enough, they were burned in ovens specially made for getting rid of countless human beings."

Madeleine's eyes were to the ground.

Sara's eyes were to the ground. A tear ran down her face. She was not one usually given to letting people know what she felt or thought ...*but when she did...*it was as if God himself chose to break into creation to transfigure humanity. Sara's mouth grimaced and her nose clenched as if her nostrils were beating back the stench of hell. She placed her palmed hand over her eyes and there came the *in-breaking* from the *Other Side*:

Yit-ga-dal v'yit-ka-dash sh'mei ra-ba b'al-ma di-v'ra chi-r'u'tei, v'yam-lich mal-chu-tei b'cha-yei-chon u-v'yo-mei-chon u-v'cha-yei d'chol beit Yis-ra-eil, ba-a-ga-la u-vi-z'man ka-riv, v'i-m' ru: A-mein.
Y'hei sh'mei ra-ba m'va-rach l'a-lam u-l'al-mei al-ma-ya.
Yit-ba-rach v'yish-ta-bach, v'yit-pa-ar v'yit-ro-mam v'yit-na-sei, v'yit-ha-dar v'yit-a-leh v'yit-ha-lal sh'mei d'kud-sha, b'rich-hu,
l'ei-la min kol bir-cha-ta v'shi-ra-ta, tush-b'cha-ta v'neh-cheh-ma-ta da-a-mi-ran b'al-ma, v'i-m'ru: Amein.
Y'hei sh'la-ma ra-ba min sh'ma-ya v'cha-yim, a-lei-nu v'al kol Yis-ra-el, v'i-m'ru: Amein.
O-seh sha-lom bi-m'ro-mav, hu ya-a-seh sha-lom a-lei-nu v'al kol Yis-ra-eil, v'i-m'ru: A-mein.

Jonah said, "A-mein."
Madeleine said, "A-mein."
Ida Belle was in silent screaming shock.
Jonah said to all, "Sara has recited a Jewish prayer giving thanks to God for everything—including those who have left us...Jesus used this prayer as the basis for his *Lord's Prayer*....so that all people might live someday in God's king-dom where all children will have their bread." He looked straight at Ida Belle. "No, Ida Belle. The *JEWS* did not kill Je-sus. Let me repeat in no uncertain terms, Ida Belle:

The...Jews...Did...NOT...Kill...Jesus.

The Romans crucified Jesus. The Romans. And I know. I'm the pastor."
Feigning a mock impressed look, Ida Belle started shaking and thrust her hands into her skirt pockets. "Well. I stand cor-

rected. I should write this down so I can *remember* it." She took out a little note pad with all kinds of scribbly notes from bible verses to telephone numbers and set to the first blank page available. "Yes, let me write this down. I surely do not want to *forget* things that I am taught. Knowledge is such an important thing you know…yes," she jabbed her pencil lead to the pad in thrusts:

'THE …JEWS…DID…NOT…KILL…JESUS!'

"So yes, there it is. I will take this teaching home and study it THOROUGHLY with my Bible and my *Prayer Partners*. Thank you very much, Pastor….thank you very much, all…for a very ENLIGHTENING experience!"

Ida Belle stormed up the church basement steps and out the church door.

"She didn't take any bread," mourned Liam.

"She didn't want any, dear," answered Madeleine.

Chapter 4

Blessed are you, O Lord, who delights in repentance.

Dulles International Airport, Washington, D. C.
Saturday, May 19, 8:23 A.M.

Eduardo chugged his way down the aisle of the small United Airlines DC 3 with his carry-on, trying not to bump too many heads of those already seated. Throwing the small duffle in the overhead compartment, he kept his laptop bag and plunked down into the window seat. *Shit! No leg room.* At least he was only going to Dayton. And he had more than enough work to keep him busy for the short hour and twenty minute flight.

A woman dropped into the seat next to Eduardo. He didn't notice. He should have. She was gorgeous.

Eduardo was tired and distracted, thinking about the meeting with Bill Blanche not many hours earlier at Chez Paul. *Why was Bill so hyped about this case? Or rather...why was Blackpoint so hyped?*

Ashman Blackpoint was a mysterious man. Although he had long been the unseen benefactor of Eduardo and Carlos, they knew of him only by his varied and colorful reputation—depending on whom one asked. To some, he was a seasoned diplomat and intelligence operative—a patriot, who had ably served several administrations in top-priority missions, albeit, in a very low-profile manner. To others, he was *Satan Incarnate*. The many stories about Blackpoint at least agreed that he had been a key facilitator of the secret anti-insurgent forces in Nicaragua in the 1980s. The forces, operating out of Honduras, were backed by the CIA, and received their funding through various shadowy American sources. While defenders of the scheme preferred to employ terms such as *counter-insurgency* forces, straight-talking opponents plainly called them *death squads.*

To be sure, the stories were lurid...unbelievable, actually...dozens of villages taken out by US backed death squads...thousands of innocent peasants including the aged, women, and children...*even nuns,* murdered in cold blood. The bodies were often found in mass graves with only competing accusations of blame from both sides in the conflict to add to the death stats. Indeed. *Truth is the first victim of war.*

Of course, Eduardo did not allow himself to give any credibility to the death squad stories. After all, his own father was a part of the operation and had often called the leftists *the enemies of democracy.* So, no. Eduardo did not believe the stories, but *they did bother him.* Somewhere in the back of his mind, they did bother him.

In short order, the plane was in the air and the cabin's passengers were quieting down. Eduardo set out his laptop, booted up, and got to work. Cramped as his space was, he deftly made the fold down table his desk and the seat pocket in front of him, his filing cabinet. In the pocket he placed the genealogies that Bill had given him the night before. A DIA friend had provided him a list of good genealogical websites, including one run by the *Church of Jesus Christ of Latter Day Saints.* He started there by entering various personages of the Van Meter genealogy into the web-site's search engine. Within a few searches, Eduardo recognized the site was flashing up the same Van Meter genealogy as that sticking out of the seat pocket before him. It was a rather full exposition of data—birth and death dates/places, marriage dates/places, names of spouses and children and allied family trees. It was amazing to Eduardo that anyone put the time into collecting and preserving such information...let alone publishing it, but there it was.

Eduardo's eye focused on the name information. Amid all the names and family trees, it was Jonah Van Meter's immediate paternal ancestors that jumped out at Eduardo. Jonah's father's name was:

Daniel Ragel Van Meter

And, Jonah's grandfather's name was:

Daniel Ragel Van Meter

And, Jonah's great grandfather's name was:

Daniel Ragel Van Meter

...all of whom lived in Columbus, Ohio.

But then, the next generation in the patriarchal line finally changed names to a William Van Meter who hailed from Noble County, Ohio. Eduardo noted the town where William was born in 1815:

Mt. Zion, Ohio

And the town of his death in 1889:

Sarasville, Ohio

Interestingly, William's father was an earlier Daniel Van Meter born in Frederick County, Virginia in 1792. He died in 1819 at:

Mt. Ephraim, Ohio

The dates caught Eduardo's attention. The eldest Daniel Van Meter died a young man—only 27 years old. His son William was only 4 years old when he passed—the same age as Eduardo's brother Toby when Eduardo's father died in the car crash.

As Eduardo clicked along, a pop-up ad flashed for airline fares to France. Eduardo instantly x-ed out of it. He could have installed pop-up blocker and spyware programs to the hilt, but actually he was rather interested in the backfield lurkers. He found it fascinating to have a running peripheral notice of who was *interested in his interests*.

The *viral* dimension of the web had long been a fascination to Eduardo since his training at the University of Chicago under Ashman Blackpoint's brother, Andras Blackpoint.

Andras Blackpoint was always keen to keep the history of computer science in his students' minds. The world of the computer had progressed from old main frame machines that took the better part of a building to contain...to the PC laptop that could sit on an airplane seat-table connected wirelessly to the world-wide web: *Viral*—lighter, stronger, faster, and able to multiply its connections exponentially. And, as Andras Blackpoint reminded his students, *Viral* was the emerging path of social structures.

In the old days, nations went to war with mainframe armies run by top-down leadership. Today was different. International conflicts increasingly took on a viral nature. Comrades in arms increasingly found themselves bound together horizontally from loose network to loose network...indeed, using the web to find and communicate with each other. Thus, in the new viral world, *Al Qaeda* exists all over ...and *nowhere*. And this fact itself had changed the whole nature of warfare in the present age. When it becomes apparent that old-style mainframe armies are hardly the largest worries—what then? When you can't find the *real army* you need to attack? Answer: *You must do as they do.* You must get down into the weeds where viral conflict begins—in the small places where word-of-mouth and trade-of-cooperation goes with a pack of cigarettes and a case of booze....you must root them out at their initial cells...*before the virus expands*. You must *eradicate* the disease before it spreads. You must *inoculate* the situation. It was all part of what bothered Eduardo in the back of his mind—the connection between *viral communication* and *viral politics*—and the possible connections between Andras Blackpoint's social theories and his brother Ashman's real-world deeds.

Eduardo heard a clicking coming from the seat next to him. His eyes shifted out of his cyber dimension to the real world....only to find someone else in front of her own laptop with graceful fingers flying over the keyboard. Together, side-by-side, the two machines looked like a mini *Mission Control*. She was *beautiful*. Her short blonde hair was done in a curled-in 1920s flapper style, framing a round cheery face and small ears adorned by large funky Indian-looking bronze hoop earrings with concentric circles in them. Her pearl white skin was bright against a low cut pink sleeveless top favoring ample cleavage over a split denim skirt, accented by a carelessly slung on wide brown belt. She alternately typed and scanned her screen intensely with far away pearl-grey eyes. But she was also at ease, leaning forward, her legs comfortably crossed and revealed, shapely and buxom, through the side slit of her skirt. Without hesitation, Eduardo *accidentally* nudged her arm with his.

"Oh, I am so sorry. Please accept my apology!" he began with effusive Latin respect heavy on the old country accent.

"Apology?!" she laughed. Her brisk English accent chirped from a wide-eyed angelic face. "Actually I've wondered if you knew I was even here! You've been ever so into your computer...I thought, Oh well, if there's no one to visit with on this flight, I suppose I could work." She brashly leaned forward to him. Her nose and eyes wrinkled coyly, "...to tell the truth, Love....I am dreadfully tired of working!" She waved her hands about. "Look at us! There must be a half dozen of us on this plane staring into these bloody screens! I don't know why we do it!" She blew a small puff and shook her short blonde hair in wonderment.

Eduardo did not know what to think. He liked her. He like her *a whole lot.*

"Hello. Permit me to introduce myself. I am Eduardo Mendoza. I must tell you again that I am very, very sorry to have been so rude to such a lovely lady. It is not the way that my mother, God rest her soul, taught myself. God willing, I would be most blessed if you accepted my repentance." Eduardo really turned it on with a short head bow.

She giggled. "Of course, good sir!" she replied with a playful medieval bow of her head. "Very pleased to meet you. I am Elaine. Elaine Armstrong." She held out her hand.

"Yes. Very pleased to meet you Elaine!" he softly joined his hand to hers and kept with the flow of the flowering impromptu play script. "Yes, we *are* quite a sad techno-pair here, are we not?! We waste good time trying to save time...and I fear we only succeed in working *all* the time, yes?!"

"Yes, exactly," she chirped. "It's all *so* important...our work...isn't it? So... Eduardo...may I call you *Eduardo?*...I so like that name," she played.

"Yes, certainly. *Eduardo,*" he nodded like the hare in Alice in Wonderland. *Man, this is going somewhere.*

"So, what work glues thee to thy bloody electronic chunk of plastic?"

"Security systems." He nodded matter of factly. "You?"

"History."

"History???"

"Yes, love. I teach."

"Oh. I am afraid that history was not my best subject in school. I do hope you are kind to all the boys in your school!"

"Oh!" She laughed falling into him closely and playfully batting his shoulder. "No, no, no. I do not teach *boys*...," her eyes widened playfully. "... I teach *men*! And alas,...women too. At the *university*, you understand...that's where I teach...History."

Eduardo was *electrified.* He could not think. Somehow he uttered, "Ahh...At what university do you teach?"

"*Oxford*, of course!" her grey eyes batted.

"You are a professor at Oxford?"

"Yes, I am afraid so. A boring academic...by day! But...*by night*...well, *other things* altogether you understand."

Eduardo nodded listlessly, his enchanted eyes wider than plates. "So...", he slowly came to consciousness. "You teach History? History of ....?"

"Early Christian History...the whole bloody mess!"

"Really. So what are you doing in here in the States?"

"I'm guest lecturing actually. It provides a bit of extra spending money for my summers and it's jolly good fun as well. I have a little circuit of schools that keep inviting me back. Last week, I was at the School of Religion at Drew University…a lovely little school in New Jersey…this week, it was George-town…"

"I see…" Eduardo's mind raced. Being turned sideways in his plane seat, he was lost enough in thought to bump his laptop causing the cover to drop closed. The genealogy sheets stood revealed and suspended in the seat pocket like playing cards in a dealer's hand. Elaine instantly caught sight and grabbed them up.

"What's this we have here?"

Before Eduardo could protest, the stewardess hovered above with offers of refreshments. Eduardo abruptly ordered rum and coke with a wild eye on the documents waving in Elaine's lovely hand. But as there was no hard liquor on a short flight, they both settled on lemonade.

"So. *This* is interesting, Eduardo….looks like you are into *History* a little bit more than you let on." She leaned over tapping his chest.

Oh Jesus.

Elaine scanned the first page of Jonah Van Meter's genealogy and her eyebrows instantly popped high. Eduardo caught the glint-flash in her deep grey irises.

"So…Eduardo…," Elaine's tone a bit more methodical. "What sort of *security work* do you do?"

He knew he was *into it* already. He decided against cover. *Maybe she could help.*

"*Homeland*," he uttered softly.

"Uh, huh. I should think so," she replied in a very even tone never taking her eyes off the papers which she shuffled back and forth like cards as if seeking a sensible ordered hand. Finally, she looked up and set her eyes softly to Eduardo's, a bit less serious but with an air of curiosity. "You have *VERY* interesting documents here, my good man. You must be on a very *top secret* mission….*James Bond* and all of that!" she whispered closely upon his ear.

Eduardo rolled his eyes and panned the cabin, front to rear.

The stewardess arrived to collect the drink cups and direct the fold-down tables be secured away. The plane would be landing in Dayton in ten minutes.

"You are looking for this man?" asked Elaine out of the blue, pointing to the name of *Jonah Van Meter* on the genealogy.

Eduardo nodded. His mind raced. With only a few minutes left in the most strange...what? *experience*?...or *fortuitous opportunity*? He decided to risk it. "Tell, me Elaine. Do you see anything *extraordinary* with these lists? It could help me with the work I need to do."

"...for the *Homeland*?"

"Yes, for the *Homeland*?"

"Well, tell me Eduardo. How ever did you obtain a *Vatican Secret Archives* document?"

"*WHAT*?!" Eduardo burst in a whispered panic. "How do you know *this*?"

"Well. You know... the pages have a watermark?" She traced the faint outline of a papal crown with double crossed keys and the Latin words *Archivo Secreto* with the tip of her exquisitely manicured pastel nail.

Eduardo thrust his eye almost to the pages themselves. "El Dio! He gave me the *ORIGINALS*?!!!" He could not believe it.

"Who, love?" she played on.

"My boss..." Eduardo's head shook side to side in disbelief. Now he knew he was really *out there*. He thought, *Can anything be salvaged out of this mess? Maybe she could be the expert Bill wanted me to find.*

A sudden drop in the plane's altitude jolted Eduardo. Looking out the window, he realized the plane was hovering just over the front of the runway. His mind lunged forward.

"So, Elaine...." Eduardo nodded to the documents still in her hands. "...is anything else notable there...besides what is giving me an ulcer at the moment?"

The landing gear boomed on the runway pavement. The cry of the reversing engines enveloped the cabin as passengers absorbed the thrusting change from air to ground. Within a few seconds, people began their pre-escape body shifting and stealth-grab of bags. Eduardo though, kept his eyes fixed on Elaine's placid eyes, hoping for a rewarding answer.

"Yes," she said. She gave Eduardo the genealogies and also began scooping up her belongings from under the seat and straightening her blouse and skirt which Eduardo found profoundly distracting. "Actually there is something quite odd that I see in the lists…a *pattern*."

"Pattern? What kind of *pattern*?"

The plane had stopped and people had burst their belts and sprung to reopen the overheads. Chatter floated like a cloud all about.

Elaine stood above Eduardo reaching upward for her carry on. Eduardo remained seated gazing up at his beautiful voluptuous mysterious oracle, *in a slit skirt,* who had something to tell him.

"Yes, a pattern!" She thrust her hand out to his and pulled him up to her closely. "Walk with me, Love. I've friends waiting to pick me up." She looked at her watch. "We're a bit late, so I don't want to keep them. You know?" She found his tagged carry-on in the overhead and thrust it in his arms. He grabbed his laptop and they proceeded down the aisle arm in arm. "This is what I see in the documents Eduardo…"

"Yes…"

"There are *three* different types of people in your lists. And these different types just keep appearing over and over again through the generations of the list…you know…as in a *cycle*…"

They cleared the plane doorway saying goodbye to the cabin crew and headed into the beige accordion hallway leading to the main terminal.

"What groups? Three?"

"Yes, *three*. You have three groups. You have *Merovingians*. You have *Jews*. And you have *Roma*…"

"Okay, Jews I know…and everybody knows Merovingians from the books and movies…" Eduardo was trying to think fast. "But, *Roma???*…"

"Yes, *Roma*—also commonly known as *Gypsies*, but they prefer to be called *Roma* or *Rom*. So anyway, Love…What I see in your genealogies is what I would call an *intentional cycle.*

Each generation has Merovingian, Jewish, and Roma connections...at least back to *one man.* Did you notice that the genealogies for both Jonah Van Meter and his wife Madeleine *go back to the same man?*"

"No. I missed it. Who is that man?"

"His name was DuBois. Cretien DuBois."

"So...What about him? Who was he...?"

Elaine stopped. Looking beyond the partition dividing arriving passengers from their greeters, she waved on her tip-toes and flashed a huge smile.

Waving back to Elaine were two grey-haired ladies in modified Catholic *nun* garb. One wore very retro cat glasses.

"My friends," Elaine smiled.

"Friends???!"

"Yes, they're my *sisters* in the *Order of the Sacred Host* at the convent of *Maria Shrine*, a little north of here."

"What? You are a *NUN*?!!!" Eduardo's heart sank to the floor and he immediately felt sick to his stomach.

"*Used* to be...my dear Eduardo. *USED* to be." She wrapped her arms around him tracing her finger down his breastbone. "We must stay in touch you know, Love....would you like that?"

"*Uh, huh.*" Eduardo deliriously agreed, his eyes totally lost in hers. She reached into her shoulder bag and retrieved her business card placing it softly in Eduardo's hands.

"Call me. Especially if you get into any trouble. But call me just the same, won't you, Love?" Eduardo did not know what to say. But what he did say came from somewhere he knew not.

"El Dio." He muttered.

"*El Dio!???*" Elaine's eyes burst into grey rays. "Are you *Jewish!?*"

"*No*, I'm Catholic, like you!" blurted Eduardo looking very confused. "Why do you ask if I am *Jewish?*" His eyes winced trying to process the moment.

The nuns looked on with questioning eyes.

"Got to go, Love. Now it is I who must beg you to accept *my apology.*" Suddenly, Elaine kissed him fully on the lips while the nuns' heads pivoted to each other's in shock.

As Elaine backed away taking leave with her friends, she called out, "Call me, Eduardo. I assure you...I'm really very good at *repentance.*"

Chapter 5

Blessed are you, O Lord, who is merciful and always ready to forgive.

Montra, Ohio.
Saturday, May 19, 12:12 P.M.

Sara trudged back down the lane toward the parsonage carrying a cardboard box filled with left over supplies from the bread-making. Jonah and Madeleine remained in the church kitchen baking the last loaves. The rest of the kids had gone home.

The morning sun and clear sky were disappearing with a line of dark cloud coming from the west. The wind kicked up signaling the coming storm. Ohio was always like that. Nice weather one hour, terrible the next. It was one of the first things Sara remembers being taught when she first arrived in Ohio at the age of seven.

Entering the garage, Sara managed to hold the heavy box on her thin but strong dark left arm and with her right hand throw open the kitchen door. As she crossed the threshold, she tapped the *mezuzah* affixed to the door lintel and touched her lips.

Hoisting the supplies onto the kitchen counter, she gazed out the kitchen window toward the horse farm. Jal and Rupa galloped joyously around their ring as the first drops of rain flew down with a strong gust of wind. The horses' owner scrambled to get her valuable *pets* into the barn, although Sara knew the pair would just as soon stay out in the storm.

Sara was tired. The bread-making had made for an early morning, and she had to leave soon again for basketball practice. She rolled down the hall to her bedroom and flung herself on her bed. She flipped her stereo on—with an already loaded Ziggy Marley CD. Immediately lost in the back-beat of the reggae, Sara laid prone on her back gazing into her pantheon of posters on the ceiling: a rainbow Peace sign, horses in swirling electric colors, an old Sarajevo Olympics poster, a dreamy Marc Chagal print of a happy peaceful village, the Taj Mahal, Brutus Buckeye, and singers—Ziggy and Bob Marley, and Alicia Keys. She *loved* Alicia Keyes. Indeed, Sara looked a good bit like the soulful artist. In 4th grade, she entered the school talent show and performed as Keys down to having her hair corn-rowed by a Black friend. The audience was *stunned* by the performance in two ways: It was very, very well done; and it was very, very *Black.* The applause was muted.

Over the music and the winds outside, Sara heard the gravel in the driveway churn and then the quick slam of two car doors.

The doorbell rang.

"Oh shit," moaned Sara peering into Alicia's eyes. *Incoming*—her Dad's term for *in-laws*. She padded sluggishly down the hall to the front door and hesitated, staring at the knob. *Do I have to do this?* She opened the door.

"HI SARA!!!"

And in they came, shaking rain droplets off their designer clothes and perfect hair.

Sara stood there, in standard teenage feigned muted awareness, and offered a silent short palm wave for her aunt and uncle, Margot and Hunter Calvi.

Margot flashed a broad smile and leaned back with hands on her hips revealing the girth of her pregnancy, which equaled that of Madeleine's.

"My goodness girl! You're getting taller and taller," exclaimed Aunt Margot. She reservedly patted Sara on the head— she had *never hugged* Sara.

Uncle Hunter offered a brisk business-like handshake. "Good to see you again, Sara," he intoned.

"So, where's Maddie?" asked Margot with a fake smile and nervous goose-necking eyes into the kitchen and down the hall.

"Mom and Dad are still up at the church finishing up some stuff we were doing in Catechism class. They should be back any minute." *NOW, goddammit!*

Sara hated Margot and Hunter…ever since she first met them. And they never liked her. Sara just knew it….the way Black people know how some White people are prejudiced, even though they deny it. *You just know*—You know by how they act, and how they say things, and what they *don't* say, and especially by what they don't *do. THE Calvis,* as Jonah called them, had *never* invited Sara to their country club home in suburban Boston. The official story had always been that it was easier for them to come to Ohio.

After an awkward pause, Sara asked if they wanted to sit in the living room.

The three of them were terrible company for each other.

Sara plopped alone on the couch clad in her worn basketball practice clothes with faded *OSU Buckeye* logos.

Margot eased herself into a loveseat with Hunter. She smiled nervously, looking around, and just patted her brilliant white lacey maternity smock overflowing her dapper khaki trousers.

Predictably, Hunter was in his polo shirt and khakis, deck shoes, webbed leather belt, and gold Rolex. Jonah called it the *Uniform*, as legion at *the club* as the drab grey Kim Jong Il uniform for the North Korean masses.

"So. Sara," intoned Hunter. "School is going well?"

"Yeah." She looked around the walls wondering how long she would be pinned down.

Margot continued to pat her lacey maternity smock, nervously. "Well Sara, are you looking forward to being a cousin?...Well, sort-of-cousin?" She beamed right through her obnoxious qualification.

"Yeah."

"Would you like to know what we are going to name our little boy…did you hear? The baby is a boy…"

Sara nodded silently in teenage robot mode.

"So. We have decided to name our precious little boy: *Hunter Logan Calvi II.* Doesn't that just sound wonderful?! It was my idea, and Hunter agreed….and the rest is *history!* Don't you just love it?! We think the name has a rather regal sound to it. Don't you agree?"

Sara remained expressionless. She looked into the kitchen at the wall clock.

"...and what will you all be naming your little......*brother*, isn't it? I think Maddie may have given me the name...but I forget it just now. Can you remind me Sara?"

"*Daniel Lazare*...after Dad's dad and *your dad*," Sara monotoned with an overt, backstreet girl *You-have-shit-for-brains* look.

Finally. Sara heard the kitchen door bang open.

In came her mother and father laden with boxes of freshly baked bread.

Hunter and Margot rose to greet them in the kitchen and Sara bolted for her room. The door closed and the stereo instantly found decibel enough to cause a slight vibration through every wall in the house.

"What on earth have you two been up to!?" exclaimed Margot as she cast her eyes over Madeleine and Jonah's flour tinged clothes.

"What else? Baking bread!" chimed Jonah.

"You look like a couple of union workers, Jonah," chided Hunter giving up a mocking *A-okay* sign.

"Jesus, Maddie! Didn't you and Jonah get enough of that craziness when you were kids?!" cried Margot.

"Oh, no! We're all about Bread here! Look at my kitchen!" Madeleine pointed upward to a highly positioned running wall shelf that bordered all around the kitchen. On the shelving resided an attractive collection of antique plates with different floral decorations, but all had the words *Give Us Today Our Daily Bread* on them....all in English, except for one in Hebrew.

"Oh my God! You're nuts! The both of you are just simply nuts! I think when you have that baby boy, he's going to come out the *Pillsbury Dough Boy!* No....I will purchase bread at the market if need be...of course I have no need...with the *low carb* diet that keeps me looking splendid....you ought to try *low-carb*, Maddie! It will do wonders for you! But for me? Oh, no! No more baking for *moi*. I hated every second of it when we were kids!"

Madeleine shrugged. "Well, to each his own, I guess…Our kids sure had a rip-roaring old time with it today…Jonah had the idea of them making the Communion bread as a service project."

"Hmm," replied Margot.

"Well, sister…want to help me straighten up and get lunch ready? You guys…you just go in the living room and we'll tell you when we're ready," directed Madeleine.

Sara entered the kitchen.

"I gotta go to basketball practice in Jackson Center, Momma. I'll get a ride with Jessica Schenck. Can you pick me up if Jess's mom can't bring me back?"

"Actually, sweetie…I was thinking I might just come over later and watch …at least the end of your practice."

"Cool. Whatever. See ya." Sara gave a short wave but no departing words to Margot and Hunter. She knew it was rude, but she also knew that her so-called aunt and uncle thought *all* teenagers were rude.

Jonah slugged into the couch not unlike his daughter would.

The Hunter took the nearest thing to a throne in the form of Jonah's second hand *Lazy Boy* inherited from a parishioner now residing on the mount.

"They give you a little time off, huh?" Jonah started.

"I decided to *take* a little time. Yes. Actually, I've raised so much money for them already this year, they're all on vacation…what do they know?" Hunter was a professional fundraiser in the Boston area for *Tri-County Catholic Charities*. From his braggart tales, the bulk of his business apparently came from shaking down corporate donors.

"Really," said Jonah flatly. "Like, how much?"

"Oh, about 5 mil. And that's approximately 30% over last year…I was able to net some larger corporate fish this year beyond the old blue-hair retirees, you understand. That's really the story. You have either the corporate types looking for some high profile goody-two-shoes PR…plus some back sheet write-off for a good price…or you have the *old money* Catholic families. It's all fundraising…but you know… the reality is: dealing with the corporate boys is the way to go. *That's* where the big money is. Yeah…They always try to jew me down. But the bottom line is:

They want their names on the top of that published donor list. Yeah…they can be tough…like I said…jew you down and all that…and let me tell you…if you're dealing with *actual Jews…they're the toughest.*

"*Really*?!" Jonah leaned forward with wide eyes. "How so?"

"Oh, Jesus. You wouldn't believe it. Jews just can't give the goddamn money and get their name in lights…oh, no! They always have a fucking laundry list of questions, a mile long…*Who gets the money? Who does your accounting?*…yeah like, *hey goy-buddy, my cousin Sol does accounting…*you know? On and on. They want to know exactly what percentage actually goes to *the people*, and what goes to overhead. They want to know this…they want to know that….The damn kikes treat us like we're some kind of goddamn Jimmy Swaggert operation. Actually, I think they just fucking hate Catholics…the whole Hitler thing and all…the Pope didn't save their asses…*whah, whah, whah…*, which I think was their own damn fault…but that's beside the point. Money is money, even if it's kike-money."

Jonah gripped the arm of the couch, his finger nails tearing at the fabric. He held it together. And probed.

"So…like, who *does* get the money? Do you ever go on-site to the agencies that get it?"

"Oh shit, no. We're *first class* in our office. It's really like any high-scale financial operation….most everything is done electronically. We wine and dine. Meet and greet. We click the money in. We click it out."

"…to soup kitchens and homeless shelters, and such, right?" Jonah pressed.

"Yeah, yeah, yeah. The knocked-up teenage mother's club; free food for little Black Sambo who's daddy don't have no job….the whole deal."

Jonah pursed his lips and bit the insides of his cheeks. Since his guest was disrobing his fake gentility down to the crudest levels, Jonah decided to play *How low can you go?*

"…so is there ever…" Jonah lowered his voice. "A little *fun money* left over for *the office,* so to speak?"

"Oh, hell yes. You know it, my man!" Hunter nodded with a smug sneer. "We have NICE Christmases, I can tell you that.

And we take good care of our friends. You need friends in this business….you can be sure of that."

"*Friends?*…Friends in Boston?...or other places?" Jonah probed.

"Yeah, yeah, sure. Boston…New York….Rome…"

"…You have a lot of friends in Rome?"

"Yeah, of course!" Hunter waved his hands wildly as he went into a fake Italian accent. "As they say, *All roads lead to Rome!*"

A long hovering pause filled the room. Jonah cocked his head slightly, his eyes sailing evenly to Hunter's as a great ship navigating a straight. His memory told him it was an inherited skill.

Hunter smiled slightly…ever so slightly…and did not blink.

And Jonah knew. He *knew*. His father had taught him well to read the signs. *It was happening.* Daniel taught him how evil infiltrated the ordinary—what it felt like—what it looked like—what it smelled like. *Yes.* Evil was paying a visit upon the Van Meter Family…and its *Secret*…*again.*

Madeleine and Margot were chatting it up in the kitchen. They stood side by side laughing, comparing girth. They decided that Madeleine slightly won the contest – she had always been the hardier of the two. Margot, three years younger, perennially competed with Madeleine. But Madeleine never took it seriously. Margot did. In the early years, it started with *looks* and clothes and boyfriends in school. Madeleine always had a rare dark *madonna* look that captivated people. Margot was a plain looking child. Her true dish-water blonde hair was now a glossy platinum, highly maintained by a most exclusive day spa. And today, Margot's physical image—weight, clothes, skin was impeccable—so *she* thought.

"That's a really pretty smock, Margot. Where did you find it?" inquired Madeleine.

"Oh, we had an exclusive private designer whip this up for us in her shop…We ordered a half dozen …and I must confess I was a little nervous about it…but I do think they turned out quite nicely. I was so desperate to find something suitable. I tried *Lord & Taylor* and *Sax*, but it's such a frustration to go to the racks anymore with the masses —I think every girl out there must be having a baby!"

"Oh, wow!" And Madeleine *was* wowed. "I just go to Stein Mart in Columbus. They have some pretty cute things for not too much."

"Oh, I remember that place. The *Jew store*...they had a lot of *wild* clothes...but some cute things, yes." Margot eyed Madeleine's multi-colored *madras* skirt. "So did you get this at Stein Mart?"

"Yes, isn't it fun! I just love it!" Madeleine beamed.

"Very colorful, yes. But you know...I'm just not into the *peasant look*...just not *my* thing, you know?..."

"Well..." Madeleine faltered, a little bit hurt. "...it sort of reminds me of Mamma."

"Oh, well. Let me tell you, sister...you might romanticize Mamma as a quaint little peasant...but let me tell you: She was just *poor*. And Daddy made her that way with that damn bakery...him and his old Dutch buddy, Danny boy...no disrespect now, you understand...I hope Jonah has left most of that nonsense behind. It's fine to bake a little bread with the kiddies, but it's nothing to make a life out of."

A bit stunned, Madeleine suggested setting the table for lunch.

Margot made a quick hop to her tote bag, and retrieved a dark bottle of wine which she presented to Madeleine.

"Oh, my," exclaimed Madeleine, squinching her eyes. "Do you think we should?....You know what they say about alcohol and pregnancy."

"Oh, hush. Worry wart! Just a little tiny bit won't do any damage! After all, we need to toast our good fortunes...both of us...after we've had so much trouble getting to this point."

Margot referred to their mutual infertility problems. Madeleine and Jonah had tried for a good while to conceive a child, with no luck. At last, they decided to adopt and had the good fortune to find Sara in Bosnia...which had infinite internal meaning and continuity with the *family secret*. But then, all of a sudden, out of the blue, Madeleine was pregnant. *Amazing.* It was as if God appointed it. An heir—to continue the secret family lineage, destined for redemption of the world...if not with *this* child in *this* generation, perhaps with another child in the same lineage five or ten generations into the future.

Margot had her own agenda. It was strange that she and Hunter, after such a long period of their own fertility problems, suddenly announced they were pregnant three weeks after Madeleine announced. Madeleine wondered if they had secretly undergone an *en vitro* procedure and just claimed to become pregnant the old fashioned way.

Beyond conjectures, the realities of Margot's pregnancy were very dark and complex. Madeleine just had no way of knowing. She *did know* that Margot had *not* been informed of the *family secret* in childhood, as she and Jonah were. But, on the other hand, Madeleine had no clue that Margot *now* knew some of the *secret* from *another* source outside the family…at least, the *immediate* family. And, Madeleine had no idea of the depth of her sister's jealousy and ambition. She did not know that the danger that haunted her dreams every night, in fact, resided in her own sister's dark heart.

Margot stuck her head in the living room and gave Hunter a signaling look. "Honey, we need your help in here."

The two men followed to the kitchen and Margot handed her husband the bottle of German Riesling. "Would you do the honors dear?"

"Certainly." Hunter plunged the corkscrew into the spongy cork and twisted away with great force.

Jonah looked frantically at Madeleine.

She gave a slight shrug.

The cork popped and the dark aroma filled the air. Jonah felt sick. His nostrils contracted and again he glared at his wife.

She stealthily nodded that she knew his concern…she understood.

He rolled his eyes.

Out of the blue, Hunter shouted, "My God, look at those wonderful horses out there!" He marched over to the kitchen window and proclaimed, "They are simply grand!"

"Maddie!" exclaimed Margot. "Why don't you and Jonah just take Hunter out to meet the horses, and I'll set the table. Go ahead. You've done so much. Let me do my part!"

"Lovely idea, my love!" chimed Hunter. "My friends, would you be so gracious as to introduce me to your equine friends?"

Madeleine agreed.

Margot stated she needed to go to the bathroom first, so Jonah pointed her down the hall.

Madeleine and Hunter had already proceeded out the kitchen door out toward the horses. Just as Jonah reached the kitchen door, he heard a cell phone ring to the tune of a German symphony rift. It was Margot's phone. She had left it on the kitchen counter. Jonah answered the phone.

"Hello?"

There was no reply, but the line was not dead. There was that *certain kind* of background noise...the sound of somebody not saying something. But, there was *another sound*—a confusing, vaguely familiar sound—a distant metal clanging. Jonah winced.

"Hello?" No reply. And then the line was dead. Jonah put the phone down where he found it, and went out the kitchen door.

Margot exited the bathroom and re-entered the kitchen. She was alone. Looking out the kitchen window, she saw them at the fence petting the horses. *Now is the time.*

Spastically, she flew to the cupboards and selected dishes for the table. She reached for glasses and grabbed four. And then stopped. *No. Not four of the same. Four different. Let's not have a mistake.*

Margot slammed the plates down, and then the glasses, the one for Madeleine especially chalice-shaped. Hastily, but gingerly, she arranged silverware and napkins. She filled the glasses, intently, with a steady hand, not spilling a drop. Grabbing her purse, Margot pulled out a small plastic zip-lock pouch with powder in it. Deftly, she poured the powder into the center of Madeleine's glass with no residue to the sidewalls. She stuck a knife in the glass and gave a few slow stirs. And with perfect malice, she spied the dog's bowl. She had always hated the species which had always returned the favor with knowing growls and shimmer of teeth. There was a little powder left in the pouch—enough to get that job done as well. Finally, Madeleine's place was marked with a small gift-wrapped present. *Done.*

Margot stepped back from the table to survey her work. She nodded to herself with approval. Grabbing another glass from the cupboard, she poured a great measure of the Riesling and gulped it forcefully down. She paced in circles around the table, surveying every angle, *thinking* every angle…And *her* angle: *My son, NOT Maddie's, will take his place in the Bloodline.*

Margot basked in the irony that the two immortal enemies over the *Bloodline*, the Vatican and the *Order*, converged in her own marriage *and pregnancy*…and she held the strings of all the marionettes dancing on the stage. Margot was *finally* pregnant, but *not* by Hunter Calvi. The baby was Wal Holloway's.

Only Margot knew the whole story. Wal didn't know about Hunter's connections with the Vatican. And Hunter didn't know about Wal. The only knowledge of the proposed crime the two men shared was Margot's source for a weapon. As a hospital administrator, Margot had access to any drug or *combination of drugs* she wanted.

Truly. Margot's whole story was her own dark journey. Years before, when Margot was single, Wal had propositioned her. When he discovered she had not been informed of her own *family secret,* he briefed her on his own knowledge and pressed his proposition all the more. They would marry, have children, and wrest *The Secret's* power from her sister Madeleine.

But, Margot and Wal did not marry. Armed with secret knowledge she hoped would lead to great riches, Margot had no wish to simply leave *the driving* to a man…or anyone else for that matter. Margot calculated she could maximize the power of *The Secret* more than Wal. And, he miscalculated when he let her know that the Vatican was as interested in *The Secret* as the *Order.* No doubt, he name-dropped the Vatican as part and parcel of selling the importance of his proposition. Unknown to Wal, his ploy totally backfired.

Margot's goals were not marriage or relationship, or even children...for themselves, but only: great money, status, and *power.* That was it.

In her calculations, Margot dispatched Wal to go on with his life and marry another. Which, he did. At the same time, through a college friend who was a member of *Opus Dei,* she networked herself, *and her secret,* into the bowels of the Catholic under-world. And it was there she met and made her deal with Hunter Calvi and his powerful moneyed friends. And so they married.

The plan was simple: a) facilitate the prevention or termina-tion of Madeleine's ability to have children—*there were ways;* and, b) supply an alternative bloodline more amenable to doing business with the Vatican.

But the project hit a snag. Apparently Hunter was sterile. Af-ter much trying, nothing was happening. While Margot assumed *it was Hunter,* she said nothing to him. But she *needed to be pregnant* to keep her whole scheme intact. Given her dark calcu-lating mind, it was an easy hop back to Wal Holloway. She propositioned *him.* She filled *him* up with all kinds of promises of later divorcing Hunter and the two of them going on together in grand fashion...and of course, Wal would have to divorce as well.

In response, Wal flatly stated that divorce would be *no prob-lem.* He bought Margot's con-job hook, line, and sinker.

And Hunter bought that she was pregnant by him.

It would work out fine. Both men had roughly the same skin tone, and hair color...*it would work.*

Of course, none of it made any sense. There was no explana-tion for the evil in Margot. It was not due to her parents, her upbringing, nor her environment. Evil is a *mystery,* but a *stupid* mystery. The dazzle of riches and the world's kingdoms blind the souls of the evil. Their dark dreams with which they go down to the pit make them forget...forget what ordinary folk think about in the broad light of day. A *Bloodline*...even of Jesus? So what? The nobility of Europe had bandied the myth amongst themselves for centuries—what does it matter to the accountant or school bus driver? Evil can't think straight. Jonah and Made-leine's *secret* was worth money to the *Order* and the Vatican, but not their actual *blood.* But Margot was so consumed by great evil, all she could see in her sister was an impediment. And in the logic of Evil, impediments must be destroyed…the task of destruction enveloping everything and blocking out the light of discernment—which might have provided the fact that Jonah and Madeleine presided not over a *Bloodline*, but rather: a *Bread Line.* But blood begets blood—a self-propelling evil like a kid with a violent video game—all that counts in the moment is the *boom.* It's like going to war, and not planning for the peace.

Margot gazed up at the long train of *Daily Bread* plates as she spun herself in faster and faster circles. Her dark heart filled to the brim with hot anger and hatred. Out loud she crazily addressed the bread plates, jabbing her finger, "There'll be NO tomorrow for YOU! NONE!" She grabbed the spare glass and filled it again, immediately devouring the dark spirit. Finally, she took the bottle itself and sucked a long chug. She slammed the bottle down, and nodded gutturally. *It IS finished.*

Out at the fence line, time with the horses was cut short when Rupa bit Hunter's hand, and Motzi followed suit by nipping his ankle. They all agreed it was best to head back inside.

As Madeleine was walking through the yard back to the house, she tripped in the grass and fell. In the fall, her *tefila* cord broke.

The men picked Madeleine up, and she laughed, clutching the broken cord together. But Jonah was filled with dread. He could feel, taste, and smell Evil in the air. Every nerve in his body and soul was on alert. As they entered the kitchen door, Jonah grasped the *mezuzah* with all his strength.

"My goodness!" exclaimed Madeleine as her eyes set upon the table before her. Everything was in its place: food, drink, present, and a thorny rose in a slender vase in the middle of the table.

"Madame!" Margot dramatically drew out Madeleine's chair to seat her as a queen.

Madeleine giggled. It was like playing house when they were children. "Jonah, would you say grace?" she asked.

He nodded, thinking prayer supremely appropriate.

Blessed are you, O Lord our God, King of the universe who brings forth bread from the earth.

"A-mein," said Madeleine and Jonah.

Hunter and Margot said nothing.

Jonah took up a *Daily Bread* plate with a loaf of bread baked that morning and offered it to Hunter and Margot.

"Oh, no!" sang Margot as she began to fill her plate with other food. "Not for me. I'm doing the *low-carb* thing, you know. I've got to watch every pound!" Waving her hand over the dishes of Greek Salad and assorted Mediterranean cheeses and relishes, she exclaimed, "But Madeleine, I owe you an apology—most everything here is SO *low-carb!* It's wonderful! You know Hunter is doing *low-carb* too. He's lost 20 pounds! I'm so proud of him. Yes, I really am, honey bunch!" She was sickening.

Hunter, working unenthusiastically on the salad, added, "Yes, but usually I do a lot of protein, which I do not find here today. Are you *Vegetarians*, Jonah and Maddie?" he inquired slipping back into his fake sophisticate accent.

"Yes!" piped Madeleine. "Actually, we didn't start out that way....we really never did eat that much meat to begin with, but Sara became interested in vegetarian diets through a report on India she did for school....and she wanted to try it. And we just found that we really like it..."

"Isn't that interesting...," prattled Margot. She waved her hand over the glasses. "Drink! It's wonderful wine! It's from Germany!"

"But wine is NOT *low-carb,*" Jonah quickly injected with a piercing look to Madeleine.

"Oh, Jonah!" exclaimed Margot. "Maddie can drink just a smidge. We're big strong girls! We can handle it! Drink, drink! To the future and all it brings!"

Margot raised her glass to which Madeleine and Hunter responded with clinks, and they *drank*.

Jonah did not move a muscle. Jonah did not drink.

"Maddie, dear! You must open your present!" declared Margot.

"Oh, forgive me sister! I don't have one for you...yet! I guess I just haven't found the right thing...you know—we live out here in the country..."

"Oh, I don't need a thing dear...my friends have been dropping all sorts of *gar-baje* at our little shanty...I don't know what to do with it all! I just ran into this and thought it was entirely perfect for you? Go ahead dear!...Open!"

Madeleine carefully unwrapped the present in the slow manner she always did. It always drove people nuts that she refused to rip either paper or ribbons. After what seemed an eternity, finally the gift emerged. It was a book. A brand new weight-loss guide book.

"Gee...," said Madeleine in stammering low tone.

"It's a really good one Maddie. My fitness trainer at the spa highly recommends it."

"Gee...."

Margot leaned over and flipped the pages to the table of contents with her perfectly manicured middle finger.

"...and here's a really wonderful chapter on weight loss during pregnancy!"

"Gosh...I guess they cover it all," was all Madeleine could think to say.

Hunter took a quiet drink of Reisling.

Jonah's face was stone neutral, but his eyes and brain were in very deep penetrating analysis of every syllable, sound, and move...indeed the very air. The switches inside him, long dormant, were on. The gears were turning. He looked straight into Hunter's eyes with the expressionless look every ghetto kid knows to have before the fight.

"You don't drink, Jonah?" inquired Hunter.

"No." His eyes were steady.

"I see you have a pony tail tucked down the back of your shirt...kind of neat how it doesn't stand out that way. But you know...I always associated free-spirit hippie types with *drinkin' and partyin'*...as they say."

"I don't drink and I don't cut my hair." Jonah remained rock-steady.

Madeleine interjected. "Jonah is very principled. His idea is not to drink or cut his hair until there is peace in the world. It's a religious discipline—going without certain things to remind one-self of the plight of others."

Hunter took another drink of wine. "Hmmph. Sounds a little extreme…going without the good things of life when you can easily have them."

Jonah nodded with deadpan eyes. "It's a *workin' man's* thing. Like Johnny Cash wearin' black 'cause of the world's troubles."

"So, Jonah. Do you think there will *ever* be peace, or will you *never* drink wine or cut your hair?"

"There will be peace. Someday. Someday, all God's children will have bread." Jonah grabbed a chunk of bread and bit into it, piercing into Hunter's eyes.

"You seriously believe that?"

"I seriously do."

Jonah and Madeleine stood on their front porch and watched as the BMW cleared the mount.

"Maddie."

"Yes."

"We hoped it would never happen. But, it's happening. They know we're here. They're coming. We've sensed it in our guts and our nightmares lately. Calvi is one of them."

"I know."

"The *Signal* is operative at this moment. If you hear it from me…you know what to do."

"I know."

"Are you going over to Sara's basketball practice?"

"Yeah…..You want to come along, babe?"

"No. I have some phone calls to make."

"I know."

"Don't cry."

"I know," she said, wiping her eyes.

Chapter 6

Blessed are you, O Lord, the redeemer of Israel

Washington, D. C.
Saturday, May 19, 12:12 P.M.

Bill Blanche entered Chez Paul and proceeded briskly to the shadows beneath the Tiffany chandelier at the end of the bar.

Ashman Blackpoint was waiting for him, sipping ouzo.

Blanche sat down and waved quickly at the barkeep, who brought the Bordeaux without a word.

"Our boy get off?" Blackpoint inquired.

"Yeah," nodded Bill. "He's in the air about now."

"Good." Blackpoint took a long drink and passed a dark meditative hand over his mottled balding forehead. Tugging the sleeve of his elegant pin-striped suit, he spoke slowly and methodically. "I want you to inform me as to any and all information that comes from Eduardo at once...as soon as it comes in."

Blanche nodded. "I intended so."

"Good. We're on the same page....or shall we say, *post office box*?" Blackpoint smiled wryly.

"Yes." Blanche raised his glass.

"Yes, indeed. We need, Bill, to watch the *mail* very closely here. When we have *Pony Express* coming out of Rome and Zurich at the same time...to the same address....*Something* is on the verge..."

"...and that is?"

Blackpoint cocked his head side to side and sipped his ouzo. "Well, I am an honest man. Rome and Zurich are much older entities than all of our agencies combined. So…it's their game. We are interested *observers*. But. From reading the signs of the age, as it were, I think we have some mutual interests with them. They are our *canaries in the coal mine*. If they perceive a threat, we should as well."

"So what's the threat?"

"Well. That's the question, now isn't it? We are not entirely sure. We are guessing, yes. But, we need to guess well. So. We use our brains. We know that the Vatican and the *Sovereign Order of the Temple of Sion* have been in, how shall we say?…an *ancient* struggle. Over what? Well, the more romantic followers of the tale, say the *Grail*. Fine. So, *what is the Grail*? It's this. It's that. Whatever it is, it's supposedly a potent secret that somehow has the power to un-do the base of Christian infra-structure…*and we can't have that.* That's important. *Infrastructure* is crucial to us all. Not that I personally care what that means for the Vatican and *Sion*. Fuck them. But *WE*…here in the U.S., cannot afford to have our agenda or our party base upset and distracted over religion. We use that religion for a lot of grease. We don't want to lose that. In fact, we want to utilize it more than we have. So, whoever…or whatever screws with our base infrastructure here…could…effect infinite change …and that, as they say, is *NOT* in our national interest…or *something like that.*

So, is the Grail some type of proof, some artifact, some device with a capacity to alter popular understanding of Christian tradition among the masses? Not sure. Is the Grail actually a group of people…the supposed descendants of Jesus…or people who believe they are Jesus' descendants who *DO* have some sort of leverage over the Vatican? Not sure. So. It's true. We do not know—we are behind the eight ball. But *something* very impor-tant is at stake. And *that* my friend gives us every reason to watch the *mail.*"

"I have to admit something." Blanche looked a little lost as he took a drink of Bordeaux and leaned his head into his hand as if trying to think how to phrase his thought.

"Yes?"

"The Vatican, I understand…some of the basics. They have a company to run, and they don't want anyone fucking with their bottom line."

"Yes."

"So. This *Sovereign Order of the Temple of Sion*?—I have the sense they're all blue-bloods, but what's the *Sion* part?…*Sion* with an *S*?—or *Zion* with a *Z*?…Are they Zionists?—Do they have connections to Jews? –to Israel?" Bill threw his hands out. "I just don't understand the connections."

Blackpoint laughed for the first time, his shoulders jiggling. A sip of ouzo and a drag on the cigarette was the beat before the punch line.

"Well, don't feel bad, Bill. It's a little involved. So, here's the skinny:

Gentiles sometimes use the *S,* and Jews always use the *Z*, but that's really nothing more than a language difference.

But more to the core of your question—The relationship between the *Sovereign Order of the Temple of Sion* and Jews…Well. Actually, there is very little relation—of a positive nature, anyway. I'll try to put in a nutshell.

For Jews, the word *Zion* developed over time. Originally, it referred to just Jerusalem—the whole city. And then later, they applied *Zion* more narrowly to the Temple Mount—where the Jews actually had their temple before the Romans destroyed it in 70 CE. And then sometime later, the word *Zion* was applied to another spot: A small hill just outside the walls of Jerusalem— on the southwest corner of the Old City. Now today, for Jews, the word *Zion* today still applies to all of these things—the City…the Temple Mount…and the small hill. And then. There's a certain mystical meaning Jews give *Zion*—in terms of how they see their manifest destiny in Israel with Jerusalem as its capitol. A *Zionist* will *never* give up Jerusalem—or anything else for that matter. But, I digress…

Now. The *Sovereign Order of the Temple of Sion*—that's something entirely different. You're correct. They're *blue- bloods,* as you say. They're the noble and royal families of Europe—or people descended from them. And they have this mythology that they're all descended from Jesus and his family...*thus Jews*...in a *very* figurative sense. But it's not like they're interested in eating *kosher.* They don't hang out with *real Jews.*

So, how do the blue-bloods connect to Sion? Well. It has to do with the Crusades—when these blue-bloods were over in the Holy Land. During the Crusades, the grandaddy of these guys was a fellow named Godfroi de Bouillon. He was in this supposed bloodline of Jesus...at least, *he* believed so. And so anyway, as a military general, de Bouillon ends up taking Jerusalem in the year 1099. He sets himself up as a *de facto* king...sort of reclaiming the family throne, as it were. And so, here's the *Sion* part: In the same year—1099—Godfroi establishes the *Priory of Sion*—on the small hill outside the city walls. It was an elite order of Crusader knights—which the present *Sovereign Order of the Temple of Sion* claims descent from. And so, over the span of centuries, the history of *Sion* is very murky—all kinds of legends and rumors—they have the Holy Grail...or they have the Bloodline of Jesus...and all of that."

"So...the *Order*...or the *Priory of Sion*, or whatever, doesn't have much to do with Israel today?"

"No. Not much—just the history of originating in Israel. You could do a little archaeology show on the *History Channel,* and that's about it. The little hill outside the walls is still there, and it's still called Mt. Zion. But it's really nothing more than a tourist stop with a couple of dubious holy sites—the *Last Supper Room* and *David's Tomb.* It's pretty much *Lincoln Slept Here* kind of stuff."

Blackpoint took a long drag on his cigarette, and his eyebrows arched. "Now, geopolitically...the *Sovereign Order of the Temple of Sion* and the Zionist State of Israel are on a veritable collision course with each other. *Sion* champions the ambitions of the elites in the European Union. Their most fervent desire is to see the EU supplant the US. Now, mind you. The EU doesn't want to kill us...our economic contribution is much too important to their own interests, but...a little shaking of the American cultural foundations?...Well, that wouldn't hurt them one bit. For all practical purposes, the Europeans have already jettisoned

Christianity. But, it could shake America up enough for us to lose our edge. And *that* is what the battle is for: *the edge*—who calls the shots. So, in this battle…Oh, yes. *Sion* and *Zion* are quite *contrary*. And to top that off…all these blue-bloods in *Sion?*…Despite their cherished mythology as to their pedigree, they're all anti-semites. They have *nothing* to do with *real Jews.* Indeed, to a man, they're pro-Palestinian…pro-Hamas…pro-Hezbollah, et cetera…especially the Germans, of course. They're pretty slick about keeping it under their vests, but you know how that goes. So…with our two dead men…our *Sion* fellow had some kind of documentary connection to a Palestinian, huh?"

"Yes."

"Well, there you go. That's consistent with my observations of *Sion.*" Blackpoint shrugged. "Now, on the other side….*Zion* with a *Z*? To be frank, the Jews are just going to get fucked over again from the current vicissitudes of history. Israel is not going to get any more meaningful help from us…indeed, we'll be basically pulling the rug out from underneath them. Iraq is going down a fuck hole…Afghanistan could go down as well…and we can't afford to let Lebanon fall into the same toilet….we just didn't get to this goddamn radical Islamic virus quick enough. Our whole Middle East policy is going down a fuck hole. So. We've got to make some deals with the moderate Arab states— their governments, you understand…*not* the peoples. The masses are falling sway to the radicals…so, we have to prop up our Arab kings and dictators, best we can. No. Israel's on her own. She'll have to rely on her God for her redemption, not the US.

"So," Bill continued. "What do you think the deal is with this Van Meter guy and the whole *Lutheran thing*? The Palestinian connected to the dead *Sion* guy is Lutheran."

Blackpoint scrunched his eyes upward. "*The Lutheran thing*? Could be just a coincidence. It happens in this business. Not every fucking thing in the world is tied together, you know. Or…it could be an angle of history that's not jumping out at us at the moment. That happens a lot as well."

"…and Van Meter?"

"Yes. Van Meter. He worries me. I've hired a genealogical expert. It appears the good Pastor Van Meter is a descendant of Godfroi de Bouillon."

"So…he's *Sion*?"

"Ehhhh. Kind of yes…maybe….and mostly no…probably. My gut tells me this guy's a *renegade*."

"*Renegade?*"

"Yes. Renegade. Every organization has them. They're a problem. So, if this Van Meter fellow is *renegade Sion*….that's something to worry about. He knows stuff, and renegades who know stuff are a problem—A problem an organization has to deal with….like a *virus*…you have to stamp it out. And, you usually want to dig things out a little bit—to see how widespread the virus is, before you kill it. It was that way with us in Honduras, for example. We busted our asses training the Contras and the other support units, but…it's a law of nature…you're going to have some of these people you train turn on you…for money or position…or they just change their minds…or whatever…and you just have to deal with it. As quietly as you can. So, for whatever reason, this Van Meter fellow and his wife may very well be a virus that needs *attention.*"

"Eduardo has forwarded a little info. He's found a census record indicating they have a daughter…"

"Yes, I've seen that…she's adopted….so, that's not the deal. But, here's the real deal: We ran all their medical records and it turns up, Van Meter's wife is pregnant…*THAT'S* what all the excitement is about….there's nothing like *New Blood* in dormant royal lineages to get genealogy freaks going…and whoever else. So. *Whatever* this virus is…it's on a new growth cycle." Blackpoint finished his ouzo and set the glass down firmly. "Finally, back to something else…You're watching our boy Eddie closely?"

"Sure. Actually, I'm quite impressed with Eduardo. Good kid. I feel bad for him with his only brother stationed in Mosul."

"Hmm. Yes. Eduardo has *no idea* how well his brother is being looked after…just like him. So. You gave him the original genealogies as I requested?"

"Yeah. Sure. Mind me asking why that was?"

"*Fly paper.*" Blackpoint shrugged.

"*Fly paper?*"

"Yes. Hang it out there, and see what comes buzzing around and sticks. So, it's your job to inventory what sticks…even if it's Eduardo himself."

"You have concerns?"

"Well, I suppose it could be a *genealogy* thing. Eduardo's father—one of our assets in Honduras…He turned up on fly paper one bright and shiny day."

"So, what happened to him?"

"Oh. Well. He had an unfortunate mishap in a traffic accident. DUI they said."

"Did he have a drinking problem?"

"No. But most of them down there do…so, it all worked out. His boys and the wife were already up here in Georgia under our *protection,* as it were. And so, ever since their father's untimely passing, we've been keen to keep a good eye on Eduardo and Carlos *wherever* they are.

Something stirred in Blanche's peripheral vision.

Out of the blue, coming down alongside the bar were two grey-haired women carrying shopping bags and walking intently with loud clops of thick heals. Both were stout and sixty-ish. Both wore mid-calf navy blue skirts, plain white blouses with small gold crosses on the breast pockets. One had thick black plastic 1960s cat glasses with disorientingly thick lenses that magnified her black eyes and bushy eyebrows. The duo stopped dead behind Blanche and Blackpoint.

"It's absolutely BEAUTIFUL, Maria!" exclaimed the one with glasses. Her Hispanic accent was thick. She waddled with great speed around Blackpoint and took hold of the Tiffany chandelier shade with both hands. "It's just stunning!" she reiterated.

"Oh Marta, it reminds me of one that hung in the Mother House years and years ago. I'm sure it was donated," prattled Maria in an equally thick accent.

Twirling the shade lightly, Marta raised her glasses to her forehead and focused one eye deep into the interior of the shade. "Just fantastic work, I must say."

A slight shower of dust and other nasty small debris fell down onto the fine suit of Ashman Blackpoint.

Bill Blanche's mouth was wide open.

"Do you MIND, ladies?" exclaimed Blackpoint pushing back his stool, tugging and brushing his sleeves, and glaring at the duo.

"Oh, we are so terribly sorry, sir...," cried Maria. "We just *HAD* to inspect this wonderful Tiffany lamp. One does not see many like these anymore, you know?"

"Oh my, yes!" Marta grinned in full teeth at the two men. "We truly get excited when we see a genuine Tiffany lamp! So sorry for the dust....We just got a little bit excited...you know?...My, my. There IS quite a bit of dust up here, isn't there? OOOPS! And there's a little *bug* too!"

"Alive or dead, sister?" sang Maria.

"Dead *NOW,* sister!" Marta pinched her prey, popping it to the floor behind the bar where it made a slight tic sound on impact. "Now, THAT'S better!"

Blanche and Blackpoint looked at each other in disbelief.

"Well, we should probably be going Marta....how are we doing on time?"

"Oh dear, I'm afraid my watch has stopped working." Marta tapped the watch dramatically and held it to her ear. She shook her head negatively.

"Sir, could you be so kind to inform us as to the time," Maria asked Blackpoint.

He was speechless.

"Oh, I see a clock Maria...over that mirror down there...see it? It's saying 1:35 or so."

"Oh, good. Not as bad as I feared! Yes, we have *plenty* of time." Marta looked directly into Blackpoint's eyes. "We have a 3:16 flight to catch."

Blackpoint's head bolted back and his face squared with a cold grimace. "*Really?*" he replied in a low aggressive breath.

"Yes. *Really,*" nodded Maria with a matching breath. "You boys really ought to eat something when you drink." She reached into her shoulder purse and flipped out two Communion wafers embossed with a wheat sheaf design onto the bar. Looking directly into the eyes of Blackpoint she offered a soft "*Kali Mera.*"

Blackpoint's eyes matched the woman's. With a soft sneer and a nod, he replied, "*Buenas tardes, Sisters.*"

And the pair departed the tavern, disappearing into the mid-day sun.

Blackpoint's eyes were in complete glare to the furthermost edge of the universe.

Did we just get a visit from the Vatican?" inquired Blanche directly.

"No," he replied slowly. "Not the Vatican. *Vatican rene-gades. Viruses. Sisters Of The Precious Host.*" He picked up one the communion wafers off the bar and twirled it around in his fingers like a baton, deep in thought, staring into the wafer. He held it up to Blanche. "The Sisters worship crackers by day, and fuck with the US government by night. They came up against us in Honduras in the '80s, especially our 3-16 Counter Insurgency Unit which we trained in Georgia." Blackpoint nodded to him-self, half shaking, from anger and some fear.

"This thing is connected to what went on in Central America a quarter century ago?" Blanche winced at his own question.

"Have your people at ICE monitor all Hispanic Catholic Re-ligious personnel coming in and out of the country. All of them. This *thing* is larger than I thought."

Chapter 7

*Blessed are you, O Lord, the healer of the sick of his people Is-
rael.*

Montra, Ohio.
Saturday, May 19, 3:13 P.M.

Jonah had just put the phone down. It rang again.

"Daddy, Daddy, Daddy!!! Come quick!" Sara's voice was
hysterical. "There's something wrong with Mommy!
She's really, really sick, Daddy! I think it might be the baby!"

Jonah's jump into the *Caravan* and arrival two miles east at
the Jackson Center High School gymnasium defied conventional
measurements of space and time. He found his wife on the gym
floor surrounded by a huddle of people. Madeleine's body was
on its side drawn in fetal position. She was semi-conscious,
faintly groaning.

Sara held herself around the middle sobbing.

"Quiet!" barked Jonah ferociously. His shaking hand lovingly
stroked Maddie's face down to her neck bearing the repaired *tefila* cord soaking in her sweat. She burned. His eye pierced to
hers as he lifted her eyelids to reveal an oblique sickening gone-
ness. Her head shook with small convulsions. Jonah's shoulder
was gently tugged by a firm hand.

"Sir..." the paramedic said.

Jonah retreated and took hold of Sara, oblivious to the surrounding two dozen on-lookers equally in shock.

The paramedics quickly went through their protocols. The
squawks of their radios were disorienting. Jonah answered seven
medical background questions fired at him in rapid order. And

immediately the group hustled with the gurney to the ambulance waiting outside, its running diesel engine seeming as a roar. With the gurney loaded, Jonah, Sara and paramedics tumbled in. The engine's roar was immediately joined by the shrill siren wail from above. The chariot thundered forward with terrible vibration and light.

Twelve minutes later, the ambulance arrived at the ER of the Bellefontaine Community Hospital. The vehicle doors flew open and the people and equipment surged forward like troops storming the beaches of Normandy. Flashes of grey walls, beige carpet, and glass strobed through Jonah's eyes as he raced with the gurney blasting like a tank through two huge grey double doors. And the firm hand, again, pulled him back.

The grey doors closed.

Jonah was on the *other* side of *another world*.

Madeleine Garmu Lechem Van Meter was not sure if she heard a voice or not. All was black. She felt as though she lay trapped at the bottom of a well in complete darkness. She was frightened. She kept hearing a voice. *Maybe* it was a voice. But she could not climb to it. She could not. She saw, or imagined, or thought?—of dim faces—her mother and father, her grandparents, and other *old ones* she did not know. She saw a little boy's face—a little Jewish boy with neat little side-locks flowing in the wind. It was her *Danny*. Jonah's boy. Sara's brother. For an instant, she saw his little shining face so brightly, so vividly, she thought she might burst through the darkness to the light. But then he was gone. And all was black again.

Sara Kali Van Meter was a strong girl. She marched through the large double grey doors behind her father with her head held high and straight. Her stark dark eyes pierced all existence. Through the long antiseptic grey and beige corridor they marched behind the nurse—no sound, beyond their shoes ticking on the cold tile.

The nurse delivered them to the door of the room. And Sara did something quite extraordinary. She forbade her father to enter the room. She told him to wait until she said it was time for him to enter. Being in shock, Jonah complied.

Sara stood at the foot of her mother's bed. Madeleine lay almost sideways, in a no-direction position. Her hair was plastered by sweat to the side of her face and neck; her eyes closed and twitching; her breathing under the fogged plastic oxygen mask was strangely shallow, rapid, and struggling all at once. There was stench of vomit and feces and antiseptic in the air. The machines with their lights and blips worked the tubes going into Madeleine with gurgles and drips. Sara looked at her own thin dark arms, and then at her mother's. There was not much difference. Madeleine was sorely depleted. Her mother looked small. *Too small* under the sheet. *O God.* It hit Sara. *O God.* The baby. He was not there. Danny was gone. *O God.*

Sara dropped to her mother's side. Looking into Madeleine's closed struggling eyes, Sara recalled the first time she saw her mother's face. It was in the orphanage in Sarajevo. She was six years old. It was another room full of stench and cries to God. The beautiful face. The beautiful dark, somehow familiar face with soft gentle eyes and a knowing smile, framed by shining black hair that came to hover above her. And beside the beautiful face, the strange funny man with long hair—gods come down from somewhere to save her.

The flood of memory pushed up against the back of Sara's eyes to flow, but she held. She held. Her eye pierced, and her lower lip trembled in spasm.

"Mommy. O Mommy." She let her soul flow, blowing her breath into the air.

"Mommy. You are the best Mommy in the whole world. You *remember* that Mommy. *Remember. Remember. Remember* that you are Roma. And I am Roma. Remember the poem you taught me by the Englishman…about the Gypsy Songs?

> The faery beam upon you,
> The stars to glister on you;
> A moon of light
> In the noon of night,
> Till the fire-drake hath o'ergone you!

The wheel of fortune guide you,
The boy with the bow beside you;
Run ay in the way
Till the bird of day,
And the luckier lot betide you!
To the old, long life and treasure!
To the young, all health and pleasure!
To the fair, their face
With eternal grace
And the soul to be loved at leisure!
To the witty, all clear mirrors;
To the foolish, their dark errors;
To the loving sprite,
A secure delight;
To the jealous, her own false terrors!

And *remember* Mommy. You are a Jew. A special Jew. *Remember* how many grandmas and grandpas have had the recipe for your bread. And now I have it Mommy. The same bread that the first baby Sara ate in the boat. In the boat Mommy, get back in the boat and sail. Sail away to freedom. Sail away with me, Mommy. We can make it. We can. We will live, Mommy. We will make the bread. I will make the bread....with my own daughters, and my own sons. I will, someday, Mommy. You are a Jew, and I am a Jew." Sara reached out and stroked her mother's feverish face and long graceful neck. Suddenly, she spied something on the tray table beside the bed. Lifting it up, she found it to be a very old leather cord with a small pouch. She had never seen the cord and pouch before...but then it dawned on her. She *remembered*. It was from the story her father had told her of the first Sara. It was from the boat.

Standing herself up straight as an arrow, Sara addressed her mother.
"You are Roma, and I am Roma. You are a Jew, and I am a Jew. And Daddy is a Jew. And Daddy is a special Jew. We need Daddy. I'm going to get Daddy, Mommy. Hang on....I'll get him right now."

In the hallway, Sara faced Jonah, "Mommy needs you. You have to do something Daddy. You have to *do something*."

Chapter 8

Blessed are you, O Lord, who blesses the years.

Bellefontaine, Ohio.
Sunday, May 19, 6:13 P.M.

Jonah stood with Sara at Madeleine's bedside. Standing with them was a petite dark-haired woman in a white coat: Dr. Susan Gellman, Chief Resident.

"Not sure what is going on here, Mr. Van Meter. Perhaps, it would be better if Sara, stepped outside a minute," said the doctor in a low voice stepping back from the bed.

"No," said Sara.

"No," confirmed Jonah shaking his head.

"Yes. Certainly." Dr. Gellman nodded in respect. "I am a direct person Mr. Van Meter. So, I don't wish to burden you more than necessary, but neither do I think it fair to withhold any facts. You have a right to facts, so that you may choose the course you see fit. The facts are: Madeleine is not doing well—at all. We extracted the fetus, which you understand was no longer living, to prevent further toxicity to her system. She continues to be in a profound state of septic shock which would suggest some sort of bacterial infection. On the other hand, her symptoms in regard to the extreme stress to her whole digestive system correlate to what we sometimes see with heavy metals poisoning. I suppose it would not be outside the realm of possibility that she's been subjected to a combination of factors. We're waiting for the blood work to come back…unfortunately the weekends are slower on that."

"Can alcohol do this?" asked Jonah bluntly.

"No."

"Will she live?"

"We are doing what we can with chelation therapy. We inject an agent called *calcium disodium edetate.* If there are heavy metals in her tissues, the agent will bond with them which enables them to be passed into the bloodstream and then from the body with the urine. It may help some."

"Is she going to live? Will this therapy possibly save her?"

A long silence hovered in the air.

"Unlikely. I am *very, very* sorry Mr. Van Meter." Dr. Gellman raised her hand to wipe her eye. She stroked the silver Star of David pendant about her neck and then took Jonah's hands into hers. "Would you like me to call someone from our *Pastoral Care* staff, Mr. Van Meter?"

"No. Thank you," said Jonah softly. He was stung by the irony.

Sara's dark thin arms took to Jonah's, locking them together.

"Daddy, you have to *do something.* You have to *do something.*"

Jonah wheeled around and slowly walked toward his wife. His memory strobed through his brain. His eyes were wild and wide, and his mind ticking like a time bomb... a time bomb...*A time bomb.*

"You say *she will die,* Dr. Gellman?"

"Yes."

Jonah slowly grimaced and cocked his head. Trembling, he slowly and slightly began to shake his head *NO.* His head sliced the air horizontally wider and faster, and he went to Madeleine's bed. He began to pray in a low voice, rocking forward on his feet:

Baruch atah Adonai elohaynu melech ha'olam oseh ma'asey Sara

Baruch atah Adonai elohaynu melech ha'olam oseh ma'asey Sara

Baruch atah Adonai elohaynu melech ha'olam oseh ma'asey Sara...

Jonah rocked and prayed the same words over and over again, faster and faster, twelve times.

And then he stopped.

"You say, Dr. Gellman, that my Maddie will die?" Jonah stared into the air. His face started to twitch and turn red. His mind burst into spontaneous combustion. A roar deafened his interior hearing and consciousness. Fire flushed through Jonah's entire being rolling out from some unknown central source, and out of his mouth came the Word:

NO!

I – DON'T – THINK – SO!!!

"Daddy!" Sara wheeled her father around and took his arms. "Put Mommy in the *boat* Daddy! Put her in the *boat*. With *me*. Remember? *Remember* Daddy. Put Mommy and Sara *back* in the boat. Send them from France Daddy. Send them from France. Send them *Home*. Send them Daddy. Mommy and Sara want to go home…where the *bread* came from. You *remember* Daddy. *I remember.* I remember *everything* you've told me. You make Mommy *remember*, Daddy. Put her in the boat, *Abba*. Please, *Abba*!"

Jonah's jaw set square and solid. The drummers of all existence inside his head immediately ceased. He turned directly to Susan Gellman who was not sure what she was beholding.

"I want you to take Sara, and have your staff take care of her. I want you to have some bread—any kind, sent to this room. When I am beyond your state of consciousness, hook me up to an I.V….do whatever you have to do—to keep me going…."

"What?" Susan was incredulous.

"Do it!" he blurted. "Finally, I want you to absolutely follow this order. No one outside this department….I repeat, no one, is to know that my son Daniel is dead. No one. Someone did this to my wife—to my son. We will not give them information as to their deed. Will you promise me that?"

"Yes…for as long as I can, Mr. Van Meter. For as long as I can," replied Susan.

Montra, Ohio.
Sunday, May 20, 10:30 A.M.

Eduardo slipped into the back pew of Emanuel Lutheran church just before the service began. He felt a strange juxtaposition of the familiar and alien. Stained glass and a richly carved altar bearing a statue of Jesus were not far from his Catholic youth. But the music was different—heavier and marching, like an army on orders—not like the ethereal pleas for grace in Latin chants. And the service started with a ritual quite unknown to Eduardo called a *Brief Order For Confession Of Sins.* At first, the ritual struck him as a very practical thing....make confession *easy*, right at the regular Sunday service....no need for a special trip to church during the week to confess. But maybe the ritual was *too easy.* The words of the ritual were quite foreign to Eduardo. The congregation said together:

> *We confess that we are bound to sin and cannot be free. We have sinned against you by what we have said and done. We have not loved you with our whole devotion; we have not loved our neighbors as ourselves. For the sake of your Son, Jesus Christ, have mercy on us. Forgive and deliver us, so that we may ascend to your will and walk in your light, to your peace everlasting. Amen.*

Eduardo was confused...*bound to sin???*....and...*cannot be free???* Did this mean that *there is no hope for people?—That people will never in themselves be able to improve the kind of people they are?—That there is no such thing as moral progress in humanity?* This was not what his mother Zara taught him as a boy. She taught Eduardo that he must go out into the world and make the world better by doing good.

Eduardo became even more confused when the pastor stepped forward to speak. The pastor was certainly not Jonah Van Meter.

Eduardo was looking at an old man....*Am I in the right church?* Eduardo checked the bulletin. Indeed, it indicated *Emanuel Lutheran Church, Montra, Ohio.* Then he saw it. An announcement that Pastor Jonah had a family emergency—*Prayers are needed for Maddie*, and Pastor Stuck was filling in.

The old pastor looked like Moses. He held up his right hand and intoned the words of absolution:

> *The Lord God has mercifully given his Son to die for us and, for Jesus' sake, forgives us our many sins. Therefore, by the authority of Christ and His Church, I proclaim to you the forgiveness of all your sins, in the name of the Father, and of the Son, and of the Holy Spirit. Amen.*

The pastor made a sweeping sign of the cross, and the congregation responded in a resounding *Amen.*

Eduardo found all the words strange. *What? Forgiveness of ALL sins...just for showing up at church? Easy to sin, easier to be forgiven?* By the sound of it, these Lutherans believed forgiveness was all up to God, and that their own actions had very little to do with it. Eduardo liked his mother's theology better. *Eduardo, you are a child of God. So, act like it.*

The old pastor, having finished his absolution, motioned the congregation to sit. He stepped down from the chancel to make announcements. All eyes and ears were alert due to what was already in the bulletin about Madeleine. The pastor had very little additional information. He asked for the congregation's prayers. Madeleine had collapsed the previous afternoon at the high school gymnasium. She was in critical condition. No information was available beyond that. There was no word of any effect on her baby. The sanctuary buzzed in fast whispers as the pastor went on to other announcements.

Eduardo looked across the aisle to see an elderly woman in a wheelchair at the end of the back pew. She was bent over and sobbing. Eduardo slid out of his pew and hunched down next to the old woman.

"Mam?...Do you know what has happened to Pastor Jonah's wife?" Eduardo asked gingerly.

Barbara Weiss looked up and stared through wet eyes. "Danger," she said. "I told him there was danger. I told him to be careful. He knew there was danger."

"Danger? To who dear?"

"The baby, of course. Who are you? I don't believe I know you. Do you know Jonah? I know Jonah. He's a dear friend of mine. I came over here first thing when my friend called me with the news," rattled Barbara, quite shaken.

"Jonah is a friend of mine also." Eduardo instinctively lied.

"Well, you know that Maddie is at the Bellefontaine Hospital. Will you be going there?...since you're his friend? I won't be able to get over today, but there's something I would like to say to Jonah. Would you take him a message for me?"

"Surely," agreed Eduardo with genuine pity on the old woman in her distress.

Barbara fished around in her purse and finally found a pen. She took a collection envelope from the pew rack and struggled a moment to remember what she wanted to write. But it came. Her hands gripping the pen fiercely and shakily, she wrote out something. She quickly folded the note and gave it to Eduardo.

"Make sure he gets this, will you sir? It is very important that he receive that message."

"Yes, mam. I will be sure that he gets it. You take care now. I'm going to leave right now and go to the hospital."

Barbara nodded and quickly cast her eyes back to the deacon standing in the narthex who she called over to her. She directed him to remove a small portion of the Communion bread waiting on a small table nearby. She gave it to Eduardo.

"Put it in your pocket. It will bring you good luck...God willing," said Barbara as she patted Eduardo's hands, scanning the lines. She was comforted by what she saw.

Eduardo slugged out the church door toward his car. Lost in thought, he meandered in the gravel parking lot with his head to the sky. The sun, bright and hot, hit his eye as it bounced off the silver orb atop the church steeple. He winced at what looked like a giant clown hat looking down on him, laughing. Fishing for his keys, he felt something else in his coat pocket. It was Elaine Armstrong's business card. Eduardo's eyes lit up. He immediately flew to his car. He grabbed his laptop and fired it up. In no time he had a map to the address on the card. *Not far. Not far at all. Thirty minutes, tops.*

In one seamless movement, Eduardo's tires spit gravel and his hand grabbed the cell phone. He called Elaine Armstrong.

"Maria Shrine. May I help you?" the scraggly nun-voice answered.

"Yes. I am looking for Professor Elaine Armstrong. She informed me that she would be staying at your facility…"

"Ah, yes. Sister Elaine….well, we like to think of her as *Sister*. Yes, she is here. Let me try to ring her room. May I tell her who is calling?"

"Certainly. This is Eduardo Mendoza….she knows me from United Airlines." *That was a stupid thing to say,* thought Eduardo.

"Yes, Mr. Mendoza. Please hold."

"Thank you."

Within a minute Elaine answered the phone. "Cheerio, Sexy!"

"Cheerio, Sexy!??? Are you allowed to say that *there?!!*"

"Well, love. The *NSA* may tap our phones, but Mother Superior does not. Lovely to hear your voice Eduardo…."

"Elaine, I need your help."

"What Eduardo?…You sound worried."

"Yes. Well. You know the man we were discussing on the flight?…Jonah Van Meter…you remember?"

"Of course. I've been thinking about that situation ever since the flight. Is everything alright?"

"Uh,…No."

"No?"

"No. I went to his church this morning to check him out, and he wasn't there. The story is that his wife collapsed yesterday and she is in the hospital. Apparently, she is pregnant and…"

"What about the *baby*?" Elaine was *suddenly* urgent.

"Well…I do not know…if she is *still* pregnant…you know?

"Oh, God. The baby has to be in trouble..."

"Yes, that is the thing, Elaine. There is no information out of anyone except that the woman is in the hospital...no condition...no word on her baby. Sounds weird, you know? Feels weird. I would like to talk to you some more about these genealogy lists...like,...Is there a reason that someone wants to harm this family?..."

"Yes. Eduardo." Elaine's voice was even more urgent and emphatic. "We must talk. *Now*. Where are you?"

"I'm already headed toward your place...hoping you would see me. I should be there in twenty minutes."

"Yes. Good, Eduardo. Pick me up and then we must go to the hospital. Where is it?"

"A town called Bellefontaine."

"Good. It's not very far. Hurry Eduardo. There are *things— secrets*...about this family's genealogy that are *very important*. I indeed fear they are in very grave danger."

"I will be there," said Eduardo.

In no time, Eduardo pulled off a country road surrounded by wheat fields to another world. Maria Shrine rose up from the grain as a surreal mini city of God. The old brick complex was L shaped with a lovely courtyard in its center. A walk led through the courtyard to the main door at the base of a tower supporting a soaring cross-topped spire. Entering, Eduardo noticed a white statue of St. Joseph tucked in the alcove above the door.

"Good Morning," said Eduardo to the grey-haired nun behind the sliding window of the reception office. "I am here to see Professor Armstrong..."

"Oh! Sí, Señor Mendoza!" cried the grey-haired nun, her eyes and bushy eyebrows googling large hehind her thick cat glasses.

"Yes?..." blustered Eduardo, befuddled by the nun's instant recognition complete with Hispanic accent and address.

"Certainly," continued the nun. "Sister Elaine is in the *Relic Chapel* taking a shift with our *Perpetual Adoration*..."

"I should wait then," stated Eduardo. He knew that *Perpetual Adoration* meant prayer before the Blessed Sacrament on a continuous basis. His memory instantly recalled how his small town church in Honduras held such adorations for stints of time. It was not an easy thing to do. Enough dedicated people, of good repute, were needed to man shifts on a 24 hour basis in order to attend to the *Host* reserved in a special receptacle on the altar.

"You can come with me Señor Mendoza," the cheery little grey-haired nun chortled. "I am Sister Marta. It's my turn about now anyway. So it all works out nicely you see!"

They trooped down the hall to the cadence of Sister Marta's choppy walk of clunky shoes on old slate floors. Memories of his early youth flooded into Eduardo's mind.

They arrived at the richly carved oak doors of the *Relic Chapel*. Pulling open the doors and stepping inside was like landing in *Oz* out of the twister. Directly facing them arose three large intricately ancient oak altars, the altar in the middle being the highest. Each altar was a virtual topography of niches and alcoves, all with something very specific enshrined in each. The side walls also were lined with altars, each bearing a cache of sacred relics secreted somewhere. The chapel was dim in a purple haze, illumined only by stained glass windows and a few votive candles at the various altars. An alluring aroma of incense and freshly baked bread flavored the air with an other-worldly pull upon the soul.

Elaine was in the front pew, kneeling in prayer. Her head was positioned full-up and directed at a special silver cross on the central altar. The cross, called a *monstrance*, had a large round compartment at the center of its cross-beams which held the *Blessed Host…the Body of Christ… in reserve.*

Sister Marta genuflected and motioned Eduardo to follow her down the aisle. Instinctively, Eduardo genuflected and followed the clopping small feet on the slate.

The pair knelt in the front left pew opposite Elaine. She did not move, her face locked in a laser beam gaze to the monstrance upon the altar. Even though she was in prayerful posture, Eduardo could not see her *as a nun*. He could not help but trace the lines of her figure under the shadows of the towering high altar, and he felt very consciously, and indeed… agreeably conflicted.

Sister Marta coughed.

Elaine turned her head and smiled. Immediately she arose. With a soft nod to *her sister*, Elaine took Eduardo's hand and they departed up the side-aisle and out the door into the arched gothic hallway.

"I hope that I did not interrupt you," Eduardo was quick to be polite.

"No, not at all. I was just taking a turn at the *vigil* for old time's sake."

"Yes, I know this practice. Our church in Honduras did the same, although we called it the *Blessed Sacrament* instead of *Blessed Host*..."

"Yes, it's the same thing....just a little different wording. It's still the *Bread* representing the *Body of Jesus* being reserved for us."

"Hmm...yes. I must admit Elaine, there are many things about religion I do not know. Like, as a boy, I always wondered about little things that are probably not important...like why they called it *Blessed SACRAMENT*...when it was only the *bread* they put in the cross-thing... what do they call it?..."

"Monstrance."

"Yes, monstrance. So...like...the priest blesses the bread and *the wine*, but they put *only bread* in the monstrance thing, but they still call it *Sacrament?* I am afraid religion can be very confusing to me," shrugged Eduardo with a sheepish grin.

Elaine laughed. "Well, I'll let you in on the back room secrets of how it all works. Really. The main reason that wine isn't reserved is simple: Wine is like *blood*...very messy. Not an easy substance to contain and control. It can just leak out here or there and everywhere...and you don't want that. If something is holy, you want to keep it holy. That's rather difficult with a fluid substance. How do you keep it where it's supposed to stay? I suppose it is like our own bodies....you know? We keep our blood on the *inside*, not the outside.....it works much better that way, you know? Bread, on the other hand, is more stable...more *outsideable*...how do you like that for a new Word, love?...so, being more *outsideable*...out in the everyday world...like our own bodies...*bread* and *body* really are themes that go quite well together. Bread is a universal symbol that applies to all people, no matter what kind. We all have bodies working out in the world and we all need the basics to keep going, basics like bread…"

"So…the wine?" inquired Eduardo weakly, his tone suggesting that he still felt theologically challenged.

"Ah, yes. How then do we say that we adore the whole Blessed Sacrament when we behold only the Host in the monstrance. It's simple!" she exclaimed spiritedly. "What body does not have blood *in* it? Just because we look at a body and do not *see* the blood, doesn't mean the blood isn't there!"

"Ahhhhh!" Eduardo nodded. He got it. After so many years. It *was* simple.

"And I'll tell you a little extra secret about our relic chapel here." She drew close to his face. "In the monstrance along with the Host is a splinter of the True Grail hidden in the bottom of the receptacle. It's something we keep to ourselves in the order generally, but really, in today's world it wouldn't mean much even if you went around talking about it."

"A splinter? A splinter of metal?….the grail was metal wasn't it?"

"No. Actually the True Grail is wood. The wood of a common carpenter's family. It's amazingly simple isn't it? The real Jesus had simple things in his life. Simple bread and wine…simple plates and cups…what have you. It was really much later that people with power came along and imagined what powerful people always dream of—gold and silver and gems, and all the rest."

"Wow." Eduardo *was* amazed at how simple and direct his new beautiful catechism teacher made things. And then he was brave. "You really believe all this?" He waved his hand toward the relic chapel. "….All the stories in there with all the holy things from so many places and people and their secrets? Like when you see the statue of Mary in there, do you think she is looking at you from somewhere?"

Elaine smiled a professor's smile. "Well. I suppose I *do* have my own spin on it all. But my whole life, I've lived with a certain sense of history as a living breathing thing. So yes, in some way I can think about Mary in the here and now…but of course, you know there is *more than one Mary* in there…"

Eduardo felt stupid again. "Well…there would be Mary, the mother of Jesus…. and….???"

"…and Jesus' *special friend* who just happened to be a *girl*…Mary of Magdala…popularly known as Mary Magdalene—a *very special friend* as we say today with a wink and a nod."

Eduardo's eyes went wide. "Well, we all could use a special friend," he mused in accordance with his new favorite inner-conflict. "So…what do the *Sisters Of The Blessed Host* do with their time when they are not praying in the chapel?"

"Well, largely the order does two things. They do social service in developing countries…like in Central America….you are Honduran, yes?…"

"Yes."

"I thought so…from your accent. *And* we bake *Bread*."

"Yes, I smell that. Wonderful! So why *bread*…because of the *Host* in your name?

"Well, yes of course that's the spiritual base…but there's the practical as well. The order typically supplies altar bread for neighboring parishes. It's a good source of revenue, and we have a very good product. And there *is competition in the field.* But you can be sure you are getting the very best in altar bread if you see the Order's symbol on the bread…"

"And what is that?"

"Well. We need to get to the hospital, but I can show you very quickly. Follow me."

Elaine led Eduardo down the hall toward the source of the bread aroma. They passed through a heavy steel door into a large, brightly lit kitchen: The bakery. Several of the sisters were busy removing sheets of round flat loaves from old ovens and placing them on stainless steel topped tables in the middle of the room. On the ends of the tables were several old large round wooden stamps used for marking the tops of the loaves.

Elaine picked one up and displayed it to Eduardo. The design was a circle with a large equal armed cross. In the very center was a tiny Star of David. Under the circle were some Latin words: *Hoc Est Enim Corpus Meum*. Within the design were smaller rings and divisions and individual dots within each ring and the whole circle was outlined with individual dots.

"It's a very ancient Middle Eastern Christian symbol," instructed Elaine. "Note how it symbolizes our Global Community as having inner and outer layers and all the individuals are organized according to their section but related to all the other sections as well."

Eduardo's brain jumped into high gear. "It's a *network!*" he blurted.

"Exactly" Elaine smiled. "A very sophisticated network. Common...Ancient...and strong as God."

"What do these words mean?" Eduardo pointed to the Latin under the globe: *Hoc Est Enim Corpus Meum*.

"Simple: *This is my Body*." Elaine's eyes searched Eduardo's for understanding.

Eduardo continued his questions. "So. The *energy* of this network?...Does it come from the center?....from the Star of David out to the Cross?....or does it come from all these *dots* on the outer ring?"

"Both...and everything in between," answered Elaine plainly.

"The perfect *virus*." Eduardo nodded. "No way to kill it."

"Exactly," affirmed Elaine. "A *Community*, like this..." she pointed to the sphere, "...has been blessed with *years beyond years*."

Eduardo looked up to a sky light flooding the room with the morning light. His task compelled him to be direct.

"Elaine. Perhaps God has brought you to me, or me to you. You know that I need quick help with this matter about Jonah Van Meter...and....God help me, I don't have time to check you out. You know that I work for an intelligence service, yes?

"CIA?"

"No, DIA. Different building. Similar job."

"Our order has a history of doing battle with the CIA. Did you know this?"

"No...I know what you are saying...I understand. But, there are good people everywhere. I am *good people*. And I must ask you to consider that...and I must ask you to somehow trust me...to...."

"...to...act...on *faith?*"

"Yes....maybe *faith*. I need to understand why the family of Jonah Van Meter is under attack. I need to know why he is important...if this is part of a terrorist attack being planned or whatever. I hope you can help me Elaine. I am using my gut and breaking all protocol in asking you this, but my gut tells me you know many things and that you can help. Will you help me?"

"Yes. Of course, love," affirmed Elaine as she softly laid her hands upon Eduardo's face. "I can see you are a good man Eduardo, notwithstanding who you may work for. Let's go, love. Quickly. I will help you."

Eduardo's rental raced east toward the town of Bellefontaine.

"Eduardo. If I am to be of help to you, I must ask you some questions."

"Okay," replied Eduardo unflinching.

"Do you remember when we first met on the plane and I told you about the man *Cretien DuBois* who is the common ancestor of both Jonah and Madeleine Van Meter?"

"Yes.

"Did you Google him as I suggested?"

"No, I am sorry I did not have time."

"Okay. Well. I need to help you there. First, let me ask you about the *Vatican Secret Archives* genealogy list you showed to me...."

"Yes..."

"Was that the *only* genealogy list you have in this matter?"

Eduardo's eyes widened. He hesitated for a moment as to whether he should divulge the whole story of the two murders.

Elaine beat him to the punch. "I am assuming that you have also encountered the agents of the *Sovereign Order Of The Temple Of* Sion."

"And how do you know about them?" blurted Eduardo.

"Our order's motherhouse is in Switzerland and has long done battle with them there and throughout Europe. They know us well. We know them. Unfortunate neighbors we have been."

"I see," said Eduardo. His gaze over the road was pierced by the sun reflecting off the church spire of Emanuel Lutheran high upon its mount. Speeding past the town of Montra, he did not immediately notice the white car that pulled out onto Route 274 from Montra-Pasco Road…and another car from a nearby farm lane shrouded by overgrown brush. "Uh, yes, Elaine. There are *two* genealogies. They are similar. But as you say. One is from the *Vatican*. And the other is from the *SOTS—Sovereign Order Of The Temple Of Sion.*"

"How did you obtain them. Eduardo?"

"Murder."

"Murder?"

"Yes. The Vatican agent murdered the *SOTS* agent. Shortly after this, the Vatican agent was murdered in the Boston City Jail. The genealogies came to us from the crime-scene evidence."

"The Catholic was poisoned?"

"Yes. How did you know?"

"It's text book Vatican *m.o.*"

"What do you mean? YOU are a Catholic! You are saying… your own leaders murder people all the time?!!

"It is like you have already said, love. There are good people everywhere. There are also bad. There are Catholics, and then there are *Catholics.*"

"On the plane…" Eduardo stuttered.

"The plane?" Elaine replied.

"Yes. You asked me if I am Jewish. Why did you ask me if I am Jewish?"

Elaine gently stroked Eduardo's face. "Well, my dear. You may be Catholic, but you are a *special kind* of Catholic."

"What do you mean?"

"It's like this, love. The reason I asked if you are Jewish is because you used the word *El Dio*. Where did you learn that word?"

"What? *El Dio*? It's just *God*…I thought you knew Spanish!"

"But Eduardo. *Dios…God…* is Spanish. *El Dio* is more than Spanish."

"Different forms of the same thing…it happens in every language," Eduardo shrugged.

"But Eduardo, where specifically did you learn *El Dio*?"

Eduardo shrugged again. "My mother of course. *El Dio* this. *El Dio* that. *El Dio's watching you*, she would say. So what's the big deal with one Spanish word? You know, I know a lot more Spanish words…and what does *El Dio* have to do with being Jewish?

"Tell me, love…," Elaine probed. "…did your mother light candles on Friday nights?"

Eduardo looked quickly at Elaine and then back to the road racing before him. He looked at her again. His eyes pierced. "Yes," he blurted. "How could you know that?"

"….and when your mother baked bread, did she pinch off a little piece and throw it in the hot oven and burn it up?"

Eduardo's eyes blinked wildly. His head snapped in a shot to Elaine's searching eyes. "*HOW* in the world would you know about something like *THAT*? YES, my mother did these things? What are you telling me?" his voice rose in confused tremor.

Elaine drew close and stroked the back of his neck. "Eduardo. *Jews* light candles on Friday night…at the beginning of *Shabbat*. And *Jews* pinch off a piece of dough for the oven in memory of the sacrifices their priests made when they had a temple. And the word *El Dio*?...is *Ladino*—the dialect of *Spanish Jews*—*many of whom were forced to convert to Christianity out of persecution.* Even when families forgot they were once Jews, they kept some of the old ways, passed from one generation to the next. Yes, Eduardo. You are a *Jew*. More accurately, love…you are what they call a *Crypto-Jew*…or *secret Jew*. In the year 1492 all the Jews were expelled from Spain in one of the largest persecutions of Jews down through the centuries. A lot of Jews in Spain and Southern Europe coped with the persecution by officially converting to Catholicism on the outside. They took on Christian names and ways, acted Christian in public, but at home…Eduardo, they lit candles on Shabbat, and they pinched bread into the ovens and they prayed to the One God, *El Dio*."

Eduardo stared ahead into the racing highway in absolute silence, blinking his eyes. He was in shock. A torrent of memory flooded his mind. The early misty years in Honduras. Then the years in Georgia. He thought of the last time he saw his father. It was an ordinary morning. He left for work. Got in the car and drove away. Never came back. Until then, everything was looking so much better. His father had a good job at the secret training school. Yes, it was stressful. His father always looked very worried. Once, *and only once,* he confided to Eduardo that not *everything* the Americans did was right and that he was trying to help show them a better way. Eduardo had no idea what his father meant, but it sounded good to him. Mother was much happier in America, and his little brother Carlos had already forgotten Honduras. Carlos was a *true* American.

Then it all crashed and burned. One day, after school, the soldiers in their fancy uniforms came to the door. It was a Friday. He remembered how his mother crumpled in the chair beside the candle table, rocking back and forth with her hand held strangely over her eyes. She was muttering something, perhaps a prayer, with words and soft sobbing that Eduardo could make no sense of whatsoever.

"Eduardo? Are you alright?" Elaine's soft hand touched the side of his face.

"Yes," he replied shaking the past vigorously out of his head. His eyes darted up to the rear view mirror. "Hmph," he uttered.

"What?"

"*Company.* Do not turn around to look. Just keep talking to me normally." Eduardo tracked the movements of a white rental car, very similar to his. And another. A black one, several car lengths behind the white. Same model. "Stupid shits!"

"What? Who?"

"All of us! Out here…we're all using the same goddamn car rental agency! Not very *James Bond!*

"Just two of them?"

"Yes. But two is enough for trouble."

"Well, love. It's two *now*…but a good deal more to be sure very soon."

A blue *Escort* with two grey-haired ladies suddenly passed them and sped ahead.

Eduardo turned full face to Elaine and with wide eyes exclaimed "*Really*?!" He studied her soft blue eyes intently. She had just given a glimpse that she indeed had some grip on what was going on.

"Okay, Elaine. Who *is* Jonah Van Meter? Why are we and the *Budget Rent-A-Car-Club* all chasing him?"

Elaine was direct. "Actually, the question is: Who is Jonah *AND* Madeleine Van Meter? There is a short answer and a long one."

"My GPS says we have 3 miles to the hospital…give me the short one."

"Alright, then. Jonah and Madeleine Van Meter are like you, Eduardo. They are *Crypto-Jews*. And very special ones, at that. In a nutshell, their story goes back to the man I have been telling you about: *Cretien DuBois*."

"Okay."

"Okay. Jonah and Madeleine are *both* descendants of Cretien DuBois who lived in the early 1600s. Cretien was from a French Merovingian family very concerned with its Merovingian status and the whole legacy of a *bloodline* from Jesus and Mary Magdalene. In a word, Cretien caused a scandalous breach with his family. *He married a Jew.* And in that marriage, Cretien created a new crypto-Jewish lineage with an agenda much different than that of the Merovingians.

"What agenda?"

"Yes. Well. There have been rumors for years, in the back channels of the Church, that there was indeed a family *out there*—a split-off from the Merovingian lines. And the Word has been that this new line opposes the entire core of mainline Merovingian values. This split-off family reportedly scorns elitism, royalty, and all the pride wrapped up with the elevation of a certain group of people on the basis of *blood*. And. The word has also been that Cretien's line possesses a *Secret* that the Merovingians do not have…"

"Why would that be?"

"…short answer?"

"Yes…short answer." Eduardo turned the car hard into the hospital parking lot, almost careening on two wheels to a parking space front and center to the door.

The two other cars landed in more outlying spaces.

Eduardo snatched the keys and looked Elaine square in the face.

"…the short answer, love, is: The Jewish woman that Cretien DuBois married was a direct descendant of Mary Magdalene."

Eduardo paused a moment in thought. "You will tell me the long answer?"

"Yes. But we have to race now, love. Madeleine and her baby are in danger. Do you have the genealogy documents with you."

"Yes, of course."

"Good. From here on…you should keep them constantly on your person. They will guide us every inch of the way. Let's hurry."

Jonah Van Meter's right hand gripped the IV bag pole in the grey of the darkened room. His bowed head was shrouded by the curtain of his exposed long Merovingian hair. Hunched and wincing in a torrent stream of prayer accented with short subtle rockings of his body frontward and backward, his visage paralleled that of the late John Paul II hanging upon his staff. Jonah's right arm was strapped up with Madeleine's *tefila*. It was the *tefila* passed from Yeshua to his wife Miryam of Magdala…the first Madeleine…and then down through the generations of the *Family*.

Jonah was *gone*. He was *somewhere else*. Somewhere in time and beyond time. His skin was on fire exploding into a thousand suns.

Madeleine also burned. She laid sweating, her eyes twitching ferociously, sometimes open, sometimes closed. Strangely, a small piece of bread laid below her nostrils wedged under the plastic oxygen mask. She also was *gone*. She was *somewhere else*. Madeleine was with Jonah.

Dr. Gellman sat lurched forward in a chair next to Jonah, her eyes wide and intrepidly intent, recording every muscle tick and sound. She did not know what she was beholding. She was in a land not tread before. Madeleine should have been dead, but she was not…*yet*. Gellman constantly checked the vital sign monitors wired to both Madeleine and Jonah. Somehow, it was all *one circuit*. Gellman was completely bewildered and entranced.

As a Jew, she could not imagine the meaning of what she beheld: The woman before her struggled for life with bread under her nose. The man beside her prayed in constant cycles of Jewish blessings attached to various Hebrew names. He would chant a blessing with a pair of names three times, and move on to the next pair with the same blessing:

Baruch atah Adonai elohaynu melech ha'olam oseh ma'asey

Daniyel v'Miryam Garmu...

Elaine and Eduardo slipped silently into the room. Elaine immediately latched onto Madeleine's sweating countenance. Madeleine's body heaved with Jonah's in an other-worldly struggle. Elaine immediately began to cry and shook her head violently *NO* as she clenched Eduardo's hand. Then. She caught sight of a small temporary cardboard coffin positioned at the head of Madeleine's bed. Elaine went directly to it. The index card taped on top read:

Daniel Lazare Ragel Van Meter 5/19-5/19

Elaine fell to a heap on the floor before the coffin. Her clumped body gave out a muffled wail, low and throbbing.

Eduardo, though stunned, gingerly pulled Elaine up and circled his arms around her — this woman who knew so much. In her sorrow, he could see that whatever she knew, had to do with *that which is good* in the world—*that in which people place their hope.*

"Who are you?" asked Susan Gellman.

"I'm her *sister*," whimpered Elaine, instantly stretching the truth. It was a better story than what she used to get into the room. Elaine had flashed her old *Precious Host* ID-card, presenting herself and Eduardo as a *pastoral counselor* and *assistant*. Eduardo was impressed with her instant manufacture of an alias.

Madeleine was sweating profusely, sometimes giving out short strong grunts as if trying to pull herself up from somewhere deep.

Jonah was heaving back and forth like a machine, as if trying to pull a body up from a well. His skin was totally red. On fire. He was chanting in an agonizingly hoarse spasmic rhythm:

Baruch atah Adonai elohaynu melech ha'olam oseh ma'asey

Yehuda v' Chana Garmu

Jonah fired out the blessing three times in short bursts. And then another,

Baruch atah Adonai elohaynu melech ha'olam oseh ma'asey

Yosef v'Sara Lechem

This too received a set of three. And then he began again, "*Baruch atah*"…and ended the blessing with another set of names,

Ya'akov v'Rachel Garmu

Three times. And then the next blessing and its names,

Efraim v'Leah Lechem

And the next,

Shimon v'Sara Garmu

Elaine bit her lip.

Eduardo cocked his head and pulled Elaine to him. Looking her directly in the eyes he whispered, "What is he doing?"

"He's been doing this for hours," Susan Gellman interjected, escorting them back from the bed. She shook her head in wide-eyed bewilderment. "I don't know what he's doing, but, by *God*, it's *working*. She should have died seven hours ago,…but…." She lifted her hands in an unknowing reach to the heavens. "…he's pulling her…he's *somehow* keeping her in this world...*somehow*. *Somehow* he keeps on with her wherever the two of them are, and I just watch. I just watch her vitals get a little stronger and stronger...very gradually."

"*Stronger?*" Eduardo shot back with a piercing eye.

"*Stronger.*" Gellman matched him eye to eye.

Eduardo pivoted to Elaine. "What is he doing Elaine? What are these words he is saying?"

Gellman cut in again. "The words are Hebrew. He's using Hebrew blessings and names. I don't understand it. The chart says they are Lutheran...that's Christian, right?" Gellman's eyes reached also to Elaine for an answer.

Elaine could not respond in an instant. Her eyes fled through the ceiling to the heavens, as tears fell from both eyes. She brought them back down to earth, to Madeleine and Jonah. She followed Jonah's back and forth rhythm ....

Matanyahu v'Miryam Lechem

"What *is this* Elaine?" Eduardo emphatically repeated in a low voice.

Elaine nodded and swallowed. "He is chanting an old Jewish blessing. She looked at Susan Gellman. "You know doctor, from shul."

Gellman nodded.

Elaine continued, "He is saying: *Blessed are you O Lord, King of the Universe, source of*...And then...he fills in a pair of names. And then another pair."

"*Names?*" Eduardo shot back. What are these names?"

Elaine slowly cocked her head and looked softly into Eduardo's eyes. Taking his hands into hers, she whispered, "Eduardo. Remember. *Remember*? Remember how I told you?"

"Told me *what?!*" Eduardo was on the edge of panic, trying to lay grasp of what he could not yet understand.

"Remember, Eduardo. You must *remember*. You must remember to keep the *lists* with you at all times." She patted his coat's breast pocket. "You have *Jonah's names* in your pocket."

Eduardo blinked, and the gears in his brain immediately began to shift and drop into place spinning like a fine Swiss watch. He plucked out the list and squinted at its text in the dim grey room. He began walking toward the blind-drawn window which was suddenly pierced by a shaft of sunlight streaking through the slats. Eduardo veered directly toward the light as Jonah chanted on,

Yonah v' Miryam Lechem

Eduardo flipped page after page searching and listening at the same time for Jonah to announce the names again,

Yonah v'Miryam Lechem

By Jonah's third repetition,

Yonah v'Miryam Lechem

the sun streaking through the blinds hit the mark. Eduardo found the names on the *list*. And then Jonah was off to the next set,

Raguel v'Miryam Garmu

Jonah rocked and sweated the blessing three times heaving to Madeleine. Then the next set,

Tobiyah v'Chana Lechem

It was on the *list*. And then Jonah was on to the next generation,

Tobiyah v'Sara Lechem

Eduardo circled wildly around Madeleine's bed. Looking at her. At Jonah. At the small coffin. At the pages flapping in his hand. Circling…circling….as if carrying the very world in the palm of his hand. And Jonah continued rocking and chanting his same low song into the next names,

Jean Brunell et Jeanne Jariot

Three times.

Elaine, in multi-faceted shock, watched Eduardo wildly increase the speed of his encirclements—like a *new Joshua* around a *new Jericho*. And then Eduardo stopped. Stopped dead still. His eyes went wide to the heavens. He was *somewhere* with *SomeOne*. And then his eyes came back down to earth as a dove to Elaine's.

"I know what he's doing," Eduardo nodded his head vigorously in the affirmative. "I *know* what he's doing he reiterated keeping his voice low."

"You do?" replied Elaine, her eyes locked onto his.

"He's *encoding*." Eduardo stepped back and waved his hand over the *crèche*. "Actually, he is *re-encoding*."

"Re-encoding?" winced Dr. Gellman.

"Yes. Re-encoding *memory*. In graduate school, we conducted human memory research....specifically, in how human memory compares to computer memory. There are *some* similarities. Information is imputed, or *encoded* into short-term memory. With more reinforcement, or *re-encoding*, the data is transferred to long term memory. And then...there is *recall...retrieval...*and perhaps?...*restoration?"*

Eduardo stepped around the crèche of Jonah, Madeleine and their dead child. He stood directly above Jonah as he rocked back and forth entranced in never-ending blessings and names. Eduardo studied closely the flow of energy of rocking and chant coursing through Jonah's body, and down his left arm to his hand laid flat and vibrating like a piano tuning fork to Madeleine's face with the bread laid under her nostrils, and then beyond, on the other side of the bed, the child's coffin butted up to the metal bed rails. Several times, Eduardo's pierced eye traced the map of the flow. He cocked his head. *Something* clicked.

"Yes," he said. "We devoted quite a bit of our study into the possibilities of memory being a *facilitator* of bodily repair." Eduardo nodded and stepped back from the crèche. "But," he continued looking directly at Gellman and raising his finger.

"After the basics, the comparison between the human brain and the computer breaks down. Yes, they both have a hard drive. But the computer's hard drive is really a simple machine....it simply spits back what you put in it and does so perfectly—often, *too perfectly*. But the human hard drive is *something else*. First, where is it? The human brain can lose many cells, and yet...still...research proves...memory can be retained. Not perfect memory...not like an exact copy of the original...but a memory with the most important aspects of the original."

"Are you a doctor?" asked Gellman.

"No, I'm a computer guy. But computers come from human beings. So then, you have these questions, you understand?" He motioned his arm at the combo of flesh and machine before them.

Gellman nodded.

"So...," Eduardo continued. "...a big question is *where* is human memory stored?...if not in the actual neurons of the brain...then where? So, some scientists theorize that it's in the connections *between* the neurons...I think they call them *synapses*?" He looked at Gellman.

"Yes."

"...which of course, is very strange, because these synapses are nothing...they are the *gaps* between very closely placed neurons." Eduardo stepped back to the crèche at work. He looked at Elaine and Gellman. "I think what we have here is a *composite brain* working on something...certainly working on coming out of a coma...but working on *something else* to work out of the coma. Part of the brain is dead, but the brain still works...the question is: What is this *something else* this brain is working on? Then, I am thinking about another question about the entire idea of a human hard drive. Okay, for the sake of argument, let us say there *is* one...and it somehow is transferred generation to generation...like animals in the forest are born with certain instincts. But with human memory...memory is so much more complex because humans are complex. So, again. If there is a hard drive, why then doesn't every human being remember every bit of human history? I mean...You either have a hard drive or you do not. If you are going to apply the logic of computer memory to humans, then you should be able to get the same perfect recall out of humans...but, we do not. So what is missing? We do not know. But. There are some alternative theories. Some have argued that *logic* may NOT be the base of human memory..."

"Then what Eduardo?" asked Elaine. "What would be the base?" Her eyes searched his for a Word she could hope in.

"*Emotion.*" he said. "Meaning. Purpose—things that people decide are of ultimate importance to them...important enough to *encode in one-self*...and *one's children* over and over again. Consciously or subconsciously, human beings remember things because *they want to*—because *they will it.*" Eduardo paused gazing over the crèche. He waved his hand over it. "But what is this all about? There is something very extraordinary here. These are people engaged in some kind of *manipulation of memory*....but they do so as others do not. These are rare people. They know things we do not know. Why does this woman have bread under her nose? I have a theory." His eyes widened. "Tell me Doctor, is this man left handed?"

"I don't know. Why?" shrugged Gellman.

Eduardo eyed Jonah's pulsating left hand on Madeleine's face. "I think this man is left handed. In school we looked at a rare group of people who had phenomenal memory...most of them were left handed. They have a congenital condition in which their senses mix together in their brains and the result is that their memory is enhanced fantastically. One of the most famous of these rare people could memorize an unbelievable long stream of numbers. The reason he could do it was because his brain converted numbers into colors and then he would arrange a picture story in his mind of different landscapes in different colors along a path....so all he had to do was take this nice little walk along this beautiful pathway in his mind, and the numbers were all there."

"That's *Synaesthesia!*" sparked Gellman.

Jonah's chant became louder. Sparks were shooting all over the room.

Eduardo nodded. "Yes. The Synaesthete is an amazing mystery. Their traits really sharpen the question of *emotion* being the base of memory instead of *logic*. If a man can remember a thousand numbers in a row because he finds them beautiful — *that's* something to pay attention to. The potential implications are fantastic—that people can have long memory, not because they're smarter, but because they *care*...care about something very deeply.

On the other hand, is it really so hard to believe? The bread under this woman's nose now makes sense! Many articles on Synaesthesia report that when people experience the aroma of fresh baked bread, it takes them back to a pleasant memory. It is true for me. I *remember*. I remember coming home on Friday after school...and I would walk in the front door...It was wonderful...I knew my mother was in the kitchen. I could not see her, but I could smell the bread she always baked on Friday. That smell *meant something to me*. To me...it had the smell of...of..." Eduardo struggled against the sky for a Word, and it came and he brought it down in his eyes and he gave it as gift: "...*Peace*...it had the smell of *Peace*. Yes, *Peace*. You know...it is very strange. Article after article that I have read mentions this bread idea. And actually, the rarest type of Synaesthete is the one who does conversions with smell and taste. Most do it with hearing and touch. The literature also says that most Synaesthetes do memory conversions between their senses and numbers. Doctor, have you heard *any numbers* in the words Jonah has been chanting?...I have not."

"No, not that I've heard...just the blessings and names," she shrugged.

"Hmmm. Usually there is some connection between Synaesthetes and numbers. But. This woman has bread under her nose. And this man is calling on her memory with his Words and the bread in, with, and under her nose. Yes, the rarest form of Synaesthete is the one who does conversions with smell and taste." Eduardo turned directly to Elaine, "And guess what?"

Elaine's eyes widened.

"Synaesthesia is *hereditary*...And...it has specific personality traits—like, being religious and, uh, like sensing spirits or like, God around you, you know?...other things like umm, clairvoyance and telling the future, and that thing where you think you have been somewhere before...?"

"*Deja-vou*," supplied Elaine.

"Yes! That's it!" confirmed Eduardo.

"They believe in psychic healing!" shot out Gellman. "I had a synaesthete patient like that...He had cancer that he described in very specific ugly colors. But. He did recover...and we didn't know why..."

Eduardo nodded "Yes. Exactly. *Faith healing*." He pointed to the *holy family*. "These people know things we do not know. Whatever it is—they have passed it down generation after generation....and that is why our friend here is going through the *genealogy list*...he is guiding his wife down the yellow brick road of their minds...of their mutual stored memory.

"*Mutual* is right," added Elaine. "They share a *common ancestor*."

"Ah, yes! Cretien DuBois," Eduardo remembered.

"Exactly. Cretien DuBois." Elaine nodded.

"Hmmm. Here is a thought: A common ancestor would mean *double the memory power.*"

"At least *double*," assured Elaine. "...but, I can tell you, *a lot more than double*...based on the constant intermarriages in the genealogy lists."

"Hmm." Eduardo nodded. "So, doctor. How is your patient doing *now* compared to when Elaine and I *first came in?*?

Gellman flashed over to the monitors with chart in hand. "Wow," she said.

"What?" replied Eduardo.

"BP...better. Pulse better. Temp better. Blood oxygen better. Wow!" exclaimed Gellman softly.

Eduardo looked at Elaine.

"So," Eduardo continued. "It appears that our friend here is successfully re-teaching his wife her place in this world, Doctor?"

"Perhaps!" she said, flipping out her hands with a tentative exuberant laugh.

"...Makes me wonder." Eduardo slightly smiled. "I wonder if a Synaesthete's faith healing method could be taught to common people...I mean, many people like to think they believe in something like this....like with Jesus in the Bible...you know?" Eduardo motioned to Elaine for a response.

"Well. Jesus did have *students*...or *disciples,* as the *New Testament* calls them...from all walks of life. And he did *teach* them using some very basic physical symbols...like *bread*. He taught them to eat bread in *holy meals of community*...which the Church calls *Holy Communion.* He taught them:

Do this in MEMORY of me.

"Completely synaesthetic." Eduardo nodded.

"Yes. Exactly." affirmed Elaine. "It is doing things, as you say, to *encode* important ideas into long term memory to live on into future generations."

"Why *bread*?" Eduardo quickly interrogated.

Looking at Gellman, Elaine replied, "Well, the *Jews* started it...*bread* at every event having to do with *Life* and *God*...bread is the most basic common denominator of human sustenance...it is what keeps us going."

Gellman nodded. "We always do the bread blessing before our shabbos meal."

Eduardo nodded. "Makes sense."

Suddenly, something *changed*.

Jonah's chanting stopped. All was silent.

Then, Jonah's right bicep, strapped within the leather *tefillin* straps, flexed and bulged. Jonah's forearm, plumbed to the IV pole, raised the whole apparatus into the air.

And then.

Suddenly, he slammed the pole down to the floor with a loud metallic

CRAAANGGG...

And then again,

CRAAANGGG...

And again,

CRAAANGGG...

Silence.

With his eyes still closed, Jonah sat upright, his long hair draping evenly about his shoulders and neck. His lips in slow motion went to form a sound so slowly the witnesses thought it would never come. And then it did. In a long breath, like a *wind* that came from *the Unknown*, the room filled with a resonating

Bahhhhhhh....

and then finally,

ruchhhhhh!

The word landed with the thud of a heavy stone dropping from heaven to God's dusty earth.

Bahhhruchhh!
Bahhhruchhh!

Jonah repeated the Hebrew word, meaning *Blessed,* sitting straight up, his eyes closed, twitching in a sweating fervor, and his soul lurched forward into the Blessing,

atah Adonai elohaynu melech ha'olam oseh ma'asey,

Cretien duBois et Jeanne Masic Brunel

Cretien duBois et Jeanne Masic Brunel

Cretien duBois et Jeanne Masic Brunel

The IV pole slammed the floor tile again,

CRAAANGGG...

Madeleine answered the call.

A low crying moan came out of somewhere deep within her, and then…breath. Her lips reached out to the air above, and those in the room heard softly…thinly,

Eloi. Eloi. Eloi. Lahma sabachthani?

Jonah rang-slammed the pole again fiercely.

The IV needle blew out from the underside of his wrist and blood burst forth spraying over his *tefila* strapped arm.

Baruch atah Adonai elohaynu melech ha'olam oseh ma'asey,

LOUIS DU BOIS ET CATHERINE BLANCHAN…

Jonah ordered loudly with clenched eyes and a violent whip of his head.

Madeleine's response came as one from across the wide ocean, thin and floating,

Yeshua….Yeshua….Yeshua….

The metal pole fiercely clanged again and blood sprayed widely over Jonah and Madeleine. Jonah called again loudly in a deafening bellow,

*BARUCH ATAH ADONAI ELOHAYNU MELECH HA'OLAM
MA'ASEY*

SARA!!!

Madeleine Garmu LechemVan Meter let forth a high pitch wail such as middle-eastern women give at the grave. She called strong,

JONAH!…….JONAH!…..JONAH!!!

Jonah heard the call. And his eyes burst open. He shot to his feet, the metal and tubes flinging off as debris falling away from a launching rocket. Jonah furiously whipped off the *tefila* dripping with blood and crowned Madeleine's forehead with the pouch bearing the Word of God. Jonah pinched the bread upon his wife's burning face, stirring the aroma from its core. He bent lowly to Madeleine's ear and breathed the Word lowly but strongly,

Sh'ma Yisrael Adonai Elohaynu Adonai

ECHAD!!!

Madeleine's larynx and eyes fluttered violently.
Jonah took his dear wife's hand in his. He made the final call:

TALITHA CUMI !!!

Silence hung. And then...

JONAH!!!

wailed Madeleine out of a sputtering choke. Her eyes opened. Her arms thrust out.

JONAH!

And immediately they were one. Wrapped in muffled wails and heaving trembles.

"Jonah."

"Oh, my God! Oh, my God! Oh, my God!" sputtered Dr. Susan Gellman. She instantly threw Elaine and Eduardo out of the room to the hallway and frantically called for the station nurse.
In no time, the room was flooded by staff.

Elaine and Eduardo stood outside the closed door listening to the sounds of resurrection.

Eduardo mindlessly stuffed his hands in his coat pocket and felt a wrestling of paper. He pulled out the note and bread piece the old woman had given him at the church.

"I was supposed to give this to Jonah."

Elaine looked at the piece of paper. It read:

Sh'ma Yisrael Adonai Elohaynu Adonai Echad

Elaine gave a soft incredulous laugh. It's Hebrew. It says, *Hear O Israel, the Lord our God is One.* There's your synaes-thete number, love. The Lord is *One.* You know…like…*El Dio.* I think Jonah has gotten the message. Maybe it is the rest of us who need to get it."

Chapter 9

Blessed are you, O Lord, who gathers the dispersed of his people Israel.

Eastlawn Cemetery. Columbus, Ohio.
Monday, May 21, 7:00 A.M.

In the mist of grey morning fog, a silent throng gathered around the open grave. Rhythmic clops of a horse and wagon approached from the west. The sounds came closer, and then stopped. Then, a shuffling of feet together in unison. A thin mournful foreign music pierced through the fog with a jingling of what sounded like small pieces of metal. The notes rose louder. An old Roma man, in black coat and white satin vest, broke slowly through the fog to the grave clearing, his chin clenched to a fiddle calling out for God. Slowly he stepped toward the grave, leading the pall bearers forth with a small pine-wood box.

Behind the coffin stepped Jonah Van Meter, his head and upper body shrouded in an all-white Jewish *tallit* prayer shawl. In his left hand he carried a crude wooden staff bearing small flags of Israel and of the Roma. In his right hand, he held out the corner of the *tallit* with its fringe hanging including one blue cord.

Then followed Madeleine and Sara arrayed in white peasant dresses. Belts of jingling coins slung about their hips joined with the fiddle-wail in the otherwise silent fog.

As the coffin was brought to the scaffold above the grave, everyone took their place.

Jonah stood at the foot of the chasm. Silently, keeping a steady eye on all those gathered, he removed a knife from under his *tallit*. With its sharpness, he tore a hole in his shirt on the left of his chest. His fingers tore the hole into a ripping tear down-ward in the shirt. Likewise, he performed the same sign of the left of Madeleine's dress, and then to the right of Sara's.

Jonah breathed deeply, closing his eyes. He uttered a prayer lowly. Then suddenly: His arm ratcheted back and hurled the knife high and far into the sea of grey out beyond the people.

He began the service.

God is our refuge and strength,
 a very present help in trouble.
Therefore we will not fear though the earth should change
Though the mountains shake to the heart of the sea;
Though its waters roar and foam, though the mountains tremble with its tumult.
There is a river whose streams make glad the city of God
The holy habitation of the Most High.
God is in the midst of her, she shall not be moved;
God will help her right early,
The nations rage, the kingdoms totter;
He utters his voice, the earth melts.
The Lord of hosts is with us; the God of Jacob is our refuge.
Come, behold the works of the Lord
How he has wrought desolations in the earth.
He makes wars cease to the end of the earth;
He breaks the bow, and shatters the spear,
He burns the chariots with fire!
Be still, and know that I am God.
I am exalted among the nations, I am exalted in the earth!
The Lord of hosts is with us; the God of Jacob is our refuge.

Jonah gazed into the mist of faces floating in the fog. Jews. Roma. *Who else? How many? A hundred? Five hundred?* There was no way to tell in the grey.

Jonah announced the Blessing:

Baruch atah Adonai Elohaynu melech ha'olam hamotzi lechem min ha'aretz.

The congregation responded: *A-mein.*
He addressed the congregation:

"How does one say a true thing about a soul one never knew? I do not know. I do not know if Daniel Lazare Ragel Van Meter was the *door* to the *Age To Come,* or not. Indeed, to be completely honest, I prayed that he was not. My parents felt the same way about me...as did Maddie's about her. To be sure, there was more comfort envisioning the *Age To Come*...down the generations...beyond us. Then all we needed to do was add our small contribution by guarding the *Secret* with our memory...our deeds...our prayer.

So. Now what?

Evil has broken into our *House*. Once again. It has happened before....to those before us. So. We face now the oldest, most central question of our *House*. We know that we cannot live by *Bread alone*. But the question is: Do we have the *courage*? Do we have the *will*?—To make *God's Bread* of *Peace On Earth* which proceeds from *His Will*....to be enough for us???—to be our song of *Dayenu*?...Over against?...Over against all the powers and kingdoms of the world scratched together by *Blood*...Blood for what? For blood itself, of course. Never-ending bloody king-making where *nothing* will ever be *Dayenu*....

.....even to the slaughter of innocents."

Madeleine immediately fell to the ground. She grabbed her hair on both sides of her head and let out a choked scream.

Sara grimaced and gritted her teeth wrapping her arms around her mother and pulling her haltingly to her feet.

Jonah moved not a muscle. *Grief was fitting*. He continued:

"Today, we *are* again at the pinnacle of decision—Between eternal war and eternal *Shalom*. We hear the voices on both sides calling us.

On one side, out of the darkness, they take us up to show us, what *THEY* say, we could have....through *Blood*. This Yeshua faced...as do we.

On the other side, on the common ground...of every good
and common man and woman....rises the call not for glory and
riches, but for the simple bread of *Shalom*. It is not easy to walk
away from the *bloody darkness of war* and all its empty promises, but we've been doing it for centuries—by the power of *The
Secret* of which we are guardians.

Those who went before us, certainly *Cretien* and *Jeanne*, did
as our father *Abraham*. They left their pavilions of privilege and
joined their workers in the wheat fields. Why? Because of what
was in them. The *legacy unfaded*. The *Promise remembered*.
Because of :

Lahma Mahar....

The Bread Of Tomorrow...

Shalom

That is why we stand here now. In mourning, yes. But not
only mourning. We. We must answer the question today. And
we must answer it *now*. Will we keep the truth of *The Secret*
burning within us? I will answer. If I lead in anything, I will answer for us all. We *will*. Surely, we *will*."......

Jonah paused, letting the words sink deeply. He gave Madeleine a strong look with pursed lips, and a strong nod. He raised
his voice much louder.

"I know what all of you are wondering. Are we on the eve of
some sort of final battle? I will tell you truly....I think we may
be. The agreed upon *Signal* will go out when our destiny is fully
apparent. Yes, a battle. But on our terms. Not a battle for dominion, but for *Shalom*. And if I should fall? No matter. I, here and
now, confer the heirship of our *Beit Lechem*, our *House Of
Bread*, to my daughter Sara. It is fitting. For by the *first Sara* we
have this *House*, not by *blood*....but by *Love*. And, in love, we
revere here our *Daniel Lazare Ragel*. I thought him hidden from
the world, but I was wrong. I think now, the days of running and
hiding are coming to an end. We stand here among the tombs of
my family...among stones with no names or symbolic names,

even false names. It is time to go the other way now…and with that I will place a *Tziyun* here with just his real Hebrew name:

Daniel Ragel…

……a *Tziyun Mahar*."

Out of the grey mist came forward two old men. One in fedora and vest, the other in a black suit and *kippah*. With slow stepping dignity the two carried their ends of a modest sized grave stone. On the stone, above the name, was an engraved pictograph of an eastward bound wheeled wagon bearing a large menorah with a double hexagon base. The old men carefully set the stone down to the ground at the head of the grave, gave short bows to Jonah, to Sara, and finally to Madeleine, and returned into the grey.

Jonah bowed in response and intoned, "Let this *Tziyun Mahar*…this *Sign Of Tomorrow* be engraved in all our hearts today…even as our *Kaddish* was engraved upon our people long ago unto this very day.

Immediately Sara stepped forward. She said the first word and the congregation followed.

> *Yit-ga-dal v'yit-ka-dash sh'mei ra-ba b'al-ma di-*
> *v'ra chi-r'u'tei, v'yam-lich mal-chu-tei b'cha-yei-*
> *chon u-v'yo-mei-chon u-v'cha-yei d'chol beit Yis-*
> *ra-eil, ba-a-ga-la u-vi-z'man ka-riv, v'i-m' ru: A-*
> *mein.*
> *Y'hei sh'mei ra-ba m'va-rach l'a-lam u-l'al-mei*
> *al-ma-ya.*
> *Yit-ba-rach v'yish-ta-bach, v'yit-pa-ar v'yit-ro-*
> *mam v'yit-na-sei, v'yit-ha-dar v'yit-a-leh v'yit-*
> *ha-lal sh'mei d'kud-sha, b'rich hu,*
> *l'ei-la min kol bir-cha-ta v'shi-ra-ta, tush-b'cha-*
> *ta v'neh-cheh-ma-ta da-a mi-ran b'al-ma, v'i-*
> *m'ru: A-mein.*
> *Y'hei sh'la-ma ra-ba min sh'ma-ya v'cha-yim, a-*
> *lei-nu v'al kol Yis-ra-el, v'i-m'ru: A-mein.*

O-seh sha-lom bi-m'ro-mav, hu ya-a-seh sha-lom
a-lei-nu v'al kol Yis-ra-eil, v'i-m'ru: A-mein.

At the conclusion of the prayer, Jonah gave a nod to Sara and Madeleine as an attendant removed the lid from the child's coffin revealing a very small figure completely shrouded in white muslin. Sara stepped forward and placed a gold foiled chocolate coin and a small dreidel on the child's breast. Madeleine took a step forward. She placed a small boy's light blue sweater vest on top of the Chanukah gifts. Then came Jonah. And over the heart of the child he gave a handful of earth from *eretz Israel.*

Madeleine fell wailing into Sara who stood upright.

The attendants replaced the coffin lid and lowered the holy ark into the earth.

"Sara. Lead us in the final prayer," directed Jonah. Holding her mother tightly, Sara began and the *House* followed.

> *Our Father, hallowed be thy name. Thy kingdom*
> *come. Thy will be done. Give us today our bread*
> *for tomorrow. Forgive our debts, as we forgive*
> *our debtors. And let us not fall to temptation. A-*
> *mein.*

Jonah's left hand took up his staff. He stretched out his arms from his shrouding *tallit*, lifting his head and voice much louder… as if calling out to the *nations*:

"When the *Day* comes for us to fight, we will fight. But only with *HIS* strength….the strength of *Bread*…the strength of *Sha-lom!*" Jonah held up his *tefila*-strapped arm flexed to a fist.

> *He breaks the bow, and shatters the spear.*
> *The Lord of hosts is with us;*
> *the God of Jacob is our refuge.*

And the whole assembly responded, "A-mein!"

Immediately a chorus of violins sprayed a terse vibrant wail through the mist.

Out of nowhere, sprang hands bearing ark shaped loaves of bread, each being broken and passed from one soul to another. A circle of women in white peasant dresses began to dance in a circle, arm to arm, around the *tziyun*. Out of the mist came a rhythmic low chant quickly rising as more disparate voices joined the claps and stomps of feet in the dance.

Jonah, Sara, and Madeleine turned and proceeded quietly away through a double line of guardians.

At the end of the line, Jonah stopped before a man. He was tall and refined looking, with close cropped beard and shoulder length hair.

"Geoff, I'd like very much for you to take Maddie and Sara to your house now." Jonah looked in all directions for any suspicious faces. "I'll call you in a few hours. I have an appointment with *The Inquisition*."

The tall man nodded knowingly. "We will take good care of them Jonah. No more mistakes. I promise."

"It's not your fault Geoff. Not your fault. It's mine. I got too used to the idea that they would never find us."

And without further word Jonah Van Meter departed.

Eduardo and Elaine followed.

Out of the mist, two grey-haired ladies also followed at a distance.

Chapter 10

Blessed are you, O Lord, the King who loves righteousness and justice.

Columbus, Ohio.
May 21, 9:11 A.M.

Jonah parked the *Caravan* and trotted across High Street toward the old brick building housing the *Ohio District Lutheran* headquarters. Peripherally, he noted the construction project down the street on the corner where workers were just arriving for the day. Gone was the old *Market Exchange Bank* that had stood on the corner for a hundred years. A great uncle of Jonah's had owned it.

Jonah entered the foyer, a musty old hall of dollar-bill green floor tile. It led directly to an ancient elevator with double opaque chicken-wire glass. The door clunked open. Jonah listened to the straining gears of the shaft pulleys hoisting the car. He hoped they were good enough for one last ride. The doors opened. He took a deep breath, and a few steps, and then through the opaque glass District Office door.

"Good morning Mrs. Steele. I'm here for my nine-thirty with the Bishop and Pastor Holloway."

"Of course, Pastor. I'll let them know you've arrived. Please make yourself comfortable." She motioned to the non-descript office couch before her.

Jonah nodded and plunked himself. He hated the place—always incredulous at the sterility of the décor. The carpet and walls were all a shade of metallic silver-gray. Word was that Mrs. Steele, the Office Manager, had seen to all the accoutrements, down to the non-religious metal framed generic office art prints from *Staples*. Jonah always told Madeleine *it looks like a goddamn insurance office.*

"The Bishop will see you now," announced Mrs. Steele. She briskly escorted him across the expanse of the reception area to the Bishop's office situated toward the front of the building overlooking High Street below.

"Jonah. Good to see you," greeted Bishop Virgil Hoyer. The brusque square-headed German in black suit, purple clerical shirt and plain silver pectoral cross, grabbed Jonah's hand in a hard grip. "Please have a seat," the Bishop directed Jonah to a small conference table near the windows. "Wal will be here shortly...he's finishing up a call. So. How's the family...Maddie and...and uh...is it, Sara?"

"Yes....Sara. Everyone's fine," replied Jonah carefully.

"Now, if memory serves....Maddie's expecting soon?"

"Yes," answered Jonah smoothly with keen study of the Bishop's every facial movement.

"Well, what a blessing. I'm sure you're looking forward on pins and needles...do you know?....boy or girl?"

"Boy."

"Well, that's wonderful. Just great. Oh, here comes Wal."

In strode Wallerund DuBois Holloway in his customary por-tentous gait and slickness. He wore a fine pin-stripe suit and perfectly starched gleaming white clerical collar against a very smooth chubby-boy face which gave no sign of a life touched by arduousness. Somehow, he got away with wearing a larger and more ornate pectoral cross than the Bishop, complete with a large dark ruby jewel in its heart. A gent. A dandy in a collar.

Wal dropped an expensive looking black leather portfolio on the table, carefully positioned his cell phone with the time facing him. He sat down next to the Bishop, across from Jonah who faced the windows and God's clear blue sky.

"I am so glad you could meet with us this morning Jonah," announced Wal with pompous crisp enunciation.

"No problem," nodded Jonah, eyes steady.

Wal blinked.

"Well good.....How are things? Maddie? Sara?..."

"Jonah says Maddie's having a boy," interjected the Bishop.

"Wow....well...that's great." Wal blinked twice. "Things are going well?..."

"Everyone's fine. Perfectly fine," answered Jonah with complete opaqueness.

"Well....great....glad to hear that. Sounds good." Wal's eyes fluttered as he reached for his portfolio and handed it to the Bishop.

"Well, Jonah," the Bishop began. "The reason we felt it good for us to get together here today is some concern we have out of discussions with several of your parishioners who have contacted us about some issues."

"Bishop, I've noted the major points there in the folder," Wal cut in.

"Yes. Thank you, Wal." The Bishop opened the folder and scanned with a few eyebrow raises. "Well. Jonah. ...uh, there are a number of *concerns* relayed here, but they would appear to have a common theme, *that* being the question if perhaps you may be employing some *non-Christian* elements in your ministry..."

"*Non-Christian?*" replied Jonah in complete poker face.

"Yes," inserted Wal. "Non-Christian...As in *Jewish* motifs, Jonah."

Jonah rocked his chair back and pursed his lips, nodding slightly.

"Ah, yes," the Bishop continued. "It appears there is some concern over what people describe as being certain teachings and practices you employ that would seem to be *Jewish* rather than *Christian*..."

"I wasn't aware of mutual exclusiveness in that area," retorted Jonah. "Has the Lutheran Church suddenly gone *Marcionite*? I didn't get the memo. Last I heard, the book of *Isaiah* was high on Jesus' reading list."

The Bishop glared. He was not a man accustomed to being *talked to*. He flipped his eyes to Wal.

"Well. Let us be specific." Wal took up the inquisition. "We have reports that you teach that Our Lord Jesus Christ was crucified solely by the Romans...that no Jews participated in the crucifixion...that you deny the accuracy or, how shall we say, the historicity of, say, John's Gospel which clearly alludes to Jewish participation in the crucifixion. Now, granted...our faith is that we *all* are participants in the crucifixion...that all of humanity's sin made the *Cross* necessary. But, I must say, we are deeply troubled if it is true that you are denying Scripture." Wal had made his first serious move on the chess board.

All of Jonah's pilot burners immediately flamed up. He mentally stationed himself in his tank, turned its turret, and its tracks lurched forward.

"*Jews* didn't and wouldn't participate in crucifixion. It ain't *Kosher*.

"Oh, really? King Herod had nothing to do with it?"

"Herod wasn't a Jew. He was a puppet *Idumean* appointed by the Romans."

"...and how about Caiaphas? He wasn't a *Jew*?"

"He was a sell-out to the Romans. You sell out to the pagans, you're not a *real Jew* anymore. The Jewish populace hated the sell-outs."

"I see. And how about the throngs of folks in John's Gospel crying out to Pilate *Crucify him!*...they were not Jews?

"John's Gospel is cooked. It simply reflects the Jewish-Christian arguments of its day—in the first century, after the Romans kicked them all out of Judea."

"Oh! So you *DO* question the Scriptures!"

Jonah laughed. "Oh, no more than established Lutheran professors that train the rest of us!"

"Like who?"

"Oh, like Dr. Norm Beck...that's who! He's so out front with it, you don't even have to read his book, he puts it right in the title: *Mature Christianity: The Recognition and Repudiation of the Anti-Jewish Polemic of the New Testament!* Jewish scholars *do* like to quote Norm. So round up your horses Wal, and fire up the Inquisition for Norm and all the professors! YOU guys keep paying the guy....I just read his books!"

"I've met the man...not a bad fellow," added the Bishop, trying to think of something half-way intelligent to say.

"Well, Jonah," Cal continued the attack. "We also hear that you never seem to preach on Pauline texts. What about that?"

"True. I never liked Paul. But, neither did James, who I'm kind of partial to... seeing as he actually *knew* Jesus...'cause they were brothers and had the *same Mom and Dad and all!*"

"Well Jonah," Wal surged. "Your insult to Our Lord's paternity aside, how in blazes can you possibly call yourself a *Lutheran pastor* and totally negate the central theological focus of The Lutheran Church: The Pauline doctrine of *Justification by Faith?*"

"Again, I side with James: *Faith without Works is dead.* As for Lutheran identity, there are options. Luther, I never had any use for. He was a fraud and a coward. He never once went to the *Cross.* When his *Excommunication Bull* came down from the Pope, he ran to his prince buddies to protect him. So, it wasn't any big deal for him to go swaggerin' like he was some kind of new pope himself. To Luther...it was *all or nothin'.* With him, there was no finessing anything...no different from the Pope he was opposing...it was all *My way or the highway* power-playing crap...same ol', same ol'...all the way down from the first bitchout between James and Paul. Power, Power. Power—*the same exact thing Jesus walked away from.* So what did Luther do when he got his power? He did *worse* than the Pope! When someone wouldn't line up with his doctrine, they had to suffer the sword! So he turned on the *Peasants* that supported him in the beginning....And he turned on the *Jews,* huh? Yeah. Luther talks nice-nice to them in the *beginning*...but when they don't convert as a result of Luther's oh-so obviously correct Gospel....well then, *to Hell with the Jews!*....burn their houses, burn their talmuds, put them to the sword, drive them out of Germany! Gee, does any of this sound familiar?! Have you ever read Luther's tract *The Jews And Their Lies*???....of course you have!!! But you know...he wrote a *WORSE* tract that American Lutherans haven't even had the *GUTS* to translate into English...a little dandy called *Vom Schem Hamphoras*...an incredible piece of filth—a piece of theological pornography! And all this fucking shit Luther wrote went straight into the collective consciousness and memory of Germany—down the generations—and then straight to Hitler…who knew just how to call on those demons and make THAT fucking word FLESH….."

"THAT IS ENOUGH! You can't talk like that here JONAH," yelled Wal.

"Have you lost your MIND, Pastor?!!! Has SATAN entered your heart?!!!" the Bishop flashed out his hands. "THIS is a CHRISTIAN house. You CANNOT speak thus!"

Jonah gave a quick cock of his head and a snarl. "Tough Shit. It's happenin'. NO! I repudiate Luther completely. But you know, Luther wasn't the only Lutheran. His right hand man Melancthon was a decent guy…a liberal to be sure…somebody more interested in making a deal and making peace. But hell, let's talk about Luther's *Justification By Faith* doctrine. He took it from the Apostle Paul who basically used it to sell easy religion to the Gentiles at the expense of betraying his own Jewish people. YEAH!…Let's talk EXACTLY about THAT!…about how German Lutherans turned their heads while hoards of Jews were carted off by the trainload to the slaughter house…and then they go to church and take care of it all with a piddly little *Brief Order For Confession and Holy Communion*…then back to the killing! So, YEAH….You know this thing where you people *JUSTIFY* YOURSELVES just by saying you believe certain correct doctrines???....Well, that's just a bunch of bullshit!…A complete *rip-off* of God….A complete rip-off of *Jesus*! You call it GRACE when you get forgiven for putting a bullet in a Jewish child's brain… just for saying *I'm a Christian*???.... *I believe in Jesus???!!!!*….For saying to God, I'm sorry for being such a complete scum bag of maggots!…Yeah, well. That's *Fake Grace*…it's *Satanic Grace*…it's complete bullshit!!! As for me and my *House*, we'll have nothing to do with it! So, fuck Luther!!!…fuck Paul!!!…"

"JONAH!!!

Have you NO decency?!!! Is THIS the kind of language YOUR house uses?!!!…" shot Wal.

"OUTRAGEOUS! I am absolutely OUTRAGED!" barked the Bishop hysterically pounding his fist on the table in spasmic thuds.

"YOU"RE outraged!!!???...YOU"RE OUTRAGED???!!!" yelled Jonah. "How 'bout the Jewish parents who were forced to watch BAPTIZED Nazi soldiers take their little babies up by their feet, and then swing their bodies like baseball bats exploding their babies' heads onto a brick wall out in an alley???...and then put a bullet in Mom's face, and then Dad...after seeing all Hell on Earth....GEE, do you think?...maybe just for a second?....when you get to that point?...that maybe?...just maybe?...Something went WRONG somewhere with Christianity!!!???...While the vast majority of German Lutherans do nothing???!!! And the POPE does jack shit! You think, maybe those Jewish parents just might be a little PISSED OFF down in HELL... because of course that's where they are, even after NAZI HELL, because their ancestors didn't listen to LUTHER???!!! I mean, do you EVER stop and THINK about this GLORIOUS Christian tradition of slaughtering those who do not recite YOUR catechism???!!!....So, it started with Constantine! He hears *GOD???* Say?: *By the sign of the CROSS*...You are to go out and put your enemies to the sword and conquer! And then, all the same SHIT in the Crusades!!!...you have Godfroi de Bouillon, who by the way, I have the inglorious privilege to be descended from...what does he do?....he goes to the Holy Land to win it back for Jesus and *HIMSELF* and the Pope and whatever other stupid shit going through his brain....and so what is the FIRST thing he does???...when his army crashes into Jerusalem? He slaughters *every* Jewish and Muslim man, woman, and child he can lay his hands on....and you know...they ain't forgot about that shit over there!!!....."

Wal's eyebrows popped.

Jonah cranked on. "YOU'RE OUTRAGED???!!!....YOU'RE OUTRAGED???!!!...YOU'RE OUTRAGED!!!???...And it just keeps going on!...Hell, look at *Bosnia*. You had complete ethnic genocide going on...The Serbs were going Nazi all over the Muslims! But, as CHRISTIANS you know....we have an IN with the Serbs....Did WE raise holy hell with the *Serbian Or-thodox Church???* Hell, no! We didn't say shit! My kid *Sara* was caught in the middle of all that shit! We found her wasting away in an toilet of a orphanage on the edge of death...She saw her own birth parents butchered....She was left to experience *Nothing* in the world that even suggested to her that she was of any value to anyone....she was the lowest of the low...because she was *Roma...Gypsy...complete refuse,* of both Christians and Muslims! AND, before we finally got the adoption papers signed there was some stupid ass missionary group that came to the or-phanage telling the kiddies they HAD to learn about Jesus so they wouldn't go to HELL!

YOU'RE OUTRAGED???!!!

YOU'RE OUTRAGED???!!!

You TWO! You sit here and prattle in your stupid little office building here waiting for your checks to roll in from your rich suburban churches when YOU YOURSELVES ought to be out in those goddamned pulpits taking on the WAR MONGERS in Washington....

WHO AIN'T SPREADIN' FREEDOM!!!....THEY'RE SPREADIN' GUNS AND BOMBS AND GENOCIDE! YOU'RE OUTRAGED???!!! ....

I'M OUTRAGED!!!
Let me tell you:

GOD DAMMIT, I'M OUTRAGED!!!"

Jonah bitch-slapped the table with an open left hand and fire-glare in his eyes.

"Jonah-You-Need-To-Calm-Down," the Bishop paternalisti-cally ordered, lowering his eyes, as to a boy.

Wal half smirked and rocked his chair back with his arms folded in smug satisfaction. And then he fired a shot straight across the bow. "I hear Jonah that you do not observe the Sacrament of Holy Communion properly."

"Meaning what?..."

"Meaning: I hear that you personally do not take the *Cup*, but only the *Bread*."

Eyes of both men were as Patton to Rommel, and vice-versa, positioning their tanks on opposite ridges. Jonah calibrated the sites of his gun.

"...Never drank wine. Never did. Besides, the practice in the *early* church was for the common folk to take Communion in *one kind—the Bread.* After all, the *Body* already contains the *Blood*, not the other way around. Jesus always made sure there was Bread for the folks...If the wine gave out, it gave out...You make do with what you have." Jonah nodded with goading in his eyes.

Wal pressed on. "Well. We also hear....that you practice *non-Christian* RITUALS in your *home*!...rather, I should say, the Parsonage!...owned by the Church!"

"Really? Do tell," snarled Jonah.

"Yes!" Wal snatched up and opened the portfolio. "We have a report here that your family was observed in a ritual whereby some sort of incantation was being made with exotic hand movements over bread and lighted candles."

"What is THIS?!!" blurted the Bishop.

Jonah laughed, rocking his chair as if it laughed with him. "*SOME SORT???!!!*....You forgot to mention it was FRIDAY NIGHT!!! You might want to check ol' Roy Metz's police record and see if he has any arrests for peeping in other folks' winders!"

"What in the world are you talking about Jonah?!" demanded the Bishop.

"Oh, Virgil. You DO understand, don't you?....that this is all an inside Cain and Abel hatchet job, don't ya?...." Jonah kept his eyes on Wal with a smirk-snarl. "...right, *COUSIN*?!"

"*Cousin*?! You're not making any sense Jonah!" The Bishop pointed his finger.

"Oh! He never 'fessed up, Virgil? Yeah! Wal and I are COUSINS! Wal-Boy is sittin' here pretendin' not to know what a *Friday night Jewish Shabbos* blessing is...isn't that right, *Cousin*?" Jonah was already re-loading.

"Goodness Jonah! Why are you having *JEWISH* prayers at your home on the *JEWISH* Sabbath?!" the Bishop barked.

Jonah returned fire, "And why do you allow your churches to have mock Passover Seders on Maundy Thursday, Virgil?"

Wal shot back. "The *BISHOP* asked YOU a question, Jonah. Answer the *BISHOP'S* question!" Wal pierced his eyes and his own snarl came up with the next thunderous shell to be fired.

"The *MAIN QUESTION* here, Jonah is:

ARE....YOU....A....*JEW*?"

Jonah's eyes went to clock-work calculation fragmented in a million separate milliseconds. The silence hung for an eternal life.

And Jonah said:

"Ego Eimi Ioudaios.

I AM."

And Wal replied,

"Oukoun Ioudaios ei su.

So, you *ARE* a Jew...

...And do tell us, Jonah....Can a man be *both* a Christian *AND* a Jew at the same time?"

Jonah stared out the window at the clear blue sky. He heard a noise. *Familiar and jangling.* Metal against metal. Slowly he got up and went to the window. Down on the corner the workmen were in full stride at the construction site. A huge crane was dropping a iron weight on steel pilings, driving them into the ground creating a terrific clanging, like a bell, that reverberated through the whole street into the buildings, into the very air.

CLANG... CLANG... CLANG...

Immediately, Jonah's head began to hurt. He felt dizzy.... sick...and began to sweat. He had to steady himself on the ledge, his stomach deep down began to heave, and his esophagus was getting ready for the sick.

CLANG... CLANG...CLANG...

Jonah's eyes squeezed as his inner gears started clacking in response to the clangs. Something within him was trying to make a connection.

CLANG...CLANG...CLANG...

Suddenly. A surge came into him from somewhere. It overpowered. His eyes went wide to the sky. Jonah stood straight and hard. And he turned and faced Wallerund DuBois Holloway.

"No. One *cannot*," answered Jonah. "One cannot be a Jew and a Christian at the same time. A son can learn from his father, *but a son cannot be his father.*"
Jonah eyed Wal's cell phone laying on the conference table. The metal tolled.

CLANG... CLANG...CLANG...

Jonah slowly walked to the table, tracking Wal's eyes all the way...not making a sound. Slowly...Jonah's hand dropped lightly on the table. In a flash, he snatched Wal's cell phone like a cobra. Immediately he flipped the cover and scrolled the address file.
"WHAT THE HELL!?..." Wal leaped at Jonah in outrage and fear.

Jonah thrust a stiff left arm to Wal's throat catapulting him back onto the conference table. Jonah kept scrolling the phone.

"STOP! JONAH! STOP!" screamed the Bishop, and he ran out of the office yelling for Mrs. Steele to call the police.

Wal lunged again. Jonah backhanded him across the nose and blood exploded into the air with Wal's shocked scream, "YOU GODDAMN SONOFABITCH! YOU FUCKING SONOFABITCH!" Though wounded, Wal tried to move toward Jonah, but Jonah just kept walking away in circles around the table scrolling the cell phone. And then, it *hit*. There it was. Big as shit: Margot Calvi's name and cell phone number. And the whole call history.

"YOU!

YOU & MARGOT!!!???"

Jonah bellowed the declaration.

The Bishop ran back into the room.

Jonah leaped and violently jacked Wal's throat up against the wall with a vice grip. Jonah pushed hard.

The instant choking sound was like blood in the water that sharks like, and it made Jonah push harder.

The Bishop screamed and screamed.

Mrs. Steele screamed.

Blood poured from Wal's face down Jonah's strangling hand and arm. Somehow, with blood dripping from his mouth, Wal gritted his teeth and spit out a seething, defiling, whispering taunt,

"...whatsamatter Jo-Jo? Did you lose your little *loaf of bread*?

Yeah. So now...you like blood too, don't ya Jo-Jo. Yeah. Now, you're just like the rest of us Jo-Jo. You like the power too, don't ya...yeah you want to rule the world...you're not any different."

Jonah roared from his bowels and pressed harder, squeezing gags of spit and blood out of Wal.

Again, Wal taunted through the blood, his eyes bulging to pop under Jonah's grip.

"Yeahhh, do it Jonah. DO it! Step on down....to the rest of us. You can do it....you can make it work...If you're a Merovingian....you can do YOUR will...not His..."

Jonah's brain flashed out.

The Bishop and Mrs. Steele screamed and beat on Jonah's back pulling on his immovable rock solid pulsating body.

Jonah was falling through time off the Temple pinnacle calculating in a still panic the time to impact. He fell past *the man in the chair*—feverishly trying to choose Good or Evil...Bread or Blood, as the silver witches spun 'round and 'round. He fell and fell and fell through the aeons, and he saw the ground coming fierce at him, and *The Cup* standing on a huge Rock...*Take it? Or pass?...Take it? Or pass?... Take it? Or pass.*

Then. In a last half-breath, Jonah saw *Sara*...her dark sweet arms and face calling out to him. She cried, *"ABBA!"*

In a shot, Light hit.

Jonah exploded off Wal.

The malevolent wreck dropped to the floor.

The Bishop and Mrs. Steele fell to their backsides, yelling. They ran back out to the phones in the reception area. "Where are the police?!" screamed the Bishop to no one in particular.

Wal coughed out blood and sucked fresh air. He sprayed out, "...KNEW YOU COULDN'T DO IT...KNEW IT!"

Jonah put his face on top of Wal's. "I'm gonna do ya worse Wal-Boy," Jonah nodded. "You know what I'm gonna do? *I'm gonna bring him in*...You know what I'm sayin' Wal-Boy?...Yeah. I have *him*...you know that, don't ya, Wal-Boy? Your Granpa Max knew it too, didn't he Wal Boy? Yeah. I have *him*. And, *I'M GONNA BRING HIM IN!* Yeah. I'm going to finish it...for *good*...but not with *death*..."

Jonah stood up.

"...but with *Life*." And Jonah plucked out the white tab of his clerical collar and flipped it in Wal's face.

In the distance, the sound of police car sirens approached.

Resolutely, Jonah whipped off his jacket and placed his hand into the ripped hole of the side of his shirt. He forcefully ripped the shirt wide and off, revealing a short white *tallit* with *tzit-tzit* fringe.

Jonah stood over the bleeding Wal-Boy on the floor. With stone-cold countenance Jonah said:

"Truly, truly I say to you, *a son is not his father*....

and there comes a time, when a son becomes a man on his own." Jonah threw his old ripped black clerical shirt onto Wal's bloody face. "Clean your own self up."

And Jonah spied a silver chalice on the office bookshelf. He grabbed it and hurled the vessel savagely at Wal's head, and in a bound, bolted from the room. Like an act-of-God, Jonah blew past the Bishop and Mrs. Steele and blew out the office door with a slam of thunder exploding the glass in a super nova gush of a million pieces...like a big fish expelling that which never belonged in its belly in the first place.

And as Jonah heard the police pulling up out front, he hoisted on his sport coat and beat it down the stairwell to another office on the second floor just long enough for the police to pass. Then he was off again running out into the bright morning sun.

And even before he got back to his car, he put out the *Word*.

Madeleine answered the phone, and Jonah gave her the *Signal*:

"*Lahma Mahar! Tziyun Mahar! Tziyon Mahar!*

Tell Geoff to gather the Council there tonight. I will be there."

Madeleine understood. *It was here*. A shock, but not a surprise. "Jonah, where are you going right now?" she implored.

He gave her one word,

Sarasville

Chapter 11

Blessed are you, O Lord, who smashes enemies and humbles the arrogant.

Sarasville, Ohio.
Monday, May 21, 4:30 P.M.

The small eastern Ohio village was comprised of a dozen houses in need of repair, a post office, and a mini-mart across the road from the cemetery where Eduardo and Elaine observed.

Jonah exited the *Caravan* and went directly to a spot in the front half of the cemetery. A billow of white cloth flew up over Jonah's head, and his shrouded figure stood alone among the stones. After some time, his hands emerged from the *tallit* and cast a crumbling substance upon the ground. Jonah returned to the *Caravan* and drove away.

Eduardo and Elaine hurried over to the cemetery and found the crumbled bread strewn before two grave stones.

William Van Meter	*Sara Van Meter*
Born 1815	*Born 1813*
Died 1898	*Died 1909*

Elaine nodded to herself as if it all made sense. "Let's go, Love. We need to keep up with Jonah. I'll drive. I want you to get the lists out." She hopped into the driver seat and they streaked northwest back up Highway 146—the same path they had taken from Columbus.

"Our *friends* are still with us." Eduardo informed.

"Uh-huh." Elaine confirmed checking the rear-view mirror.

The narrow country road and its inferior paving stirred up wafting clouds of dirt. But through the clouds, outlines of the familiar rental cars could be seen. Elaine and Eduardo gave short laughs—things seemed to be in their proper slots. Elaine was watching the rear-view mirror when something suddenly happened.

"Holy shit!!!"

"What?!" cried Eduardo.

"One of those cars!—It just fell off the road!"

Eduardo jerked his body around and peered down the road into the dust to see one of the cars indeed on its side in the ditch. Then. From out of nowhere, a smaller car swung around the remaining rental car still following them. The small car, a rusty old blue *Escort* missing its *Ford* nameplate, passed them in a swoosh. Two grey-haired women rode in the front seats. The one in the passenger seat wore black cat-like glasses and waived at Elaine as they passed. The *Escort* streaked ahead leaving Elaine and Eduardo far behind. In the distance they could see the small blue car settle back to the proper side of the road behind Jonah's *Caravan.*

What the hell was that!?" exclaimed Eduardo, looking backwards and seeing the other rental car further back at a more respecting distance.

"Not sure, Love. But as things are getting a little freaky, I suggest we study a bit. I would like you to boot up your laptop. Google us a map of Noble County, Ohio, would you?"

"Okay...." Eduardo replied slowly in wonderment as he followed orders.

As the machine fired up, Elaine began her lesson. "I'm a history teacher, Love. I do hope I shan't bore you. I'm afraid, in my experience, the only students who even pretend to be interested in serious history are the *brown-nosers*. You know what I mean?"

"Yes...I guess so. And I suppose if you were not so blessed beautiful, you would not have even *them*!"

"Mmmm. I do so like your accent, Love. Mmmm...What was I saying....?....Oh. Yes. *History*! Do you have the Noble County map up?"

"Yes."

"Splendid!" Elaine gazed over and quickly pop-pointed to Sarasville, Ohio on the screen. "We were just there."

"Yes."

"Now, look straight upward." She pointed. "See the town of Mt. Ephraim?"

"Yes."

"And look over here....see the town of Mt. Zion?"

"Yes...okay...so? What does this all mean?"

"Well, Love. It's in your genealogy lists. Turn to the couple whose graves we've just visited: *William and Sara Van Meter...*"

"Yes....okay...."

"As you see...When the Van Meters came to Noble County, they settled *first* in *Mt. Ephraim.* Then, they moved to *Mt. Zion.* And then...when William Van Meter married *Sara Stewart* of *Sarasville*...he moved there...and *there in Sarasville* we find them."

"Yes...So what does this mean Elaine?"

"Alright. Hold on. I want you to save the Noble County map, and bring up a map of Israel. Alright, Love?"

"Okay." Eduardo minimized the Noble County map, and in a minute was able to pull up a suitable map of Israel.

"Good, Love. Now. This area ..." Elaine pointed to the northern part of the Israel map "...is the region of Galilee. This, of course, is where Jesus grew up. Specifically, he was from the town of Bethlehem—right here." She pointed to a small dot slightly left of center within the region. "As you can see, the map calls the town *Beit Lechem*—which means *House of Bread* in Hebrew. But, we in the West, call it Bethlehem. Anyway, the town sits high upon the northern banks of the Jezreel Valley, which has always been excellent for wheat farming. It's entirely why *bread* figured so highly in Jesus' preaching and ministry. It just went with the area. He had a rather simple spiritual message, actually: Everyone needs *bread.* And everyone needs *God.* And one can't live with one and not the other. *Very Jewish.*"

"Okay..." Eduardo replied slowly. "I am with you." He nodded.

"You're such a good student, Love. Well. Let's talk about this Galilee region a bit...specifically the area around Bethlehem which is typically called *Lower Galilee...*"

"Okay...I am with you."

"Alright, then. The Galilee region had a popular ancient nickname...and that was: *Ephraim.*

Now, *Ephraim* was an ancient Jewish patriarch whose tribe settled in the North. Ephraim was the son of the patriarch Joseph, the eleventh son of Jacob...or as his name became: *Israel.* Now, I could bore you with a lot of very, very complicated Jewish history...but let's just say the *Galilee...or Ephraim* tradition is rather like what happened in America between the South and the North in the Civil War. The Jews had their own split a thousand years before Jesus. In this case, the Northerners...or Ephraimites came up much shorter in history than the Southerners...the Jews in the Jerusalem region. So...you know....it's not unlike what you have in America where the side that came up short...*the South*...has always had *The South shall rise again* idea.....So, there was something of the same in the Ephraim-Galilee area in the day of Jesus...a sort of *The North shall rise again* spirit. But the different thing in Jesus' day was that *all Jews*...both South and North, were oppressed by *foreigners*...by the Romans. And even though the Southern Jews in Jerusalem claimed superiority to their brothers in the North...they weren't doing anything dramatic to throw the Romans out. In fact the priesthood in Jerusalem had just rather given into the Romans...or at least, that would be the way Jews in Galilee would see it. In some sense, the Roman occupation presented an opportunity for Galileans, who rallied around their Northern Ephraim tradition....which included an idea that some day, *their* region in the North, would someday raise up a *Champion* who would reunify *all the Jews...North and South...*and *THEN*...the Messiah would come to redeem the whole world and do away with the oppressive Romans and anybody like the Romans. So...Jesus growing up in the North...grew up in an area saturated with expectation of the North rising again...with the expectation of a Northern *Champion* rising up to be the hero for all Jews. Galilee was a hot-bed of anti-Roman insurgent groups. Jesus had some of those insurgents in his own circle. Certainly Jesus was very interested in the themes of the northern Ephraim region. The old capitol of Ephraim was the town of Shechem…which in Jesus' day was inhabited by the Samaritans…who were a people related to the Jews…a sort of prodigal son split-off of the Jews…which had caused a good amount of strained relations between the two…but nonetheless, Jesus went to Shechem and met with the people there. And even when Jesus was in the Jerusalem area, he used to stay in a little town north of Jerusalem called Ephraim. The *Ephraim thing* was huge in Jesus mind.

"Okay….I am with you…but how does this all explain the Israel map?"

"Yes. Okay. On the map….from Galilee in the North…or *Ephraim* as I've explained…go directly south to *Jerusalem*—see it?"

"Okay. This is important: Another name for Jerusalem is *Zion*…or even *Mt. Zion.* So the North has the nickname of *Ephraim*…and the South has the nickname of *Zion.* Okay?

"…okay…."

"Alright then. I see that your Israel map includes the border with Jordan. That's good. Look here…" Elaine pointed to a spot on the right side of the Jordan River approximately mid-way between Galilee and Jerusalem. "That's the town of *Pella.*"

"Yes. I see it. What is your point?"

"Okay. I am going to give you the story in one breath, okay?"

"Please do."

"Jesus began his life, and later, his ministry in Galilee—or Ephraim. During his ministry he also had a base of operations across the Jordan in the Pella area…it was a convenient escape hatch when hostile forces were threatening to undo his ministry—he would just hop across the border and let things cool off. But finally, he went south to Jerusalem—or *Zion*, as it were. And there, he and his whole operation really got into trouble. He was arrested and charged. Somehow. Don't ask me how—I don't know—Jesus, either escaped a near execution or somehow survived a botched execution. Whatever. *He survived.* So. Jesus, his brother James, and most of the organization again fled to their base across the Jordan—to Pella—except…his wife Mary Magdalene and their daughter Sara."

"Why would they split up?" Eduardo was quick to ask.

"Well…perhaps Jesus did not have confidence they could last long in Pella…and so, he sent his family away. Think about it. Think about any man in a land where insurgent forces are battling a super-power. The sporadic nature of such situations makes everything and everyone unpredictable. The super-power at hand gets very nervous and it takes to horrific methods of war where weapons are used on a massively wide scale…something akin to *insecticide*…against mass numbers of the *enemy*…men, women, children, babies, the elderly, the handicapped—*whatever—kill them all.* You know…that's what *genocide* is…*insecticidal war.* It's a certain logic that pops up in every generation. *Sherman's March* into the South during the American Civil War was a foreshadowing of later *Total War* thinking. Sherman went into the South with a total-assault strategy against the entire culture and infrastructure of the South—*burn everything.* It wasn't a long jump to what followed less than a century later…*Auschwitz, Hiroshima, My Lai, Central America, Bosnia…Haditha*—and on and on.

So when one is in the theatre of *total war*…What man?…what *good man*, could stand to have his wife and child endure that? No. Jesus sent his wife and daughter away…*while he could.* It must have been an agonizing decision for him."

Eduardo sat in stunned silence. A whispered sigh slowly blew out of his mouth. He looked directly at Elaine. "Tell me. How does all this misery so long ago have something to do with the Noble County map?"

"Yes, Love. Do pull that map up again. There. Good. Again. You see the Van Meters going from Mt. Ephraim…to Mt. Zion…and then on to Sarasville…"

"Okay."

"Yes. Now pull up the Israel map again. Okay, *remember….* Jesus' overall path in one sentence was: He started out in Ephraim—or Galilee…and then, he went to Zion—or Jerusalem. And then he went out to his old hideout base at Pella. Now. I want you to compare the positions of Ephraim-Galilee, Zion-

Jerusalem, and Pella on the Israel map.....with....Ephraim, Zion, and Sarasville on the Noble County map."

Eduardo flipped back and forth several times. "El Dio! They are the *same*!"

"Exactly. The Van Meter family was among the pioneer families who first settled Noble County. And...these pioneers all came here together as one group...in a wagon train from Virginia and before that, from New York where they landed when they arrived from the *old country*. So these pioneers named the Noble County towns. They placed the towns, and *the way* they named and placed them shows that they were in possession of *a Secret....*"

"....*A secret???*...But..." Eduardo's brain gears spun. "...the region names are not *totally* the same...you have *Ephraim* and *Zion* on both maps...but what is the connection of *Sarasville* to *Pella*?"

"Good eye, Love. Alright, then. *Sarasville* is a nickname for Pella. It has to do with Jesus' own secret word-play. The name *Sara* goes back to the Jewish matriarch Sara, the wife of the patriarch Abraham. But before Abraham and Sara migrated to what would later become Israel, they had different names. Abraham was formerly *Abram*. And Sara was formerly *Sarai*...which was a Persian name from her home country of Ur. *Sarai* means *house alongside the road for travelers*....which was entirely what Pella was. It was a well known and widely used stop on the trade route that went up and down the east side of the Jordan River in the area known in ancient times as Gilead. In Jesus' day, the Romans called the area The Decapolis because it had ten cities. Jesus knew the area well...had preached there often. He was mindful that Abraham and Sara had come through the area long ago in order to cross the Jordan River and proceed to the holy city of Shechem....which would later become the capital of Ephraim.

So...the words *Sarai*...*Sara*...*Sarasville*...all have to do with typical Middle Eastern word-play in Jesus' mind...*and his HOUSE*...his descendants and followers of his descendants. Think about it. Think about Jesus marooned in a remote camp— on the run—totally separated from his wife and only daughter....and how natural it would be for him to think about his *travelers' house* in Pella...or *sarai*....being all for *his* Sara...*his* child who would, hopefully, go on...out into the world...and *live*...It was a *very meaningful hope* to Jesus."

Eduardo gazed into Elaine's soft eyes. A flash of his own mother's face crossed his mind. Her name was Zara. And then he saw his father's face. And he thought of his brother Carlos and himself...and how they were both *alive*...and *well*, despite all the perils of their early lives. Eduardo's eyes widened. "*Meaningful* hope...based on *meaningful memory?...*" he offered with his eyes searching into Elaine's.

"Exactly." Elaine smiled gently and touched Eduardo's face. "Yes....*a long memory of Sara*....a memory that leans into the future. The name *Sara* in Hebrew means *princess*. Jesus, like any father, would think of his only daughter as his little *princess*...but also as a *princess*....of a *sarai*...a *traveler's* or *traveling House*. Sara has always been the symbol of the *future* of *Jesus' House*. Jesus and Mary Magdalene named their daughter *Sara*. William Van Meter, a descendant of Sara DuBois, married a woman named Sara and lives in Sarasville....after he's lived in Mt. Zion....after he's lived in Mt. Ephraim. And the theme just keeps marching on. You *do* realize that the name of Jonah and Madeleine Van Meter's daughter is *Sara*?

"Yes, but I know from my conversation with people at their church, that their Sara is adopted."

"Yes. And Sara, daughter of Jesus and Mary Magdalene, was also adopted. And this gets to the crux of Jonah's *Secret* that the Merovingians could not fathom if they tried. Jonah represents a family, not of blood, but of righteousness...a righteousness that all people of the world are called to. Jonah's got a huge *Secret*....to use one of your American sports metaphors...he's running with the *football*, and they want to take him down before he gets to the end zone—but at the same time, they need to know where the end zone is."

"So what is the *football*?...Is it the *Holy Grail*?"

"Oh, no. The Merovingians have their Grail. The Grail is *nothing more* than the Bloodline of Jesus that seeped into the

European nobility and royalty. No, they have their *Blood*...but what they *do not have* is......?

Eduardo's mental gears churned. W*hat is Elaine leading to?* And then...their previous conversation about the Sacrament kicked in. *They have the Blood...the Cup...the Grail...but NOT the...BREAD!...the BODY!* Eduardo paused for a second to check where his logic was leading. Suddenly, he turned to Elaine with wonderment in his eyes. "Jonah has: *The Body of Jesus???!!!!*"

Elaine nodded with a soft smile. "Jonah knows where it is....in Pella...or *Sarai...or Sarasville.* Jonah knows. They don't. And they know he knows."

"So how in the world does a secret like Jesus in this Pella come all the way down to Jonah and Madeleine Van Meter?"

"Well, Love...This brings us back to their common ancestors: Cretien DuBois and his wife Jeanne Masic Brunel...you see them in the list?"

"Uh...Yes. Cretien was born in Wicres, France, 1597. He died 1655. Jeanne Masic Brunel was born 1599 and...it doesn't say when she died....

"...1655...I can tell you...same as her husband Cretien...they were *martyred* together..."

"*Martyred???* Why?!"

"Well, it's quite simple, really. Cretien Du Bois married outside the family—*far* outside the family. His bride Jeanne was NOT a Merovingian. She was a Jew. And not only that—she was a *special* Jew. Jeanne was descended from a unique tribe of Jewish and Gypsy families that had intermarried in Southern France. And in that mix, Jeanne was even *more special*. She was a direct descendant of Mary Magdalene.

Cretien Du Bois' father Jacques was *upset*! You see, Jacques Louis Wallerund Du Bois, the Marquis Du Bois, had not always had a title! Originally, he was simply a social-climbing employee of a Merovingian family. But, he got very lucky, and married *up*. Jacques married Madeleine Renne De Croix d'Anjou. Now, the Anjou were mainstream Merovingians—going back to the Crusader king Godfroi de Bouillon who founded the original Templar order on Mount Zion in Jerusalem.

And so, Papa Jacques devoted a good amount of thought to his scheme...He even named his son after the author of the original Holy Grail romances—Cretien de Troyes.

But then, Cretien Du Bois destroyed it all. He fell in love with a girl from across the proverbial tracks—a girl he met by happenstance as she traveled north in the great Huguenot exodus of the day. Yes, for Jacques Du Bois, it was a complete catastrophe! His son had married *out* because Jeanne was not a Merovingian. He had married *down* because she was a Jew and a Gypsy. And worst of all, Cretien had married *into* a potential rival family—a family with a more authentic ancestry—directly descended from Mary Magdalene. A more complete catastrophe could not have been achieved.

Given the stakes, Cretien Du Bois must have agonized terribly over his decision to marry Jeanne. It meant giving up his title, all his money and possessions, all his connections to his family and the Merovingians...and ultimately life itself. Yes. Cretien and Jeanne were murdered by the Merovingians to keep their precious *Bloodline* pure and un-assailed. Attempts were made to erase their memory from the Du Bois family records and the whole history of the Pas de Calais region—a history which gloried in the legacies of Godfroi de Bouillon and William the Conqueror.

"But...obviously, it did not work....the *erasing...,*" Eduardo concluded.

"Exactly!" Elaine laughed. "You can't kill Jewish *memory...it just isn't going to happen!* So what *did* happen? Did they stamp Cretien and Jeanne's line out? No. Their son *Louis* and his wife *Catherine Blancon* escaped France through Holland and emigrated to New York. And they just started the Jewish Du Bois line over again...from scratch. And they even made their line *even MORE Jewish*...talk about going Jewish....look at *their* family...they had *twelve* children...look:

Abraham
Isaac
Jacob
David
Solomon
Rebecca
Rachel
Ragel
Luis
Matthias
Magdalena
and then...
Sara....

Now, as you see on the genealogy list, Sara DuBois married Joost Van Meter. And, she was, by all accounts, a most unusual woman. Although married to a Van Meter, she always identified herself as *Sara DuBois*. She was known as a terribly strong-willed woman. There is a story of she and her mother Catherine being captured by Indians in the wilds of New Amsterdam...later New York. The story goes that the Indians were about to execute the two by burning them at the stake when Sara saved the day by singing Psalm 137. Her voice was so beautiful to the Indians that they delayed long enough for her father Joost and his company, who were in pursuit, to hear them and rescue them in the nick of time. It's a beautiful Psalm...it must have held great meaning for Sara....

By the waters of Babylon
There we sat down and wept,
When we remembered Zion.
On the willows there
We hung up our lyres.
For there our captors
Required of us songs.
And our tormentors, mirth, saying,
Sing us one of the songs of Zion!
How shall we sing the Lord's song

In a foreign land?
If I forget you, O Jerusalem,
Let my right hand wither!
Let my tongue cleave to the roof of
My mouth,
If I do not remember you,
If I do not set Jerusalem
Above my highest joy!

.....And that's just *Jonah's* side of the genealogy!—Jonah is descended from Sara. But Madeleine, on her Merovingian side, is descended from Sara DuBois' sister, *Magdalena.* And do you see...how the same family names and their derivatives keep recycling over and over again? Well, the same thing happens on Madeleine's Jewish-Gypsy side. You have the same Jewish and Roma surnames from Southern France over and over again in Madeleine's geneaology: *Lechem, Garmu, Karo, Brunel, Tzigan, Calo, Masik,* etc...they just keep revolving back into her genealogy...And, I should point out, that it was the Roma side that did the heavy lifting on guarding the family *Secret.*"

"What do you mean?" asked Eduardo.

"Well, Roma have always been a migratory people...and *The Secret* has always been a migratory secret. It was a match meant to be, I suppose. Originally, the Roma migrated out of India around 1000 CE, working their way northwest out of India. Because they were strangers, erroneous legends grew about them—like, they were from Egypt because they were dark skinned—thus they were nicknamed *Gypsies.*

By the time of the *Crusades,* the Roma were in the Middle East, having been forcibly conscripted by the Muslims to fight the Christians. Through the natural course of the Christian-Muslim battles and taking of prisoners in the Trans-Jordan area...where Pella is, the Crusaders came into contact with the Roma...who in turn were in contact with the descendants of Jesus' followers still in the area. And so, *secrets* were passed from the Roma to the Crusaders...most probably from Roma prisoners trying to buy their freedom.

So, what *secrets* were passed? Well, it can be no coincidence that the Templars under Godfroi de Bouillon set up their headquarters on Mount Zion in Jerusalem. For, it was on that very mount that Jesus' own *House* had maintained their headquarters before fleeing to Pella. History tells us that the Templars discovered something in those environs that made them very rich and powerful. How did they know *where* to look? How did they know to look at all?....for things hidden a thousand years? Simple...the Roma gave up *secrets* including the *Bloodline* of Jesus...but apparently *not all the secrets*—as in: *The location of Jesus himself.* So then, it is also no coincidence that all the Grail lore starts coming out in Europe after the Crusades...as the Roma continued migrating west out of the Middle East into Europe. By the early 1400s, the Roma were in Southern France...mixing with Jews...mixing with people they already knew about...the *descendants of Mary Magdalene, Sara, and Jesus of Pella.* So then it's easy...*The Secret—as to the location of the Body*—went out of Southern France into the Huguenot Exodus...to Cretien DuBois...to the Van Meters...and there you have it. And as they say, *The rest is history.*"

"Hmmm." Eduardo pondered. "Yes...history. But this is a very different kind of history...*These people*...they are different. They are not just searching for lost memory—they are...uh, Well, it is...as if...they are *building* memory!"

"Exactly." Elaine leaned to Eduardo and softly kissed his lips.

He looked out over the road before them and the distant outlines of the city they approached. He looked at Elaine with a sudden new insight. "This is not about the past...is it? It is about the future."

Elaine nodded. "Yes. *Jonah Oskar Van Meter* and *Madeleine Garmu Lechem Van Meter* are people of the future. Look at the full name of Jonah's mother on the genealogy:

Zara Mahar Pancasa

"*Mahar* is Hebrew for *tomorrow*," said Elaine.
Eduardo's eyes jumped.
"What, Love?"

Eduardo was strangely silent. "My mother's name...it was *Zara*," breathed Eduardo.

Elaine's eyes puzzled. What was your mother's maiden name?"

Eduardo thought. "I have no idea," he said in an awed tone signaling something that had just dawned on him.

Elaine kept this revelation in her heart, noting especially that the mother of Jonah Van Meter bore a Hispanic surname.

The Bread House. Bexley, Ohio.
Monday, May 21, 8:30 P.M.

The old grey three-story farm house stood at the corner of Bellwood and Cassingham as one among other adjacent homes on a normal older residential street. But originally, the house stood alone in fields of wheat when it was built in 1900—before the village of Bexley ever existed. The structure had a certain shabby grace including a classic wrap-around porch. And, high atop the peaks of the house, were small attic windows taunting gazers to wonder what secrets might lie so far up in the dark.

The interior of the house was another matter. It had been radically remodeled into a secret Jewish synagogue. Walls had been moved, removed, and added. Hidden places created. On the first floor, the dining room ceiling had been raised to a high gothic peak reaching to an open second floor overlook balcony. A huge four foot square sky-light ceiling window brightened the room in addition to a Victorian chandelier suspended over a large roundtable in the center of the room.

Adjacent to the dining room was an open area which served as the synagogue's sanctuary. Its floor was raised to a low platform above two steps. The outer walls, on the east and south, were of a deep blue color and lined with sitting benches. In the center of the platform resided a modest wooden table for the reading of the Torah. Behind the table on the east wall stood a wooden cabinet housing the Torah scrolls. And in the southeast corner of the room there was wooden bookcase full of Hebrew prayer books.

The house was owned, officially, by Geoffrey and Faith Sinclair. Geoffrey, a college French professor, had an understated but refined European bearing. Faith, a vivacious African-American woman, was an artist. And then there was Destiny, their daughter—a raucous cherubic thirteen year old of caramel complexion and finely arrayed dreadlocks.

Jonah stood on the porch of the house. He rang the doorbell. Immediately there was the muffled sound of quick padding feet.

Sara flung the door open. "Daddy!" Sara took hold of her father in her dark sweet arms.

Holding onto his daughter, Jonah entered the foyer leading into the open sanctuary room where some people were milling about in conversation. Madeleine emerged from the adjacent dining room with the Sinclairs and a number of others. In the hum of people and Madeleine's tearful embrace, various guests called out, "Shalom, Jonah. Shalom... Shalom."

Jonah made the rounds of greeting old friends not seen in many years.

As Geoffrey Sinclair shepherded the group into the dining room, Faith stayed close to a somber Madeleine.

The dining room was grandly lit by the august chandelier over the large central roundtable. Wall sconces flickered on the interior side wall over a serving buffet built into the wall.

Jonah looked up into the high ceiling, nodding to the attendants on the overlook balcony. They monitored the gathering below while keeping watch outside the house through the large skylight window. Not far from the attendants was a stairway to the house attic—the main Command Center of *Beit Lechem—The Bread House.*

A fair amount of kibitzing ensued as the group negotiated their chair positions at the roundtable. In the center of the table lay an antique white ironstone bread platter with embossed words upon its rim: *Give Us This Day Our Daily Bread.* Upon the platter were placed two stacks of six *matzah* squares.

Jonah motioned everyone to take their seats. Jonah sat Sara in the center on the west side of the table facing east. He sat to

Sara's right and Madeleine to her left. Opposite Sara were seated Destiny and her parents Geoffrey and Faith, facing west.

On the north side of the table were seated local Jews led by their affable rabbi, Howard Golden.

On the south side were seated two groups of secretly converted Jews. One group represented the various Roma and Traveler groups of the House. Their leader was Waldon Johnson, a tall grey-haired man clad in a white shirt and a blue silk vest. A bright gold pocket watch chain draped his vest over crisply pressed black pants.

To Waldon's right was another leader: Raina Langevin, a young woman of fair skin and long black hair. She wore an earth-tone knitted cap and a rough hemp-looking blouse that only made her fair skin stand out all the more. She and several others represented the converted Merovingians. In all, there were about thirty people in the room.

Jonah asked Sara to do the *Motzi*. The girl stood. She stood in a way that indicated to Jonah that she was going to say something in addition to the blessing. The thin dark girl's eyes looked at all the faces with direct eye contact. Some she knew, and some not. Raina Langevin smiled sweetly to her, as to a sister. Rabbi Golden's eyes adopted her as his own. Waldon Johnson cast a knowing eye to Madeleine. The others searched Sara's eyes as she searched theirs. And although her father had already announced that Sara was the leader in reserve, she could not but wonder what that meant to them—not being in line by blood, but by adoption. Sara felt she had to say *something*. And so she did.

"There is a place in the Passover seder where the youngest child gets to ask some questions. The first one starts out, *Why is this night different from all other nights?* I know from the Torah, that Passover is about when the Angel of Death passed over the Jewish homes when they were breaking out of Egypt. I think…it's like…today the whole world is in Egypt…trying to breakout. So, like…I remembered the Passover question tonight. But, this night…this night *is different.* Tonight, I do not want an angel of death for anyone in the world. I dream about an *Angel of Life*…for the whole world. That is what I think about tonight."

Jonah wept. He did not have to look at Madeleine to know her heart. From his coat pocket he took a fine velvet violet kippa and placed it on his head.

Sara held a piece of the matzah and did the blessing.

Baruch atah Adonai elohaynu melech ha'olam hamotzi lechem min ha'aretz.

And the whole assembly said *A-mein.*

Sara broke a piece of matzah and ate. She passed the bread plate to the people.

Jonah stood. He nodded. He addressed the gathering:

"Yes. Tonight, the Angel of Life takes flight. And we will not fear. We will not fear those who corrupt faith in God. We will not fear those who dream only of power and might. We will not fear racists or terrorists. *We will not fear.* Even though the opposition has wounded my family…*our family….We will not fear.* And our answer to Death tonight….will not be death…but Life. Only when the world sees the true power of Life, will it cast off the fear that propels it to death. No. *We will not fear.* We will live. We are Jews. Everyone one of us. We will live."

And the whole assembly said *A-mein.*

"I will now turn things over to Geoff, who will outline the tactical plan."

Geoffrey Sinclair arose with a nod to Jonah.

Two attendants drew down a map affixed to the south wall of the room.

"We are going to get the job done," Sinclair began. "I know that everyone will do his or her job, and be proud to do so. Let me first echo Jonah's admonition: Fear not. Fear is a luxury we cannot afford. We will not tolerate fear in ourselves. It is simply not an option. Yes. They are out there. They're out there as I speak, actually. I could take you upstairs and have Ehud and Chaya show you close-up video of them all. So, it's okay. They're there. We know where they are and that's always more comforting than not knowing. Indeed, I should think Jonah, that you probably spotted a couple of our people keeping an eye out for you?..."

"um-hmm." Jonah smiled and nodded. "Yes, your ESCORTS are quite interesting!"

Madeleine gave Jonah a perplexed look.

Jonah whispered into his wife's ear and her eyes went wide.

"Yes!" Geoffrey beamed. "Aren't they grand?!!—the best illegal aliens the House can muster!"

The room rolled with laughter.

Well, anyway. Let's get down to it." Geoffrey slapped a yardstick to the map. "Here's Jonah, Maddie, and Sara in Ohio. And. Here is the *Package of Pella* we will transport in our *Operation Bodyguard.*" He pointed to a spot on the east side of the Jordan River.

"How will we guard against interference from the Jordanians?" asked Rachel Benjamin from the rabbi's group. "The Jordanian Army will spot the convoy from their posts in the mountains."

"I'll defer to Rabbi, who serves as our liaison to the Israelis," answered Geoffrey.

"Well." The rabbi shrugged. "We are certainly not going to trust the Jordanians, but…we are not too worried about them either. It is a very short drive from Pella up Jordanian Road 65 to the border crossing at Beit She'an. And then it is straight across the bridge to Israeli Road 71 in the land of Ephraim. As long as our vehicles look like all the other traffic, there should be no problem. But. We are prepared. Yes, we are always prepared. Israeli Air Force helicopters will monitor everything from the west side of the Jordan. No harm shall come to the *package*. I guarantee it."

"I also guarantee," stated Waldon Johnson with a firm nod. "Our *Rom* men running the convoy…or I should say, *Dom,* as they call themselves in that country, will be 100%. No mistakes! With God as my witness—they have maintained perfect security over the *House* there for a thousand years. Yes, I guarantee it!"

"And. I too guarantee!" echoed Raina Langevin with a playful bounce of her closed fist. "NO mistakes in Europe either!"

"What path will you take the convoy, once across the bridge?" called Rachel Benjamin.

Good question, Rachel." Geoffrey nodded. "The *Dom* convoy will, straight away, take the *package* up Road 71..." Geoffrey traced the pointer on the map. "...to Road 70...to Road 73...then to Road 75...and then to Road 77...and that's a lot of 7's!...and then straight up to *Bethlehem*. I hear they are having a census there."

The room roared in laughter.

"And so, the next day...," Geoffrey continued. "...they'll go up Roads 77 and 65 through upper Ephraim...up to 85 and 866 and 89 straight into Tzfat where they'll stay the night with the *House* there. And then. The next day, it's simply straight south from Tzfat on Road 90 along the west side of the Jordan. We will, of course, have air cover going through Samaria....not that we are worried about the Samaritans...they're with us too—they keep tabs for us on potential problems from Palestinian extremists. So...They'll come straight down 90 to Jericho where our Ethiopian brothers and sisters have a base and they will join the convoy...and then it's a straight shot west on Route 1 through the Wilderness of Judea to Bethany and straight up to the Mount of Olives overlooking Jerusalem."

"So what about *The Furniture?*" Rabbi Golden prompted.

"Right. Thank you, Rabbi." Geoffrey nodded. "This brings us to the fact that we will have *two convoys*. We've been talking about the *first* convoy which will transport the *Package*. But, there will be a *second* convoy. You've probably heard the rumors throughout the *House*—and I can assure you now that they are true. We *will* be bringing the *Jewish Temple Treasure* the Romans stole 2000 years ago back home. We know where it is, and we're just going to get it....AND....and...We will ALSO have the supreme privilege of bringing back the original *Tablet of the Law* from Aksum, Ethiopia...our Ethiopian brothers and sisters have decided to move their whole operation back *home*."

The room rolled into controlled shock and awe.

"So, yes. *The Furniture.* It is my job to coordinate the movement of both convoys here at our Command Center. Quite simply: *The Furniture* comes into Ben Gurion from its departure points. And Jonah, Maddie, and Sara will arrive at Ben Gurion a little behind *The Furniture…*

…So. It's very simple….*The Furniture,* and the Van Meters, will go straight east from Ben Gurion on Route 1 to Jerusalem…." Geoffrey carefully traced the pointer to the north side of the City and then down to East Jerusalem. "And, *The Furniture* convoy goes up the Mount of Olives Road past the village of E-Tur on top of the mount and straight to the Tomb of the Patriarchs in front of the Seven Arches Hotel at the NORTH side of the Jewish Cemetery. Now. On the other hand, the *Package* convoy will simply stage on the SOUTH side of the Cemetery on the Jericho Road…which is Route 1 from the east. Both staging points, NORTH and SOUTH, have roads that go down the Mount of Olives and then the roads converge at the bottom of the mount in the Kidron Valley below the walls of the Old City. So, then…we head for *Zion.*"

"Geoffrey…?" called Rachel Benjamin. "Okay. The Dom will lead *The Furniture* convoy down? But, who will be leading the *Package convoy* down the mount?"

A fair amount of hushed whispers rolled throughout the room.

Geoffrey shot a look to Jonah, his eyes wide and searching.

"Haven't assigned it yet," snapped Jonah. Quickly changing the subject, he continued, "I want to mention some logistical and security details…First, we'll be using flags at the head of the convoys and on Mt. Zion. We want the convoy commanders to be able to track where they are heading as they come down the Mount of Olives. We'll get the gear there of course, which will be more involved on *Zion* because we need about 30 feet of flag staff. Our *Ground Zero* is on the backside of the mount.

Second, as we've said before, we'll have Israeli air support…over both convoys. Now, at the base of the mount, not only will we have Israeli cover, we'll also have the assistance of the Jerusalem Dom community at the Lion's Gate of the Old City directly on the opposite side of the Kidron Valley. The Dom neighborhood is just inside the gate. We can be sure they'll have first hand knowledge of anything in the works from *Hamas, Islamic Jihad,* or the like. And the Dom *WILL* fight, if they have to.

"So, how do we get to Zion?!" Rachel Benjamin shouted.

"Yes! Of course, to Zion!" Jonah chuckled. "Well, simply: Once we are at the bottom of the Mount...and we have both the northern and southern groups all together...We turn south on the Ophel Road and we go along the southern side of the Old City walls. We will enter the Old City at the Dung Gate, which of course overlooks the Western Wall under the Temple Mount...And so, we just simply go along inside the wall on Batei Masseh Road to the next gate, which is Zion Gate." Jonah quickly traced the route three times with the pointer. "And then. We'll simply proceed out the Gate, and then on to our terminal point on Mt. Zion."

"I disagree!" cried Rachel Benjamin. "Jonah. Going down the Mount of Olives is all fine and good, but have you really thought through *Arab reaction?!!!* You know...they will be watching every move we make from the Temple Mount, and you know damn well they're going to assume we are coming *for them...on the OLD Mt. Zion!* I am really very doubtful that we are going to have the opportunity to say, *Relax, we're heading to the NEW Mt. Zion...and by the way, you can keep the rock!*

So, okay Jonah. Fine. You've got air cover...and you envision us just trotting down the Ophel Road under the choppers for the Dung Gate and then we're *home free?!!!* Hell, Jonah. Look at what you're talking about! You're wide open on that road from the Arabs across the valley in Silwan. Their houses sit pretty high over there...no trick to launch rockets from over there. And, then Jonah...you've got Arab houses right on the side of the Ophel Road as you take the curve toward the gate...perfect vantage for IEDs or a hell of a fire fight. You'll be damn lucky to get to the Dung Gate! And personally, I just don't like the thought of taking the future of the Jewish people and the world through the *DUNG Gate!*"

Jonah looked at Geoffrey widely.

"Do you have an alternative to suggest Rachel?" asked Geoffrey.

"Yeah. Do it the *Jewish* way!...the *Israeli* way! Straight up from the base of the Mount to LION'S GATE...up the Via Dolorosa...just like Moshe Dayan in '67!!!"

Jonah rolled his head and eyes. "And you're worried about the *Arab reaction!???*" That's *THEIR* quarter! You've got everything you don't want in that neighborhood! *Hamas...Islamic Jihad...* the whole thing!"

"AND the *Dom!*" Rachel Jacobs retorted. "You said they would fight!"

"Well, yeah. If they have to. But why pick the fight if you don't have to?...and in narrow streets...you can't take a car in there....well, not a large one anyway...and we're haulin' considerable gear, you know?"

Rachel Benjamin nodded grudgingly. "Well Jonah, you have a point there about getting bogged down in the Muslim Quarter."

"Tell me about it..." affirmed Jonah.

Rachel Benjamin shifted gears. "There's another Lion's Gate option I was thinking about..."

"What's that?"

"The Kotel Tunnel. It runs from the Kotel plaza along the Western Wall.... "

"Yes..."

"...and it dumps out right on the Via Dolorosa...uh...about 300 yards from Lion's Gate. The IDF are always there guarding the tunnel entrance on the Via Dolorosa. If you had to, you could shoot through the tunnel into the Kotel, and then straight through the Jewish Quarter to Zion Gate."

"Hmmm. Interesting to think about..." Jonah agreed. "But I'm not so sure about *shoot* through. The tunnel is pretty tight in a lot of places, but it would be secure." Jonah had another thought about the tunnel which he kept to himself. "It's food for thought, Rachel. I assure you we will study this further and possibly work into our contingency plans. Obviously, our commanders on the ground will make decisions on the spot as they are needed."

Geoffrey Sinclair rose to take the lead again. "Switching back to our Command Center here, I wish to introduce our technical directors, Mr. Will Aaronson and Mr. Rodney Fridenmaker, more affectionately known to us as *The Rod Man.*" With a wave of his hand Sinclair pointed the men out on the southwestern side of the table. Will Aaronson, chubby with blonde hair, had an impish over-grown teenager personality. He was a text-book computer geek. Rodney Fridenmaker was a thin man of dark complexion with stark black hair. The Rod Man was confined to a wheel chair. He had Multiple Sclerosis. The movements of his head, facial muscles, and limbs were all contorted into spastic gesticulations. His speech was terribly labored and beyond the comprehension of others—except for Will, who was The Rod Man's interpreter. The two had been best friends since grade school. The man in the wheelchair knew more about technology than anyone could guess. He also had theories about *potential technology* between God and those seeking to be healed of disease. The Rod Man had an agenda. *The Bread House* had an agenda. And in God, it was all the same agenda.

"Will and Rod are very excited," continued Geoffrey Sinclair. "They've never had such a budget to go gadget shopping! They'll be lining up all the equipment for *The House* for both our Command Center here and on *Zion.*

"So what's the equipment for?...what kind of equipment?" called out Raina Langevin.

"Lights…Camera…Action!" Geoffrey laughed. "We're going to broadcast the whole event! And…The Rod Man here, is going to hack us into the Net and all the major TV networks.!"

"Cool!" celebrated Raina.

The Rod Man forced a guttural laugh of glee out of the back of his throat with some fast rocking forward and backward.

Will nodded *YES* spastically with a grin stretching ear to ear. "It's gonna be cool!" he laughed. "Serious cool!"

Geoffrey checked his watch. "It's getting late…So, let me point out the major monitoring sites in Jerusalem.

Our opposition has two main high places: The Lutheran Church of the Redeemer in the Old City, and the Lutheran Augusta Victoria Hospital on the Mount of Olives. Both have tall bell towers. Interestingly, both structures were built by the Kaiser Wilhelm in the 1890s. I guess the German-Palestinian connection has a tradition.

On our side, we have several sites in and about the Old City. First, we have a base on Mt. Zion where Rabbi's colleague, Rabbi Avraham, runs a yeshiva and holocaust museum. Then, we have another yeshiva which stands over the Kotel. All events on the Mount of Olives will be monitored there by the Chief Rabbinate of Israel and the Prime Minister's Office.

And then, just outside the Old City, we have two sites. One, is the Pontifical Biblical Institute at 3 Paul Botta Street. It is a very tall building which houses on its top floor the Vatican Communication Center for the entire Middle East region. You may wonder how such a Catholic site is one of ours...Simple: The *House* has infiltrated the Communications staff and they will be working with Will and The Rod Man on the video feeds which all the world will see.

Finally, I wish to point out the Rockefeller Museum. It's situated caddy corner across the road from Herod's Gate in *Arab East Jerusalem*. So, yes. It's in the wrong neighborhood, but it's ours, and supremely defensible. It was a key *IDF* position in '67, and we should remember that..."

"Now you're talkin' Geoff!!!" called Rachel Benjamin with her fist in the air.

Spirited shouts of *A-mein, A-mein* circled the room.

"...Jonah and I have decided this is our *Plan Bet*, if you will...that is...if things, somehow, get really freaky, we can head for the Rockefeller and hole-up there...until we figure something else out.

So, then. All we have to do is start. And so, here is the first step. As we all know, Jonah is being constantly tailed...Now, Jonah...You told me that you spent some meditation time this afternoon at the *House* graves in Sarasville..."

"Yes. And I had *company*."

"Of course you did. Like I said before, it's good to know where the *company* is. So let's keep it that way, shall we? Uh...Let's keep *the grave thing* going. Let's make a *bread crumb* trail for them...the more they see a path...the more they want to see what is at the end of the path, huh? So, yes. What we are going to do is send Jonah, Maddie, and Sara on the safest and most circuitous route possible *through Europe* as they make their *aliyah* to Zion...but of course in our very narrow time-frame! Not too quick and not too soon. We need the better part of a week to line everything up in Jerusalem. So, we'll have Jonah & Co. visiting graves...dropping bread crumbs along the way. And, we'll have *House* crew schlepping as decoys here and there along the way.

Jonah, Maddie and Sara will leave tonight by car for Chicago where they'll fly out of O'Hare tomorrow. Besides, we can't fly this *outlaw* out of the *Columbus* airport!...seems I saw something on the local news about somebody assaulting a Bishop's Assistant???...My, my, my! *What is this world coming to?!!!*"

Whoops and shouts filled the room.

So. Jonah, Maddie and Sara...get some good sleep tonight en route. We have a good driver and good *escorts*..."

"...the best illegal aliens the *House* can muster?!!!" laughed Jonah.

Geoffrey nodded and chuckled with the whole room. "So, then. It's from here... to Chicago-O'Hare...to Europe...to *Mount Zion...and the rest is history*...the *new* history of the *Israelites*...no longer slaving for bread...but the *Defenders of Bread for All...the Bread of Tomorrow*...which begins tonight...here...this very moment."

Geoffery looked at Sara.

"My dear. I have a few ancient questions for *you* as we conclude our Seder."

Sara nodded and stood.

"From where have you come?"
"I have come from Egypt," answered Sara.
"Where are you going?"
"I am going to Jerusalem," she answered.
"What are you taking with you?"

Sara pointed to the *matzah* on the table. She collected the squares into a cloth bag and slung the bag over her shoulder.

Geoffrey Sinclair nodded. "Jonah," he called. "Do you have concluding words for this august assembly?"

Jonah stood. Not a sound breached the air.

"Yes," said Jonah. "I think of the words that come at the end of the Passover Seder:

> *I was a young man and now I am old,*
> *yet never have I seen a righteous man deserted*
> *nor his children lacking for Bread."*

And the whole congregation said *A-mein.*

Chapter 12

Blessed are you, O Lord, the support and stay of the righteous.

Chez Paul, Washington, D. C.
Tuesday, May 22, 12:12 A.M.

"Eduardo just texted," stated Bill Blanche, pouring Bordeaux into a glass.

"…and?" Ashman Blackpoint demanded.

"Van Meter's headed north…most likely for Canada."

"That can't happen."

"Yes, of course. I've already put word out to ICE all along the border."

"What do you know about the woman Ed has been consulting with?"

"She's on faculty at Oxford, Professor of Christian History…"

"And they met, how?"

"Eduardo says, happenstance…on the plane."

"*Happenstance.* I don't like *happenstance.* Notify me immediately of *any* new developments.

"I will," confirmed Bill. He studied Ashman Blackpoint's eyes. They were facades, like two-way mirrors in a gray cement interrogation room.

Blackpoint abruptly stood hitting his head slightly on the Tiffany chandelier hanging over the bar. Turning on his heels, he departed briskly and out the tavern door to his waiting car.

"White House." Blackpoint ordered.

"A little late, no? Mr. Blackpoint." inquired the driver.

"Let's hope, not *too* late."

Johnstown, Ohio.
Tuesday, May 22, 12:59 A.M.

The *Caravan* pulled slowly into the cemetery creeping along
the narrow way. The driver, a sharp-eyed Hasidic Jew wearing a
black kippah, methodically navigated the winding path between
sections of gravestones, their forms outlined only by the light of
the moon. Using a crude map drawn earlier by Jonah, the old
man found the correct stone.

Jonah, Madeleine and Sara slumbered deeply in the back of
the van upon each other and a few bags of supplies. The driver
tried not to disturb the women as he tugged on Jonah's sleeve.

"Mr. Van Meter, sir?" he whispered carefully.

"Hmm? What?" Jonah stirred.

"We are here Mr. Van Meter. As you wished. The tomb of
Yitzak Van Meter."

"Ummmm. oh…" Jonah mourned his break from sleep, but
his hand floated to his coat pocket and found the matzah.

"Make a big show of it," Jonah directed groggily.

The old man exited the vehicle and stood upon the grave. He
raised both hands together with the *matzah* in the air in the manner of the *Cohains*. He said the *bread blessing* and made a
shower of crumbs upon the grave. The old man returned to the
Caravan.

"That is all, Mr. Van Meter?" he asked incredulously.

"Yeah. I'm deader than Yitzak. Keep going north, no delay."
Jonah immediately returned to his former state.

Best Buy Store, Easton Mall. Columbus, Ohio.
Tuesday, May 22, 9:33 A.M.

"Tom, honey. We're gonna need yer authorization for a sell,"
the Appalachian voice sounded on the back room office inter-
com where Assistant Manager Tom Hartlan sat at a paper strewn
desk trying to figure out the next two-week shift schedule. The

tall heavy man patted his bald head, pushed himself up, and lumbered toward the front of the store thinking about the application he had just put in at Target.

Tom arrived at the checkout to behold the conveyor belt chock full of high ticket electronics, and three carts full of similar ware.

"OooWeeBuddie!" exclaimed Tom under his breath. "What the hell is this?" he whispered to Wanda the cashier.

She shrugged blankly chewing gum, awaiting her orders.

"Hi guys...," Tom greeted Will Aaronson and Rodney Fridenmaker stationed in his *command chair.*

Both grinned like the noonday sun.

"Uh....so...uh...these are all items you are purchasing today?" Tom inquired in a wary retail store manager tone.

"Yes!" chirped Will Aaronson as The Rod Man rocked forward and backward in complete joy.

"Okay... uh. How are we paying for this order today?"

"American Express!" blurted Will.

The Rod Man spastically pitched out the *Gold Card* from his chair pouch onto the conveyor belt.

Tom turned to Wanda and frantically whispered, "What the hell is the total on this shit?"

"Seventy-seven thousan', twelve dollar, an' one cent."

Tom leaked a restrained laugh and he shook his head. He picked up the *Gold Card* which read: *Bethlehem Productions, Inc.* "Uh...You guys in some kind of religious TV station business or something?"

"Somethin' like that!" snort-giggled Will Aaronson sideglancing The Rod Man rockin' on in his *command chair.*

"Uh...Okay," said Tom. "We're gonna need to see some ID."

White House Situation Room, Washington, D.C.
Tuesday, May 22, 9:33 A.M.

Ashman Blackpoint hunkered down with a senior member of the Mid East Watch Team at the end of the conference table in the small cramped room.

"We've been tracking the *Sufas* all night," the analyst informed, referring to a squadron of twelve Israeli F-16s launched from central Israel. "They're all armed to the teeth. At first they stayed together, but about an hour out over the Mediterranean, they split. Six are still westbound, but the others hard banked to the south very low over the *Suez,* and then west toward Ethiopia. *AND*...they're towing a Hercules C-130 transport with them. *AND*...the westbound Sufas have a 707 riding shotgun"

"Analysis?" probed Blackpoint.

"Well. The Israelis use 707s as refueling tankers. Looks like they're on a long haul trip with the westbound *Sufas*. On the other hand, the Ethiopia group looks like a short tripper...no refuelers, but with the *Hercules* transport tagging along...Looks like they're going to pick some thing up."

"What?"

"Well...don't know. The Israelis have been working for years on transferring Ethiopian Jews to Israel. There's been a move the last several years to get the last of them out...and now...it's always dicey with radical Muslims often carrying out operations along the Somalian-Ethiopian border. But the thing is...you're not going to get *that many people* on just one C-130...so, this may just be the beginning of something much larger...some kind of *preparatory* mission. I'm troubled though by the port they've landed at."

"They're on the ground?"

"Yeah, 'bout an hour ago."

"Where?"

"Aksum, in northern Ethiopia."

"*Aksum,*" repeated Blackpoint. His eyes sharpened.

"Yeah, Aksum. You would think if they were picking up *people* they would do it from the main airport...Bole, in Adis Adaba...certainly for the PR value of it. So it's something else...whatever blessed thing there is in Aksum to fly all those birds for. And, as for the ones coming our way, they're following a pretty normal flight pattern over the Mediterranean..."

"...such as a commercial carrier would to the US?"

"Yeah, sure."

"…except…with a tanker…they're not planning on landing anywhere"

The analyst gave a quick nod, his lower lip protruded. "That would be a safe assumption, sir."

"…and Van Meter's course? Still northbound?…Crossing the lake by ferry or going around the long way or what?"

"No sir…."

"What?"

"Van Meter veered northwest through Fort Wayne, Indiana and is presently heading west on Route 30."

"Shit. He's heading toward Chicago."

"Yes, sir. He's about an hour east of Chicago as we speak."

"Okay. Put all agencies in Chicago on alert at O'Hare—especially at the *EL AL* counters. Wait for my instructions. I have a meeting." Without further word, Blackpoint bolted from the room.

Pearson International Airport, Toronto, Canada.
Tuesday, May 22, 1:11 P.M.

Agitated, Wallerund DuBois Holloway paced in front of the departure schedule monitor in the blasé beige airport hall. A necessary layover from Columbus, it was still the most direct flight to Tel Aviv. He pulled at his clerical collar and shifted a weighty brief case from his left to right hand. He floated through the newsstand shops blankly, forced himself to sit down and appear to be reading a newspaper, paced the monitor again, and then posted himself at the huge square windows of his gate section looking out to the wide flat expanse of asphalt, grass, sky, men and machines. Watching a pilot conversing with other flight crew behind the cockpit window of a Lufthansa Airbus, he had a flashing daydream of himself in the seat before the controls, dry and cool in dead-lock check-listing for a mission, certainly a combat mission, in a race of time. He wondered, *Where is Jonah now?* Perhaps in the very same airport. Wal's eyes kept searching faces and figures in clumps of people on carpet and tile for an emergent dogfight. Throughout all of Wal's nerves and muscles there was a spitting grit of anger and his jaw clenched into a rock. Images of his fallen grandfather Max and his pantheon of aspiring Merovingian emperors marched across the dark interiors of his mind. His cell phone sounded.

"Yes?" Wal moved quickly to a corner of empty plastic seats.

"Pastor Holloway?" greeted a woman with a European accent.

"Yes. This is Pastor Holloway."

"Yes, Pastor. Hold one moment please. Mr. Khouri, is concluding another call. He will not be long."

"Yes. Fine." Wal quickly surveyed the people traversing the tiled concourse beyond the carpeted seating area.

"Hallo Wal, I am happy to find you! Where are you?"

"Toronto. The most boring airport in North America, I can tell you."

"Ha, Ha. Yes, I quite agree. But, I am afraid it is the best way, if one does not fly Jewish. Can you believe what *EL AL* charges? Oh, my god! The bastards! Ha, ha. We shall correct that too, yes?"

"Certrainly, Mr. Khouri...but we have much work to do first."

"Yes of course, my friend. When shall we see you in Jerusalem?...Actually, I shall have my people receive you because, as you know, I am still in Zurich. And I must tell you that it has been a very fruitful time. I think our brotherhood is in very good position for all things, you know? When will you arrive in Jerusalem, Wal?"

"...should touch down about 9 am."

"Very good. Very good. You will have first class service, my friend. I shall have you picked up at *Ben Infidel Airport*! Yes, I tell you. My assistant Munib will pick you up. He is very short but he will hold a sign for you. Maybe it should say *Follow me to Palestine, Pastor Holloway!* I shall tell him to write in *German!* Ha, Ha, you like?"

"Uh, maybe just my name."

"Okay. Okay, my friend. Ehhh....You' *special friend*—Mister Van Meter? He is where now?"

"I'm not sure. But I have no doubt he's en route…through some means."

"Yes, of course. You know, my friend….I hear today on the radio that the Pope has left Rome for his palace at Castel Gondolfo. It seem' to me it is very early for his summer vacation, yes?"

"Well. I am sure it will be a *working* vacation."

"Yes, I think you are correct Wal. Very correct. You are a very smart man, my friend. That is what I tell everyone. Well, my friend…I can assure you that everything will be ready. I look very, very much forward to seeing you and conducting our business."

"Yes, Mr. Khouri. We will get *that* done."

"Yes, of course, my friend. We shall. I see you soon in Jerusalem, Wal…with our souls and blood for you, my friend…our souls and blood."

"And mine for you Mr. Khouri. Mine for you."

Northern Indiana.
Tuesday, May 22, 1.11 P.M.

Jonah's *Caravan* rolled into Valparaiso, Indiana on Route 30. The group was refreshed after having slept part of the night at a truckstop in northern Ohio. Jonah directed their driver Reuven to stop the vehicle along side the road directly in front of *Valparaiso University.* Jonah got out of the passenger side and bid the old man to move over and take a break.

"I'll do the driving from here on." said Jonah.

The old man was grateful. Even with the nap at the truckstop, it had been a long night.

Jonah stepped into the middle of the wide grassy field in front of the university's *Chapel of The Resurrection,* a huge modernistic edifice resembling a battleship at dock with an octagonal tower of glass on one end approximating a mock canon turret. Jonah planted himself squarely in the grass before the great ship and spoke lowly unto the air:

*Pour out Your wrath upon those who do not know
You and upon the governments which do not call
upon Your name. For they have devoured Jacob
and laid waste his dwelling place.*

"…but, not for long." added Jonah.

Jonah returned to the *Caravan* and took the driver's seat. With a quick wrist on the ignition, he gunned the wagon down the road.

"A little quality-time with the ol' *alma mater*?" chided Madeleine.

"Yeah, right. It wasn't my favorite school…not to mention they have a shitty basketball program. You know what their team name is, don't you?

"What?" asked Sara, the family basketball expert.

"*Crusaders.*"

"Hey that's what *Capital University* in Columbus calls their team! They're Lutheran too." cried Sara.

"Yeah…all the Lutherans think they're *Crusaders.*"

Reuven made a quick turn of his body toward Madeleine and Sara in the back seat. "Do I understand that *YOU* play basketball, little girl?"

Sara made a quick nod with a beaming smile.

"Best center the school ever had!" chimed Madeleine. It was the most cheerful she had sounded in many days.

"What is your team called?" asked Reuven.

"We're the *Lions!* Which I think is really cool and all, but my favorite team is the *Buckeyes!*"

Reuven immediately looked perplexed. "What is *Boch chai*? I am from Israel. There are many American things I do not know. Ehh….We have Lions in Israel, but what you say…*Boch chai*? What is *boch chai*?"

Sara laughed. "I really don't know what it is. It's like this stupid brown nut-thing that grows on trees…"

"On *Buckeye* trees! They're an Ohio tree!" explained Madeleine.

Jonah was enjoying the banter he started.

"Oy." Reuven nodded. "In Israel we have...ehh...date trees...ehhh...we have olive trees. I do not think these would make good names for basketball teams.

"Oh-oh-oh! Here! Look here, Reuven!" Sara thrust out her *Brutus Buckeye* key chain. "THIS is a *Buckeye*!"

"He has eyes!" the old man mused.

"He's like a mascot or somethin'....at all the games this dude comes out in the *Brutus the Buckeye* costume. It's like, all fuzzy and stuff. And he dances around and gets people to yell and stuff. It's so cool. I think I want to marry *Brutus Buckeye*!"

"Oy! I am sure you will make a lovely couple....*Brutus and Sara Boch chai...stein.*" The old man raised his finger.

Madeleine giggled hard and joy filled the *Caravan*.

"Well, I'll tell you..." joined Jonah. "When I first laid eyes on this girl, I saw her long fingers and legs, and I said, didn't I Maddie?....I said: Looks like a basketball star to me!"

"Yep!" agreed Madeleine. "That's what Daddy said!" Her smile rotated all over the car and brought gladness to Sara and Jonah.

"You are from where?" Reuven asked Sara. He noted Sara's facial features and dark skin.

"I was born in Bosnia. I'm adopted." the girl answered matter-of-factly.

"Oy." nodded Reuven, shaking his head. "Very hard. Very hard." he said nodding again and patting Sara's hand. "My father and my mother also..." he said pointing his finger. "...they come from Budapest, which is not so far from where your people come. My father...during the Great War...they took my father away. It was in the night. I did not know. I was only a small boy, you see. My mother... she did not see Father again. After the war was over, she brought me up to Israel. It is strange. Though I was only a small boy, I feel as though I do remember Father and Budapest. I think it is from the stories that my mother told me. This is what I think."

"What was your father's name?" winced Sara, her heart going out to the old man.

"His name was Chaim. Chaim Kohen. Thank you." he patted Sara's hand. "Any Kaddish you ever said, you said for my father, Chaim Kohen...even if you did not know his name. You know. This is the Torah."

Sara nodded with understanding. "Are you a rabbi?" she asked.

"No. I did not have chance to study. My mother and I live on kibbutz....that is a farm, you know. We work very hard. After my schooling, I went to the Army, of course. This is what everyone in Israel does, you know. Even the girls, yes?"

Sara nodded. "What did you do in the Army?" she asked.

"What I do now!" Reuven laughed. "I drive the trucks. When the trucks broke, I fix the trucks. I assure you, if this truck breaks, I can fix it. I am Reuven the truck fixer. I think this is what I want them to put on my *tziyun*: Reuven The Truck Fixer Kohen. Nice sound, yes?"

Sara giggled as she hung on the back of Reuven's car seat like a granddaughter.

"So, like. Did you get married? Did you have kids?"

"Oh yes. I met my Raziela in the Army. We were married after I was...ehhh...how you say....ehhh: got out. The girls. They do not stay in Army as long as the boys. So. Raziela. She left before me. And I was very glad she wait' for me. She was very pretty girl....like you Sara."

Sara beamed. "And your kids?..."

"Yes, we had two wonderful children. Both little girls, Abbie and Tziyona. They were trouble the two of them were, I tell you. They were born two years apart. But it was like they were twins, you know? So much trouble. Always making such mess...with drawings....they draw pictures on everything in the house...on the walls...on the tables...pictures all kinds...of prince and princess...trees, maybe *boch chai trees*...I don't know....they draw animals...they draw all kind *mashuga* things. They were crazy little girls."

"So what did Abbie and Tzi--?"

"Tziyona."

"..and Tziyona do when they grew up?"

There was a long silence.

Reuven answered. "The girls...they did not grow up. They were killed. With their mother. It was a bomb. In the market."

The drone between the asphalt and the rubber wheels hung in the air. Facts oppressed.

Madeleine scanned the heavier traffic around them on the highway. There were many cars full of families of all shapes and color. Her thought was stark: Her sister Margot had killed her baby. *My own sister. Blood counts for nothing.* Madeleine leaned forward and kissed the old man on his temple. "*Shalom aleichem,*" she whispered. In her strong right arm, she took her daughter Sara. In her strong left arm, she took the nape of Jonah's neck which had turned to a rock formation to guard his tear-swollen eyes locked on the road before him.

"*Aleichem shalom.* We are all working on *Shalom,*" said Reuven evenly.

"We are, Reuven. We are. We shall build the *Third Temple* for your father, for your wife, and for all the children. We will do it," answered Madeleine.

Eduardo and Elaine followed fast behind Jonah's *Caravan* into Chicago Heights, on the south side of Chicago. The road, now less than a freeway, gave more opportunity for other cars of interest to stand out. The *Caravan* was escorted on all sides by other vehicles that appeared associated, including the familiar blue *Escort* with missing *Ford* nameplate piloted by the animated grey-haired ladies.

Eduardo could see that Jonah was driving the *Caravan* and his older man in *kippah* rode shotgun. In the escort cars, there was clearly no attempt of their passengers to hide their Jewish identity as several wore *kippot*, and two of the cars had Jewish bumper stickers. One sticker depicted an Israeli flag with the caption: *Blue & White Forever!*

"I like that one," laughed Elaine as she pointed to an old Honda *Civic* with two stickers. One said: *Never Pay Retail,* and the other: *Optimists See A Bagel. Pessimists See A Hole!*

Eduardo had to laugh too. "I'm starting to like these people, whoever they are!"

"Yeah love. More likeable than those bloody twits behind us." said Elaine glancing behind at several cars each full of several men. The cars had been trailing them since Ohio.

As the various squadrons of cars proceeded out of Chicago Heights toward downtown Chicago, Eduardo and Elaine were suddenly shocked. On both sides of the road, stood people. Hundreds of people. Men, women, children, old folks. All were jumping, waving, thrusting fists in circular *go-go-go* fashion, yelling and hooting. And *waving flags* to and fro toward the blue and white *Caravan.* There were Israeli flags and flags of the Roma people bearing the red spoked-wheel. There were Ethiopian flags bearing Lions and *Stars of David* with crosses in their middle. There were Honduran flags and Jamaican flags.

In response to the people on the street, the windows of the *Caravan* and the escort cars came down. Hands, arms, and even half-bodies jutted out to join the air with shouts and *go-go-go* circling fists of joy.

Eduardo sped past the block-long street party. "What in the world was *THAT*?!!" he exclaimed scanning the pulsating crowd in his rearview mirror.

"Did you see all their flags, love?" chimed Elaine in a joyous tone.

"Yes! All kinds of different flags! I saw the Jewish flag, but there were lots of others too!"

"Yes! Did you see the Roma flags!?...the ones with the red wheels?"

"Yes! There were many..."

"Remember?...I told you about how the Roma carried *The Secret* to Southern France?...and how the Roma mingled with the Jews there...and then how the *secret* went to Cretien DuBois and his Jewish-Roma wife Jeanne?!!!!"

"Yes! I *remember!*"

"And here they are today, love! Cheering on the descendants of Cretien and Jeanne!...along with all manner of other friends, I might add!"

Eduardo's cell phone sounded. He grabbed it and pushed the speaker-phone button.

"Where are you?" demanded Bill Blanche.

"I am in South Chicago heading north on I-94 behind Jonah Van Meter...and I might add, his *entourage*...."

"What the hell are you talking about?"

"Well. Van Meter appears to have quite extensive support. There are four escort cars surrounding his vehicle on all sides, and I just passed through a crowd of a couple thousand people cheering his vehicle..."

"What?"

"Uh, yeah. He's got cheerleaders standing out on the road waiting for him to pass by."

"What?"

"Yeah...and waving flags...Israeli flags...and Roma flags and some other kinds of flags."

"What the hell is a *Roma* flag? Israeli I know. But what the hell are you talking about...*Roma flag*?"

"Well, Roma is the proper term for the *Gypsy people*. I learned this from the consultant I hired."

"...jesus...what the hell do *Gypsies* have to do with anything?...jesus...Uh, Eddie. That consultant? Where is *she*? Are you alone *right now* Eddie?"

Never could a glance between a man and woman have been so split-second, and without skipping a beat, Eduardo answered. "Sure. I wrapped things up with the consultant back in Columbus."

"Okay Eddie. We need to pick this Van Meter guy up."

Elaine immediately laid her hand on Eduardo's thigh.

"We have a half-dozen units at O'Hare, inside and outside *Terminal 5*. We've already scoped out their tickets...their going *EL AL* to Tel Aviv. So, you bring up the rear and we'll get this goddamn thing clipped. What's he drivin'?"

Elaine's hand moved up Eduardo's thigh.

"Uhh....He is driving...uh....let me get closer here....uh, yes. He is driving a grey Honda *Civic* with Ohio plates: MSD 007, and the car sort of stands out because of the Jewish bumper sticker..."

"Jewish bumper sticker?"

"Yes. It says: *Never Pay Retail*. And the dude driving is wearing a Jewish hat...you know, the *beanie* kind?"

"Yeah."

"So, I do not think you should have any problem spotting him."

"Okay. Goddammit. Let's get it done. Out."

Eduardo shook his head in absolute stunned silence.

"What, love?" Elaine cajoled.

"What the hell am I doing? What the hell am I doing? I just lied to my boss. I just lied to a freakin' Deputy National Intelligence Director! What the hell am I doing?"

"Taking advice from a pretty girl?" she gunned the coy look, her full breasts lodging upon Eduardo's side.

"Jesus! I lied to the DNI." Eduardo shook his head violently and re-fixed his eyes on Jonah's *Caravan.*

Jonah and his escorts sailed through the downtown Chicago on I-94 and then northwest onto I-90 which turned due west toward the airport. Jonah saw the South Cumberland St. exit sign and immediately hit the off-ramp.

"Where you headed, Jo-Jo?" Madeleine was surprised.

"I've got a message to deliver to some more *bloody Crusaders,*" replied Jonah. He dumped out onto Higgins Road running parallel with the interstate and proceeded at a great clip for about a half-mile. Suddenly he turned sharply left into a driveway entrance leading to a larger oval drive at the center of an office building complex. Jonah roared the *Caravan* directly toward the largest building at the end of the oval. Slamming the vehicle to a stop before the doors of the building, he leapt out.

"I'll be right back".

Jonah blasted through the doors of The Evangelical Lutheran Church in America headquarters, and presented himself to the receptionist at the center of the lobby.

"Good afternoon. I'm Pastor Van Meter from Emanuel Lutheran Church in Montra, Ohio. I'm here in Chicago en route to the Holy Land...we're taking off shortly from O'Hare, but I just wanted to drop off some written reflections on our family's trip for His Holiness, The Archbishop, because I know that he is vitally interested in the Holy Land...would that be possible?"

"Why, certainly Pastor."

"Oh, good." Jonah withdrew a sealed envelope from his sport coat pocket. "I'll just put his name on it...there: *Mark*...he always likes it when we call him *Mark*. He's a very down-to-earth guy, you know."

The middle-aged lady's eyebrows lifted. "I'll see that it gets to *The Archbishop*," she replied.

"Thank you *so* very much!" answered Jonah in grandiose mock-deference.

"Jonah!" called a voice from across the lobby. A tall blonde Nordic figure in a clerical collar came bounding toward him. "Jonah, how are you!? I haven't seen you since seminary!"

"Hey, Brad!" exclaimed Jonah as he punched his old class-mate on his shoulder. "So...you're working in der Fuhrer's House."

"Yeah...I guess. I work in The Archbishop's Office."

"Oh really? Boy, I was more right than I knew. Well, I just dropped off a note to *The Archbishop*...I should have waited and just given it to you."

"So, you know *The Archbishop*, huh?"

"Nah. I just had some info I thought he might be interested in."

"Yeah?"

"Yeah. I told him, Jesus is gonna fire him." Jonah hit his classmate's shoulder again, laughing.

"...Same ol' Jonah!" laughed Brad.

"Same ol' Brad!" Jonah gregariously yucked it up. "And, you know, Brad...I never liked you."

And Jonah popped his *kippah* on his head and bounded out the door.

Eduardo struggled to keep up with Jonah's sailing *Caravan* as it turned left off of Higgins Road onto Mannheim Road leading to the airport.

"Here we go!" exclaimed Eduardo. "Elaine...Could you...like...duck down, because you're not supposed to be here, you know. And my *bros* are here."

"Going down, sir!" she saluted tucking herself below the dash.

Eduardo tried to keep a steady eye on the *Caravan* and the other vehicles, but he found himself distracted in a most profound sense. His eyes blinked. "Oh!" he exclaimed. "You are definitely *NOT* a nun!"

"*USED* to be!" she sang. "Believe me *now!?*"

The string of various cars took the Airport Exit ramp off of Mannheim Road and rounded a loop under the I-90 overpass and headed for *Terminal 5*. The terminal building itself looked like a giant airplane with two concourse wings coming off a center entrance hall.

As Eduardo drove into Parking Lot D, he noticed it was extremely full. All of the entering cars were forced to search for spaces at the far east and west ends of the lot. Finding a space on the east, Eduardo directed Elaine to head toward the terminal entrance first. He would follow some paces behind.

Elaine made her way across the parking lot to an enclosed pedestrian bridge spanning a service road below and leading to the terminal entrance.

Eduardo, following some fifty yards behind, noticed many cars that just popped out at him. There were many with Jewish window decals or bumper stickers; quite a few old smaller RV's painted in bright colors; a good number of hippie-mobiles—odd little foreign cars bearing anti-war, Rastafarian, and other various alternative culture statements. The various people making their way through the lot corresponded to the cars: quickstepping Jewish couples, jazzy looking east-Europeans; young twenty-somethings in artfully frayed and funky attire, black people in dread-locks—all gabbing at jet-speed as they headed for the bridge. In his peripheral vision, Eduardo caught sight of a large clump of men and cars at the west edge of the lot. In the middle of the clump was the grey Honda *Civic*.

Sara, Madeleine and Jonah, each wearing bright light blue t-shirts over their street clothes, strode swiftly into the crowded pedestrian bridge. The narrow tunnel erupted into applause and shouts of *Lahma Mahar*! Showers of crumbled *matzah* were hurled. Short bursts of song, fiddle, and foot stomp spiced the cacophony. The trio gave high-fives to all in reach along the passage way, and called out to some by name. But, they did not stop. They stepped quickly and smoothly along.

When the trio reached the end of the tunnel, as was planned, they were quickly plucked from the crowd by comrades, and instantly a new look-alike trio popped out of the crowd clad in the same light blue T-shirts.

The decoy family immediately made a hard right turn into the western wing of the terminal's *Concourse M* and headed straight down the row of gates which were engulfed with an even larger and noisier crowd. *EL AL Flight #300* was docked at the very end of the concourse at *Gate M1*.

The real Sara, Madeleine and Jonah were quickly disrobed of their blue t-shirts. *House* agents silently hustled them down to the opposite end of *Concourse M* where a chartered *Romar Airlines* jet awaited at *Gate M21*. The family boarded the 707, and it began taxiing from the terminal before they sat down. In three minutes, the plane was over Lake Michigan and heading for Canadian airspace.

By the time Eduardo arrived at *Gate M1*, several of Bill Blanche's men had already cornered the decoy family.

"We're screwed." stated one of the men laying a hand on Eduardo's shoulder. Eduardo gazed at the blue t-shirted family in disbelief. The decoy family was somewhat similar to Jonah, Madeleine, and their daughter, but the woman and the girl were African-Americans. The man appeared to be eastern European. Eduardo knelt down to the girl, her cherubic face framed by a spray of dreadlocks that made her look like a little lion.

"Who are you? What is your name?" Eduardo pleaded.

"I's *Destiny!* You's must be Eddy, ha, ha!" she giggled with a broad flashing grin.

Eduardo's eyes went into orbit.

"We are *REALLY* screwed," reiterated Eduardo's colleague.

Elaine stood at a distance watching.

Immediately the *Company* men, in suits, buzz cuts, ear-pieces and dark glasses all set out in a frenzy down the corridor inspecting all the gates whether they had waiting passengers or not. Eduardo among them—secretly reluctant and disoriented, hurried past Elaine with a *What do I do now?* look.

Elaine's mental gears turned methodically as she followed the group at a even pace.

The *Company* men reached the center of the terminal between the east and west wings. A man that seemed in charge frantically studied the suspended departure/arrival video monitor. He named various carriers out loud: "Lufthansa...SAS...KLM. Air India...EL-AL? NO! Iberia...no...Kuwait Airways...don't think so....Air Jamaica...Aer Lingus...Alitalia...Air France..."

"Maybe, *Air France*," inserted Eduardo.

"Why?"

"Because they have ancestors in France."

"Eh," the *Company* man shrugged. "AeroMexico...British Airways..."

"Maybe that one?" Eduardo again suggested.

"More ancestors?" the *Company* man sarcastically asked.

"Well. London is a hub for many outbound flights to anywhere..."

"Maybe. Japan Airlines...Singapore Airlines...Turkish Airlines... Romar..." The Company man squinted his eyes and turned to Eduardo. "What the fuck is *Romar*?"

Eduardo gazed at the monitor, cocked his head, and said, "Damned if I know. I have never heard of it."

"That's it. *Gate M21*. Let's roll!"

The *Company* men sprinted to the eastern end of *Concourse M* only to find a completely empty gate. The lead man was furious. He holed up in a corner and made several loudly muffled angry cell phone calls while the rest of the men bantered among themselves various theories of *What went wrong?*

After a quarter hour, the lead man rejoined his troops and delivered the post mortem.

"*Romar*. It's a Romanian airline. They haven't run passenger business out of Chicago for years. The plane just took off...a charter. They screwed us good."

"So...are we gonna intercept or knock it down?" asked one of the others.

"Not over Canadian airspace. No way. We'll have to see when it gets over the Atlantic."

The lead man directed his squad to start interrogating O'Hare officials, gate workers, the tarmac crew, *and the decoy family.* A subordinate had the sorry job of informing that the family had slipped away while the men searched the concourse. The lead man blew up in a torrent of expletives.

Eduardo excused himself to make a cell phone call.

In the course of talking to Bill Blanche for about an hour, Eduardo learned he was correct about one thing. The *Romar* flight plan stated London as the destination, but curiously, did not cite the specific port of arrival. Blanche directed Eduardo to board the next plane to London. He might not be needed there, if events were resolved beforehand, but all contingencies were to be covered.

Eduardo snapped his cell closed with a sick feeling in his stomach. But then, he looked out onto the concourse and found a shining face: Elaine. Something *other* spurred Eduardo into his own dogged agenda. He needed to see what the Jonah Van Meter business was all about. That was the first thing. Then he would decide what to do about it after he had sized things up. He snatched Elaine by the arm and led her to the *British Airways* counter. If he had to do his own counter espionage, he might as well do it in style with a pretty British girl. *Bond, James Bond,* would.

Chapter 13

Blessed are you, O Lord, who rebuilds Jerusalem.

The Bread House, Bexley, Ohio.
Tuesday, May 22, 4:04 P.M.

On the attic-level of the house, Rodney Fridenmaker and Will Aaronson sat at their monitors among the two-dozen staff along parallel lines of computer stations.

"Ooop, there she is! Geoff! Come 'ere!" shouted Will Aaronson. Full face in the monitor was Destiny Sinclair waving over the heads of two grey-haired lady passengers.

"Hey Rod Man! Hey Will! Hey Daddy! Say Hey to ever'body, Momma!" The monitor flashed with tilted obtuse angles until it focused on the rolling eyes of Faith Sinclair.

"On our way, Daddy! Can you see us?" called Faith.

"Oui, Oui, mon amour," called Geoffrey Sinclair through his headset standing over The Rod Man's monitor.

"Coolest video phone I ever did see! I'm happy!" announced Will.

"Everything okay, dear?" Geoffrey checked in.

"Sure enough, babe. Everthing's lookin' fine."

"Great! I'll be with you soon enough…we'll just have to play it by ear."

"I know, babe. Don't worry. And Rod Man…You take care of Geoffrey!….make sure he eats good!"

"Hmmm-Hmmm," replied The Rod Man rocking and laughing in his chair. With pen in mouth, he pecked on the keyboard: *You will be happy to quit matzah for sweet bread in Zion. I love you all.*"

"Yes, Rod Man. We love you too. Bye everyone…Bye Geoffrey. I love you!" Faith called.

"I love you Daddy! *Lahma Mahar*, Daddy!" joined Destiny.

"*Lahma Mahar*!" called out the whole control room.

British Airways Flight #1301.
Tuesday, May 22, 4:14 P.M.

Eduardo and Elaine finished their cocktails and replaced their seat trays. Elaine slowly raised the partition between their seats. Eduardo, a bit buzzed amid Cognac and French perfume, acquiesced as Elaine laid softly upon him. Her full lips came to his. A rare moment for a man. A dream all men harbor: To sail the skies in heroic cause and love eternal all in one time, to win life's glory in a woman, and not die, *after all.* Suddenly, the moment was broken.

"Hey guys! Ever hear, *Get a room*?!!! Hee, hee, heee!" Destiny, the brown lion-faced cherub, giggled in glee.

Eduardo knew he was *not in Kansas anymore.*

Romar Airlines Flight #001.
Tuesday, May 22, 6:09 P.M.

As the plane had few passengers, Sara made a whole seat-row in the center section her bed. She slept alone. The high altitudes over Newfoundland made the cabin remarkably cold and Sara sheltered herself with a blanket over her *OSU Buckeye* hoodie. The dull low roar of the engines caused her memory to spin a dream reversing her life's wonderland experience. She was once a child of the east…sent west. *And now*? Sara dreamed: She again laid small on a rusty broken bed screaming into the gray-brown walls with only the antiphonal cries of other children in response. Filth and stench stuck to skin and air, a deep raging infection of suffocating mucus stuck inside the head, an interminable winter's disease punctuated by unceasing rhythmic concussion thunder bolts of coughing pain, hard-hacked enough to shake crumbly powdery paint flakes off the walls of a city once called home; home enough, for common folk who bought their bread in the market on the street. Beyond the windows of the gray walls, the minaret towers pointed heavenwards. But no man called, nor would he have been heard over the harmonized screams of the small who called and called and called...for somebody...*somebody*...anybody...to make themselves into a prayer and answer all in One. *Why do they not come?* she cried to the minaret. *Can the minaret not hear the babies call?* Her parents gone, she still ached to know where they were...her mother, who often screamed at the deafening sounds of war from the air and street. Her father. She had seen him, a few times but not many, on his prayer rug ...*for luck,* he would say. *But where was luck? What was supposed to happen after the man on the tower called, and the rugs were rolled up? Why do they not come NOW?*

Then shone light into Sara's dream. She stood naked in warm and perfectly clear-clean water. *Immerse!* The Rabbi called three times through a door by which he could not see, but hear, the making of a Jew. And then she was re-clothed in a fine new clean dress. And the Rabbi called her: *Sara bat Avraham Avinu v'Sara Imeinu.*

Madeleine dreamed a dream. She stood naked in the water, and the Rabbi called. *Do you present yourself voluntarily and with intention? Do you understand that entrance into the Jewish faith replaces your former religion? Do you faithfully promise to raise your daughter as a Jew?* Three times she went down into the clean warm water. Then she arose as a new mother to her family. And the Rabbi called her: *Miryam Channah bat Avraham Avinu v'Sara Imeinu.*

Jonah dreamed a dream. He stood naked in the water, and the Rabbi called. *Do you commit yourself to the Torah and to the Jewish people in every place and time?* Three times, he re-entered the water of his mother's womb and was, indeed: born again. And the Rabbi called him: *Yonah ben Avraham Avinu v'Sara Imeinu.*

Sara, Madeleine, and Jonah dreamed a dream. They called back to the Rabbi, *Entreat me not to leave you, to turn away from joining you. For wherever you go, I will go. And wherever you stay, will I. Your people will be my people, and your God will be my God. Where you die, will I die, and there I will be buried.*

Jonah woke. He recited the *Shema*. A streaming hiss of locusts pierced through the cabin from somewhere outside the plane. He lifted his window slide to the first streaks of dawn spraying out over the sea and a faint grey-green outline of Britain on the horizon. In the light purple sky swarms of gyrating F-16s screamed, hopping and darting in flash-fast maneuvers. Some had Israeli insignia. The others were American.

The jets were all jockeying for attack-geometry. An American F-16 made a hard circle turn heading for the control zone behind the lumbering *Romar* 707. But an Israeli *Sufa* lit his afterburner and dived in a roll and came up with great acceleration behind the *Romar* for a pure head-on attack line with the American. Luckily, the American's speed was too great and his arc sent him too wide to get right behind the *Romar*. Around he came on Jonah's side, and Jonah eyeballed the pilot in mutual assessment. The American fighter came so close, Jonah caught the pilot's scripted kick-name below the cockpit window: *JUDE*, accented with a cartoonish *Star of David*. Jonah Van Meter shook himself and he bolted for the cockpit.

"Quite a party we have here," said Jonah to the pilot and flight officer as streaks and screams of bouncing F-16s danced above, under, and alongside.

"Yes, sir," stated the pilot in Slavic accent, his eyes and hands working together in repeated checks of the controls.

"Do you think they will actually attack?" Jonah noted the under-wing missiles of the American fighters.

"Very difficult to say sir. I think, right now, they are trying intercept, you know? They want us to land with them at the *Fairford Air Base*, west of London."

"Well, we're *not* going to do *that*."

"No, Sir. Right now, they are trying to scare us with their maneuvers, you know? I am afraid sir, we are...ehh, how you say?....*playing chicken*, you know?

"What do we have defensively?"

The pilot shrugged. "We have the *Sufas*. We have the new *Flight Guard*. It automatically shoots flares to throw off the missiles, but it is really designed for the shoulder fired missiles from the ground, you know? I do not know what it can do for close range...maybe nothing. It is all automatic...when the plane's radar see the missiles fired. But, we do not know that the Flight Guard has started until we see the flares shoots out...or until it is too late. Who can say? We also have the DIRCM...this is infared jamming for missiles, you know? And we have the chaff...it is...ehhh...packages...of little aluminum pieces...they fly out...and they tricks the radar. But all these things...like I say...they are designed for the missiles coming from the ground. I think sir, our best defense are the *Sufas*. We have six. They have four. But it only takes one shot, you know."

"Yeah." Jonah paused for a long moment, scanning the screaming sky. "How long has this been going on?"

"Since we leave Canada airspace."

"Well. If they're going to take their shot, they only have twenty minutes. They're not going to do it over land."

"Yes. I think you are correct." The pilot nodded.

"Can you do evasive maneuvers yourself?"

"...ehhh....limited, I am sorry to say. Very risky. Very hard on the plane. But we will see, you know? The most possible trick is to steer the nose straight at them, you know?"

Jonah nodded, and then his brain jumped. He caught a skiff of the blue *Jude Star* flashing as the fighter cut diagonally in front and dived. "See that guy?" blurted Jonah.

"Yes."

"Keep your eye on him! You got...uh...some blank paper and a black marker?" fired Jonah.

The flight officer's eyes screwed up while he immediately ripped pages from a flight planner and fished a marker from his flight bag.

Jonah hastily wrote some words in big letters on the paper. "Now…" directed Jonah. "….I want us to pay my friend a little personal visit…When you see him come up, run right at him!"

"Yes, sir." The pilot warily side-glanced his flight officer.

On the near horizon, the western coast of England laid wide and green. Field and hills segmented by stone grey fences immediately became the *promised land*. The screaming of the F16s suddenly spiked near. The radio sparked up with American accented orders and expletives. Jonah saw the blue *Jude Star*. "There!" he shouted, pointing upward at two o'clock, and the *Jude Star* banked left. "Go at him! Go at him!" shouted Jonah.

The pilot accelerated abruptly with no emotion and Jonah was slammed against the side cockpit window with his message on the glass. In a flash, the two planes almost destructed each other, but not. Before the *Jude Star's* nimble craft rolled out, he caught Jonah Van Meter's sign:

YOU'RE A JEW FIRST!

MOT!

The *Jude Star* arced around again. The two men stared at each other. Jonah Van Meter slapped his *kippah* to his head and jutted his pointed index finger to the heavens. He drew out a pocket Bible from his breast pocket and slapped its open Hebrew text to the window. He gave *Jude* a nod and a clenched-jaw smile.

"*MOT?*" crackled the radio.

Jonah plucked the flight officers head set and popped it on his own head. "*Ken. MOT!*" Jonah kept his stare fixed with *Jude's*.

There was a long pause, and then the radio cracked: "Me too….Who are you?"

"I am *Joseph*….your *brother*," called Jonah, his stare locked.

There was silence of word against the pealing streams of jet engines for what seemed an eternity.

The radio sparked, "Shalom, my brother. Shalom."

The *Jude Star* banked, and with him, his cohorts.

Oval Office, Washington, D. C.
Tuesday, May 22, 9:01 P.M.

"The intercept was unsuccessful," informed Ashman Blackpoint.

The room flamed and raged with fury and incredulity.

"Any fuckin' word from Jerusalem?"

"No, Sir," replied Blackpoint. "They say the Prime Minister
is *engaged in a security emergency*."

"Well. You know. We should'a never put them sonsabitches
back in a state in the first place. You give 'em an inch...you
know what I'm sayin? I'll tell ya, Ash. I'm a startin' to think like
Dick Nixon. You know what he said...about the Jews, don't
yuh?"

"What's that, sir?"

"He said, *Fuck 'em...They never vote for us anyway.*"

"Hmm. I wonder if they're saying the same about us."

Chapter 14

Blessed are you, O Lord, who causes salvation to flourish.

London Luton Airport.
Wednesday, May 23, 7:33 A.M.

Sara, Madeleine, and Jonah toted only small carry-on bags. Their exodus from the *Romar* and through customs was a speed-bullet affair. It was *Yes sir, been on holiday in the States and we're going home...* and straight through they went. The Van Meters carried Israeli passports.

Quickly they strode through the halls heading for the far side of the airport where the trains to London were stationed. Three Rom escorts followed thirty paces in tow.

"Oh. Oh. Oh. Stop!" cried Sara pulling Jonah back by his sleeve. "Cappuccino time!" she sang, pointing to a coffee bar amid other brasseries in an open food court including a *Burger King*.

"Alright, but we need to hurry," advised Jonah with a stern eye.

"Moolah..." Sara directed with a rub of her fingers.

Handing over several pounds Sterling, Jonah and Madeleine took to a nearby table while Sara ordered. The Rom camped out at various tables at the edges of the seating area. Madeleine noticed several *other* men spread out at different tables pretending to read newspapers. Her face tightened.

"Getting the lay of the land, dear?" Jonah said knowingly. His eyes panned side to side without turning his head. He nodded.

"It's strange," she said with an ironic half-smile. "They remind me of something when I was a kid....when Bubbe Maggi would take me out to see Zayde Tobar at the race track—in the barns where he worked with the horses. Bubbe would always point out all the wild cats in the barns that would just sit around pretending not to be watching each other.

"Well, just remember. They're the kitties, and we're the *lions.*"

Madeleine nodded.

"It's really good!" Sara exclaimed nestling a steaming cup below her lips. "Double Mocha!"

"Well, at least you didn't go to *Burger King!*" mused Jonah pushing himself up from the table set for others. "Okay. Let's roll," he ordered.

"What time do we have to be at the church, Jo Jo?" huffed Madeleine as they booked down the hall.

"Our appointment's at nine-thirty." Jonah picked up their pace toward the trains.

Sara picked Jonah's pocket for *matzah* to dunk in the double mocha.

Castel Gandolfo, Italy.
Wednesday, May 23, 9:01 A.M.

The ornate chair turned from desk to window. He gazed out over Lake Albano, one leg crossed upon the other under the loose rich fabric of a white cassock just arrived from the tailor. He approved its fit. At the cassock hem peeked a fine-made shoe. It flamed red in the glint of the morning sun, adding sparkle to the deep aqua gem of the lake below his mount. He was a man on top of the world. All was fine at the pinnacle. And yet. He wondered. Indeed—What was going on in that *other* Holy Land where Jesus had loved another lake so far *below* the level of the sea?

A knock sounded at the opulent apartment door.

"Yes...."

"Good morning, Your Holiness," greeted Sister Scholastica Begleiter, his personal assistant.

Turning slowly from the window, he received her with a soft smile and a flowing hand direction to the smaller chair opposite the desk. "A fine day, we see over the lake, Sister. We should like to walk along the shore, but..." His hands shrugged. "...there is so much to do."

Sister Scholastica nodded smiling weakly. "It is early in the season. There will be time for walks yet, yes?"

"Perhaps, my dear. Perhaps. But today...we must *do*. But before we *do*, we must *know*. But that is the problem, no? We do not know what is going on in the world beyond us." He mused with a small laugh. "Strange, is it not? For all of our people and all of our associations, we still do not *really* know what is going on in the world!" A sudden flash of sternness crossed his fair face. "But, we *must* know!" he effused with pointed finger.

"We do know *some* things, Your Holiness." Sister Scholastica was ready to report.

"Yes, of course. What do we know today, my dear?"

"Yes, Your Holiness. Let me first confide that there are things I am able to share with you that are of two natures. The first, what we have actually observed. And the second, that which we feel confident in predicting."

"Very well. Let us begin with the first, my dear."

"Yes, Your Holiness. In regard to our observation of the subject, Mr. Jonah Van Meter, I can tell you that he and his family have fled America. They have today landed in London and are, as we speak, en route to the center of the city...."

"Yes...And *two*?"

Sister Scholastica nodded. "In our observations we have noted Mr. Van Meter's appearance at a succession of tombs..."

"*Tombs*?" He leaned forward.

"Yes, Your Holiness. *Tombs*. Specifically, tombs belonging to his ancestry. So...ah...we feel confident that he will continue to pursue this course of action in accordance with his ancestry in Europe."

"His *Merovingian* ancestry?'

"Yes, Your Holiness."

"To what end, Sister? What do these *tombs* accomplish for this man?" His face belied lostness, but then sharpened. "Do you think these tombs contain hidden things, as is the custom with our Merovingian and Masonic adversaries…with all their devilish rites and books cloaked in false words and symbols?"

"No, Your Holiness," stated Sister Scholastica flatly. "Mr. Van Meter *is* a Merovingian, but not a faithful one. Actually, he is a *Jew*… a *secret Jew*. He is a man of secrets, but his secrets are his own, not of the Merovingians. He is a man who *prays*. He prays at the tombs. He prays as a Jew. I believe he receives strength from his prayer. We have heard stories that exceptional powers belong to this man…"

"Such as…..?"

"He raised his wife from the dead."

His Holiness winced. His hand, bearing the *Fisherman's Ring*, beckoned explanation.

"Our Merovingian adversaries…poisoned her while she was with child. The child did not survive. And…by all medical protocols, she should not have as well. But. By some power, we are told…Mr. Van Meter was able to rescue his wife from what was, by all accounts, the *irreversible.*"

He turned and gazed again out the window over the serene lake below. "A Jew who raises the dead," he mused. Rubbing his temples deeply, he was profoundly silent. And then, "Well. The Jews are not our enemy, my dear. On the other hand, their concerns are not always ours. I assume, then, you are saying that this man has Jewish comrades?"

"Yes, Your Holiness. But *more* than Jews."

"More? *The Masons …the Templars…the brothers of Sion?*"

"No. Not they. This is the greatest mystery. We seemed to have encountered something quite unexpected in our observations of Mr. Van Meter, and that is: *Another House…* beyond our own and that of our adversaries."

"A *House?*"

"Yes. This man acts not on his own accord, but as a leader— A leader of a large community previously unknown to us."

"Jews?"

"Yes, Jews…but, many of them…apparently *converts*. And some of them quite poor. It is, for lack of better words, a secret community of quite ordinary people."

"Their goal, then?" He gestured in summons of declarative word.

"I think...." Sister Scholastica paused pensively. "I think they wish to see the ordinary become the extraordinary. *The last, become first.*"

"...and *the first, last?*"

"Yes."

"How shall they do this?"

"By ending *our calling.* They possess the body of Jesus. They mean to produce it. It is that which we have always feared."

"Your prediction of their steps in this campaign?"

"Yes. Mr. Van Meter, no doubt, is currently approaching the *Temple Church* in London. From there, we are quite confident, he will proceed to the *Pas de Calais* region of northern France, from whence his Merovingian ancestors came...including God-froi de Bouillon. From Calais, we expect him to arrive in Paris at the tomb of the Magdalene, his ancestral mother. And... in due course, we certainly expect him to enter Jerusalem...to open the *Pandora's Box* which we cannot allow. For now, we will have our people proceed to Calais. They will be ready for any order that Your Holiness may render."

He was silent in a long moment. He held out his hand. She kissed the ring and departed.

Sister Scholastica's thoughts were her own. She had lied about the poisoning details, and kept other matters undisclosed.

Gatwick London Airport, North Terminal.
Wednesday, May 23, 8:08 A.M.

The landing gear of British Airways flight #1380 kissed the tarmac. In short time, passengers began to collect themselves and navigate their way up the aisle.

"Now what do we do?" asked Elaine.

"We follow the girl and her mother." Eduardo glanced back-wards toward Destiny who was rasta-dancing up the aisle to her MP3.

Destiny and Faith zipped through *North Terminal* as if they had done it before.

Elaine, a Londonite, had no trouble helping Eduardo slip into the rhythm. Following Destiny and Faith, they immediately boarded the *Inter Terminal Transit* train which delivered them to *South Terminal*. A short sprint through the building brought them to *Gatwick Train Station*. Eduardo and Elaine queued for tickets not far behind Destiny. She was still dancing, but turned quickly to wave at Eduardo. He weakly smiled back.

"I need two of the same passes you just sold to that girl and her mother," ordered Eduardo at the ticket window. He gave himself a small self-amused laugh. A £22 swipe on the *American Express* bought two Thameslink *DaySave* passes. *Done.* Eduardo and Elaine followed Destiny and Faith onto the northbound train for London.

Ben Gurion Airport, Tel-Aviv, Israel.
Wednesday, May 23, 3:13 P.M.

Wal Holloway picked his man out of the crowd immediately.

"Welcome to Palestine, Pastor" greeted Munib, emissary of Mr. Sabeel Khouri.

"Salaam!" Wal responded with a cheek-to-cheek embrace.

"Your trip was good?" inquired Munib as he quickly snatched Wal's luggage and briskly headed him for the terminal exit where a car for Jerusalem awaited.

Wal shrugged. "As good as Air Canada can get, I suppose."

"Ooh. Air Canada not good?"

"Oh, they're okay I guess. But you have to put up with the Jews. I was sleeping *so* well this morning, and what do I wake up to? A flock of damn Jews with those stupid boxes on their heads and their arms all strapped up...and they are just rattling away their morning *heebyjeeby* prayers, rockin' and rollin' right in the damned aisle!"

Munib laughed vigorously. "Well, pastor. You will need to develop a measure of *tolerance*...yes, *tolerance*. There is much of the *heebyjeeby* here, you know."

"Be my guide, Munib. Be my guide." Wal returned the laugh.

The rear door of an old black Mercedes stood open and the comrades climbed in. The chauffeur, a young Palestinian with a slick tough-guy air, closed the door while looking in all directions.

The Mercedes dodged into departing airport traffic and onto Route 1 toward Jerusalem. The car's air conditioning was apparently inoperable as all the windows were half down. Wal's senses were immediately jarred and disoriented. The pungent aroma of the driver's Turkish cigarettes spiced the hot dry air rushing in through the widows. The terrain beyond the modern highway was an expanse of pale-golden rock and scrub punctuated by working class houses and small businesses. To Wal, it looked like Jamaica with fewer trees.

The highway itself was a mosaic of the unfamiliar: quirky-modeled cars transporting everyday families, workers, students and soldiers. Hebrew road signs were strange. Some had secondary English translation, but most did not. Wal studied a small poster he repeatedly saw plastered to light poles and overpasses. It featured a photo of an old Hassidic rabbi hovering over an open Hebrew text. The rabbi even appeared on the back of a white van that whisked past the Mercedes. Cal winced at the Hebrew caption below the rabbi's photo. His seminary training in Hebrew was moribund, but he could make out the first letters of *mem* and *shin* in one word. He figured it had something to do with *messiah.*

"Who is *that*?" Wal queried pointing at the rabbi on the back of the van. Israeli army vehicles cruised around the van.

"Oh, that is *Schneerson!*" sang Munib gleefully.

"That's who?" laughed Wal.

"Oh yes. That is Rabbi Schneerson. He is the Messiah!"

"He's the Messiah?!!"

"Oh yes. Certainly. He is the Messiah to the Crazy Jews. He was some kind of rabbi...actually from you' own country...from New York...I think. He was like super-star. You know?"

"Was?"

"Yes. Yes. The Messiah died...so sad! Ehhh...I would say it was about ten years ago....would you not say, Mitri?"

The chauffeur grunted an affirmative.

"Yes. Yes. From that time...the followers of the rabbi...they claim he is the Messiah. How he is both dead and Messiah, I do not understand. But I am not crazy Jew, so I leave it to them. But another mystery I tell you…how they put up so many signs, you know? They put them on everything…you see how they do, yes? I think they must do it at night. Perhaps this is how one begins in the messiah business. Perhaps the people of Jesus did the same. Who can say?"

Wal rolled into the chuckle. "Maybe so. Maybe so."

The trip up to Jerusalem on Route 1 took only 45 minutes.

The outskirts of Jerusalem appeared to Wal as a transition from the pioneer environs of rock studded fields to a dense urban center of diesel exhaust, apartment towers under construction, and golden domed roof lines. As the highway led into greater Jerusalem, it narrowed to an ordinary avenue called *Jaffa Road* which, from ancient times, ran from the coastal city of Jaffa to the Jaffa Gate on the west side of the ancient walled Old City.

Proceeding along the road through modern Jewish Jerusalem, Wal noted the fervent bustle of the street with all manner of eateries, sidewalk vendors, clothing and book stores, banks and urban transit busses. People strode briskly in a multiplicity of attire—traditional Orthodox Jewish men in black and white, other men donning modern knit *kippot*, young girl soldiers in green with automatic rifles slung over their hips. All made their way on the stone sidewalks. Everything was made of stone—the same stone. The buildings. The spires of church and minaret. The walks. The streets. The walls. All was made of the same golden, luminous *Jerusalem stone.*

The Mercedes came to a chaotic five-point intersection. Standing over the intersection was an old municipal building scarred at its top with bullet holes from the '67 war. Beyond the intersection sprawled a mythic view of the walled Old City. The notch-top walls stood against a skyline of dome, steeple and minaret. Wal's eye followed the trajectory of Jaffa Road down to the monumental Jaffa Gate with its exotic Arabesque arched portal.

But the Mercedes turned left on Ha Tzanhanim which curved around to the north side of the Old City. They passed the smaller and unadorned New Gate leading into the Christian Quarter.

Soon the Mercedes came to a stop. From the street, Wal gazed upon the surreally magnificent Damascus Gate. Its ramparts were adorned by small minaret-like spires and its arched entry flanked on both sides by huge square towers. Before the gate, lay a grand esplanade hosting an amphitheatre of steps descending to a stone bridge leading to the great portal.

The chauffeur opened the door informing Wal that his luggage would be delivered to his quarters.

"I thought you would enjoy a walk through our community," advised Munib.

"Certainly," responded Wal in awe. "I had no idea how magnificent this place would be."

"Yes. It is like a woman you cannot forget...or leave...to fight and die for. You understand?"

"I think so," breathed Wal, descending the steps, his eyes taking in a scene that was at once so foreign, and yet...somehow, vaguely familiar.

The stone bridge was lined on both sides by Arabs in all manner of dress and endeavor. There were close-kept conversations of old men and the open loud banter of the young. There were carts of fruits and sweets. A beggar woman in tattered traditional dress and jingly-cheap jewelry sat on the ground with her children, calling out for alms in a shrill staccato voice. Her outstretched hand was as searching as her opaque blind eyes.

Munib led Wal into the cavernous gate, which at once turned left. The structure was built in an L configuration, an ancient defense strategy designed to slow the aggressor.

Coming out of the gate, Wal beheld an open pedestrian avenue flanked on both sides by money changer offices, small convenience markets, and souvenir shops. Many Arabs went briskly to and fro carrying small plastic bags from shopping in the *suq*. Young boys steered wooden push carts laden with clinking soft drink bottles. The flow of people bottlenecked at a fork in the road ahead. The split was the beginning of two smaller streets that delved into the dark *suq*.

Munib led Wal into the tunnel-like entry on the right where plastered on its wall was the street name: *Suq Khan ez-Zeit*. Wal immediately found his senses assaulted by a myriad of sound, color, and aroma. Arab music buzzed and whirled through the air from radios in shops and small eateries lining both sides of the way. Canopied by stone arches which amplified voices, the narrow street was chock full of people within inches of each other—everyone briefly nudging someone else. Muslim women in head-scarves guided tottering children, while their well-dressed fathers harnessed the boundaries of their outing with stern eyes. Shop owners, older men in fine suits and their sons donning Euro sports wear, lingered at their shop doors calling to each other over the street-flow, keeping their eyes out for tourists needing a *very good deal.* There were shops full of sweet breads and other pastries. Other stalls offered mounds of fruits and nuts, and unwrapped candies spiced by hungry circling gnats. Wild concoctive aromas wafted from dealers hawking exotic coffees and spices. Open-air butcheries displayed whole carcasses of beef and lamb hanging in their sinews within blue-tiled stalls made all the more garish by florescent lighting. The sweet fracturing smell of blood, fruit, and spice grabbed Wal by the throat and he was both repelled and drawn to it in the very same breath.

The course of Suq Khan ez-Zeit led along the backside of the Church of the Holy Sepulcher. From the street, an unassuming flight of stairs ascended up and out of the bustling bazaar to a landing that turned to another flight leading to the Ethiopian chapels on top of the Church. Going beyond the stairway, Munib and Wal soon came to an intersection of streets in the *suq.* With a short right turn and another left-right zigzag, they came to an opening into the Muristan plaza. To the right, the plaza was centered by a grand ornate Turkish fountain. To the left, stood the Lutheran Church of the Redeemer. Munib showed Wal a historical marker giving the history of the grounds upon which the Lutheran church was built:

Here in the Muristan was situated the first hospital of the Knights of St. John of Jerusalem during the twelfth and thirteenth centuries. In 1882 the Grand Priory in the British Realm of the most Venerable Order of the Hospital of St. John of Jerusalem established an ophthalmic hospital in emulation of the humanitarian and charitable efforts of its Medieval predecessors.

"Ophthalmic hospital?" asked Wal.

"Yes. For the eyes. Many problems with the eyes in Palestine." answered Munib.

"I see," said Wal.

Munib led Wal through the Muristan and then left onto Muristan Road to a small outdoor café in the *suq.* They were immediately and formally received by Na'ila, the wife of the café owner—Mr. Sabeel Khouri. The severe sixtyish looking woman, wearing an olive wood *Jerusalem Cross* pendant, began to seat them. Suddenly, a voice called out loudly, "SALAAM!"

Mr. Sabeel Khouri appeared from a back room of the café to embrace Wal cheek-to-cheek. Behind the short businessman in fine pinstripe suit were two other suited European looking men.

"Salaam! My friend! God gives us such sweetness and grace today in bringing you safely to us in Jerusalem! So. How do you find the *Holy City*, the mother of our faith?"

"It's unbelievable, Mr. Khouri. Unbelievable!" said Wal shaking his head.

"I bring Pastor Holloway from the Damascus Gate through the *suq,"* boasted Munib.

"Ahhh! What you think?" cooed Khouri, stroking his mustache. "It is very wonderful, yes? I tell you, my friend...there is no place wonderful like Jerusalem in all the earth!"

"I must confess, Mr. Khouri...," Wal stammered to rise to his host's effusiveness. "...it leaves me speechless. No doubt, Jerusalem will be a source of reflection for quite some time." Wal's response, vague and passable, was his standard *running-for-class-president* tone that had served him well for so many years, the currency of official mediocrity in corporations and governments around the world.

"Well. Good. Very good, my friend," replied Khouri, deflating a bit. He patted Wal softly on the arm. "Well. Shall we begin?" He motioned the two Europeans to sit down with him at the small round café table. Na'ila brought hummus, pita, and strong Arabic coffee.

"Allow me to present: Mr. Martin Carion, and his assistant, Mr. Prescott Pierce," stated Sabeel Khouri. "Mr. Carion and Mr. Pierce are, respectively, the Grand Regent and the Grand Inspector of the *Sovereign Order of the Temple of Sion.*"

Titles aside, both men were dressed in normal, if fine, western suits. Carion, a large affable man, had a certain military air about him. Pierce, on the other hand, was a short bespectacled man of annoying diminutive features reminding one of *Jiminy Cricket.*

After a bit of further introductions and small talk, discussion began upon the topic of their mutual concern: Jonah Van Meter...and the threat he constituted. The threat had a history. While it had been long understood by both Merovingians and the Vatican that a potential problem lay in the recesses of a Cretien DuBois cadet line, it was—in general, an impressionistic understanding. History itself had made the very idea of a royal line descended from Jesus and Mary Magdalene rather impressionistic. As to the role of monarchy in the Western world, time had marched on. Still, the Merovingians had hopes—vague hopes that the tradition could some day be used for some positive benefit to their house—certainly, including leverage over the Church, which did not want to be embarrassed—which could not *afford* to be embarrassed—any more.

Carion, Pierce, and Khouri also had a history. Khouri was recruited to the *Order* in late September, 1970. He was a Lutheran student in Switzerland and glad to have his family with him at the time. They were, for all practical purposes, privileged West Bank Palestinian refugees. Khouri's extended family and friends back in Palestine had fled the West Bank for Jordan during the '67 war. But they found themselves in deeper trouble when their own PLO went to war with Jordan itself, and Jordan won the argument slaughtering several thousand Palestinians. With his family and friends streaming back to the West Bank, Khouri was keen to return home. The *Order* could help. Fellow students Carion and Pierce were members, and they became conduits in the *Order's* proposition to the young Palestinian. The *Order* fervently desired to secure a presence in the *Holy Land.* Financing a future Palestinian businessman was a prudent investment toward building a base of operations in the region. While Khouri could not have predicted that Carion and Pierce would ascend to *Order* leadership, neither would they have predicted Khouri would develop a *contact* with intimate knowledge of the long-rumored renegade Merovingian line. But once Jonah Van Meter was identified by Wal Holloway through his grandfather Max's contacts, the *Order* leadership thought it best to get a handle on the situation. But the devil, *and God,* are in the details. The *Order* didn't expect such a heavy and immediate competition from the Vatican. And it certainly didn't expect the Vatican to move in and do a *hit.* And then Jonah Van Meter's completely unexpected reaction of engaging his adversaries—whoever they may be, raised a more troubling question. It was one thing to *stop* his bloodline, but quite another to destroy him completely. *When should a cancer be totally cut? When it is first found? Or only after one discovers how far it reaches?* It was a terrible quandary for those who had good reason to be paranoid.

"Our people report that Van Meter has arrived in England. You believe that he will come to Jerusalem?" Carion queried Wal directly.

"Yes." Wal nodded. "He told me."

"What *exactly*-did-he-tell-you Pastor Holloway?" inquired Pierce emphatically.

"He told me *I have him*".

"And *that* to you means...?" Pierce circled his hand for Wal to elaborate.

"He has the *body.* He has it. My grandfather—who was much more versed in the history of Jonah's line than I...He told me when I was a boy that Jonah's family has custody of the body of Jesus. He always taught me: *The Merovingians have the Blood, but the Van Meters have the Body.* And he would always say to me: *It's a problem. The Body and the Blood ought to be together, but they are not.* I am here, gentlemen, to help you with that task."

Carion and Pierce's eyes met sideways.

"And how do you propose to do *that* Pastor Holloway?" Pierce pressed forward.

Wal blinked and cleared his throat. He shifted and tugged at his clerical collar. *This* was his moment. His unveiling. His *pitch.*

"Well," Wal began. "Your problem is straightforward. On one hand, you cannot afford to have Van Meter undo you. On the other hand, you have the question of what you lose if you liquidate his entire line. Is there an intermediate option?—perhaps some extraction of information before liquidation? Hmm. Highly uncontrollable…it could get very messy. So, what to do? But, I am here to tell you of another option…another factor. And that is: The fact that my own bloodline is as good as Van Meter's. We are related by blood—my mother's family goes back to Cretien DuBois just as Van Meter's does. You *DO* understand, I trust, that Van Meter's *capacities* are the result of repeated re-marriage back into the Merovingian lines?"

Carion and Pierce glanced at each other without expression.

"Yes, we have studied that issue," stated Pierce flatly.

"Good. Very good." Wal shifted nervously in his chair. "Well, I would like to explain how my own bloodline is vitally important to our mutual concerns. You know, life is strange—full of twists and turns. Some things are unfortunate but then they produce other beneficial things. In my own case, it is unfortunate that my wife and I have grown apart…for all practical purposes, our marriage is over. We are still working out the details…we've not disclosed these facts publicly yet. But, they *are* facts. Also not public…and I must confess, it is not easy to divulge, even here, matters involving…how shall we say?…my own personal frailties. But the truth is: I have *another relationship.* And that relationship is with Margot Calvi. She is the sister of Madeleine Van Meter. And…as unwieldy as the situation may sound, Margot is expecting a child…*our* child…that we are having together. All these things will be brought together once the divorce is finalized and Margot and I are married. But the main point here is: If Jonah and Madeleine Van Meter were...uh...somehow...uh...no longer a factor...Be assured: Margot and I could replace that bloodline."

A good bit of silence hung in the room. Pierce leaned over to whisper something in Carion's ear.

"So, Pastor Holloway. You are...our *Plan B messiah?*" Carion mused.

Wal's countenance turned to a fluster. "I...uh...seek to serve...uh, as I am given ability to serve," he replied searching the inscrutable eyes of Carion and Pierce.

Carion stretched back, capping his hands atop his head and searching the heavens. After a long moment, he slowly enunciated his reply. "Well. There is much here to ponder. *Over time.* But the *immediate question* is the location of the *tomb* that Jonah Van Meter has access to. *That* is what we need to know in the present moment."

"It's on *Zion,*" Wal blurted. I know, from my grandfather, that Jonah's group has a mantra they chant about *Zion.*" Wal was most emphatic and authoritative.

Pierce laughed. "Do tell, Pastor Holloway! Sion indeed! But *where* on Sion...and *which* Sion?"

"What do you mean *which Zion?*" Wal shot back in obvious annoyed defensiveness.

Pierce's eyes rolled. "Well...*Pastor* Holloway.....there is Sion which is on *Mt. Moriah*...you know, *The Temple Mount???*...where now resides the Islamic *Dome of The Rock.* Or. There is Sion, the small mount outside of *Sion Gate* where our *Order* was founded by Godfroi de Bouillon in the year 1118. *Both* are known as *Sion.* Which *Sion* does Jonah Van Meter mean, *Pastor* Holloway?"

"I don't know," stated Cal in flat panic.

"Well. We need to determine that, do we not, *Pastor* Holloway?"

Sabeel Khouri and Munib exchanged quick glances.

Now Khouri was panicked. It was his financial backing on the line.

He broke in with an authoritative tone. "I can assure you Mr. Carion, we have sufficient intelligence resources in the City to determine what Van Meter is doing."

"Really," replied Carion. His eyes added the question mark.

"Yes, of course." Khouri's voice lilted and his hands gestured flippantly. "We have many people with many eyes. Even our buildings have the best eyes. Come, come. I will show you. You will see Jerusalem as we see Jerusalem." Khouri sprung to his feet and herded the group out of the café into the *suq*.

The troop proceeded out into the Muristan and with a short walk, arrived at the door of the Lutheran Church of the Redeemer. The stone church received them into its grey echoes. Their heels clacked on the stones under rays of suffused light emanating from the rosette window above. Sabeel Khouri led them to the back right corner of the nave. There, a small elevator to the church's bell tower was stationed. He pushed the *up* button and the door opened.

"We have *THE supreme* view of Jerusalem at Redeemer Church. The Supreme!" cheered Khouri, his index finger raised skyward as he packed the men into the small chamber.

The ride to the tower's pinnacle was smooth. The elevator door opened to an enclosed platform. In the center resided a huge bronze bell framed by a low square retaining wall. Each of the four exterior tower walls bore double arched open-air windows looking out over Jerusalem. With a clear blue sky, the incomparable view of the Golden City immediately drew gasps from the men. Khouri escorted them to the east windows.

"There is the first *Zion*." He pointed over the City toward the golden Dome of the Rock. "The Jews call it the *Temple Mount*. The Muslims call it *al-Haram al-Sharif*. If you look beyond… you see the Mount of Olives. See the Russian church with the gold spires? That is the Church of Mary Magdalene in the Garden of Gethsemane. Then. Look up to the top of the mount. There, on the left. You see a tower. That is our Lutheran Augusta Victoria Hospital. It was built by Kaiser Wilhelm, as this church was also built. The bell tower of the hospital also has very good view of everything in the area. Then…come, please…" Khouri crossed over to the southwestern corner of the observation platform. Pointing outward again, he directed, "There is the *second Zion*. You see? The hill with the big dome-church. That is the St. Mary Dormition Church, also built by Kaiser Wilhelm.

"What does *Dormition* mean?" Wal asked, immediately regretting his ignorance on display.

"*Dormi* means *sleep,*" Pierce broke in with a scholarly tone. "The *tion* ending is *Sion*. So, the name meaning S*leep of Sion* refers nebulously to a legend that *St. Mary slept there*. But. Of course, what most people do not realize is that the *St. Mary* referred to was not the mother of Jesus, but rather, Mary Magdalene." Pierce turned to face Sabeel Khouri, looking him square in the eye. "Indeed. A sleeping Sion may be more dangerous than the first Zion. You say, Mr. Khouri, that you have people on the ground?

"Yes, my friend. *Many*. I assure you."

"Yes..." Pierce circled the platform inspecting all the vistas. "You know....we hear from *our people* on the ground that *Jonah Van Meter* has *many*. And yet. We do not know who they are, Mr. Khouri." Pierce faced Khouri directly again. "Do you?"

Khouri winced. He looked at Wal Holloway.

"Jews, perhaps," Wal supplied. "Margot tells me that her mother's people were Jewish generations ago."

"Yes, Pastor." replied Pierce. "Have you noted their surname....*Lechem*?"

"Yes. That's it. *Lechem*. That name always sounded Jewish to me." Wal confirmed.

"Yes, it does sound *very* Jewish," concurred Khouri. "It must be the Jews!...these *many people* you speak of!"

Pierce's eyes rolled to Carion with a sick slosh in his gut.

"What do you think Carion?....*Lechem*?....Jewish? Could it *possibly* be?!!!" seethed Pierce incredulous over their stupidity. He whispered to Carion's ear, "*Shall we throw ourselves down now or later?*"

Pierce and Carion meandered to the northeast corner of the platform. Carion's attention was caught by something he saw down below.

"What is all this, Mr. Khouri?" inquired Carion. He pointed downward to a flat roof-area on the adjacent Church of the Holy Sepulcher complex. Carion saw what appeared to be some kind of small village on the roof. Rudimentary mud huts were arranged in a courtyard accessed by stairs coming up out of the Arab *suq* below. Outside the huts sat black men in cassocks conversing with each other while women tended wood-fired cooking pots some yards away. In the center of the small village was a dome with small windows around it. The dome was actually the top of St. Helena's Chapel within the church below. On the west side of the roof-village was a modest oblong chapel. The front of the building was draped with a huge flag of green, yellow and red horizontal bands. And on the back of the structure was an incongruous shiny new aluminum antenna. Next to the chapel rose a large tent, such as those used in America for revivals.

Khouri looked down and frowned. "Ethiopians. They are too poor to have a chapel *in* the Church, so they live on the roof like they are still in Africa. A rather worthless group, actually. But, *one thing* is strange."

"And what is that, Mr. Khouri?" asked Carion.

"*The tent.* They usually raise their tent only *one day* each year."

"What *one day* is that?" Pierce blurted.

Perplexed, Khouri thought for a long moment, and then answered, "*Palm Sunday.*"

Thameslink City Station, London.
Wednesday, May 23, 9:13 A.M.

Sara, Madeleine, and Jonah jaunted out of City Station across Ludgate Circle to the south side of Fleet Street. A few minutes later the Gatwick train arrived also at City Station.

Destiny and Faith also traversed the circle. Eduardo and Elaine followed. And *others* followed.

"Are you sure you know where you're going Jo-Jo?" huffed Madeleine as they strode quickly down the sidewalk.

"Oh yeah! It used to be a little hard to find, but all you have to do nowadays is look for the tour busses and turn left!" laughed Jonah.

Indeed. They soon approached the block where tour busses were dumping off their morning loads of *tomb pilgrims*. The sidewalk was quite the *mardi gras* as various groups, including a troop of third-grade Brownie scouts, collected themselves for the tour.

Jonah and crew briskly rounded leftward down the walk leading to The Temple Church.

The church presented itself augustly. Made of golden Caen stone, from across the channel in France, its color was not unlike the shrines of Jerusalem. Resembling an ancient ship, the round front part of the church indeed looked like a ship's *bridge* constructed of two wheel houses, one on top of the other. The bottom wheel was large and strongly buttressed. The upper wheel was smaller and notched on its rim with the look of a hundred eagle eyes gazing down upon the land. Behind the bridge of the ship-church followed the main decks of the longer basilica.

Jonah, Sara, and Madeleine approached the church door at the narthex attached to the bridge. Sara caught sight of a handsome altar boy in a cassock posted at the open door.

"Daddy, who's that there dressed in white?"

"Shhh, child!" Jonah laughed lowly. "He's a friend to the Israelites!"

"JONAH-DUDE!" intoned the cassocked teenager.

"MICHAEL-DUDE!" responded Jonah with a *high-five* slap to the boy.

Breezing through the doorway, Sara's head whipped back.

"Oooh Mama. He's cute!"

Madeleine giggled.

They brisked through the narthex hall to the entry of the *bridge-wheel*. The massive arched portal was flanked on each side by four columns, each topped with exotic bulge-eyed stone creatures.

Entering the wheel of the church, Sara was immediately jolted back by dark stone effigy knights lying on the floor with shield and sword.

"Woahhh! I see dead people!" exclaimed Sara.

"They won't bite," assured Jonah. "They're all losers. Come. Follow me," said Jonah taking his daughter's hand.

They crossed over the center of the sanctuary as Sara made creepy-eyes at the stone men on the floor. Passing through the portal on the opposite side, they entered the larger open nave of the basilica. Bright and airy with high vaulted ceiling, it was immediately apparent that the basilica was not just a museum, but in current use as a parish church. Behind them, bus-tourist voices echoed from the round church and a few had begun to find their way into the basilica. A loud prattling tour-guide woman entered with the bulk of her group. Indifferent to setting or audience, but keen to stick to the clock, she nearly shouted for the *Canon* of the church.

"Where *is* he? He should be here." she whined.

Fortunately, the silver-haired cleric immediately entered from the sacristy and took to a small lectern midway on the center aisle for his daily talk on the history of the church. While the good Canon addressed the group, Jonah quietly led Madeleine and Sara to the main

altar at the back of the church.

The altar was really nothing more than a simple wooden Communion Table covered with a fine linen cloth. Behind the table rose a finely carved wooden altar screen backlit by a triple-arched stained glass window casting rays of soulful blue light. The center of the screen was a Judaic double-tablet of the *Ten Commandments*. Above the Decalogue, scribed in gold, was:

Exodus – Chapter XX.

"A little bit of home," mused Jonah.

Sara counted the commandments. Four on the left, and six on the right.

More tourists came into the basilica, their voices threatening to overwhelm the Canon's lesson.

"Oooh, look Mommy!" Sara pulled Madeleine by the hand to an odd tomb recessed into the sidewall of the church. The niche hosted a brightly painted figure of a medieval man in fine costume. He was less scary than the stone knights in the adjacent round church. Jonah observed with a smile his daughter's curiosity of all things, apparent and hidden.

Sara and Madeleine continued to peruse various attributes of the church from gargoyles to stained glass windows. Even more tourists flooded the sanctuary. Destiny and Faith arrived. Then, Eduardo and Elaine. And then, men in suits and dark glasses.

There were so many people and voices in the church, it was impossible to discern who was with whom, as lookers and gawkers meandered to and fro. Everyone was rather on their own and all together at the same time.

Eduardo, having detached from Elaine, made his way up the center aisle. Passing Destiny, she gave him a big wink-wink. He just smiled at the mystery of her being.

Elaine gazed over the crowd and saw a man standing at the Communion Table gazing intently at something on the stone floor under the table. She quietly saddled up next to Jonah.

"Good morning, *Pastor*."

"Good morning, *Sister*."

"What have you found there?" she asked.

"A rock," he replied, not diverting his eyes.

Elaine knelt to inspect the small inscribed flagstone. "Hmm. 'Tis the season for good rocks, Pastor, yes?"

"I think so, Sister. I think so." Jonah slipped a piece of *matzah* to Elaine's hand. She laid it on the stone.

"Your man that you are with....?" broached Jonah.

"Yes?" replied Elaine.

"He looks familiar to me somehow. What is his name?"

"Eduardo. Eduardo Raguel Mendoza."

Jonah turned his head slowly to Elaine. "Raguel?"

Elaine nodded, and winced in hesitation. She said to Jonah, "And...his mother's name was Zara..."

Jonah's eyes went very wide. He turned fully and cast his eyes across the basilica looking for Eduardo. Spotting him, Jonah just stared in study of the man's face. "Is his mother still living?" asked Jonah softly.

"No," answered Elaine.

"Did she die in peace?" asked Jonah.

"Yes." Elaine turned Jonah to herself directly. "Jonah...you don't think...?" her voice trailed.

"I think..." said Jonah, his eyes swelling a bit. "...I think that today I believe in God...some days...every once in awhile, He actually shows up..."

Elaine looked out over the crowd at Eduardo. She nodded. "I think you may be right, Jonah. You may be right. *Lahma Mahar*, my brother."

"*Lahma Mahar*, my sister."

And Elaine departed back down the center aisle.

Up the aisle came Sara and Madeleine.

Sara's eyes flashed upon Elaine's. "He's soooo CUTE!" squealed Sara with a hop to see where Eduardo was on the other side of the sanctuary.

Elaine nodded with a girlish feigned swoon. With hands on hips, she leaned backward to get a good look at Madeleine. "Girrrrl! You lookin' GOOD, huney-child!" exclaimed Elaine in faux black accent. "I've been chatting with Destiny *'bout y'all!*" she whispered.

Madeleine blushed. "You too, girl! But, you have to tell us Elaine...just between us girls...ah, you and *handsome* over there...Are you and he...uh...well, *you know...*?"

"Uh-huhh...," Elaine let out with her own blush.

"Oh, my GOD!" squealed Sara. "This is *so awesome!*" she squealed stammering her feet upon the stones.

"We'll talk!" declared Madeleine flipping a hand wave.

The trio broke up back into the crowd.

As if the church was not burdened enough, the Brownie troop entered. The decibel in the sanctuary jacked several notches making the Canon's eyebrows hop. Clumps of the little troopers darted crazily about with short shrieks and wispy shoe-skips upon the stones.

Somehow, Destiny got into a verbal altercation with a particular little Brownie girl sporting a cable combination bike-lock around her neck.

"Oh yeah?!" Destiny's hand sliced and diced the air while her head slid left and right Egyptian-style. "You wouldn't know a *secret* if it was right in front of you'alls stuck-up nose!"

"Oh, right!" The spindly little girl screeched with her little white knuckles on her hips. "Well, you certainly do not look like a Merovingian! My family, on the other hand, comes from a very long, very important line of Merovingians! My Daddy has all the proof in a book he has!"

"O Yeah? What book is that?!!!"

"It's a BOOK! A true book. My Daddy got it from some other man. But it's a TRUE book!" the Brownie's nasally little voice crescendoed.

"Oh, right. True like the Bible. And tell me little Miss Browwwwnie…what makes you think that I am not a Merovingian??? Huh?! How do you know?!"

"Oh, that's simple!" the little brat declared with her nose up in the air. "You can't be a Merovingian because you're BLACK! And….you're FAT!" Little Miss Brownie stuck her tongue out and ran back into the crowd.

Faith came up to Destiny. "Child, whatchoo been doin'?"

"Oh nuthin', momma. Just playin' the dozens with a foo'"

"Oh, okay." Faith smiled.

Madeleine spied Jonah still standing at the Communion Table and so she took Sara up to him. Jonah was deep in prayer with his eyes closed, but twitching in spasms of alternating currents within his brain. Sara had seen this before. Madeleine softly stroked the back of his shoulders and his eyes slowly opened. Jonah smiled, and kissed his wife.

Madeleine looked down and beheld at Jonah's feet the small flagstone. She bent down to trace the words with her finger. She gave a short gasp. Her head slowly turned up to Jonah with mist in her eye, and then a full teardrop. He nodded, stiffening his lip. The stone read:

Here Lies

Sara

Wellbeloved

A Stranger

The trio recessed from the Communion Table in absolute silence. They reentered the round church. Jonah noticed a marble plaque on the wall. It read:

Restored After The War Damage

The Round Was Re-Dedicated On The 7ᵗʰ November 1958

By The Archbishop Of Canterbury

Standing in the middle of the round church, surrounded by the stone knights, Madeleine wiped her eye. "Well....Shouldn't we look like we're doing something official here to keep up appearances?" she strained out a chuckle.

Jonah nodded with a smile. "Guess so. Let's see…What can we do in a round church for our little audience?" Jonah's surveyed the church wall. It had a low sitting stone bench all around backed with graceful gothic niches. A variety of tourists sat here and there on the bench, including some men still wearing dark glasses in a dark church.

"Me-ow," Sara cried softly. "Momma told me her cat story, Daddy!" she whispered.

"Me-ow," cried Destiny as she hooked her arm around Sara. "She told me the cat story too, Jonah," whispered Destiny.

"Me-ow," cried Madeleine as she perked to a hearty laugh under the multi-color rays streaming through the ancient stained glass windows.

Then it came to Jonah. He grinned to himself. He took the hands of his wife and daughter and they formed a small circle. Jonah began to hum a small Jewish melody with a soft smile to his lovely wife and daughter. And their circle turned. To the side, the left foot behind the right…Another slide, the right foot in front of the left…They nodded to each other and Sara began the song slowly.

Hava nagila, hava nagila
Hava nagila venis' mecha

And the circle went faster, their feet small-hopping between the rhythm of the steps.…

Hava nagila, hava nagila
Hava nagila venis'mecha
Hava neranena, hava neranena
Hava neranena venis'mecha
Uru, uru achim
Uru achim belev same' ach

Destiny entered the circle taking the hand of Sara. Then came Faith.

"JAH!" cried Sara.
"JAH!" cried Destiny.
"JAH!" cried Faith.

And their cries, their laughs, their gladness became the back-beat to the Hebrew song…and the circle spun faster…

Uru achim, uru achim

Elaine jumped into the circle pulling Eduardo. Smiles and jumps of feet soared high with gothic stone and window. The song rose louder, and the circle spun faster, and the echoes in the sanctuary called even to the stone dead brethren on the ground…

Uru achim uru achim!!!

"Oh, my God!" called a short-pint tourist woman with a New York accent. "David! Look! David! David!"

"WHAT, Miriam?!" the older man sniped at his wife while he fiddled with his hearing aid.

"They're doing a HORA! In the CHURCH! Oh My GOD! I can't believe it! Come on, David, We HAVE to do the HORA in the CHURCH! Bring your camera. Come on, Come on! Leah and Sol are going to be SO jealous. Oh, I LOVE IT!" And Miriam lurched herself and David into the growing circle, doubling the decibel of the Song with megaphonic blackboard screech,

HAVA NEGILA, HAVA NEGILA!!!....

"Are you Jewish, honey?" crowed Miriam to Madeleine in the whirling of the circle.

"Uh, huh. Are you?" Madeleine laughed throwing her hair to the air.

"Oh, yeahhhh! I'm the original *Noodge*! Can you tell?!" Miriam shouted.

"Uh-huh! I can tell!"

More and more people in the Round Church were drawn into the spinning circle of joy. Altar Boy Michael broke in next to Destiny and Faith. "Cool!" he cried, making a hopping stir of his cassock. And in came the Canon, with glad bewilderment and a *lovely jubbly* beam in his eyes. And two grey-haired ladies appeared with a cackle and a gust of spirit.

As the circle of the dance swelled greater with tourists jumping in and learning the steps right quick, Sara and Destiny broke off and formed a new circle along the outlying edges of the sanctuary. Chirping children twirled and hopped their own dances upon the very bellies of the stone men and their useless swords. The dark-glasses men and the Little Miss Brownie were hard-pressed against the walls, not knowing what to do. The wind spun by the whirling circles of souls, one inside the other, was too much for them. As Sara and Destiny came round about in the outer circle, they appeared to trip on the foot of one of the dark-glasses men. Destiny fell into a heap on him.

"Sorry we're bugging you!!!" she laughed hysterically and jumped back into the circle.

The Bread House, Bexley, Ohio.
Wednesday, May 23, 3:01 P.M.

On top of the house, before their monitors, The Rod Man and Will Aaronson exploded into shrieks and screeches.
"What?" yelled Geoffrey Sinclair.
"They picked his wallet too!!!" screamed Will.
And the whole house erupted into a thunder of laughter.

Chapter 15

Blessed are you, O Lord, who hears prayer.

White House Situation Room, Washington, D. C.
Wednesday, May 23, 11:59 P.M.

Ashman Blackpoint hovered over the conference table with a maniacal eye upon the disheveled remnants of Eduardo and Elaine. Their clothes were torn and blood stained, their bodies bruised, from the Company's abduction outside the Temple Church. The two had been interrogated separately aboard the night flight and in the ante-chambers of the Situation Room. It was Blackpoint's decision as to their disposition. Rendition to Egypt for a more *thorough interrogation* was one option. On the other hand, Blackpoint had a nickname: *The Magician.* He was good at making things disappear. But in his own mind, he was more *The Virologist.* He had to get to the origin of the virus that had infected the body of his organization. Then, it would be the time for magic.

"Oh, please, Eddie. The *silent treatment?* Come now. You understand we have *methodologies...*hmmm?" Blackpoint's head dipped at a cocky angle with wide eyes straight into Eduardo's.

"Sí, Señor Blackpoint," replied Eduardo, direct and unflinching. "Now I understand many things...."

"...such as, Eddie?..."

"...such as: YOU MURDERED MY FATHER...before he could out your Honduran death squads!" Eduardo seethed and nodded with a jutted lower lip and stabbing eye.

"Oh, really?" Blackpoint's mouth turned slowly upward. "And look now how my prodigal son returns to me. You know what your mistake was, don't you Eddie? You made the mistake of thinking you would never come home. Hmmm?"

Eduardo seethed a whisper: "But your problem is not at *home*, Blackie. It is *out there*, no? It is a *virus, Blackie*. And it is spreading like wild fire...and then: it will be a nuclear chain reaction. Kill us now....All the same. Your empire will not last the weekend. You're already *DONE*."

Elaine, separated by six feet and two guards down the table, shouted: "A-MEIN!!!"

Blackpoint stepped back and huffed. "Interrogation has its side effects."

Doubting odds for survival, Elaine thought about her childhood in the fields of Glastonbury.

Eduardo remembered his mother lighting candles for his father on Friday at sundown.

A door in the room opened. They heard the hard clacking of heels on the sterile tile floor. A tall gaunt woman of severe features circled the table and came to stand over them. The figure stretched out a bony tobacco-stained finger and flicked a teardrop off Elaine's cheek.

"Oh. Please. It is not that bad. Let us be big boys and girls, shall we?" The pale un-feminine figure enunciated in thick German accent—her face square and capped by short-cropped gray hair. A gray woolen suit dangled loose upon her frame enhancing a bloodless appearance—an empty vessel looking for sustenance by preying upon the living.

"I'm *very* pleased to introduce to you..." intoned Blackpoint, sticking his menacing face directly before Elaine's. "...Doctor Ricela Kundorf, of the *Universitat Berlin Technische*. Dr. Kundorf, I dare say, is a competitor of yours Doctor...or is it *Sister?*...Armstrong...in the field of medieval history."

Kundorf cut in. "I must tell you, my dear. I am not here to ask you *questions*. No. I am here for Mr. Blackpoint....and to tell your people *out there*, as you say, yes?....that we know the facts. Yes. We know the facts of your little project!" She walked slowly and menacingly around the table looking for reaction in Elaine's eyes. Kundorf lowered her backside to the table beside Elaine who recoiled at the stale tobacco smell coming off the gray woman. "Oh what a pity, that you and your comrades thought yourselves so-oooo intelligent…sadly laughable, really. You actually thought that we would not be able to understand your plans…your *methodology*. Hmph. But we do, my dear. We do! We know *exactly* where your friends, the Van Meters, are going." Kundorf leaned down mockingly, studying Elaine's eyes. "Yes. Your Jonah Van Meter's next move is: *CALAIS*…the tomb of his sainted ancestor, Cretien DuBois. Surprise! How could we know?! But we do, my darling. We do."

Elaine blinked and stared into the eyes of the gray woman, and blinked again.

"Hah! Yes. Calais!" laughed Kundorf, taking Elaine's facial movements for confirmation.

Portsmouth, England.
Wednesday, May 23, 3:21 P.M.

The horn of the ship *Mont St. Michel* was deep and sonorous, calling into the blue mist as it pulled away from the docks of Portsmouth. Sara stood at the bow of the ark-shaped ship, waving at the gulls and watching the blue-green fields of England drift away. A certain feeling of anxiety flooded into her. She was leaving….everything. She was going home, a place she had never been. *Zion.*

"This is good," breathed Madeleine holding onto Jonah, looking out to the sea. "Thank you," she said laying her eyes into his.

"For what?" he answered softly.

"For saving me…for saving *us*. Thank you for our beautiful daughter. Thank you for the dance at the church." She laid her head upon his chest, her long hair falling down over his arms. "I miss him, Jonah…I still miss him. I wonder…I wonder where his little soul is…" She buried her face deeper and held him tighter.

"I know…But, I feel his soul, Maddie. He is with you…you still carry him with you…you always will…just as we've carried *The Secret* within us for a thousand years."

"I suppose now, I can understand how a body can harbor love for a thousand years. I'm doing it, Jonah. I'm doing it."

Jonah nodded, seeing deep within her eyes. "*We're* doing it. It's what Jews do." He looked out to the sea. "We'll dock in Caen in about six hours…at sunset. I expect the harbor will be beautiful. You're right Maddie, *This is good*, and we're all to-gether…you, me, Sara… Danny."

"Thank you." She kissed him, and looked across the deck at Sara hurling bits of *matzah* to the gulls following the ship. "Will Uncle Aaron really be having dinner with us tonight?"

"Yes, he promised. Uncle Aaron always keeps his promises."

Port of Calais, France.
Wednesday, May 23, 9:01 P.M.

The late day sun behind them, Destiny and Faith stood on the bow of their ship approaching Calais. On the distant horizon they spotted the lighthouse of the port and beyond it, the spire of the town hall. Yano, their Roma escort, lounged against the deck rail keeping an eye on the dark-glasses men.

Destiny fished a small object out of her purple jeans and flicked it into the sea.

"What was that?" asked Faith.

"A little bug I found in my pocket," the girl smirked.

"Oh," chuckled Faith. "So now Charlie-The-Tuna will have a little company?"

"Yes ma'am!"

"I heard that."

Pontifical Biblical Institute, Jerusalem.
Wednesday, May 23, 6:21 P.M.

Sister Scholastica surveyed the Old City from the top floor of the Pontifical Biblical Institute. The tall building provided per-fect oversight of the Mount of Olives and Temple Mount on the horizon. And nearer: the Church of the Holy Sepulcher, the Lutheran Church Of The Redeemer, Jaffa Gate and to the right, just outside the Old City walls, Mt. Zion.

Sister Scholastica scanned the rows of computer consoles manned by a variety of denim-clad young adults. Above the computer stations were several video monitors taking feed from cameras mounted on the Institute's roof. Beside her stood Miguel Raphael, Communications Director for PBI.

"This centre is staffed at all times?" inquired Sister Scholastica.

"Oh, yes. This is our telecommunications centre for the entire region. So yes, we are staffed at all times. And, as our students are always in need of employment, they are most happy with the opportunity…"

"I am not sure I trust students, Miguel," she countered directly. "Students are not always fond of following protocol."

Miguel chuckled. "I can assure you Sister, our students are not so studious outside of their classes to worry about the intricacies of the data we assign them to collect and transmit. They do their work and they chat ….or maybe it is they chat, and then they do a little work, yes? This is the way of the student."

Sister Scholastica turned and gazed again out the windows. She looked down upon a courtyard in the grounds next door to the Institute. Another group of college-age young people were in the courtyard having what appeared to be some kind of party or mini-rally. There was food. There was strobing rhythmic African-Caribbean music, and youth with matted hair dancing in jutting and flowing leg, arm, and pelvic gesticulations. Dogs and frisbees careened through the air. A number of tables were set up with materials for making signs. Sister Scholastica could make out some of the slogans the students were scribing: IF WAR IS THE ANSWER, WE'RE ASKING THE WRONG QUESTION!.....ZIONISM IS PEACE!....LAHMA MAHAR! One little boy was making a sign which read: MORE CANDY, LESS WAR!

"What is all this Miguel?" Sister Scholastica circled her finger about the scene.

"Oh. Our neighbors. That is Hebrew Union College. We have some cooperative programs with them....which is very good for keeping an eye on them, yes?'

"They are Jews?"

"Yes, of course."

"But why are their signs in English...well, *except for that one*?" she pointed.

Miguel shrugged. "I think many HUC students are Americans."

"What does *that* sign say? It is not in English."

"It say, ehhh, *Lahma Mahar,* yes. This is Aramaic, actually. The students must be practicing their Aramaic...ehhh...*Lahma mahar*...it means, like, *bread tomorrow*...or something like this."

Sister Scholastica grunted. "Keep watch on *everything* Miguel, including your *neighbors*. Report anything emergent or remotely suspicious to me at once. Do you understand?"

"Certainly, Sister. We will remain vigilant. We can do nothing less as we have the widest view of everything!—As you can see, yes? Do not worry. We are at your service, dear Sister."

Sister Scholastica abruptly shook Miguel's hand with a vice grip. "I must return at once to Rome. *Adeus*, Miguel." And just as abruptly, she turned and departed the Communications Room.

"*Auf Wiederschen*," whispered Miguel with a trailing finger-wave.

The students rumbled in a low roll of laughter. Leah, a neo-hippy looking girl with long straight blonde hair called, "Hey Miguel!" She hurled a bagel in a hook shot over her head at him. "The Rod Man says: *LAHMA MAHAR!!!*" Full-faced in her computer monitor was a laughing rocking Rodney Fridenmaker.

Miguel caught the bagel with one hand and snatched a bite. "*Todah rabah*, Rod Man!" And Miguel knocked on the table for *good* luck.

Port of Caen, France.
Wednesday, May 23, 9:31 P.M.

As Jonah predicted, the harbor was aglow. The fading sun trailed a soft lavender sky over the outlines of Sword Beach where a previous generation had landed to strive with the Germans.

Sara, Madeleine, and Jonah disembarked the *Mont St. Michel* to be greeted by their driver Lazlo, a spry fortyish Roma man in blue vest and black trousers. Although tired, they jabbered wildly with Lazlo as he deftly whisked the old but fine humming Peugeot on the highway toward Caen. Arriving on the outskirts of city, Lazlo took the outer-belt westward. Just off the highway, he pointed to the Memorial of Peace Museum.

"*The Failure of Peace* is the name of the first hall in the Museum," instructed Lazlo. "We shall strive to improve upon that....What do you think Sara?"

"Gitter Done!" exclaimed Sara.

"You must be speaking *American*".

"Actually, I speak *Ohio.*"

Lazlo circled around to a point west of Caen and then proceeded east into the town on Rue Ecuyere to Rue Saint Sauveur. With all the windows down, the warm evening air and the town itself came into the car. The streets were alive with people, lilting Normandie music, and the aroma of fresh bread from brasseries lined end-to-end. Graceful multi-branched street lamps illumined the golden Caen stone of the buildings, the cobble-stone ground, and the pastels of café awnings pressing against the night.

"Look!" shouted Sara pointing out her window. On the sidewall of a building with much graffiti was written in huge jagged blue letters: *LAHMA MAHAR!!!*

Lazlo made a right turn onto Rue Demolombe. Suddenly they saw a tremendous increase of people on the walks. Lazlo's hand jutted out the window grasping a small Roma flag. He laid on the car horn. Immediately the people of the street began to cheer loudly, jumping up and down. Flags Israeli, Roma, French, Ethiopian, and Jamaican sprouted out over the street curbs.

Hand-made signs scribed with *LAHMA MAHAR!* bounced and danced amid blasts from pneumatic noise-makers. The cacophony of voice and horn exploded as people rushed the car and Lazlo reduced to a crawl as Sara, Madeleine and Jonah hung out the windows *slapping fives* with all who came near. Sara, circling her small dark fist in *go-go* whirls, started the chant...

LAHMA...
...MAHAR!!!

LAHMA...
...MAHAR!!!

LAHMA...
...MAHAR!!!

Lazlo shepherded the car to the intersection of Rue Demolombe and Rue De Bras where the crowd had enveloped the whole block. He released Sara, Madeleine and Jonah to the crowd. Their hands joined to others leading them to the center of the intersection where shouts and dancing spun cyclones of joy to music of all kinds spicing the air. There were Jazz and Mariachi bands. There were klezmer and reggae bands. One loud Ethiopian reggae band, from a nearby bar, held court in the intersection with black women dancing in sun-splash color dresses and headscarves. Songs of *Zion Freedom* and *Lions of Judah* pulsed through the very stone of the street and made it flow.

At a distance, clumps of radical Muslims bandied insults and attempted incursions at the peripheries of the crowd. But the Jewish and Roma *House* guards were too many and too strong for them.

Sara threw herself in with the Ethiopian women dancing in alternating squats, kicks and shimmies.

The crowd surged and amplified along with the loud speakers, all under the watchful eye of *House* guards, the Caen police, and television news cameras mounted on scaffolds.

Suddenly, the party began to move westward on Rue De Bras. Jewish, Roma, and Ethiopian escorts surrounded Jonah,

Madeleine, and Sara as the mass of people flowed down the boulevard.

After several blocks, the crowd arrived at its destination: The Abbey Of The Men. The crowd pulled back to make way. Jonah cast his black-stripe *tallit* upon his shoulders. With Madeleine and Sara, he proceeded deliberately up the steps of the grand church to the thunderous applause and shouting of the crowd. Television cameras rolled.

Inside the ancient church, the gothic arches swelled the din of the crowd in joyous echoes bouncing off the golden stones. Jonah proceeded to an engraved stone slab recessed in the church floor: The tomb of William the Conqueror. As people loudly gathered around the grave with their flags and signs, some wearing *kippot*, others in dread locks, others in blue vests or peasant dresses, they all laughed. Jonah laughed. Madeleine and Sara laughed. With fists of crumbled *matzah*, Jonah showered the crowd with a blessing of bread confetti. Laughing roared in echoes through the church. The reggae people yelled *"JAH!"* The Jews called *"YAH!"* and *"EL DIO!"* And the Roma shouted *"O DEL!"*

"What are they doing?" a befuddled reporter whispered to a Roma man.

"Oh! The Jonah man…he is making fun with the William…ehh…in his family…long ago…sorry, my French, not so good."

"Oh…" the reporter winced, shaking his head as he watched Jonah lean his ear down to the slab while knocking his knuckles on it to the raucous laughter cascading through the church. Sara and Madeleine joined in the zany ritual, giggling all the way.

Then the circle dance began to the strains of Jewish and Roma horns and violins. Reggae drums blended in giving the down beat for the dancers to thrust their hips out and then hold their noses. The dance was a joke—unknown to the uninitiated. William The Conqueror, who married into the Merovingians, died a very fat man in 1087 AD. Through a mishap at his funeral, his body was mishandled and it gaseously broke open producing such cloud of stench, all attendees fled the church. Added to the ignoble burial, his remains were dug up and desecrated by marauding Huguenots in 1562 leaving only a thigh bone to be re-interred. As the crazy dance circled the tomb, Jonah led the revelers in his own made-up reggae song,

Jacob do de better den Willie!!!...

Israel do de better den Willie!!!...

"Who is this man?" the reporter asked a Jewish woman laughing in the background.

"He is Jonah Van Meter....from Ohio," she laughed. "He is going to Paris."

The reporter wrote it down.

The woman had lied about Paris.

While the party continued at the church, Lazlo slipped his charges out to his car. He quickly wheeled across several blocks of rumbling cobble-stone streets to Rue des Equipes d'Urgence. They came to rest in the crescent drive of a small pastel-colored tavern: *La Petite Auberge.*

With an elegant canopy over the door, the tavern was a most welcome site to the weary travelers. Entering, they found a most pleasant interior of slate floor and walls painted in the golden color of Caen stone. The tables were also arrayed in cloths of gold accented with crisp bright white napkins and contrasting jet black chairs. Bright blue curtains gave a certain cheerfulness warding off all malevolence. The aroma of the cuisine was uplifting and spirited with freshness which could instantly be seen in the impeccably presented buffet arrayed in the center of the dining room. The ambiance fit well the Van Meter style: down-to-earth, but elegant.

Lazlo immediately split off by himself, taking a table in a back corner with good visual coverage of all the windows and entries.

Madeleine, tired and needing to relax, sighed, "How wonderful to end our day with, Jonah!"

"Ummmm! Super Yummy looking, Dad!" called Sara, already hovering over the buffet.

Rivka, the owner's daughter, motioned them all to the spread. Indeed, the fare was most welcome. There was a great array of fresh vegetable and dairy dishes—Israeli with a French twist.

Sara gazed over a bin of fine fresh puffed rolls and stopped herself.

"I know. We still need to remember that we are in a hurry," she said patting her fathers coat pocket full of *matzah*.

They chose a table already set and sat down. Jonah removed a piece of *matzah* from his coat pocket and gave it to Madeleine for the blessing. She closed her eyes and prayed,

> *Ba......ruchhhh! atah Adonai elohaynu melech ha'olam*
> *hamotzi lechem min ha'aretz.*
> *Lahma mahar. A-mein.*

They raised and clinked their water glasses to each other's with a robust *L'Chaim!*

After a good amount of food and deliriously tired and stupid jokes about anything and nothing, suddenly the tavern door opened. In the doorway stood a tall elderly man with silver hair under a black *kippah*.

"Uncle Aaron!" squealed Sara as she ran to the moderately but finely attired Parisian. She wrapped her arms around his neck kissing him on both sides.

"Shalom, Sara. Shalom!" Aaron chuckled, giving her a big hug.

Rivka also rushed to greet her esteemed guest. "Your Eminence. So nice to see you this evening," she said sweetly in French.

The old man took her hand gently and brushed it with his lips. "You look well Rivka. How goes your studies?" he inquired in Hebrew with a wide grin.

"Well. Thank you very much, your Eminence," the girl replied in Hebrew.

Madeleine and Jonah also hurried to celebrate the arrival of their old friend.

"Maggid, my dear. Shalom," greeted Aaron with almost a tear in his eye.

Madeleine began to weep a little as she helped the elderly man to their table.

Aaron, the former Archbishop of Paris, was a unique spirit whose life included quite an unusual career before his retirement. Born a Jew, he escaped the Holocaust having been given to a friendly Catholic family by his parents. His protectors formally adopted Aaron after the war when it became known his parents died at Auschwitz. Out of gratitude and true religious calling, Aaron grew into a passionate young man keen to contribute love and peace to the world. So, he became a priest. But, an unusual one to be sure. He was both a realist and one to push the boundaries of convention. On one hand, he was acutely aware of Christian complicity in the Holocaust, and he openly said so. On the other hand, he was adeptly able to communicate the idea that the Church should see itself as the child of its parent religion: Judaism. Thus he could criticize the actions of his fellow ecclesial leaders and still firmly assert that the Church had a vital role to play in the world *under the lead of Judaism.* And. To the consternation of the *Curia,* Aaron always and brashly claimed he was *still a Jew.* His personal friendship with the previous Pope, grounded in their mutual experience under the Nazi plague, shielded Aaron from any meaningful attack within the Church.

"And how are you, my dear Maggid?" Aaron softly asked holding Madeleine's hand.

"Good, Aaron. Very good." Madeleine nodded in a determined burst of strength.

The old man squeezed her hands.

"I am most glad that you are here, my friends. My goodness! I think all of France is glad you are here...well, most of France!"

They all laughed.

"Yes....have you heard the news reports?" inquired Aaron.

"No, what?" replied Jonah, a bit concerned.

"Oh. Well. They say all the roads are...ah, how you say?...ah, jammed...with travelers. I think you will be greater than *The Beatles*, no?"

"Well...," Jonah mused. "...it's not going to be our show."

"No, I suppose not." Aaron smiled.

Madeleine's eyebrows lifted. "So, Aaron. The *band equipment* will be coming?" she asked with very direct eyes.

"Yes, my dear. It most certainly will." He checked his wrist watch. The twist of his wrist made the small sapphire stone of his ring catch a sparkle off the candle on the table. "Yes. They will be loading in approximately nine hours."

"Good." Jonah nodded. "Your ring, Aaron. Most interesting. On the stone…A *Cross* overlapping a *Star of David*. I can't tell if the cross is behind the star, or in the star."

"Yes. It has much meaning for me…a gift from a dear friend." Aaron smiled. "But my dear Maggid, I have noticed that you also have a special *gem*. Is that what I think it is?"

Madeleine nodded somberly. She gingerly lifted the leather *tefila* from her neck and carefully handed it to Aaron. The old man traced his finger along the ancient leather cord and pouch bearing within the great *Shema*. His hands and throat trembled a little, and he looked deeply into Madeleine's eyes. "You are taking this *tefila* home to be reunited with its mate, yes?"

"Yes, Aaron. It's time for us all to go home. We will see you in Jerusalem?"

Aaron smiled. "Yes, my dear Maggid. God willing."

A Café in Calais, France.
Wednesday, May 23, 11:31 P.M.

A muscular anglo-man in a sharp business suit leaned into the corner of a back booth. He took another drag on a cigarette and punched the *send* on his cell phone.

"Dr. Kundorf?"

"Yes."

"Sorry to report. Not Calais."

"What?! Where?"

"Caen."

"Shit!" There was a long pause. "Okay…ehh…he then…went to William The Conqueror's tomb? Is that where he went?"

"Yeah. That's where he went."

"Yah. That is logical. He will now proceed to Paris, no doubt..."

"Yeah. That's what we're picking up...How do you know? What's in Paris?"

"Simple. The tomb of his matriarch, *The Magdalen* herself...at The Louvre. Go to Paris. Wait for him."

Alitalia Flight #1307 to Rome.
Wednesday, May 24, 11:33 P.M.

Her cell phone sounded.
"Yes?"
"Sister Scholastica?....Miguel Raphael, at PBI."
"Yes, Miguel."
"Our man arrived in Caen. We are told he will go to Paris."

Swissair Flight #5013 to Geneva.
Wednesday, May 24, 11:33 P.M.

"What is it?"
"Mr. Pierce, an update for you..."
"What is it?"
"Paris. Van Meter is going to Paris from Caen."
"Not good."

Vatican City.
Thursday, May 24, 5:33 A.M.

The morning sun rayed over the obelisk in St. Peter's square, but it was still mostly dark outside the north wall of the basilica. The two grey-haired Sisters Maria and Marta, two Ethiopian seminarians in black cassocks, and two American Franciscans in grey habits waited patiently outside a relatively unknown door, listening. The men were nervous.

Maria offered some levity.

"Knock-knock?"

"Who is there?" Marta played along.

"Somebody."

"Somebody who?"

"I got *some* body, do I not?" Maria ran her hands over her sides to her hips with a *ka-boom* of her portly waistline.

Marta shook her head. The Franciscans groaned. The Ethiopians winced questioningly at each other.

Finally, the lock tumblers clunked and the door pushed out a schmidgen. Marta raised her hand waiting until the trailing footsteps of their unseen accomplice faded. Hoisting a small wheeled trolley and a dark canvas shoulder bag, the squad gingerly pried the door open and stepped into the grey morning air of the basilica.

Standing within the Blessed Sacrament Chapel, they were instantly relieved to find no one there. It was good to have a moment to close their entry door and appear as having ordinary religious business.

The chapel, largest of many on the north side of the basilica, soared to a heavenly traffic of gleaming white angels in a sky of gold. It was open to the expanse of the nave through a baroque wrought iron portal. In the quiet came distant echoes of footsteps upon marble floors and the first morning wafts of sweet spiced incense from the basilica beyond.

They stepped quietly around the main altar on their right, noting its grand golden tabernacle housing the *Host*. The tabernacle's shape, round with columns supporting a dome, seemed to model the rotunda of the Holy Sepulcher in Jerusalem. Flanking the tabernacle on both sides were golden cherubim facing each other guarding the *Host*.

Leading the squad, Marta started to proceed through the center aisle between wooden kneeling benches. But Gregorio, one of the Franciscans, stopped and motioned at his partner Daniel, directing his attention to a side altar on the left. Briefly, they gazed upon a mosaic above the altar depicting St. Francis receiving the *stigmata*.

The troop again departed pulling the trolley by a rope across the marble chapel floor and through the iron gate into the soft echoes of the cavernous basilica.

Not to be outdone by the Franciscans, the Ethiopians, Menelik and Tewahido, informed Marta they wished to briefly visit the altar of St. Michael toward the front of the nave.

Marta rolled her eyes, but led the way. Not going very far, they came to one of the massive support pillars of the basilica's dome. Recessed in the pillar was the Altar of St. Jerome. Directly below the table top of the altar was a transparent compartment housing the visible un-decomposed body of Pope John XXIII in rich crimson vestments. The Pope, who died in 1963, was exhumed for display in the illumined glass coffin in 2001.

"Check this out, Greg," whispered Daniel.

"Oh. That's just wrong!" Greg chuckled.

"Yeah. *Our man* is doing better than *that*," mused Daniel.

"Come on. We need to go," pushed Marta.

Rounding the altar, they proceeded with the trolley up the side-aisle through the north transept to the Altar of St. Michael. Above the altar, between two red marble pillars, was an imposing painting of a winged St. Michael slaying a dragon. Quickly, Menelik and Tewahido hopped to touch the sword of St. Michael for good luck.

Marta briskly led her troop around the back of the central Papal Altar overshadowed by Bernini's great canopy supported by four massive and exotic twisting bronze columns. She made a bee-line toward an entry on the opposite side of the basilica under a ponderous stone effigy of a kneeling Pope Pius VIII.

The entry seemed small, almost secret, compared to its surrounding structure. The marble of the doorway was a dark olive in contrast to the lighter golden stone above and the natural grey of the statues adorning the high areas.

They passed through the dark portal into a passageway brightened by wide windows capturing the first streams of morning light. The passageway was really a hallway bridge connecting the Basilica of St. Peter with an adjacent domed building: The Sacristy and Treasury of St. Peter. The bridge spanned over the parking areas at the south side of the basilica and had three tunnels for vehicles passage underneath. Daniel noticed a door and exterior stairway leading from the bridge down to the parking lot.

"How come we just didn't use the stairs? It'd be a shorter trip, wouldn't it?

"Oh, right." Maria laughed. "Clunk it down the stairs! Much easier to roll it straight on level ground."

"How big the relic, Sister?" asked Tewahido.

"Big as YOU, my tall friend. And it weighs almost as much as you!"

"Ooh. Then, we must be careful. I bump head many times!" the tall man patted his close cropped hair and chuckled with the rest.

Entering the Sacristy and Treasury, they found themselves in a museum of priceless liturgical ware—chalices, crucifixes, and monstrances to hold the *Host*.

A plain-clothed security officer was stationed at the entrance to the exhibits. As they passed by, he nodded silently to Marta.

Gregorio glanced back in wonder at the man who had given them no second look. "How come he just let us through like that?"

"Because we're Swiss!" smirked Maria.

"We are Swiss?" chortled Menelik. "I do not think I look Swiss!"

Marta snickered lowly. "No, our mother house is in Switzerland…We have many friends among The Swiss Guards, for a very long time now. Not all of them know us today, but…as the saying goes—We *do* have *some* friends in high places."

As they proceeded down the hallway on the perimeter of the building, Marta studied a piece of paper.

"Okay. According to Uncle Aaron's map, the freight elevator should be at the end of the hall after we go left up here."

"How does Uncle Aaron know so much Marta?" asked Gregorio.

"Well, that is simple. He was a close friend…a very close friend of John Paul. It was *Aaron* who encouraged John Paul to reach out to Jews...not the present pope, I can tell you that. I think the best friend of the current Pope is his tailor."

"How come John Paul just didn't give us our stuff back?... if he liked Jews so much?" Gregorio pressed.

"Well, you know...*giving back the Temple Treasure* is something one can do only once. Timing is important. John Paul understood *one thing* leads to *another*. The world...especially *Jews* need to be ready for the *other*.

They rounded left at the end of the hallway passing a few clerical workers who gave them little notice. At the end of the hall, they came to an old-style freight elevator with old opaque glass windows. Instinctively, Daniel pushed the bottom of the two worn round black buttons. "Going Down!" he whispered playfully, like a kid. But nothing happened.

"It does not work that way any longer," Marta advised. She placed her palm over a small glass pane next to the buttons. The scanner read her palm and the old metal door clunked to the side revealing another quite modern steel door which glided smoothly open. The group filed on and the doors closed. Inside the elevator there were again black buttons and a scan panel. Some of the buttons were marked, and some not. Marta consulted her wrinkled map again. Placing her right palm on the scan panel, she pushed the bottom unmarked button with her left hand.

"How do they have *your palm* in the system, Marta?...the Swiss connection?" asked Daniel.

"Exactly," confirmed Marta as the car began its smooth glide downward.

"Well, it just kind of blows my mind that nobody on top has us on their radar," mused Gregorio.

Maria huffed. "The bigger they are, the more stupid, you know? They are like the fat man who cannot see his...ehh...own tweeter.

"Tweeter?" Menelik cocked his head in puzzlement.

"Oh, shit. We're all going to hell...," groaned Daniel.

The elevator reached the bottom with a jiggle and the doors opened.

They stepped out into a dimly lit subterranean corridor between ancient masonry walls. As their eyes adjusted to the semi-darkness, they could see that the walls were actually lines of arched alcoves. Each archway was partially bricked in and hermetically sealed by a modern heavy steel door. On the portals of the former arches were trace outlines of ancient portraits of human figures engaged in athletic endeavors.

"What is this place?" asked Menelik, his eyes wide open.

"This, my friends..." Maria intoned with an air of didactic authority, "was the Circus of Nero. Where we are standing now...was the southern side of the circus track. The chambers that you see here...were holding cells for the prisoners who were made to participate in bloody sports, in which most died. And...as you can see...today they guard something else."

"Which one are we looking for? Do we just go door-to-door?" asked Daniel.

"Well, there are twelve chambers," advised Marta. "Would you like to guess?"

"Everyone to the end of the hall, I guess," announced Gregorio.

"Yes. Follow the yellow-brick road, and we're off to see the wizard," joined Maria.

"*Wizard*?!" piped Tewahido. "No one tell me about *wizard*."

"Just kidding, my friend. Just kidding!" Marta assured with a chuckle.

"Oh. Okay."

"Okay, my friends. Let's roll."

They marched down the ancient pavement of the corridor with the trolly and supply bag to the last steel grey door sealing an arched chamber. To the right side of the door was another scan panel. Marta slapped her hand on it, and the door slid smoothly and slowly to the left.

They stared into a black hole. The air was quite dry and artificial, from automated climate controls within the sealed chamber. Maria's hand dove into the canvas bag and came up with two flashlights. With shaking hands, she clicked the lights on and shone them double-barrel into the dark.

Immediately, flashes of gold sparkled at the end of the light beams. Maria's hands trembled casting the lights up and down, and side to side, to reveal the outlines of their dreams.

There were muffled gasps.

They stood in utter silence. Time itself stood still.

Tewahido jutted out in front of them. He laid himself down prone, and kissed the hexagon base of the great golden Jewish Temple Menorah. And then Tewahido raised himself to kneel before the golden Showbread Table, kissing its top.

"It looks exactly like the engraving on the *Arch of Titus*," whispered Maria.

"Uh, huh," responded Marta, awestruck.

The long moment of silence flowed as they filed into the chamber, circling the objects, and daring to touch the very symbols of the ancient hope of Israel. Silence had to reign…before another word could be spoken.

"It's all here," said Daniel from the side of the room. Cradled in his arms were two long silver trumpets.

"My Goodness! How long do you think these have been down here?" wondered Gregorio.

"Since the war," answered Marta. "Pius XII found the treasure in the early forty's…during excavations of the catacombs under the basilica. They kept the area secret for a time, while they developed the Tomb of St. Peter under the Papal Altar for the pilgrim business. So. After they completed their tourist tomb, they just moved the treasure over here…to the *Treasury*. Like they say…sometimes *X* does indeed mark the spot."

Marta took a deep breath. She began to give orders. "Okay, everyone. Let us shake ourselves…and get to work. Maria, I see a light fixture above. There might be a switch."

Maria traced the light beams from the fixture to the wall beside the door. Indeed, there was a switch-plate. But, above the door was a surveillance camera.

Marta threw her hand up in a stop sign. Quickly, from the canvas bag, she drew out a plastic contraption and some duct tape. She ordered Gregorio and Daniel to lift her up to the camera while Maria held the flashlight. She soon had the contraption taped to the front of the camera. "Now, the switch," she ordered.

The light turned the chamber into a heaven of gold.

"What in the world is *THAT*?" laughed Daniel.

"A *View Master*," she giggled. It has a photo-slide of a Menorah in it...$12 on eBay. I love the *internets*!" Marta beamed.

Daniel and Gregorio just shook their heads. Menelik and Tewahido gazed at the ruse in bewilderment.

"Okay people," Marta ordered. "Let us carefully carry everything out through the door and then we will cover them."

Menelik and Gregorio took hold of the horizontal traverse rods of the Showbread Table and easily lifted it to the outer corridor.

Tewahido and Daniel had to exert a good bit of heaving and angling to lift and tilt the Menorah in order to clear the doorway. But it was done with dispatch.

Marta took custody of the silver trumpets while Maria unfolded two purple velvet coverings from the supply bag. The smaller cloth was simply rectangular, just large enough to drape the Showbread Table. The larger was actually a hood sewn to fit over the entirety of the Menorah from top to base.

At first they tried placing the Menorah on the trolley and rolling it down the corridor, but the pavement was so uneven, it wasn't worth the trouble. So, Tewahido and Daniel just carefully bore it themselves to the elevator. Again, they had to carefully lean, angle and pivot the piece to clear the door, but they accomplished their task. The rest was loaded. With all the furniture and people in the car, it was rather like college students stuffing themselves into a phone booth. But there was a will. And thus a way.

By the time they passed the guard at the entrance, they were all giddy over the ease with which they had rolled the covered Menorah and carried the Table and Trumpets down the hallways. A couple secretaries took note with some surprise in their eyes, but nothing dramatic.

The troop was happily progressing back through the bridge passageway when the unexpected happened. Marta stopped cold.

"Maria?"

"Yes, Sister?"

"Why are there cars and people in the parking lot?" whined Marta pointing out the windows of the bridge. She checked her wrist watch. It was only six-thirty.

"Holy shit," whispered Maria shaking her head in abject panic. "I do not know, Marta…"

"I think I know, Sister," said Menelik.

"*WHAT*?!" demanded Marta in a squealing whisper.

"Today…how you say?…is be-a-ti-fi-ca-tion of San Nabisco. Perhaps they have changed the time for the mass…"

"And *WHERE*, pray tell….would the mass take place?" glared Marta.

"Oohh. I am afraid to say, Sister." Menelik looked down at the ground wincing.

"*BLESSED SACRAMENT CHAPEL?!!!*"

"Yes, Sister." The poor man trembled.

Tewahido put his arm around his friend to support him against the storm.

"Oh, man," whined Daniel whirling himself in a circle. "We are going to be in BIG trouble. I want my mommy. I'm too young to die."

"Deep shit, man," confirmed Gregorio as he danced about the windows peering out from their edges.

"Shut up!" barked Marta. Her eyes clocked back and forth with the gears in her head. Suddenly, she smiled, and gave a little laugh.

"What, Sister?" blurted Maria.

"Stay right here." Marta ran back down the hallway back into the Treasury. "When life gives you lemons…." her voice trailed.

In few minutes, Marta came running back with a large golden monstrance and two altar candles in her arms.

"How did you get those?" exclaimed Maria, not knowing what they were for.

"Our Swiss Guard friend, Sepp. He suddenly feels ill and is going home for the day," rattled Marta reaching into the supply bag.

"…you mean, going home to get his passport." Maria chuckled.

"Yah. Is not the EU great?" Marta pulled up a utility knife out of the bag. Quickly she had the men tilt the Menorah over. With the knife, she slit a small opening at the top of the purple covering above the center lamp branch of the Menorah. She directed Maria to hold the monstrance on top of the exposed end of the lamp branch while she melded the two pieces together with duct tape. She drew the purple covering back up over the meld and stood back to view the results.

"There. The biggest damn monstrance one ever did see! I think that San Nabisco shall feel supremely honored!"

Everyone was wide-eyed in disbelief.

Marta lined up Menelik and Tewahido with the covered Showbread Table in a front position. Gregorio and Daniel were positioned with the Menorah behind their Ethiopian brethren. She took the two altar candles and unceremoniously screwed them into the ends of the silver trumpets. Maria and Marta took their places as acolytes at the head of the procession.

"Oh, wait. I forgot!" Marta reached into Maria's bag and pulled out her camera cell phone. Stepping back, she called, "Say *Mashiach*!" They did, and she snapped the picture.

"What's that for?" asked Daniel.

"Tell you later. Let's roll!" called Marta.

"Oh man. I can't believe we're doin' this!" crooned Gregorio as they briskly took off toward the door leading into the Basilica of St. Peter. As they leaned the Menorah to clear the doorway, they bonged its top. The ring served as a call to worship to the pilgrims already traversing the nave to the Blessed Sacrament Chapel.

"Alright everyone…you know the chant!" whispered Marta. She began the low sonorous introit.

> *Dominus virtutum nobiscum*
> *susceptor noster Deus Iacob*
> *Venite et videte opera Domini*
> *quae posuit prodigia super terram*
> *Auferens bella usque*
> *ad finem terrae arcum*
> *Conteret et confringet*

arma et scuta conburet in igne
Vacate et videte quoniam ego sum
Deus exaltabor in gentibus
exaltabor in terra
Dominus virtutum nobiscum
susceptor noster Deus Iacob...

Passing solemnly through the huge wrought iron portal into the Blessed Sacrament Chapel, Gregorio intoned smoothly,

Introibo ad altare Dei

Before the altar, the men turned and faced the congregants already in the benches and those still coming into the chapel. The covered Table was in front of the shrouded Menorah with its ridiculously high monstrance top.

Maria and Marta lit their trumpet candles from votive candles on the side altar and took their positions at the sides of the *very tall monstrance.*

The eyes of the congregants were wild with wonder, confusion, and awe. Spasms of genuflections and crossings riffed across the chapel. Gregorio and Daniel side-eyed each other, scrambling for what to do next. Daniel visually checked their entry door to the side of the altar. It was still cracked open a tiny bit.

With a sudden burst of cranial clarity, Daniel intoned,

Domine vobiscum...

The congregation replied,

Et cum spiritu tuo

Suddenly there was a loud crack.

To the side of the altar, opposite their entry door, was *another door.* It swung open. Out of the doorway, proceeded two *real* altar boys bearing their own candlesticks in procession with a heavy echoing of others coming down a stairway behind the door.

"Whoooah, shit!" squealed Gregorio stammering his feet under his habit.

"Where do those stairs come from?" Daniel shot to Marta in panic.

Her eyes popped. "*Papal Apartments*! Time to go boys!" screeched Marta.

Like a manic keystone cop, Marta crammed her troops out *their* door—Table first, then the Menorah—which Daniel and Gregorio bonged again on the overhead lintel. Marta grabbed up the trolley and slammed the door behind them.

Throwing the trolley down on the paved walk, they heaved the Menorah onto it and the whole squad began to run—rolling and running the purple masses toward the west behind the Basilica.

"Oh, shit. Oh, shit. Oh, shit!!!" cried Gregorio. "We're gonna die!"

They made a mad dash on the road between the Basilica and the Ethiopian Church of St. Stefan. As the purple squad streaked past the church, two colleagues of Menelik and Tewahido posted themselves at the Ethiopian church door.

Rounding the church into a forking service road behind the Palace of Justice, Marta could make out the Vatican Railway Station a hundred meters in front of them. Behind them, the Ethiopians at the Church of St. Stefan were busy misdirecting non-accomplice Swiss Guards just summoned from their barracks north of St. Peter's Square.

Tewahido and Menelik ran with the Table in staggered sprints, as they let Maria and Marta catch up with their breaths heaving to the max. Daniel and Gregorio kept looking back over their shoulders as they ran rumbling the Menorah down the road on the trolley, alternating with laughs and Gregorio's new mantra, *Oh shit, Oh shit, Oh shit!*

With much fright and breathless sweat, they finally arrived at the train station. Passing by the front doors, they headed directly to the north end of the station, which allowed for direct access to a short freight train waiting for them on the tracks. At the end of the train was a blue box car with the door waiting wide open.

"All aboard!" called Daniel in a split-second of joy. "I've always wanted to say that!"

"Get on the damn train, moron!" yelled Marta.

With too much clanging of metal, un-sacred words, and laughter, they tumbled their operation into the box car.

The train engineer hung out of his window and called back to Marta. He wanted a couple of men to help guard the engine. She dispatched Menelik and Tewahido.

The others helped each other slam the box car's sliding door shut.

As the Ethiopians reached the engine, they heard the shouts and storming feet of the Swiss Guards approaching the front of the station. The engineer's eyes bugged out. He ordered Menelik and Tewahido to just jump on top of the engine's cow-catcher.

Immediately, the train lurched forward.

As the Swiss Guards flooded the train station platform, their last sight was of the blue box car passing through the arched portal in the Vatican City wall and two black-cassocked figures standing on the engine, waving good-bye.

Inside the box car, Marta peered out a small opening to see a huge iron gate close across the arch behind them.

"I can't believe it! We did it!" blathered Gregorio. "WE RIPPED OFF THE VATICAN!!!"

"Well, do not get comfortable...we have not done it *yet*," Marta warned over the clugging clatter of the rocking train. "We will be hearing the *doo-dah* cars very soon. So, everybody! Up on your feet *NOW*! We are getting off at the next station, San Pietro. As soon as the train stops....everybody and everything dumps out *QUICK!!!* Same drill. Go wide to the left through the freight gate, and then up the side alley to the drop-off area in front of the station. Hopefully our driver with his truck will spot us right away."

Within a minute, the train came to a screeching halt. In accordance with Marta's commands, the group deftly executed the maneuver. They were speedily out of the gate and rolling up the alley without a sound, save for the trolley wheels and their savagely beating hearts.

At the front corner of the station they stood at the curb of a large oval turn-about, set back from the street, filled with cars and busses, and trucks. The morning air was already hot from a cloudless sky and saturated with acrid diesel fumes emanating from the swarm of vehicles dropping off and picking up people and goods.

Marta's eyes watered as she frantically panned the vehicles and people for their driver. "We're looking for a blue Renault *Mascot*," she announced.

"What's a *Mascot*? I'm from *Amaricuh*," Daniel shot back in faux-hillbilly accent.

"It is a truck…very popular here," replied Marta tersely.

"Look! It say *Mascot*!" blurted Menelik pointing to a white medium sized flat-bed truck parked on the opposite side of the turnabout. Indeed, it had a Renault *Mascot* insignia on its fender. The driver, a sixtyish-man, was checking his paperwork before approaching the freight gate.

"Yes. It is a *Mascot*, but it is not *ours*….oooh, where is he?!!!" fretted Marta. Her eyes scanned to and fro over the turn-about and the outlying street Via Inoconzo III.

"Marta-aaa," called Tewahido softly, his eyes lifted to the heavens and rolled.

"WHAT!?"

"I hear *doo-dah*…"

They all fell silent, and yes. The distant but increasing pulse was meeting their ears. Marta looked hard at the ground, and then to the white *Mascot* and the driver beginning to take off for the freight gate. In an instant, Marta shot across the turnabout.

"Sir. Sir. May I speak with you!?" she blurted in the best Italian she could muster. Like an air-traffic controller, she signaled her cohorts to bring their bodies and wares to the truck.

"What do you want?" the man answered abruptly with wide eyes at the approaching gang and ridiculously covered freight.

"Sir. I know this is most unusual. But we are very desperate. Our driver has not arrived, and we have most valuable goods to transport at once…."

"This is not my problem, Sister! I have my own work! You will have to take care of your own problems."

"Please Sir. Hear me. I am prepared to pay you a great deal of money for your trouble. I can pay you ten thousand Euros....and as you can see...," she pointed to her habit and the men's cassocks, "....you would be helping the Church as well." The sirens were sounding much closer.

The man rubbed his beard and shrugged. "Ten thousand you say? Hah! You can say *ten million*....how do I know you would pay me even ten for the trouble? And I'm afraid, Sister...you have picked the wrong man to talk about the *Church*. I am *Jewish*!"

Marta blinked. "We're Jewish too!" she blurted.

"*WHAT?!!!* YOU are *JEWISH?!!!*" The man laughed hard raking his eyes up and down over their habits. "Tell me, Sister! What kind of Jews are you?"

"Well...ah...We are *special* Jews!" Marta shot back. Lowering her head close to his, and looking each direction for dramatic effect, she whispered, "You know?... *special*? We often use *disguises*."

"Prove it," he whispered back. The sirens from the streets were much closer.

Marta blinked. "I will prove it, Sir! Come, come. I will show you. You will see that I am telling you the truth!"

Marta beckoned the man out of the truck to the purple-draped objects. She instructed the men to lower the draped Menorah flat to the ground and then for everyone to stand side to side to create a wall from others who might see. Gregorio, Menelik, and Daniel held the Menorah slightly above the pavement as Tewahido quickly pulled off the purple sheath.

The gold instantly flashed strong under the sun. The man's eyes bulged. His jaw dropped. He shook his head, closed his eyes, and opened them again. His mouth gaped wider. His head cocked. He made whining grunts and slapped his cheek as he side-stepped in a circle around the Menorah, surveying every angle. Leaning down, he placed his fingers in the recesses of the base decoration tracing the outlines of the pomegranates.

Maria cleared her throat reacting to the rising sound of the sirens. *"LOOK, SIR!"* She jerked the cover from the Showbread Table and two silver trumpets resting upon it. The man gasped. His eyes bulged even more.

"You might be special Jews," he said with a tremor.

"Can we raise this back up?" Daniel pleaded. "It's killing my back…and I'm hearing *doo-dahs* big time!"

"What do you say, Sir. Will you help us?" Marta urgently pressed. "… Sir…I am sorry, I did not ask your name…Can we do business?"

"My name is David…*Business???*…I should pay *you*! My truck is your truck…"

"Deal!" Marta shouted, clasping the man's hand in hers. "We must go *NOW!* The police will arrive any moment!" Marta started grabbing fruit crates to clear the truck bed.

"Marta! Wait!" shouted Maria.

"WHAT?!"

"I just had an idea." The sirens screamed closer. "They are so close…we could very well be caught…"

Marta just burned her eyes into Maria. *"Really?"* she seethed.

"…but if we were caught…," Maria pressed. "…*Shouldn't the world know what we were caught with???* We *DO* have the treasure *OUTSIDE* the Vatican!!!"

Marta stood upright, and cocked her head. Her shoulders jiggled with a small laugh. "You think good, Maria!....Okay! Everyone! The *covers come OFF!!!"*

"Sounds like fun to me!" Maria chirped. "Let's do it!"

Immediately, the purple velvet came off the treasure. Fruit crates were thrown off the truck. The golden treasure, naked to the world, was quickly loaded on the flat-bed. The Menorah, standing big as life, was squared against the back of the cab. The truck bed, framed with low side rails, had at least a little bit of containment for the rest of the treasure and people. Marta jumped into the passenger seat of the cab, and David got behind the wheel. The others rode shotgun on the truck bed.

"David," ordered Marta. "I want you to drive us *back* to the front gates of the Vatican and then east over the *Tiber*…you understand, David?…"

"Yes, yes…"

"…and then David, we will just do a circle around the center of the city…make a big show, you know…honk the horn…make a lot of noise…you understand?…"

"Yes, yes…I understand perfectly…"

"MARIA!" yelled Marta. "There is an Israeli flag in our bag. Get it out! FLY IT! Sound the horn!

LET'S ROLL! "

David laid hard on the horn and the truck lurched forward. Everyone in back had to learn instantly how to wind surf. As they careened through the turnabout, people heading for the train station stopped *live* in their tracks with their mouths wide open.

David blasted out of the turnabout into the intersection of Via Inoconzo and Via Staz Di San Pietro and drove sternly northward toward the Vatican.

The squad on the truck bed laughed and hooted at pedestrians as they roared up San Pietro keeping the Menorah braced against the cab as well as they could.

Tewahido waved the Israeli flag wildly.

With all the noise of David's horn and the yelling on the bed, Daniel couldn't hear the sirens, but he could see the lights about two hundred meters behind them. He rapped on the back window and yelled, "DOO DAH!"

Marta nodded, but didn't look up. She was frantically doing something with her camera-cell phone.

David arrived at the end of San Pietro and took a hard right. With several zig-zags through the neighborhood, he was on Via Conciliazone, the road leading straight to St. Peter's Square. Seeing the obelisk in the distance, David grunted a little laugh.

As the white truck blazed up the road, the faces of people—clerical and lay, walking on sidewalks and in passing traffic—exploded into shock. Their eyes were transfigured in a flash of gold. David's horn blared. Dozens of car horns blared back, as antiphons in a new song being made up…on the run.

Gregorio laid hands on the silver trumpets. "Hey! I wonder if these work?" he yelled through the blessed noise being joined by all the shouting, hopping, waving people of the street.

"Give it a try, dude!" bellowed Daniel.

Gregorio pursed his lips and breathed deep. With a short wind-rip of a *ba* sound, there followed a long *ruach* sound, calling upon all the people of the street.

Menelik took hold of the other horn. With David's little horn and the long silver trumpets, the shouting and the horns of the street amplified. The buildings of the street captured the wails of the horns, the police sirens, the shouting. All the sounds of human and machine, became one holy jarring blaring din covering all of St. Peter's Square.

When David got to the Square itself, he saw the Papal Apartment windows were thrown wide open.

"Look! Look!" David yelled. "They see us! They see us! Ha-Ha-Ha!" he guffawed slapping his head as if to make sure he wasn't dreaming. He stopped the truck dead in the front of the Obelisk, and leaned out the window to the crew.

"Give them a GOOD LOOK, my friends! Lift the Table up! Show them! Show them! It is why we call it the *Showbread Table!!*! Ha-Ha-Ha!!!"

Everyone on the truck roared as lions.

Behind, a police car rushed upon the truck with two others trailing several blocks back.

David gunned the engine and easily circled out of the square proceeding back down Via Conciliazone heading for the bridge over the *Tiber*. David whizzed past the two speeding blaring police cars before they could realize they were going too fast to head the truck off.

And so, David Adamsky, a common good man, reached the head of the road, took a sharp forty-five degree right turn onto the bridge, and made a bee-line over the waters to the other side, on the *Corso Victorio Emanuele*.

Papal Apartments, Vatican City.
Thursday, May 24, 8:03 A.M.

Sister Scholastica, several assistants, and the Holy Father gazed at the *Special Report* on the television monitor. Without a word, he stared blankly into the monitor with his mouth wide open.

Prime Minister's Office, Jerusalem.
Thursday, May 24, 9:03 A.M.

The aide rushed into the office. Ignoring the Prime Minister, his Defense and Security ministers, he slapped open the sliding door on the wall bookcase. Spastically, he plucked the remote and clicked the TV on.

This just in. Live, from the streets of Rome...CNN's John Josephs reporting on an amazing mysterious development in that ancient city.

That's right Rolf. Our CNN team was in the midst of taping in St. Peter's Square for a story on the Vatican, when THIS scene erupted behind us. We'll roll the tape.

The Prime minister and associates drew near the television screen. And there flashed images of a streaking white truck bearing the golden treasure. The camera then panned down the avenue behind the truck to the pursuing police cars.

Rolf, as you can see, there is a chase going on here in the streets of Rome. The white vehicle and the people aboard it...apparently clad in Catholic clerical garb...are carrying what appears to be a large golden Menorah and other objects of gold and silver...

The Prime Minister's body just started jiggling. From somewhere down in his nasal cavities came a muted hysterical whine.

His hands covered his mouth for a second and then slapped his face about.

"It appears they need a little help!" the Prime Minister laugh-snorted and fell upon his Security Minister, pushing him out the door. "Go, go, go…pick them up!" As the minister left, another aide arrived at the door.

"Sir, the White House is on the line."

"The White House is on the line? How could *this* be?!" he laughed. The Prime Minister waved the aide off. "Tell them I have an emergency!" He returned to the TV screen, wrapping his Defense Minister in a bouncing one arm hug.

"You will have to tell them *something* sometime," the Defense minister advised with a lilt in his voice.

"Oy! Fuck them. They never vote for us anyway!"

Corso Victorio Emanuele, Rome.
Thursday, May 24, 8:09 A.M.

David's truck rounded the Piazza Venezia onto Via dei Fori Imperiale.

Maria played tour guide with her hand cupped around her mouth in a faux microphone voice. "To your right you see the Roman Forum, the commercial center of ancient Rome…"

David continued in a stretch of road that had opened up in otherwise heavy traffic. He laid on the gas and horn at the same time as the crew in the back screamed,

"CHARGE!"

The rocketing truck careened into the Piazza Del Colloseo circling the great Colosseum of Rome, but was abruptly confronted by two wailing police cars forming a blockade in front of the relic.

David instantly jerked the wheel right.

Gregorio yelled, "OFF-ROAD!!!"

Maria spied an option. "SISTER!" she shouted, pointing to a small road from the piazza going into the Roman Forum.

Marta nodded and directed David. He whizzed the truck around the Arch of Constantine and made a hard right, honking at the tourists to get out of the way. He streaked down the small road to the next arched monument.

"Go right in! Go right in!" screamed Maria.
David nodded, laughing.
"WHOHOHOHO!" Daniel bellowed.
"TSIYUN MAHAR!" whooped Menelik and Tewahido.
David abruptly landed the truck in a cloud of dust underneath:

THE ARCH OF TITUS

…underneath THE stone-carved picture of

THE MENORAH,

THE SHOWBREAD TABLE,

and THE SILVER TRUMPETS.

Stunned tourists clicked their cameras wildly with gaping mouths as Maria played prize-show model caressing the latest in archaeological finds.

And then they were off.

David looped the truck through the arch and back around to the road. With a little creative maneuvering through the park grass, he circumvented another police blockade.

"OFF-ROAD!" shouted Daniel and Gregorio slapping high-fives.

And the truck easily completed its circle of Rome, turning right onto Via di San Gregorio—which indeed pleased the Franciscan, and right again onto Via del Circo Massimo, and straight over the bridge, crossing again the *Tiber,* into the *Trastevere* neighborhood of the Jews.

With *help,* the truck was seen no more.

Oval Office, Washington D.C.
Thursday, May 24, 9:33 A.M.

Chief of Staff Josh Lieker knocked rapidly on the door and barged in at the same time. His face was contorted in panic as he inserted himself in the ring of advisors huddled on opulent chairs in the middle of the room.

"Josh! Get off my damn rug. Sit down. What the hell is wrong?!"

Lieker remained standing. His eyes glossed over the judging faces of Blackpoint, Lawn Chair, Rover, and Dr. Kundorf. He could see that he had walked in on a full court jester meeting. But, he gave it no weight.

"There's been a theft at the Vatican," blurted Lieker.

The Decider laughed. "Well, Josh. Didn't know you converted...but we're kind of busy here..." he condescended with a wince and hunch-lurch forward.

Lieker abruptly slapped open his lap-top on the center table. It was a long minute for it to boot up, but soon enough, he presented a full screen photo: A white truck whizzing past the Vatican bearing what appeared to be priests and nuns showing off large golden objects.

"What the hell is *THAT,* Josh?" he hunch-lurched forward with a flash of his right hand.

Blackpoint stared point-blank into the monitor and softly seethed, "Holy shit."

"*WHAT*?! What the hell you talkin' 'bout?!"

Blackpoint looked directly at Lawn Chair and then Rover. "*THIS* is Jonah Van Meter! He pointed at the nuns on the screen. "I've seen those two bitches before!"

"Goddammit Blackie. *WHAT is it*?!!!"

"Sir. *THAT* is Van Meter's group. And *THESE* things...it's unbelievable...but these *things* are the Jewish Temple Treasure captured by the Romans two thousand years ago. The Vatican hid them for centuries. Van Meter has stolen these objects—brought them out into the open. Clearly, he intends to totally destabilize the Middle East, not to mention the entire *West*."

"*That* certainly cannot be allowed," stated Lawn Chair flatly out of the side of his mouth.

"Where did you find this image?" asked Rover.

"It's already all over the net...on at least half a dozen blogs...and even a couple mainstream net news sites. And several different shots too. These guys paraded all through central Rome this way!"

"When?" inquired Lawn Chair.

"Early this morning," replied Lieker.

Lawn Chair nodded.

They all looked to The Decider. He flash-blinked several times. "Well....Lawn Chair is right. We have to get a handle on this shit...."

Blackpoint interrupted, "Sir, we have to *confiscate* that material. The Israelis will surely use it to stir up a move to retake the Temple Mount in Jerusalem. *THAT* would strike a match for a third world war. There's no doubt...."

"Well, we should give them Jew-boys a call...no offense there, Josh. Don't you think?" mumble-mouthed the Decider.

Josh Lieker blinked. "I *did* call...They-have-not-yet-responded," he enunciated very slowly, his mental gears suddenly gyrating backwards.

"Well, call 'em up again. Don't take no shit from 'em," sputtered the Decider.

"Sir," interjected Blackpoint. "We have to root out this whole terrorist organization of Jonah Van Meter. This stunt is only a fraction of his goals. Unfortunately, we do not yet understand the entirety of his agenda."

The Decider nodded and blinked. "Do what you have to do."

The Bread House, Bexley, Ohio.
Thursday, May 24, 9:33 A.M.

Rodney Fridenmaker squealed with delight clapping his hands in front of his computer monitor.

"Are we having a party?" Geoffrey Sinclair called from down the line of monitors.

"Oh, The Rod Man likes his new eBay account!" Will Aaronson called back. "He has successfully launched his first auction! Come see!"

"Oh my GOD! Sinclair doubled over in laughter. *"That's* hysterical!"

The screen displayed an auction for a *Vintage Temple Gear Set*, using the photo Marta had taken in the Vatican Treasury. The seller *Beit Lechem* was offering the set for a minimum bid of $9.99.

Central Intelligence Agency, Langley, Virginia.
Thursday, May 24, 9:33 A.M.

Security guards hustled Elaine into the complex from her *night meeting* at the White House. She had no idea where they had taken Eduardo. As they pushed her down a dim government-gray corridor toward an isolation room, she caught glimpse, through an open door of a conference room, a television monitor bolted to the ceiling. In a split-second, she saw the cable news coverage of the white truck with the Menorah and Table.

Elaine's heart soared and her voice exploded, "WHOOOO-HOOO-HOOO!" as her fist shot to the heavens.

"LAHMA MAHAR!!!"

Lutheran Church of the Redeemer Cloisters, Jerusalem.
Thursday, May 24, 12:01 P.M.

Wal Holloway sat in an old uncomfortable vinyl chair in the hostel lounge. Various clumps of people were in different conversations. All of them, including Wal, were glued to the television coverage from Rome. Correspondent John Josephs reported that leading art historians in Rome were declaring the *Jewish Temple Treasure found*...and *disappeared*, again. In addition to the video images of the *Treasure* on the streaking white truck, blogs and mainstream outlets had also discovered an eBay auction with one very clear photograph. *Someone knew how to shop for cameras.*

Amid all the chatter and endless analysis bandied about by sudden experts, the bottom line consensus on the *Treasure* was: It was *The Real Deal.*

Wal's cell phone twittered.

"Hello."

"WAL! You've got to come home NOW!" shouted Margot Calvi.

"What? Why?" Wal answered in a half-engaged tone as he continued to watch the television coverage.

"The BABY Wal!!! I'm in LABOR! You've got to come home NOW!"

Wal, finally jolted, shot back harshly, "MARGOT! Do NOT try to command ME! That is NOT your prerogative. Get a hold of yourself. You have NO idea what I am into here...."

"Well, Wal buddy....let me tell you. You have no idea of what I am into HERE! The baby is in DANGER, Wal....I am in DANGER..."

"What the hell are you talking about, Margot?"

"I think he knows, Wal."

"Goddammit Margot! WHO knows?...knows WHAT?!"

"HUNTER....that's who! I think he knows *about us*!"

"Why do you say *that* Margot? Have you said *something?*..."

"NO! I haven't said ANYTHING. I don't know...he's just acting REAL indifferent and...mean lately...all of a sudden. A woman can tell when something's different..."

"Margot. It's just your damn hormones out of whack! Forget about it...."

"GODDAMNYOU WAL! YOU COME HOME NOW! RIGHT NOW! IT'S YOUR BABY!...IT'S OUR BABY!..."

"Margot. You're taking the *OUR* part pretty far, aren't you? *We* have an *understanding*, but *I* have a *marriage*...a pretty sorry-ass one, but it is what it is, you know?...."

"WHAT THE HELL ARE YOU TALKING ABOUT?!!! *Understanding* MY ASS! YOU SAID YOU WERE GOING TO LEAVE HER!...or did I just imagine THAT! NO! I am NOT going to do this ALONE! You get your ASS back here RIGHT

NOW! Be a MAN and take RESPONSIBILITY for own FLESH AND BLOOD!"

Wal's eyes drifted lazily back to the TV screen replaying the Menorah tape for the twelfth time.

"Well Margot, my dear. I'm afraid the stock price of *Blood* has dipped rather sharply recently."

There was silence on the other end of the line. And then, "Well, I have options too, Wal-Boy. Guess you never suspected that *Hunter works directly for the Pope?* Yeah. How do you like that, Wal-Boy? Mama Bear works both sides of the track....And I can guarantee you, Wal-Boy...you're on the wrong side...And I can guarantee you, Wal-Boy...*YOUR BLOOD* stock price is gonna CRASH! *Ka xlia ma pe tute!*"

And the line went dead.

OMAHA BEACH, Colleville-sur-Mer, France.
Thursday, May 24, 10:33 A.M.

"This is the place, my friends," stated Lazlo.

The four of them exited the car and hoofed out into the dirty golden sand.

They walked in silence, save for the waves, white capping to the shoreline in gentle roars under a sun blue sky.

Madeleine thought of her father, a soldier lucky to have not fallen on the sand. And her mother who waited for him. She remembered him working on machinery in the shop, and mother would call him to lunch...to bread she had baked.

Sara thought of the father she never knew. *Did he die terribly in his war?* Was he devoured by the *vampires?*—as her mother called them—the fighters in the streets. In silence, Sara held the hands of her God-given father and mother. She walked with her parents in that silence which conversed with the foaming sea.

Jonah thought of his father Daniel Van Meter, also a soldier who survived the war. He was a common man who struggled with an uncommon life. Jonah remembered him sitting at the kitchen table, stroking back his silver hair, trying to figure out the monthly bills with Jonah's mother.

Her name was Zara...Zara Mahar Pancasa, from a Jewish family. Daniel met her just as the war ended, as she was fleeing what had been Nazi-occupied France. She was only seventeen, but it was a war-time storybook romance. Daniel took her back to Ohio, and they started the bakery with his Army buddy Lazare. In short time, they realized the meaning of the convergence of their ancestries. But for many years, they hesitated to have children. But then again, time went by—good common time, and nothing but sweet common life came upon them. And so finally, they put war and misery behind them and Zara gave birth to Jonah in 1964.

Jonah remembered his bright life—the bakery, playing with Madeleine, school, scouts—life. And then one day in 1971, everything changed. It was a sunny afternoon. Jonah was coming back from the corner convenience store with his mother—they were walking down the sidewalk. And *Something* happened. His memory of the event was fractured, despite his ever-straining attempt to recall it. He remembered the red convertible car, and the men. He remembered loud voices, shoves, screams...and *running*. He ran... ran... ran...away. He did not know how far he ran. He remembered his father picking him up from under a tree. It was somewhere far away—blocks and blocks away from their house. A policeman was there with his father, but not his mother. She was *gone*. Absolutely gone.

From that day onward, Daniel Van Meter was obsessed with protecting his son, even as he died slowly over the years without his Zara. The only intelligence the *House* could ever muster for Daniel was that the abduction came from somewhere out of Central America. And that was it. He died a broken man—an unknown soldier.

Lazlo pointed up from the beach to the dunes. There was a path leading upward. They followed him. Midway up the dunes, amid a patch of small tamarisk trees and blackberry brambles, Madeleine stopped.

"Would it be alright if we take a rest? We've been schlepping a long time," she pleaded.

"Sure, honey," said Jonah.

As the morning sun was already hot, they took shelter under one of the small trees, and just sat on the vegetated dune looking out to the sea.

Lazlo looked at Madeleine and saw that she was very weary. Out of his shoulder bag he passed a bottled water to her, and some *matzah.*

"You should eat a little Maggid. It will make you feel better," Lazlo encouraged as he passed *matzah* and water to Jonah and Sara also.

"I think you are right, Lazlo. Thank you. You're a life saver," replied Madeleine with a soft smile.

Lazlo nudged Sara playfully on the shoulder. "*SARA* is not tired! Ha, Ha! I think she could walk another ten kilometers!"

"Yup!" nodded Sara. "I hardly *ever* get tired!"

"Well, you wait, young lady!" laughed Lazlo holding his finger up. "Someday you will have a little one pulling you all over the world making you tired."

Sarah laughed. "What? Me…have a baby? I don't think so. Well, maybe…like when I'm really old or something.

Everyone laughed. And they resumed their trek upward upon the dunes.

At the top of the dunes and through a line of trees, they entered the cemetery.

The blue sky made a surreal postcard view of a white sea of gravestones standing at parade rest in perfect linear order, row after row after row.

Nine Thousand Three Hundred Eighty Seven

Americans

dead.

They stood in silence. No word could teach a thing. The silence itself told the story. Most of the gravestones were white crosses.

Sara spotted a Star of David stone, and went directly for it. The others followed.

The stone was inscribed:

Aaron I. Miller
May 27, 1944

"Good name," said Jonah. He took *matzah* from both his coat pockets and gave it to the others. Lifting his eyes to the blue heavens he said: "As it is written:

Place your bread on the grave of the righteous...but give none to sinners."

And they went out to the four corners casting their bread among the crosses and the stars.

Going a ways westward, Lazlo drove them to the island of *Mont Sainte Michel,* also on the sea.

"Wow!" gasped Sara, as the sapphire mount rose out of the mist reaching to a noon-day sun. Encircled by a shimmering blue sea bay, the gothic city-on-a-hill appeared to Sara as a mythical blue mountain dream—a place reflecting somewhere else in the far mist of her memory.

Lazlo wowed Sara further by driving onto a thin causeway running across the bay to the mount. They parked the car at the mount base and went into the town.

The main thoroughfare into the village was a step into the ethereal. Shops and brasseries bubbled with spirited tourists traversing golden stone streets under pastel houses decorated with window boxes of morning glories.

In a minute Sara spied a restaurant at the head of the street. With no delay they settled into a table in the La Sirene Creperie. The café was merrily abuzz at the tables and its bar. Sara insisted on trying her French and ordering a variety of fruit and yogurt along with fruit drinks for everyone. Michelle, the young wait-ress, celebrated Sara's not-too-bad French by appointing Sara her *new sister.* The food and drinks came quickly. Everything was simple and rich, accented by the lilt of street musicians just outside the open café door under an easy mid-day sun.

And then Lazlo pointed. He grunted and whined with food still in his throat as he jabbed his finger like a spear at the TV over the bar.

Madeleine instantly drew her cupped hands to her mouth. "OH MY GOD, Jonah!"

Jonah's eyes just went ballistic.

The TV screen showed the *Menorah* on the speeding white truck. And the *Showbread Table*!!!

"OH MY GOD, Jonah! OH MY GOD! They did it!!! They really did it!" cried Madeleine grabbing Sara and Jonah and Lazlo into her open arms.

Sara jumped up to the bar and bounced back. "Wowwwww! That's the Showbread Table and the Menorah, Daddy?"

Jonah just nodded affirmatively. His eyes widened wildly and panned the room.

"And we'll see them when we get to Jerusalem, Daddy?"

Jonah put a shushing finger to his lips and nodded *yes* with a grin. He looked back to the TV and strained to hear the announcer:

...Next. We'll talk with a former President who warns the recovered Temple Treasure will lead to further Apartheid in the Holy Land...

Jonah threw a lunging finger at the TV.

"OH FUCK OFF! YOU FUCKING DEVIL-POSSESSED-FUCKER! ASSHOLE!"

Madeleine, Sara, and Lazlo, immediately in panic, seized Jonah back to their table, lest he go any crazier.

Lazlo hurriedly paid the bill with cash on the table.

Jonah managed a quick *Excuse my French* to the other patrons, and they were out the door....laughing.

"Jesus, Dad!" cried Sara. "So much for *When in France...!*"

"Well....sometimes, I just get pissed off! *I'm from Ohio!*"

Everyone just continued to laugh incredulously.

"Come on," said Jonah. "I've got something to show you."

Jonah led upward on an arduously steep road toward the summit of the mount. Cutting from the road to a series of upwardly winding flights of steps, they at last arrived at their destination: The Abbey Church perched on the crest of *Mont St. Michel*.

The interior of the church was a breathtaking blend of stone and light. Soaring gothic windows stood as gatekeepers of the French blue sky beyond the stone. In the chancel, approached two grey-haired nuns draped all in white. They genuflected before the altar, laying down gifts of wheat and flowers from the fields of Normandy.

Jonah led his family out of the church. Lazlo followed.

They entered a cloistered courtyard, its periphery bordered by graceful columned archways and its gardened center open to the sun-spangled sky. On the eastern side of the courtyard, the archway was without a back-wall, being open to the air. Jonah took them to the stone rail, looking out over the bay and everything beyond.

"There lies all of France we must cross over today, my dear," said Jonah lowly, taking Madeleine's hand.

"I know. We're leaving so much behind," she affirmed with a tremor in her voice.

"We are. We are leaving hopelessness behind…breaking out from it…it's an exodus…and Pharoah's chariots will follow and we shall have no mercy on them. None. We shall utterly destroy them." There was a long moment gazing out over the bay. "Come. There is one last place I wish to show you."

From the courtyard, Jonah led them into a stone hall, down a stairwell, and into yet another long stone hall, its center divided by a row of columns supporting high graceful vaults. A tour guide instructed a small group that the room once served as a guest quarters for important dignitaries. The expanse was shadowy dim, lit only by gothic windows on the ends—the glass segmented in honeycomb hexagons refracting varying shades of lavender light upon the pavestones.

At the center of the hall, in its dimmest part, there was a shadowed entryway on the interior wall. Jonah took his wife by the hand. Sara and Lazlo followed. Passing over the threshold, the light increased somewhat revealing a small barren chapel, stark but intimately elegant and slightly illumined by narrow windows. Somehow Sara and Lazlo knew to hang back at the entry way. And somehow Sara thought it better to see them framed under the arches.

Jonah took his bride to the center of the dim chapel backlit by two opaque honeycombed windows. He put his arms around her and closed his eyes as her long dark hair fell upon his arms. His mind's eye drifted to a vision…long ago…a last embrace upon the docks of Jaffa.

"This place is called *Madeleine's Chapel*," he whispered.

"Truly?" she asked with a tremor.

"Truly," he replied, their eyes drifting into each others. Smiling gently, he put her on his arm and they stepped slowly in a circle under the stone canopy. Three times they circled the chapel. Arriving again at the center, Jonah presented a plain golden ring from his pocket and held it before her. "By this ring, Madeleine Garmu Lechem bat Yeshua v'Miryam, I wish you to be consecrated to me as my wife according to the Law of Moses and Israel."

"In a church?" she blushed.

"Hmm. I call it a *stone chuppah*. And I say: We can *convert anything* God want us to convert."

Madeleine nodded with a soulful smile, and held out her hand.

Jonah placed the ring upon the finger closest to her heart. And with his heel, he smashed a glass he had stolen from the table far below the mount.

Chapter 16

Blessed are you, O Lord, who restores his divine presence to Zion.

CNN.
Thursday, May 24.

A mazing developments in Europe and throughout the Middle East today. Following the shocking apparent theft this morning of ancient Jewish relics from the Vatican, there are wide reports of large-scale movements of people throughout France and Germany today. The movements are reportedly associated with large anti-war rallies being staged in numerous cities.

In Jerusalem, tensions continue to mount. Fears are rising in the Muslim community that the resurfacing of the Jewish Temple relics sets the stage for a Jewish takeover of the Temple Mount in Jerusalem, a site long held by Muslims.

Reports also cite wide-circulating rumors that the emerging events are associated with a Jewish messianic claimant and his followers. Several leading internet blogs report that an undisclosed White House source confirms there is grave concern over the destabilizing potential of the unfolding events. The source gives credence to the rumors of a messianic claimant and indicates the claimant to be a Jewish individual from the State of Ohio in the United States..."

Jerusalem, Muslim Quarter, Old City.
Thursday, May 24, 1:30 P.M.

A young dark-skinned boy toddled up the uneven pavement of the Via Dolorosa fiercely trying to balance his tray of three Turkish coffees without stumbling. The boy passed two Israeli soldiers guarding the open metal doors to the Kotel tunnel. The archaeological passageway ran from the Via Dolorosa to the Kotel plaza where Jews pray at the Western Wall. The young soldiers lounged easy against the tunnel doors, their weapons pointed toward the ground. They took special notice of the young boy.

The boy's name was Nawar. He lived on Salahiya Street next to the Church of St. Anne. The church was not far from the Lion's Gate on the east side of the Old City, just north of the Temple Mount. Although Nawar was a resident of the Muslim Quarter, the young Israeli soldiers made a special protectorate of him because he was so abused by other youth in the neighborhood. Nawar belonged to the small *Domari* community that lived in the neighborhood surrounding St. Anne. The *Domari*, or *Dom*, were Gypsies.

Officially, the *Dom* were integrated into the Muslim community. In reality, they were not. In the Muslim Quarter, the *Dom* were held with the same contempt as Gypsies all over the world—with the same prejudices and mistrusting superstitions as to their alleged loose and mysterious ways. Jews and Gypsies had similar experience with such prejudices, and it was precisely why some leading Jews and Christians of Jerusalem had taken an interest in protecting the *Dom* and helping them preserve their culture and language. To be sure, it was a small cause. Few knew the *Dom* even existed, and even fewer would have an inkling as to their history. Of the few, were the *White Fathers*, the order which administered the Church of St. Anne. The church, an impeccably preserved Crusader structure, had been spared destruction after the Muslim conquest by the great Saladin who made it into a Muslim school. A testament to the history remained with an Arabic inscription to Saladin above the church door. Undoubtedly, the *Dom* arrived in the neighborhood with

Saladin's contingents from wars in the Transjordan—and carried with them *The Secret* about what remained hidden in that country, at Pella.

No sooner had Nawar delivered the coffee to the Arab men waiting at the portal of the *Via Dolorosa Pilgrim Shop*, than they abused the small boy.

"Yalla!" the shop owner snarled at the boy, flinging his hand in the air.

The boy flinched, but yet managed to stammer out an inquiry as to whether he could procure anything else for them.

A second man laughed and threw some coins at the boy's small feet. "Imshi! Yalla!" he yelled even louder than the first man.

Still, unbelievably, the boy tried again to sell his services which precipitated an explosive burst from the third man.

"Halass! Halass!" meaning *it is finished,* bellowed the angry man.

Suddenly, to the amusement of the nearby Israeli soldiers, young Nawar was heard by all the neighborhood as he screamed and jabbed his finger at the shopkeeper:

ENTA HALASS!...ENTA HALASS!...ENTA HALASS!!!

The boy tucked the round brass tray under his arm and stormed back down the Via Dolorosa to the café where he did odd jobs.

The Arab men roared with laughter. But, then the shop owner dispatched his older sons armed with sticks after the boy, to teach him a lesson. If not for the Israeli soldiers, who turned the pursuing boys back to their shop, Nawar would have been beaten mercilessly. And such would not have been a rare occurrence, as young toughs in the neighborhood, many of them allied with *Hamas*, often set upon the *Dom*. Indeed, older *Dom* youth were often targeted and pressured to become suicide bombers in order to prove their families' loyalty to the neighborhood. But such ploys never worked.

Nawar returned to his café, and immediately re-emerged without his brass tray. He stomped back up the Via Dolorosa with fierce determination. With a quick eye to the Jewish soldiers, the boy cut a wide and quick path around the souvenir shop and the taunts of the Arabs hanging about its door. In a shot, the boy was gone from them, running into the *suq*.

With a few zigs-zags on the darkened covered bazaar streets, Nawar came to Suq Khan ez-Zeit. The teeming avenue ran from the Damascus Gate on the north side of the Old City and became the Cardo Street in the Jewish Quarter. Midway between those points the street coursed behind the Church of the Holy Sepulcher.

As usual, Khan ez-Zeit was chock full of pedestrian traffic, mostly native Arabs and wide-eyed tourists, some trying not to succumb to calls from the shop-keepers. Amidst such a volume of important business opportunities, Nawar was never noticed. He hopped up the steps from the street behind the Holy Sepulcher to the Ethiopian quarters on its roof. There his friend, his buddy—little skinny and joyful black Mikhael was to be found.

And there on the courtyard under the strong laughing sun they played, as children do, and as children should.

White House Situation Room, Washington, D .C.
Thursday, May 24, 11:13 A.M.

Full jester-court was in session: The Decider, Lawn Chair, Rover, Blackpoint, Dr. Kundorf, and Bill Blanche. In silence they gazed at the wall of television monitors.

Continuing developments today throughout Europe and the Middle East. Reports are increasing as to massive anti-war rallies being staged in a variety of French cities. Included in the reports are stories that a Jewish messianic claimant is traveling with his followers across Northern France. The supposed claimant, a man reportedly from the state of Ohio in the United States, has been sighted in Laval, Le Mans, and Chartes being received by large crowds. Although the claimant is rumored to be headed for Paris, no reports have emerged yet placing him in that city...

Blackpoint's eyes hardened as one monitor flashed up a grainy still photo of Jonah waving from his car passing through a town with masses of people on both sides of the street.

"I am not happy Dr. Kundorf," declared Blackpoint. "Obviously you are wrong and thus our intelligence in this operation is supremely flawed. *How can this be?* At your suggestion, our agents are posted in Calais…in Paris…in Rennes Chateau….and for what? Jonah Van Meter has proceeded to none of the places you stated would surely be among his destinations…."

"Yes. Of course," replied Kundorf. "I agree with you, Mr. Blackpoint…ehh…events are troubling and disappointing." Kundorf soberly shook her head in bewilderment. "I do not, at this point, understand why Van Meter has broken off from his path of Merovingian tombs…perhaps he shall return yet to them. I do not know. But one thing I *do* know…"

"What?" demanded The Decider. "And let me…uh…hammer this thing…uh…down. We need to know somethin'," he gestured in forward hunch-lurch. "So…uh…what is it that we *do* know?...Say, Lawn Chair…Have we heard back from the Jewboys in Jerusalem?...."

Lawn Chair silently turned his head *No* with his eyes closed.

"…well, shit. So…alright, Kundorf…What is it that we *do* know?"

Kundorf swallowed hard and nodded quickly. "We know that the end of his trail is a *tomb*…the Tomb of Jesus—at which Van Meter intends to produce the remains of Jesus…."

"Where?" The Decider's hands flipped out in anger. "Where's the Tomb of Jesus?"

"Of course we do not know," Kundorf answered carefully. "This is *The Secret* that has long haunted both the Vatican and the Sovereign Order of the Temple of Sion….that this split-off family from the *Bloodline* does know…and would someday reveal the location of the *Body*. Quite possibly it would be somewhere in Jerusalem. Quite possibly. We will need to watch…and certainly I can help you there with the likely sites."

"Well, I do not like the sound of that!" Blackpoint exclaimed nervously massaging his temples. "Your *sites* have done us absolutely no good thus far."

Lawn Chair and Rover remained silent, occasionally jotting down a few notes.

Bill Blanche was also silent. His face was completely expressionless, often staring into the low ceiling of the cramped, drab and colorless room.

"You there," the Decider pointed at Blanche. "You're kind of a *guy-in-the-trenches* feller. What do *you* think about this character, Jonah Van Meter? Is he for real?...or some nut with rocks in his head?"

Bill Blanche's eyes hopped wide as the shuffling gears in his head searched for a message the Decider could understand.

"Well, Sir. As an old military guy.....the thing that stands out to me....and really alarms me is: This guy's path in France...."

"What do-ya-mean?" shot the Decider.

"Uh. Well, Sir. It's roughly the same path that Patton took in 1944." Blanche steadied his gaze on Dr. Kundorf. "Hitler was also tricked into thinking his adversary would arrive at Calais." Kundorf grimaced and squirmed retractably like a bug under an exterminator's spray.

"So what you're sayin' is...uh...this guy is....uh...fuckin' with us?"

"Big time, Sir. Big time."

"So. Uh...what's your perdiction of where these folks are headed?...Now uh, you say he's a following Patton's path...huh? So...uh. Based on that, where do you think they're a headin' for?"

"Sir. Undoubtedly, Germany," replied Blanche giving Kundorf a hard look. "At the speed Van Meter is traveling, I should think he'll cross the Rhein by dusk, their time."

"Where do you think he is now?"

"I would say somewhere between Reims and Metz, Sir."

"Blackie. We got folks in Metz?"

"No."

"Can we get some folks there?"

"Not quick enough. We'll see what we can do in Germany." Looking at Lawn Chair, Blackpoint added, "We have far more holdings there."

Lawn Chair closed his eyes and nodded affirmatively.

Metz, France.
Thursday, May 24, 6:09 P.M.

As Lazlo drove onto the bridge over the Moselle River toward the city center of Metz, Jonah felt a wave of familiarity. So many times, water crossings had been a part of the memory he bore from of old.

As the car reached the far side of the bridge, they immediately came into a huge throng sending up torrents of cheers— *LAHMA MAHAR!!!*—over and over again, with hundreds of flags—Israeli, Roma, Ethiopian, others—flocking as birds in a park around a man casting bread.

Lazlo turned left onto Avenue de Bilda—throngs lining both sides of the road. Sara, Madeleine, and Jonah in *kippah* leaned out of the car waving to the *House*—his *House*—their *House*. They turned onto Rue des Cimetieres leading to the entrance of the old Jewish cemetery of Metz.

At the ancient iron gates of the hallowed ground, Sara, Madeleine and Jonah emerged from the car to a reception committee of Hasidic men in traditional black. The committee shepherded Jonah and family through the crowd that swarmed both the interior and exterior of the gate. With not too many steps, they came to stand before the gravestone of the great teacher, Rabbi Yehonossan of Metz.

The crowd soon became silent. Jonah stepped forward and placed his finger into the engraved Hebrew letters of the Rebbes's *tziyun*.

"Shalom, Binyomin ben Yaakov Avinu," said Jonah lowly and softly.

The Hasids said, "A-mein."

Jonah turned. He gazed over a sea of people of all kinds. He addressed the people:

"My beloved brothers and sisters.

We stand at the center of the world today, between all manner of mindlessness.

We stand at the center of the world today, between all manner of humanity. A humanity descended from Love. And the question, whether many know it or not, is: Shall humanity be able to ascend to that same Love?

We stand at the center of the world today, between war and peace, between hatred and Love. And in the nervousness of the pull between these poles in opposition to each other, the world feels sick. The world feels confused and weak. The world longs for clarity of direction so that this present feeling of sickness, this inner pulling might cease.

So what of this sick feeling? Is it a evil thing? Or is it the rumblings of the full belly in late pregnancy at the dawn of the birth of a new humanity? In short, a *Change*. Yes, a *Change*. A *Change* not only in the course of humanity's history, but even more, the very essence of humanity. Our sainted teacher Martin Buber reminds us of what the Hasids of old used to say of *Change*:

The world is a spinning die, and everything turns and changes: man is turned into angel and angel into man, and the head into the foot, and the foot into the head. Thus all things turn and spin and change, this into that, and that into this, the topmost to the undermost, and the undermost into the topmost. For at the root all is one, and salvation inheres in the change and return of things.

Many in the world may ask: *How can this be?*

Many in the world may ask: *Is not war and its affliction set in stone until the last days?*

And: *Is it not true there is nothing new under the sun?*

And: *Is it really possible to crawl back into the womb to be taught again?*

These questions stand at the center of the world today between forgetfulness and memory.

As Jews, we have the gift of memory.

We remember what Hashem said to our Father Avraham. That our descendants would number as many as the stars. And do we know?—Do we know that new stars are born everyday? We catch their sparks of streaming light in the night sky, do we not? Yes. We know. This is our faith. And in our faith, we dance—even in the middle of the darkness....in the dead of night, we dance. Because of steadfast faith.

And what is our faith? Is it only trust?...a strong version of wishing and hoping against the odds?...some sort of magician's trick? Let us leave these questions hanging for a brief moment.

Today our people have reclaimed our holy relics stolen so long ago from us, as our freedom was stolen from us by cruel oppressors. So what now?

The world worries about us, *The Jews*. The world worries that we, *The Jews*, will make war by our relics. Well. Yes. We, *The Jews*, have reclaimed what is ours. Yes. But is reclamation the same as redemption? That is a question that *WE* must ask and answer for ourselves. Much of the world today says: *It is written: When THE JEWS gain their reclamation, then shall they make for war to rebuild a Third Temple.*

Oh, Really? I say: No matter what is said about us: *The Jews*...We today, *The Jews*...must...in our present moment: *Hear*! We must hear and respond to the ONE simple imposing question: *Really???*

SHEMA YISRAEL ADONAI ELOHAYNU ADONAI ECHAD

REALLY?

ECHAD?

REALLY?

Echad.

We must ask ourselves: Is *Echad*...Dayenu? Is The *ONE*...enough?

Our Sephardic brethren, I ask you: ....is El Dio....enough?

One God?

For: One Humanity?

You know. It is funny. Hillel, his memory be for a blessing, taught us that Love of neighbor was the Torah...and all the rest commentary. And Oy. Do we have commentary! We have midrash for midrash to the point that the Christians are beyond perplexed as to how any people can run a religion like this!

Truly. We are gifted, are we not? We can write a New Midrash with the click of our fingers. They destroyed our temple...we rebuilt it in our shuls, in our homes, in our hearts. They destroyed six million of us...and we rebuilt Eretz Israel out of sand and swamps.

How did we do this? Now we return to the questions of faith I left hanging a moment ago. Faith. What is Faith? Faith is this: It is *Will*...a *Will* for the *Change* the world needs...out of Love. This is what our Rebbe Yehonossan, may his memory be for a blessing, taught us. In his book *Sefer Shinuyim*...the *Book of Changes*, he teaches us that the human soul can change *ANYTHING* that was thought to be pre-destined. And in his book, the *Sefer Tikunim*...the *Book of Corrections,* he teaches us that the human soul can change *EACH* and *EVERY* situation. How is this done? It is simple: By the holy energy spark of God within us.....Love. Love changes.

It is so easy to change. Love is simple. To the hungry, give Bread...so that they might live...and love. So what if we did....just *that*? The evil ones will not know what hit them. Do you hear the winds of *Change* across the lands today? The evil ones hear. But they do not know from whence the winds come."

From Madeleine's supply bag, Jonah took the *matzah*. He held it aloft, and blessed it.

Baruch atah Adonai Elohaynu melech ha'olam hamotzi lechem min ha'aeretz.

Jonah ate the bread and passed it to the people.

"As we prepare for our Aliyah of Bread to a *New Zion,* let us meditate on the 76th psalm:

In Judah God is known, his name is great in Israel. His abode has been established in Salem, his dwelling place in Zion. There he broke the flashing arrows, the shield, the sword, and the weapons of war.

And all those gathered said, "A-mein."

Chapter 17

*Blessed are you, O Lord, whose Name is the Beneficent One,
and to who it is fitting to give thanks.*

Sovereign Order of the Temple of Sion Priory.
Zurich, Switzerland.
Thursday, May 24, 3:13 P.M.

Prescott Pierce darted mindlessly and panic stricken amid the Priory executive offices. With no rhyme or reason, he scooped reams of documents out of some file drawers, while leaving others untouched. Dumping an armload to the floor, an underling frantically fed a struggling shredder. On breathless nerves, Pierce scampered to more file caches leaking a weak hissing cry like an old junk car on its final piston.

Martin Carion gruffly barked orders to those wiring the detonators and flammables in the corners of the floor. Although the building was a rather non-descript office building, it would soon become a news report.

Carion checked his watch. "Let's Go, Pierce! NOW!"

Pierce emerged from an office, both arms full of paper. His brain was gone. He could not understand language, and could only stare at Carion with eyes reduced to horror filled black pits of confusion.

"No.....please...," whined Pierce. "We cannot leave...Why are we doing this? WHY?!"

"You FOOL! They have infiltrated everything! The Vatican has fallen like a toy soldier to them! They'll get to us next!"

"NOoooo! Not to us!...Not to us!...," wailed Pierce sobbing with his hands outstretched and pleading.

A thunderous flash of fury streaked through Carion's veins and he felt as if all his scorching blood would gush out his eyes. Seeing that Pierce had gone fetal, he grabbed the small man savagely by his neck, and pulled him to the door of the adjacent room. In an instant, Pierce's trembling body and soul was hurled through the portal, and the door slammed shut and *locked*.

Pierce jacked himself to his feet like a like a wounded camel. His nostrils flashed, sucking in wafts of sickening sweet incense swirling in the air of the large gray room that *had been* the Priory Chapel. Pierce screamed. He screamed as if to erase his life. He staggered wild eyed to a holocaust on the floor: Dozens of black-robed bodies, each with a small head wound accented by the black-scarlet of spent life, all laid in a circle, as rays from a dead sun. In the center of the circle, a solitary object: a ball of crystal upon a small wooden altar. Behind the altar, as if it fell off, a broken wine glass and its former contents laid sprayed in tiny bits of bloody crystal on the floor. Across the front of the altar was engraved in red:

"Non nobis, Domine, **non nobis"**

Then all four corners of the room exploded to hell fire.

Gemelli Hospital, Rome.
Thursday, May 24, 3:13 P.M.

His Holiness held onto the side-rails of the bed as he gazed over the struggling body of his *helper*. Sister Scholastica's breaths were very shallow. He took her hand. It was cold with clammy sweat. Her heart was grinding down to an eventual stop.

A nurse arrived at the bedside. "Sister?...it's Jael...," said the nurse, softly calling on the woman's fading consciousness. The nurse went about taking routine vital signs. Her patient's face made no overt response beyond the rapid flittering of closed eyelids in the last attempts at control, trying to ride out the arcs of pain.

Suddenly, Sister Scholastica's hand jutted out and grabbed his arm.

"You-must-stop-them," managed the dying woman in slow torturous enunciations and breathless puffs.

"I cannot, my dear." A tear fell from his eye to her hand. "They are too many. I am afraid that we are learning that God's *Will* can surprise even us…perhaps, *especially* us. We have meant well, yes? To defend our Holy Church from her enemies, yes? But, in these last days, my dear, there is something *new*…something different. Great care is needful…so that *we* do not become our own enemy and the Church find itself on the wrong side of history. We must, I am afraid, stop ourselves rather than stop others, so that we might see which way the Spirit of God is blowing in the world."

"You…," she labored. "…can still…stop…them."

He took a small silver flask engraved with the *Chi Rho* symbol and poured golden olive oil onto his hand. Making the sign of the cross upon her forehead with the oil, he prayed,

Through this holy anointing may the Lord in his love and mercy help you with the grace of the Holy Spirit.

He took her hands into his, and he was deeply moved. He cried through the words:

May the Lord who frees you from sin, save you and raise you up.

And he left her.

White House Situation Room.
Thursday, May 24, 2:09 P.M.

Ashman Blackpoint, Bill Blanche, and Professor Kundorf huddled about the round table engaged in a high level phone conference.

"The subjects are heading toward Saarbrucken Bridge," came the squawking transmission.

"Yah!" exclaimed Dr. Kundorf. "You are most excellent, Mr. Blanche. I must say: You were very correct that Jonah Van Meter shall enter Germany." Turning to Blackpoint, she advised, "You must give this man a raise in his pay, Mr. Blackpoint. You have a most excellent and intelligent minister in him!" The charlatan patted Blanche's hand as if to bestow endorsement from a credentialed expert. Blanche's stomach squeamed in tandom with his *buzz off* look at her leather-skin face.

"Where are they?" called Blackpoint to the voice.

"Jesus Christ! They stopped right in the middle of the fucking bridge!" the speaker squawked.

"What?! What the hell are they doing?"

"They're throwing something off the bridge into the Rhein."

Blanche gave Blackpoint a hard look.

"They have guards?" asked Blackpoint quickly.

"Oh yeah. There's a shit load of people on the bridge...the traffic is all fuckin' backed up...you got a bunch of black hat Jew-kikes out their rockin' and rollin' with their books out...it's a goddamn circus! And they got their darkie friends on all the corners of the goddamn bridge...."

"They'd be armed?"

"Oh yeah....it'd be a firefight....with a lot of collateral.."

"Stand down....wait."

"Aye, aye. Out."

Blackpoint heaved a gritted sigh rocking his chair back and rubbing his eyes. He slapped the round table.

"Well. They're headed for Mannheim. I have a report there's going to be a massive anti-war rally there...." Blackpoint checked his watch. "...in about an hour."

"Patton died in Mannheim," stated Bill Blanche with an expressionless stare into the gray space of the underground room devoid of natural circulating air.

"Well," mused Blackpoint. "Perhaps we should accommodate the parallel."

Saarbrucken Bridge, Rhein River.
Thursday, May 24, 9:09 P.M.

As the sun began to sink and cast shadows against the drab non-descript city and the massive gathering of people upon the bridge, Jonah thought it a kindness. Sara must have agreed.

"Kind of looks a lot like Ohio, Daddy," quipped Sara.

"Yeah…it's probably not big on the bus tours…probably why my ancestors hid out in these parts for awhile way back when. But. We are here for a Shavuot Blessing. We shall make this place better, huh? Would you like to do the honors dear?"

Jonah handed *matzah* to his daughter and his wife. As they hurled the small pieces of bread over the bridge down upon the Rhein, Jonah prayed loudly and strongly,

"GOD WILL AGAIN BE MERCIFUL UNTO US; GOD WILL SUPPRESS OUR INIQUITIES; AND WILL CAST ALL THEIR SINS INTO THE DEPTHS OF THE SEA."

Immediately fish from the depths and birds of the air took to the Bread.

Jonah embraced his wife and daughter. "Happy Shavuot, my dears."

"Happy Shavuot, *Abba*," replied Sara.

And all those assembled on the bridge shouted, "A-mein!"

The entourage of vehicles arrived in Mannheim in full darkness. Lazlo cruised at an even speed from the east toward the city-center. They passed through some very Americanized neighborhoods. Many signs were in English and shop windows advertised all manner of familiar American brand goods. It was somewhat an American colony due to the US military bases just outside the city.

They arrived at the city-center called *Market Square* to the sound of public address speakers bantering with a very loud and exuberant crowd. In ordinary times, there was not much of interest about the square, its main attraction being an old stone water tower. But this night, the square was electrically alive with all the ambiance of a rock concert. Roving spot lights flashed over the crowd from the high scaffolding of a large outdoor stage. Huge speakers on the sides of the stage blasted out recorded music of diverse genres—reggae and klezmer bands...Ziggy Marley and Arlo Guthrie...New Orelans Jazz...or John Lennon. Protest signs waved everywhere in the crowd and off the stage scaffolding: FIGHT THE WAR ON WAR....THE LAST TIME WE LISTENED TO A BUSH, WE WANDERED IN THE DESERT FOR 40 YEARS.

The Hasidic Jews and the Roma in Jonah's troupe looked as though they did not know what to think. And Jonah kept his eyes intently on the crowd, studying it face by face. He had a very nervous feeling. A clump of signs in the back of the crowd spiked his concern :

VICTORY TO THE IRAQI RESISTANCE!...

PALESTINE WILL BE FREE FROM THE RIVER TO THE SEA!

At the backside of the stage, Jonah pulled Madeleine and Sara aside under its support scaffolding.

"I have a real bad feeling in my gut about this," fired Jonah to Madeleine.

She winced looking over Jonah and Sara to Lazlo and his men.

Sara's eyes went wide picking up that, despite the party of song and frisbees in the air, something ominous was at hand.

"Look bad?" Madeleine demanded of Lazlo.

He nodded affirmatively. "We *are* in Germany. What did you expect?" he answered matter-of-factly with a flip of his hand. He waited for her response.

"Sara, stay here with Lazlo," Madeleine instructed. "Jo-Jo, let's look at this and think about it for a minute."

Madeleine pulled Jonah by the hand and they proceeded quietly up the back stairs of the stage to the top of its platform. They took a position on the side of the stage in darkness behind the huge speakers. The sound system blasted slogan-chants led by a hysterical woman in the spotlight at the podium. About her shoulders was draped a checkered red and white Palestinian kafiyah and her fist thrusted rhythmic punches into the air. The crowds, entranced by strident calls and flickering colored lights upon their hopes and fears in the night, returned waves of shouts to the speakers.

"I am not sure night rallies in Germany are a good idea," stated Jonah in a tone of the obvious. A gentle hand from behind fell on Madeleine's shoulder and then Jonah's.

"FAITH!" Madeleine embraced her friend tightly. Destiny gave Jonah a little finger wave and a hug.

"Looks kind of freaky out there Maddie…," confided Faith.

"Yeah. Jonah and I are trying to size this thing up…*little miss Hamas* here isn't giving us a whole lot to work with…" Madeleine rolled her eyes toward the spastic human bull horn at the podium.

"Yeah. And we got *Company* too." Faith added.

"Of course…" Madeleine nodded.

"How do you know?" asked Jonah.

"I see the men I saw at the round church, Jonah," explained Destiny in a nutshell.

Jonah nodded without a word and cast his eyes out toward the crowds, especially upon the pockets of Palestinian protest signs. "Uhhhh. Let's just not do this. We should leave," declared Jonah. "My Jewish radar is all jacked up."

"Where are the bad ones you've seen, Destiny?" asked Madeleine.

The girl pointed to the back right corner of the teaming, churning square.

While Madeleine could not pick the individuals out against the near stage lights and the dark corners of distance, she got the general idea of their position. Without further word, she walked deliberately out to the podium and removed the cordless microphone from its podium receptical leaving the Palestinian woman literally speechless. Madeleine did not hear, or perhaps heed, Jonah's whispered shreiks for her to return to him. The square fell silent, save for a gentle breeze against the trees in the night.

Thus spake Madeleine Garmu Lechem Van Meter bat Yeshua v'Miryam:

"*This* is not right. That we should meet in the night with loudness and wide eyes. This is not right. That we should bring even our children into the dark to hear tales of wars and rumors of wars. This is not right. That we throw our closed fists to the heavens which ask us instead, to open our minds.

This is not right. This is not what the night is for. Night is for sleeping and sleeping well. Night is for rocking babies to lullaby music.

You say: That you want peace. Really? Then, if you truly want peace, I want you to do something. I want you to *pray*. And I want you to pray all night. Here. Pray here until the morning light. For only then, in God's morning sun, will you be able to speak the word *Peace* as it was meant to be spoken...to your neighbor...to your lover...to your child...at the beginning of a *new day*. So, I want you to pray. You do not need to worry about the words. You have brought children out here tonight, and they have heard your words of war. Now. I say to you....I want you to ask your children what a prayer for peace should sound like. And whatever they tell you...that is the prayer I want you to pray...all night...until the morning comes."

A lull hovered for a moment in the warm night air over the park. Then a cry shot up from the middle of the crowd:

ZIONIST BITCH!

JEW-KIKE!

Jonah immediately bolted out and grabbed Madeleine by the arm. "Come on, let's go!" he ordered.

She violently jerked her arm from his grip and turned square to face him.

"NO! In the Name of MY son, I WILL NOT be silent! MY son! His name was DANIEL! In the Name of MY son, you WILL relent!" The fire scorching from her soul blasted Jonah backwards into the dark arms of his daughter Sara. Madeleine stormed to the podium and cast a cold eye over the darkness. She spoke again, her voice streaming out of the speakers stridently and controlled:

"I have been told....I have been told that there are people here tonight not interested at all in peace. I have been told....that there are people here tonight who intend to *act* on that non-peace. And they intend to act in this very place. Well. When in Germany....."

Never taking her eyes off the crowd, Madeleine removed in smooth and deliberate motion all her clothes and made herself naked. She brushed back her long dark hair and arrayed it about her soft shoulders. The ancient leather *tefila* hung round her neck between her breasts. Lyrically she descended the steps into the crowd. She was fully conscious and fully intentional in the throwing sway of her thighs, her hips, and her still full brimming breasts, to one side of the sea of people and then the other. And for them, she floated as a sepia-tone ghost under the same moon which served as witness to the cries of the naked of all generations before the abyss. Over the expanse of souls she found the evil ones in the far corner and stood herself before them. She stretched out her graceful arms from her breasts with her hands open to the heavens. And said she:

"You, Warriors of Blood...We stand now at the edge ...at the edge of the sword you have always longed for. How fitting for you, yes? To be granted your desire: To shoot a Jew properly so she may fall back into the pit. Where will you shoot me? In my face? My mouth? My eyes? In my heart, between my breasts filled with Jewish milk? Or...with the logic of your kind, in my belly from whence Jews come? Decisions...Decisions..."

The evil ones stood still. Only their eyes flittered above their out-of-place overcoats in the warm night air.

"Or will you shoot me first?" said Faith, stepping forward out of the dark, naked herself, and locking her arm into Madeleine's.

"Or will you shoot me first?" said Destiny, stepping forward naked and trembling and fierce-eyed to take Madeleine's other arm.

An old Hasidic man stepped forward, naked. "Will you shoot me first?"

A young man in a wheel chair rolled forth naked, his legs missing from war, calling "Will you shoot me first?"

A young naked Gypsy mother holding her baby called, "Will you shoot us first?"

And there rose up all manner of naked voices from the pit, young and old, calling *Will you shoot us first?*, one after the other.

And the evil ones had no answer. And they departed immediately into the night beyond the city.

And there stood Jonah at a distance with strong arms around his daughter Sara. And he lifted his eyes to the heavens and said:

> *My dove, my perfect One, is only One*
> *the darling of her mother,*
> *flawless to her that bore her.*
> *The maidens saw her and called her happy;*
> *The queens and concubines also*
> *And they praised her.*
> *Who is this that looks forth like the dawn,*
> *Fair as the moon, bright as the sun,*
> *Terrible as an army with banners?*

Morning came.

And they entered into the country of France again and traveled most the day until they came into the city of Saintes Maries de la Mer.

A great Gypsy festival was being celebrated there to remember the day so long ago when Mary called The Magdalen arrived in France from the Holy Land with the girl the Gypsies call Saint Sara Kali. Throngs of people were found dancing and singing in the streets from all over France and beyond. Gypsy and Gadje alike twirled with each other, arm in arm, in bright colored clothes and smart stepping shoes to the thin joyous spirit music under a benificent sun.

The town folk received them warmly at the center of the city and escorted them to the Church of the Maries wherein lies the shrine of St. Sara Kali. The ancient church appeared as a stone ship amidst the sea of the city. The people filled the pews end to end. And the nave fell silent as *she* processed alone through the center aisle. The dark slight figure of Sara Kali Van Meter ascended the pulpit and pulled the chain on the reading lamp.

Sara's thin strong voice rang out:

"A Reading from the book of Ruth:

And Ruth said to Naomi: Entreat me not to leave you or return from following you; for where you go I will go; and where you lodge I will lodge; your people shall be my people, and your God my God; where you die I will die; and there I will be buried. And when Naomi saw that she was determined to go with her, she said no more. And they came to Bethlehem at the beginning of the barley harvest."

And Sara said:

"My father is Jewish. My mother is Jewish. I am Jewish. A brave man, named Daniel Pearl, said that just before he was killed. Because he was a Jew.

They have killed a lot of Gypies too, just for being Gypsies. My parents have taught me the Gypsy saying, *Na Bister 500,000.* It means: *Remember* The 500,000 Gypsies that were killed by the Nazis.

Some Gypsies are Christians and some Gypsies are Muslims. I do not know how many Gypsies are Jews, but I am. And I know that to killers, Gypsies and Jews are about the same.

My father and mother have told me the story of how they fell in love. It was because their parents owned a bakery together. When they were kids, every morning my father and mother got up very early to help their parents make the bread for the day. As my father and mother worked together, they fell in love with each other. They were always happy looking forward to making more bread tomorrow. Because my mother is Jewish plus being Gypsy, one day I asked her if there was a difference between Jewish bread and Gypsy bread. She said to me: *Bread is Bread.*

And that is all I have to say."

Father Jacques, the priest of the church, greatly moved, proceeded to the altar tabernacle and removed from it the consecrated Bread. He gave it to Sara and said, "By the Spirit of the One God, where you go, we will go."

The people of the church rose and gave thunderous applause sounding like a thousand lions. And they took Sara down to the shrine below the church. In that place stood a small black statue of St. Sara Kali surrounded by lighted candles of every color. Strong Gypsy men mounted the statue on their shoulders, while others did likewise with Sara.

And a great and happy throng processed out of the church and through the sun drenched streets down to the docks where there awaited a boat. And the Jews of the city proceeded also to the docks singing Psalms.

On the boat already were the Sisters, Maria and Marta. Quickly, Sara, Madeleine, Jonah, and Lazlo boarded the vessel.

The crowds lined the docks shouting LAHMA MAHAR!!! to the music of accordian and fiddle and hurling of all manner of bread to the glistening water about the boat.

Like a dream in the blue day sun, Madeleine felt herself float away from the docks. The people shouted *"Dzan Devlesa"* which means *Good-bye* in the Romani tongue. And Madeleine waved to them calling *"Achen Devlesa!"* As the water gently rocked the boat, Madeleine became aware of her husband and her daughter and their arms about her...*with her...all together.* And it occurred to her that,...at last, things were becoming right. And she looked up to the blue sunned heavens and said: *"Nais tuke O Del"*, which means *Thank you God.*

Maria, Marta, and Lazlo began to sing an old Jewish song of the sea, *Mi Chamocha.*

And when they could see the city of Saintes Maries de la Mer no more, they set their faces toward Sicily, where they would rest, before their final journey home.

Chapter 18

Blessed are you, O Lord, who blesses his people Israel with peace.

Israeli Air Space.
Saturday, May 26, 3:33 P.M.

The ROMAR 727 from Sicily approached the coast of Israel, and Jonah watched the escort Israeli F-16 Sufas peel off for their bases. He had been to Israel several times, but Madeleine and Sara had never before set eye on the Land. In wonder, they pressed their foreheads to the windows as the plane began its descent over a dream of rocks and scrubland bordered by a golden shore under a sun blue sky. The plane banked sharply as it dropped in preparation for landing at Ben Gurion Airport. As Jonah scanned the approaching terrain, suddenly his eyes flashed.

"There! Look!" Jonah pointed down toward a small harbor.

Madeleine saw. She caught sight of the outlying rock reef and the boats docking below a village of palm trees and pale saffron-colored houses cropped upon a mount.

"Oh, Sara! Jaffa!" she breathed in awe.

And they wrapped their arms around each other.

As the plane began its final descent to the Land—all the more, its sanded gold married to a blue horizon flooded the portals of the aircraft. Hasids in the front seats broke out in jubilant song—*Yerushalim Shel Zahav* which means *Jerusalem Of Gold.* Jonah was enraptured to be with Madeleine and Sara in their *aliyah* to Israel. Second by second, they measured the closing hovering distance between the wings and the Land. And with a bump, they were there. *Zahav.*

Jerusalem.
Saturday, May 26, 3:39 P.M.

Sabeel Khouri and Wal Holloway stood at the pinnacle of the bell tower of the Lutheran Church of the Redeemer. They gazed out over the Old City to the Temple Mount. Behind the Mount, below its eastern wall, was the dry and rubble strewn Kidron Valley, the site of several imposing and ancient Jewish funerary monuments. The valley, essentially a barren dirt path some 25 meters wide, ran south to the rough scrabble Palestinian village of Silwan. Above the Kidron rose the Mount of Olives in forest green splotches of olive and cypress trees out of which jutted various Christian shrines including the exotic Church of Mary Magdalene with its seven golden onion-shaped domes. On the more southern flank of the Mount of Olives laid the great and ancient Jewish Cemetery where tradition long held that the dead shall arise when the Messiah enters Jerusalem from the Mount. It was not Sabeel Khouri's favorite story of Jerusalem.

"You've seen the reports on the Priory disaster in Zurich?" asked Wal, venturing into the obvious to see where he stood in the scheme of things…or even if there was any scheme left at all.

"Yes. Of course. It is quite clear that we…how you say?…we are on our own, yes? We shall need your help Pastor Holloway. Are you willing?"

"Of course," replied Wal automatically, a bit surprised at the sudden exchange. He instantly appraised the situation as a new opportunity to find his way…or any way, that might redeem something of his former dreams.

"This man, Jonah Van Meter…You know him well, yes?" asked Khouri.

"Indeed. I know him." Wal nodded seriously. "I am related to him. I grew up in the same neighborhood and church with him. My grandfather taught me the history of his family and their betrayal of our ancestral family going back to the Merovingians.

"Yes…," said Bishop Khouri slowly and thoughtfully. "I recall you referring to some of these things…but tell me, pastor.

You say that your grandfather taught you…but what of your father?"

"He died when I was in high school. Heart attack. Heart problems run in the family. I don't remember my father very much."

"Yes, of course. I understand," replied Khouri. "But, a man cannot live in the past. So, let us speak of the present, my friend. You know this Jonah Van Meter. What kind of man is he?"

Wal's eyes rolled upward as he struggled for a concept by which to answer the question. "Jonah…" Wal slowly rolled out his thought. "….is a man…who, if he had his way, would just live in some remote area with a calm little life…and no one would ever hear or know of him. He would be happy just to pass on his little family *Secret* to the next generation and be done with it.…"

"So, what you are saying is that we have awakened a sleeping lion ….eh….foolishly encroached his territory?"

"Yes. I am afraid so," said Wal matter-of-factly.

"So you say…that Jonah would like to live…a simple life, yes?"

"Yes. But, he cannot."

"Why?"

"Because he is religious…in a childish way. He wants all the world to be as he is. He believes that people can actually choose to live simply…as they say in college philosophy classes….live *authentically*.…"

"Ah yes, the *authentic* living ones. They are the ones the girls like, yes?"

"I suppose." Wal shrugged. "He does give off a certain smug moral superiority…the kind you get with a lot of women who are always squawking about saving children and feeding the hungry masses…and so….you know what I am saying?"

"Yes, of course. Socialists without arms," mused Khouri.

"Yes…your basic liberal Jew."

"Tell me, Pastor Holloway. You are of the same Blood as Jonah. Why are you not a Jew as he is?"

"Well. Jonah and I are not really of the *exact same Blood*. He has actually *betrayed* our Blood. Indeed, he simply rejects the very idea of Blood as a basis for anything. He will not even drink wine because, for him, it is a symbol of Blood. So. He has his own little theme of Bread....the *Bread of the masses*, if you will."

"Oh. So, he *is* a child!....a sentimental child!" Khouri laughed and shook his head. "We *should* be able to easily defeat such immaturity, yes? You and I, Pastor Holloway....we will need to be the adults now."

"How do we do that?" Wal was direct.

"It depends on what Van Meter himself chooses to do, my friend. So, now. I ask you in a very certain way. What kind of man is this Jonah Van Meter? What is it that he intends to do?"

"That's simple. He intends to *end Christianity* by revealing the remains of Jesus."

"Van Meter knows where the Tomb of Jesus is?"

"Yes." stated Wal.

"Yes....tombs and more tombs. Your Jonah Van Meter appears to be interested in many tombs," observed Khouri, walking around the parapet of the bell tower deep in thought. He looked down over the ledge upon the Ethiopian chapels on the roof of the Holy Sepulcher. A wincing grimace came to his face. He noted the pitched tent, and the increased activity on the rooftop. *Something* was going to happen.

"Pastor Holloway. I have a question for you."

"Yes, Mr. Khouri?"

"You say that Jonah Van Meter intends to end Christianity by revealing the bodily remains of Jesus Christ. Would you say that he is a man given....eh....to using symbols?"

"Yes. I believe so."

"Well then. *Tomorrow* could well be his day. Tomorrow is *Pentecost*. If one seeks to end Christianity...what more appropriate day than the Holy Day of Pentecost?....the birthday of the Christian Church? Yes?"

Wal nodded. "Yes, Mr. Khouri. It makes sense. I believe that Jonah will strike tomorrow."

"Yes. We will be prepared," stated Khouri resolutely. He shook his head. "What fools...these Jews! They actually think they are going to retake the Temple Mount!...How?...By waving around their precious golden candle holder and some old bones?

They think *this* will stir the Jewish passions for triumph among all their brethren...so much...that it will *assure* them victory? They believe once the world sees that Christianity is dead and Islam humiliated, *then* the course of history will be set for them to take their final victory...to rebuild their Temple on the ashes of destroyed Arab and Christian culture? Yes, this is their plan....Well. I tell you. It is nothing more than a hope...a false hope, my friend. We shall utterly crush them.

Let me tell you something, Pastor Holloway: We have many brothers waiting for battle here in the Muslim and in the Christian quarters, *AND* in the streets outside the Old City. Yes. They will defend the Temple Mount. They will. And yes. Undoubtedly, the Jews will attack. Yes, they will attack. They will come down from their Quarter, and they will come down from the Mount of Olives. They will try to close in on us from both sides. But, ah! We are ready. We are very ready, Pastor Holloway, my friend. We see everything clearly here, yes? We have perfect observation here at Redeemer Church and also at our Augusta Victoria Hospital on the Mount of Olives. But...we shall not attack them from the hospital. No, that would be too soon. We will wait until they come down from their heights. We have, I tell you, many brothers in Silwan waiting. When the Jews come down from the Mount of Olives.....our brothers will stream through the Kidron Valley, you see?...and crush them at the bottom of the Mount of Olives. And when the Jews attack from their Quarter, our brothers will flood down from the Mount itself and slaughter them. They will never ascend to the Mount. They will not. You will see my friend....tomorrow is our big victory over the Jews and your Jonah Van Meter. Yes, you will see. Now. I want you to promise me one thing. It will be your contribution to our heroic cause, Pastor Holloway."

"Yes. Mr. Khouri. What is it?" blurted Wal suddenly struck by a sense of calling.

"If you have opportunity, you yourself must confront Jonah Van Meter. You must remind him...face to face...of what you did to his son....what you did to his wife....what can be done to his adopted daughter that he has spent so much money on...You know the Jews hate to lose on investments. Yes? You must

strike terror in his soul...and he will fall, because he is a Jew. A
Jew loves life too much, and it makes him weak. Yes?"

"Yes," said Wallerund DuBois Holloway.

Tel-Aviv-Jaffa, Israel.
Saturday, May 26, 5:15 P.M.

Jonah rented a small *Fiat* at Ben Gurion Airport and happily
sped across the scrub and rubble terrain up toward Jerusalem.
Highway 1, also known as Jaffa Road, provided Madeleine and
Sara their first exciting experience of the Land itself. While the
road was modern, it seemed not very wide. Every human-made
thing—every gas station, irrigated farm, small town or village,
road sign in Hebrew, or guard rail—all seemed rather exceptional against the untamed rock-strewn fields under a strong
clear sun. It seemed as if all these human creations gratefully
accepted their appointed lots upon a hallowed ground—their
landlord.

As the *Fiat* approached the outskirts of Jerusalem, Sara was
awed by the many tall apartment buildings. Construction cranes
hovered over the skyline. And even though the towering edifices
were obviously modern, their *Jerusalem Stone* gave off the same
golden cast as the much older and smaller dwellings below.

"We will live in one like those." Jonah pointed at the buildings. "Can you imagine the view from their tops?"

"Cool!" was Sara's response.

"I can imagine, Jonah. I can imagine. I love you so much."
Madeleine kissed him, and she felt the *tefila* around her neck
sway upon her heart.

Jaffa Road ran straight into central Jerusalem. Although traffic was light and the streets quiet due to Shabbat, Madeleine and
Sara instantly knew that they were not in Ohio anymore. As the
Fiat proceeded through tidy neighborhoods that were at once
Mediterranean and Jewish, Sara took note of the palm trees, and
the shop windows with bright-colored girl clothes, and garish
movie posters in Hebrew on kiosks, and Jewish families walking

slowly on Shabbat—their fathers wearing *kippot*. Looking at her own father with *kippah*, she was suddenly struck that *here* it was not at all out of place, not exotic, but *ordinary*, and she was amazed at the thought of being *ordinary* in such a wonderful place. And when the *Fiat* passed the Sbarro pizza place and then a Chinese restaurant, Sara blurted, "Cool!"

When the top of the Old City's wall came into view, both Madeleine and Sara gasped. The wall's mystical and timeless stones beckoned their souls. Jonah's *Fiat* came to the five-point intersection at Jaffa Road and Ha-Tzanhanim. He pointed to an old building which once served as Jerusalem's City Hall, the stone of its top floors still riddled with bullet holes. Beyond the intersection, lay a grand concourse running alongside the Old City wall to a terminus: The ethereal arched portal of Jaffa Gate. Behind the gate rose the fortress of David's Tower and its minaret from a former time under Muslim rule, long ago.

Jonah proceeded to an underground car-park near Jaffa Gate. They would enter the Old City on foot, the old fashioned way.

Ascending steps from the car-park, the Van Meters came to a wide walk leading to the ancient Jaffa Gate. Not far out from the portal, sat a poor disheveled Arab woman with her three children playing about. The woman's hand was stretched out, muttering pleas for help in a low staccato voice. Sara, instantly moved, delved into her purse. Madeleine and Jonah did likewise.

They arrived under the arch of Jaffa Gate, its height soaring and its lintel adorned with chiseled Muslim medallions on the neatly cut stones. On the side of the arch, Jonah found the old cast iron mezuzah, tilted inward and upward. Above the mezuzah were Hebrew words and a menorah symbol painted primitively in white.

"Can you read the words for us, Sara?" asked Jonah, touching the mezuzah.

She squinted at the words, some of which had quite worn letters. But quick enough she said, "Oh. Yeah. *Shema Yisrael Adonai Elohaynu Adonai Echad.*"

"A-mein," said Jonah.

"A-mein," said Madeleine.

And they entered the L-shaped Jaffa Gate striding three-abreast, holding hands. Jonah covered his left eye and recited the Psalm:

I rejoiced when they said unto me: Let us go into the House of the Lord.

Out of the gate, they strode the wide walk alongside a stone paved road filled with people and cars going in and out of the Old City. The road entered the wall adjacent to the gate through a more modern portal made by Kaiser Wilhelm in the 1890s. Streams of Jews, Arabs, and tourists from all over the world walked in clumps of families and friends. They made their way along the walk and the road which, despite the cars, was one large and open way to pedestrians. On the right side of the road, stood the high walls of the ancient fortress of David's Tower, alternatively known as The Citadel. The structure bore a long and varied history, having been a headquarters of disparate rulers throughout the centuries, including Pontius Pilate. Now, the Israeli flag waved from its upper-most point. Beyond the Tower's walls, the road opened into a square-like plaza with a variety of Arabesque Victorian shops, cafes, and hotels outlining the north and east edges of the square opposite the Tower. The path of the road within the square lay between the Jewish side of the Tower and the Arab side of the shops and hotels. In the middle of the square, the road made a right-hand turn and proceeded on through the Armenian Quarter toward Zion Gate and Mt. Zion beyond it.

"Look Daddy!" exclaimed Sara pointing to the Arab side of the road. On the sidewalk stood a stout Arab man behind an old green wooden wagon mounted on bicycle wheels. The lower wood cabinet of the wagon was surmounted by a glass bakery case full of fresh sesame-seeded bread in long oval rings. The time for *matzah* was ended.

"*Marhaba. Kum hada?*" asked Jonah pointing to the bread.
"Three Shekel," replied the Arab man in English.
Jonah laughed. "Is my Arabic bad?"

"Is okay," the man shrugged with a slight smile. "Thank you very much, my friend."

"*Shoo kran,*" replied Jonah.

The man smiled slightly again.

Jonah, Madeleine, and Sara went across the road to the Jewish side where there was a low retaining wall in front of the Tower to sit upon, eat bread, and watch people go by. Sara said the blessing, and they just sat there in wonderment that they were really eating Bread in Jerusalem.

Back across the road, behind the bread man, stood an elegant shabby Victorian hotel. Three stories high, *The New Imperial Hotel* was a sepia-tone postcard view from another time. Its two top floors were graced by tall white veranda doors opening to balconies adorned by scrolling wrought-iron railings. At the street level, the hotel hosted several Arab cafes and food stands out of which wafted rich aromas of roasted meat and spiced coffee. From the cafes rose a din of spiraling Arab music and the sharp tones of street-men, their voices bantering over sport and money.

"Come," said Jonah. "There are some people waiting to meet us."

Taking Madeleine and Sara by their hands, Jonah led them across the road, around the right corner of the hotel and down a narrow side street. Within a few paces he brought them to the hotel's modest canopied entrance. Entering the foyer, they found themselves transported back in time, to the year 1898, when Kaiser Wilhelm made his famous trip to Jerusalem and lodged at the *New Imperial*. The ceiling soared over a central chandelier and rich red carpeting leading up a grand white-spindled staircase. Even with peeling paint and frayed antique wallpaper, the still stately Victorian hall gave a suggestion of how even bygone imperialisms might age with grace—by letting go of their emperors and keeping their corded curtains.

Ascending the staircase, they came to a broad open hall serving as a lounge adorned in shabby Victorian decor. At the right end of the hall Jonah presented himself at the registration office window and asked the attendant to ring one of the rooms. While she dialed, Jonah surveyed the small office cluttered with paperwork and stacks of towels. On the back wall, he noted a cheery bulletin board full of postcards from all over the world.

Jonah returned to the hall-lounge where Madeleine and Sara relaxed on an oriental divan. They were admiring a beautiful chandelier suspended from a vaulted ceiling fatigued by peeling paint.

Suddenly, a door opened on the opposite end of the hall. An older American-looking woman with long white hair entered the lounge-hall. In white Capri pants and a green sleeveless blouse, she had the easy-look of a romantic soul who had found her *Casablanca* a distant memory ago.

"OH MY GOD!" gasped the white-haired woman with an Ohio accent. "JONAH!" She clapped her hands over her mouth, and hopped-skipped to throw her arms around him. Then, looking up and down the hall, she lowered her voice to a dim gravel, "I guess, I shouldn't be so loud, huh?!" Continuing in her low voice, she turned to Madeleine and Sara. "And Oh, My God, you are Maddie...and you are sweet Sara...I am so glad to finally meet you...you're every bit as beautiful as Jonah has always told us." The grandmotherly woman kissed both of them with a tear in her eye.

"I'm sorry," said Jonah to his family. "Let me introduce you to Patricia. I've known Patricia and her husband George for ...what?...fourteen years, now? A noble woman she is...and a *Buckeye* to boot!...Came here as a nurse straight out of OSU back in the '60's and never looked back! Patricia trains nurses for many of the NGOs around the country...."

"Call me Pat my dears...Jonah is often too formal!"

"We call Daddy *Jo-Jo* a lot!" chimed Sara.

"I call him *Yo-Yo*!" called a sudden gruff voice coming through the door at the end of the hall. Toward them waddled a short and stocky balding Arab gentleman, grinning ear to ear.

"George! You old farmer! Man, it's good to see you!" cried Jonah in a muffled tone.

"And you, my friend." George slapped Jonah's bicep and hugged him. Turning to Madeleine and Sara, he exclaimed, "And my goodness, what pretty girls you bring! You are a lucky man, my friend. A lucky man!....Yes, Hello. I am George Lamsa. I am an old friend of Jonah for a very long time. I am most pleased to meet you...after all of the things I have heard about you...good things, yes!"

Madeleine and Sara responded with demure *thank-yous*, rather blushed by the lavish and gracious hospitality.

George scanned the staircase and the entire length of the lounge-hall. He motioned them. "Come, come, please," he whispered.

Through elegant white French-doors in the middle of the hall, George escorted them into an airy formal dining room. The high walls, ceiling, and gracefully white-draped windows continued the hotel's décor of Oriental-Victorian—a sort of timeless faded-glory accented in wafts of Turkish coffee emanating from the galley. Taking a table at an open veranda overlooking the square, George called the waiter and whispered the order to his ear.

"So, George. How are your crops doing this time of year?" asked Jonah, immediately explaining to Madeleine and Sara, "George has a nice little farm up north in Galilee."

"Is not bad...could be better. But you know, the costs of petrol is very bad. The Americans think they have very bad price! Ha, ha...How they like six shekel for one liter petrol? Is terrible! But....We are still shipping much to Haifa-port for Europe...so, is okay. Could be better."

"And how are *shipments* coming along into Galilee from Beth Shean?" asked Jonah directly, his eyes calm and steady.

The waiter arrived with drinks, pita and hummus. A lull hovered until the waiter departed.

"Good." George nodded, expressionless. "A big shipment came across the border today and was received in Beit Lechem...until it comes to Jerusalem."

Madeleine nodded. Sara's eyes widened.

The group quickly changed the subject. They spent a good bit of time talking about neighborhoods, schools and shops where Sara would run her father's credit card up. The hummus was good and spicy and the fruit drinks cool and refreshing.

Pat rose to look out from the veranda down into the plaza. She noted the heavier stream of people coming into the Old City through Jaffa Gate. They were proceeding east toward the Temple Mount. "You know, Jonah...there's a big peace rally down at the *Wall* tonight?" announced Pat.

"Yes, we're on our way, actually. So. George...Pat...It's really good, my friends, for us to be together today. And, we will have many more days...but, for now, we must be going." Jonah rose from the table and knocked softly upon its fine linen cloth. "May the blessing of the Almighty rest upon our *House*."

And George replied, "May God guard you, my friends. Take *much* care." George took each of his friends strongly into his arms. Pat likewise, with a mist in her eyes. And they said their goodbyes.

And they entered again the Jaffa Gate plaza, joining the flow of people which bottlenecked at the northeast corner of the plaza. From a distance, it was not apparent what lay beyond the bottleneck. Indeed, even on days when few people were in the plaza, the entry to the Arab *suq* was not so apparent. But as Madeleine and Sara reached the entry, they could see they were indeed entering the *suq* before them on the downward slope of David Street. The narrow pedestrian-way began at the plaza entry and ran directly to the Temple Mount. Paved with handsome Jerusalem stone, the street descended in terraced sections, each lowering by a step or two to the next. The stone steps included ramps to accommodate push-barrow carts used by Arab boys to deliver goods to all the shops lining both sides of the street. Above the shop-fronts were a variety of overarching canopies meeting each other from their opposing sides, producing something of a tunneled and shadowy passageway. It was as if, by passing through the almost hidden plaza entry, one found a portal into the timeless.

The shops on David Street were open earlier than usual for a Shabbat—as it was not yet sundown. But with the unusual volume of pilgrim traffic, the Arab shopkeepers were keen to be of service. Madeleine and Sara were bedazzled amidst the throng of tourists and smooth-talking entrepreneurs who forthrightly descended out of their shops into the street. *Come, Come. Yes, come see...yes...special deal for you!* The exotic staccato of Arab music buzzed, spiraled and melded in the air with the aroma of spice, coffee, and honey sweet pastries made a little more exotic by gnats flitting above the wares.

Amid endless stalls of olive wood carvings, postcard racks, and brass, Sara spotted a young Arab boy on the corner of David Street and Muristan Road. The boy called out his offerings of colored stone necklaces, varieties of which he held up in both hands. Sara descended upon the stall which displayed all manner of necklaces on stand-up boards. And there were also a great many bins of loose stones in all shapes and colors. Surveying the bins, Sara immediately understood the opportunity: To make one's own creation.

Jonah and Madeleine let her *do the deal* on her own as they watched. As in a dance, the boy held an empty cord knotted on one end as Sara intently hopped from bin to bin, selecting just the right stones. She knew what she was doing and called off the colors as she slid them on the cord. *Green. White and Blue. And Red and Green. And Yellow and Red.* And she repeated the pattern three times filling the cord. The Arab boy was quite happy to quickly calculate the bill and begin the negotiation.

"All the stones, are one hundred shekel, but for you, I give special deal, yes? Because you pretty girl, I give you for ninety shekel, yes?" The boy pitched.

"Ummm." Sara quickly countered. "I was thinking seventy shekels."

"Ehhh. You give eighty shekel, yes? Very good deal! Only for you. Special deal for my pretty girl! The necklace look very good on you!" the boy sang out while quickly draping the necklace on Sara's hand."

"Ummm....okay. Deal!" announced Sara with a resolute nod. Fishing in her purse she pulled out American bills. "How much is eighty shekels in dollars?"

"Ehhh. Twenty dollar, please. You give twenty dollar. This very good deal, yes," rattled the boy, watching Sara's eyes closely.

Sara shuffled the bills out of her purse, and had to let him know, "Sorry, I only have 19 dollars."

Quick as fire, the boy spurted, "Okay. 19 dollar. You give 19 dollar. 19 is good number."

"Yes, 19 is a good number," agreed Sara with a broad smile. And the two shook hands, happy with their deal.

Going further down David Street amid the growing crowd, Jonah noticed Madeleine admiring multi-colored embroidered dresses displayed above the doorways of various shops. At one doorway stood a dignified Arab gentleman in pin stripe suit and charcoal sweater vest. He also caught the glint in Madeleine's eye and immediately bestowed lavish oriental hospitality pulling the entire Van Meter family into his well stocked shop. After some rounds of womanly aesthetic dialogue between mother and daughter, each point and counter point affirmed by the prudent shop-owner, finally a fine long white gauze dress with small blue embroidery about the neck was selected. Sara, having already proven her bargaining skills, negotiated the price for her mother. Jonah paid the bill, and his daughter assured he had gotten a very good deal.

"No doubt," he said.

Going a little further, they came to the central intersection in the *suq*. At the crossroad, Jonah explained that the left side was called *Suq Khan ez-Zeit*. It was the main avenue through the Muslim Quarter leading to the Damascus Gate. But, on the right, the road was called *The Cardo*, and coursed through the Jewish Quarter.

"So, the Muslim Quarter and the Jewish Quarter live right next to each other?" asked Sara.

"Yes!" confirmed Jonah. "This little street—David Street, full of people from all over the world, runs right down the middle of everything."

Not too many steps further, the road jogged right and left and its name changed to *Street Of The Chain*. Although the street led directly to the Temple Mount, Jonah took his family only two-thirds the way. Suddenly, he exited to the right on a small walk-way leading to a plexi-glass checkpoint booth staffed by Israeli security soldiers. The young soldiers were all immigrant Ethiopian Jews.

Bags and purses were duly x-rayed and retrieved from the far side of a conveyor belt. And Madeleine, Sara, and Jonah stepped out of the booth at the top of a stone staircase.

Madeleine quietly gasped. She gazed out over a sea of souls completely filling the Western Wall plaza, known also as *The Kotel*. The sun was receding and the expanse of people and stone was turned to a soft purple haze between night and day. In the foreground clumps of celebrants danced in circles clapping and shouting. The jazz of klezmer music zipped through the air. And the zings of fiddles and clinging tambourines mixed with sonorous Ethiopian drums reverberating the entire Kotel, wafting to the Jewish Quarter above.

As they descended the stairs to the Kotel, Jonah noted the many Arabs stationed on the ramparts of the *Western Wall* monitoring the crowds below.

Sara spotted a number of *Lahma Mahar* banners amid the dancing and singing people.

Stepping into the plaza, they made their way toward the *Wall* through the deafening joyous celebration of expectancy. Jonah pointed Madeleine and Sara to the women's side of the prayer area. Jonah took to the men's side.

Madeleine and Sara approached the wall through an obstacle course of other women, white plastic lawn chairs, and portable carts full of prayer books. Madeleine drew a book and stood herself before *Wall*. She laid her body and forehead upon the two-thousand-year-old stone. She wept. Sara wrapped her arm strongly around her mother. With tears falling upon her hands, Madeleine took the *tefila* pouch from her blouse and touched it to the *Wall*. She opened the prayer book and found the *Mourners Kaddish*. Sara joined her in the prayer.

They just held each other for a long time.

"Mommy, I would like to write a prayer to put in the stones," stated Sara.

"Yes, dear. Please do."

Without deliberation Sara tore a page out of her passport and wrote:

L'Daniel

She folded the page neatly three times and carefully placed it between two large wall stones.

On his side, Jonah also wrote. The wall received his prayer of one word:

Echad

When they came together again in the exuberances of the plaza, Jonah spied his old friend, Rabbi Avraham. The *rebbe,* who was the head of a yeshiva on Mt. Zion, was leading a merry band in a raucous sweaty hora in the early summer night. Around the circle, his yeshiva klezmer band played feverishly. Jonah led Madeleine and Sara through the throng, and they slipped quietly into the whirling hora. It took a few moments, but soon enough the *rebbe* spotted his insurgents. He laughed thunderously and rocketed the song's decibel toward the upper pavilions of the Jewish Quarter.

> *Im Tirtzu, im tirtzu*
> *Ein zo agadah, ein zo agadah*
> *Lehiyot am chofshi b'artzeinu*
> *B'retz tzion v'rushalayim*
> *If you will it*
> *It is no legend*
> *To be a free people*
> *In our land of Zion and Jerusalem*

Soon other insurgents slipped in. Destiny took Sara's hand. And Faith took Madeleine's.

"Move over, Jonah," called the raspy voice of Sister Marta— with Maria and Lazlo in tow. Then came also Menelik and Te- wahido. And then Gregorio and Daniel, their cassocks flipping and their Midwestern feet hopping crazily to dance the dance, creating some new form of Jewish Kabuki in the process.

The sun had fully retired, and the plaza glowed amber in the night from candles and floodlights commencing the vigils of peace. In Rabbi Avraham's hora, a sudden searing light broke upon the circle as a television news-team launched into a report. Always seeking any light, Destiny jumped in front of the cameras, her pudgy fingers thrusting out a waving peace sign to all the world she hoped that even her father would see.

Rabbi Avraham's eyes met Jonah's in prudent mutual decision to slip away from the dance. They had work to do. The Van Meters were to lodge at the *rebbe's* yeshiva that night. But first, Avraham escorted them to the north side of the plaza. There, he showed them the Kotel Tunnel entrance. It was from this point that the tunnel ran along the under-courses of the Western Wall to the Via Dolorosa in the Muslim Quarter. The tunnel would be an important component in the operation.

Their Kotel tour completed, Rabbi Avraham escorted them to the security booth on the south end of the plaza, opposite the booth where they first had entered. Again the Ethiopian soldiers were efficient and admirably vigilant in their duties.

Out of the booth, they ascended a monumental wide flight of stairs leading to the summit of the Jewish Quarter, where a number of impressive yeshivas towered over the Kotel. Going on, the *rebbe* led them on a sharply inclining road alongside the Old City wall. Rabbi Avraham explained that most of the Quarter was newly built since the '67 war. And although most of the buildings were new, they were made of the same golden Jerusalem stone as the old. The majority of the dwellings were ordinary family residences, as was true before the Romans burnt and demolished the Quarter in 70 CE.

Madeleine carefully observed a number of young Jewish families slowly making the arduous upward climb with them. They were young Orthodox couples—men in black suits and wide-brim hats—their wives in knitted shawls, long fine skirts, and reservedly stylish berets. Some of the couples had toddlers in cute miniature versions of the parents' apparel, and others wheeled baby carriages home resplendent in a holy City. It *got*

Madeleine. It got her good. She laid eye upon a small boy in a black *kippah* trudging upward on the road. He looked at Madeleine and smiled…and waved. And she smiled and waved back, her eyes welling close to tears. But. Her hands reached out and took those of Sara and Jonah. And in that very moment: Jerusalem became her life, her joy, her home, forever and ever. Amein.

Upward and onward toward Mt. Zion led Rabbi Avraham. He explained that Mt. Zion was a hill outside the southwest corner of the Old City wall through the *Zion Gate*. It was actually the second Mt. Zion, the first being the Temple Mount before the Temple was lost to Roman destruction two millennia before. The second Mt. Zion was home to a number of odd holy sites. Among them was the grandiose St. Mary of Zion Church, also known as the *Dormition Church*, a relatively modern shrine built by Kaiser Wilhelm on the remains of previous ancient churches. Tradition held that the site marked where Jesus' mother fell into final sleep before her bodily assumption into heaven. But there were lesser known traditions that the site was connected not to the Virgin Mary, but to Mary Magdalene. Then there was the Cenacle also known as the *Upper Room* where tradition placed the *Last Supper* of Jesus. And, downstairs from the Cenacle— really part of the same building, was the so-called Tomb of David. It was only a symbolic shrine, since the actual site of David's tomb had been forgotten long ago. The real tomb, the rabbi explained, was elsewhere—by tradition, somewhere on the other side of the Old City wall—on the adjacent hill just north of the second Mt. Zion. The hill was said to crown an area which had been the smaller original Jerusalem, known as the *City of David.*

"We'll find it soon enough," the rabbi assured. "Our past is our future."

They arrived at Zion Gate which proved to be a smaller version of Jaffa Gate, its structure also laid out in the defensive L position. But unlike Jaffa Gate, ordinary vehicle traffic was routed through the very portal of the gate…if it could fit. Much care was needed with even a mid-sized car in making the turn in order not to hit the walls. Indeed, the smaller the vehicle, the greater the chance of making it to Mt. Zion unscathed.

As they exited the gate, under the glow of street lamps, Rabbi Avraham showed them the outer stones of the gate severely defaced by thousands of bullet and mortar holes from the war of 1967. The rabbi placed his finger into one hole in the side of the wall, his eyes fixated as if on something not able to be seen by common light. He spoke toward the wall:

"We keep the holes to remember the reality of war that is always at our gates. But..." He turned and looked directly into all their eyes. "We, my friends, are set tonight on another mission: To remember, yes? To remember our future. To remember: Peace. The eternal Shabbat Shalom."

"A-mein" said Madeleine. And so said Jonah and Sara.

"A-mein," agreed the *rebbe*. He took Sara's hand. "Come. I am eager to share with you our humble quarters. Our klezmer band will be coming up soon from the Kotel. Do you play music Sara?"

"Yeah. I play...I mean, I *did* play mellophone in my high school marching band."

"Well. I am afraid I do not know what a mellophone is, but I am sure that our band will draft you to their cause. No doubt," assured the rabbi.

"Oh. A mellophone is a marching French horn," informed Sara.

"Indeed," smiled the *rebbe*.

CNN.
Saturday, May 26, 3:00 P.M. EST

"Breaking news from around the globe.....

Large demonstrations took place again today in many cities throughout Europe and the United States, protesting the Iraq war and calling for peace. Tensions appear high in many Middle Eastern countries as rumors increase that last week's apparent stunning re-surfacing of ancient Jewish relics was an Israeli operation. There is also wide speculation that the reappearance of the relics is connected to a mysterious messianic claimant. The rumored claimant, reportedly a man from the State of Ohio in the United States, has been spotted in a variety of European cities and received by large crowds. Some reports also include that the claimant is in transit to Israel.

In reaction to all these events, many Muslims fear that the Israelis are preparing to reclaim the site of the ancient Jewish Temple, which was destroyed by the Romans in the year 70 CE. The site is now occupied by the Muslim shrine, the Dome of the Rock, one of the holiest shrines in the Muslim religion.

A special live report, from John Josephs in Jerusalem...."

"Rolf, I'm standing now in the plaza of the Kotel, also known as the *Western Wall*—the holiest Jewish site in Israel. The *Wall* is a remnant of the ancient Jewish temple compound that existed over two thousand years ago. As you have just indicated, the Temple Mount itself, with its golden Dome of the Rock mosque, is today in Muslim hands as it has been since the 7th century, except for brief periods of Christian control under the medieval Crusaders. It is certainly true that a loss of the Temple Mount would be unthinkable to Muslims. Indeed, there is wild speculation and expectation in the streets of Jerusalem and throughout Israel tonight that some immense event is at hand. People are flooding into the City from all over the country and beyond...many Jews into the Jewish Quarter of Jerusalem, and Muslims into the Muslim Quarter...many Muslims literally camping out on the Temple Mount, Rolf....in readiness to defend it from a feared Jewish assault.

And Rolf, we are hearing reports of many candlelight vigils occurring in towns throughout Israel tonight—including the important religious town of Bethlehem in the northern region of Galilee.

As you can see here, the Kotel plaza is absolutely full—literally thousands of people with lighted candles, singing songs, and praying at the *Wall*. And...above the *Wall*...at its top, we can see many of the Muslim onlookers camped out on the Temple Mount watching out for whatever momentous event might occur. Throughout the City of Jerusalem, there is much heightened security by the Israelis…but so far, only peaceful activities are being reported. Long time residents of Jerusalem are telling us that they have never seen anything like what we are witnessing here tonight. Back to you, Rolf."

"Thank you, John Josephs, for that live report from Jerusalem…

In Washington today, things appear quiet as most government workers settle into the long Memorial Day weekend. No comment has been issued by the White House in regard to recent events in Europe and the Middle East…although, it has been noted that the President is not spending the weekend at Camp David. A source close to the White House stated that, given current events, it is difficult to imagine the President ever spending time at Camp David again.

Next, we'll be going to Christine Haman in Mosul, Iraq, for a special report on Iraq's religious role in world history, some of which can be found even in the Bible….."

Sabeel Khouri stood alone in the night atop the bell tower of the Redeemer Church. In the distance he could see the floodlights and myriads of candle flickers emanating from the Kotel. But more pressing, his very feet felt fire and panic as he looked down upon the rooftop of the Holy Sepulcher across the road. The rooftop was exploding in firelight and drums as the Ethiopians conducted a strange rite in their open air sanctuary. Khouri watched a figure in grand flowing robes, the Ethiopian Patriarch, lead a procession of white-robed followers in a circle around a roof-top dome. The celebrants rhythmically danced, alternating one foot and the next, in cadence with the sonorous drums echoing over the Old City. Candlelight was everywhere. The light on the rooftop produced glowing streams from those who danced— flickers of hope—a hope remembered by old men who told of it to children sitting under a festal leopard-skin tent. And even from somewhere within the Ethiopian Chapel, a small shimmer of light illumined some work of destiny.

Khouri nodded to himself. In the morning, he would go to war.

Fox News.
Sunday, May 27, 11:11 A.M. EST

"The Day's major stories that you and your family need to know....

"Apocalypse....or...much-ado-about-nothing? It's a question on many minds today as a nervous quiet hovers over the City of Jerusalem following wide expectations of an immanent Israeli attempt to reclaim Jerusalem's Temple Mount. The Mount has been under Muslim control for centuries. A spokesman for the Israeli Prime Minister's Office scoffed at the rumors calling them *ridiculous* and claiming that all of Israel's security forces are at normal readiness levels. The spokesman added, *Nothing is different today than the same day last month. Tomorrow?...We never know. But today...everything is quiet.*

Asked about whether Israel played a part in last week's theft of Jewish relics from the Vatican and whether Israel was in possession of the relics, the spokesman issued a flat *no comment.*

Despite apparent quiet, speculation continues throughout many Western countries concerning a so-called messianic claimant. The man, reportedly Jonah Van Meter from the State of Ohio, drew much attention last week in a trek across central Europe. Wide reports in France indicated that Van Meter intended to proceed to Israel. And today, there are scattered unconfirmed reports that he has been sighted in Jerusalem.

Turning to news in the United States...Questions continue to linger, especially in Washington, as to the President's whereabouts over the past several days. White House Press Secretary, Eva Perra, called an impromptu news conference in response to a blizzard of media inquiries. Perra indicated that The President, while not enjoying his typical Memorial Day weekend at Camp David, will be taking a working holiday at the White House. She noted that The President was scheduled for a Memorial Day appearance at which he would lay a wreath at the *Tomb of the Unknown Soldier.*

In other news, oil industry experts predict continuing higher prices for crude oil...."

White House Situation Room, Washington, D. C.
Sunday, May 27, 11:13 A.M. EST

Bill Blanche spastically rubbed his forehead as he leaned back in his chair staring at the television monitors high on the wall. He had been spending so much time in the subterranean quarters that he had procured a desk for himself. His temporary universe included a computer, faxphone, maps, and dirty coffee mugs. And, a stand-up family photo of his Vietnamese wife, Thanh Binh, and their two children, daughter Saria and son Nhat Hanh.

Blackpoint and Kundorf entered the room together. Blackpoint summoned Blanche to the round conference table in the center of the room.

"Report," demanded Blackpoint in his *s.o.b.* tone.

"Well. Van Meter's in Jerusalem. He's been pretty brazen about it. In addition to reports from our people, media's picking it up ..."

"Where in Jerusalem?"

"Old City...all over, really.

"No one place?"

"Not that we can tell...as of yet."

Blackpoint turned directly to Kundorf for her analysis. "What do you make of it, Doctor? Nothing has happened today. The day is almost gone in Israel. Should we expect something yet tonight?" Blackpoint was grasping at straws.

Kundorf replied, "No. I do not think our Jonah Van Meter prefers the night. He never visits tombs in the dark...but only in the broad light of day. And he will make his pilgrimage to tombs. I am sure of it. Certainly he must go to the *last tomb*...the Tomb of Jesus...wherever it is...to reveal the remains of the body of Jesus to the world and make his claim. So, no. Not in the night. Which day, now? Sorry to say...*now*...we do not know. We must wait...and watch, yes?"

"Well…" mused Blackpoint. "I'm wondering if the Israelis might move against the Temple Mount before Van Meter makes his play. What's the intel on Israeli military positions, Blanche?"

"Nothing." Blanche shook his head.

"So, Doctor. You say we must watch for Van Meter to appear at the tomb of his desires. What are your educated guesses as to possible locations of said tomb?"

Kundorf was so glad he asked. "Yes. Of course," she said with a wry smile as she straightened her gaunt frame into a lecture position. "First. We must understand one central doctrine about Jonah Van Meter. He is a *Merovingian—a* rebellious Merovingian, yes…but a Merovingian all the same. He has the *Blood.* And the Blood must control him, as it does all Merovingians. Blood is everything. Think about the reports we have of his travels. In France. Where does he go? To the tomb of his ancestor, William the Conqueror. How touching. But we must not let sentiment awe us. We must ask *where next*? Where is the next point of contact for this Merovingian in his epic quest to claim the prize of his heritage? Well. If one goes to Jerusalem, it is very easy: *The Church of the Holy Sepulcher.* There. You have tombs, yes? There is the tomb of Jesus. But.…also…within the church, the tomb of who else? Yes, the King of the Merovingians: The great Godfroi de Bouillon…right directly below the Chapel of Golgatha where Jesus was crucified…"

"I'm confused." interrupted Blackpoint. "The tomb of Jesus—in the church…is *empty*, is it not?"

Kundorf smiled condescendingly. "Yes.…but, you must understand, Mr. Blackpoint. The Church of the Holy Sepulcher is built upon a Jewish cemetery from the Herodian era. I can assure you there is much yet to be discovered *under* the Church. Here is an interesting fact, Mr. Blackpoint: At the far end of the Church is a most remote chapel owned by a little known sect of Syrian Christians. Good heavens, they are so poor, that all they have in their chapel is a solitary crumbling wood altar with a faded icon. But. They have other interesting riches there. There is a small opening in the chapel wall—to the ancient Jewish cemetery below the Church. I have seen it, yes! Indeed, I was there! I was, myself, half-way into the entrance when a very large Syrian priest in a black robe took hold of me and pulled me priest in a black robe took hold of me and pulled me out! He shouted at me angrily and I thought he meant to do me harm, as he was not letting me go. But, I broke free of him and he pursued. We jaunted several times around his wrecked altar in the middle of the chapel before I found my chance to dash out the main entrance of the chapel into the nave of the basilica...where of course, it was easy for me to fall into a tourist group. And he did not pursue me any further once I was outside the chapel. But another interesting fact about the Syrian Chapel: When I was chased by the Syrian priest, this was many years ago. But today? The chapel is sealed off...with a *new wall*! Completely! The ordinary tourist today would not even suspect the chapel is there. This tells me something—that perhaps something very important is being covered over in the Syrian Chapel—possibly the true Tomb of Jesus. We shall see.

But. There is also a second Merovingian possibility. At the base of the Mount of Olives, there is a shrine called the *Tomb of the Virgin Mary*. It also has an authentic empty Jewish tomb....empty because, of course, the traditions say: the Virgin Mary was taken up into heaven as was Jesus. The shrine is a very mysterious place. The entrance is just a simple Crusader doorway leading down a very long flight of stairs, deep below the earth. It is a very dark place...there are strings of ancient oil lamps hanging from the ceiling of the stairway, but they are not used. You must depend on light coming down from the doorway or candles on the side altars that are recessed into the walls of the stairway. And so. At those side altars, there *are* Merovingian tombs in the walls. And, at the bottom of the stairs is the main sanctuary of the shrine. At one end is an edicule standing over the supposed site of the Virgin Mary's tomb...before she was supposedly assumed into heaven. And again, it is very dark down there...you must buy candles from the priests to see much of anything. But my point is: On the back wall of the sanctuary is a door....a door that pilgrims are not permitted to enter. Behind that door lie more Merovingian tombs. I do not know how many, but the maps I have studied indicate the area beyond the door is quite large. So. This is another possibility. We watch. And we shall see."

Bill Blanche rested backwards with his hands folded behind his head. His face was perplexed, his eyes reflecting the gears in his head sorting disparate information.

"But," challenged Blanche. "Jonah Van Meter did not visit the tomb of his ancestor Cretien DuBois as he was going through France. More to the point: Isn't it true that Van Meter *avoided* many of the so-called Merovingian sites in France? But rather, his path through France followed very closely that of ol' *Blood & Guts,* General George S. Patton!...Now, Dr. Kundorf...I think...and this is just my personal opinion: But, I think this Van Meter guy is some kind of trickster. He's playing with us. And I don't know what his game is. But, frankly, Doctor...I don't think you know either."

Thus Blanche spoke his mind. He had spoken, at least some truth, to power. It was no small challenge, as Blackpoint's whole universe revolved around the idea that *he* was the *controller* of information. It was *he* who should capture, monitor, and control vast amounts of networked information...and kill parts of those networks, or *viruses* as he called them, if need be. Blanche looked at Blackpoint and saw that he was peeved. He looked at Kundorf. But, she was not peeved. Her half-smile betrayed a smug touché in reserve.

"My dear, Mr. Blanche...," led Kundorf. "I too, have re-searched the subject you so forthrightly broach. From my research, it would appear that Jonah Van Meter and George S. Patton share a very important singular trait...."

"And that is?...." Blanche leaned forward, his eye-gears click-ing.

Kundorf huffed a hearty laugh. "My good Mr. Blanche. It is very simple! They are *both* Merovingians! And, they are *both*, yah!....descendants of Cretien DuBois!"

Yeshiva Zion, Jerusalem.
Sunday, May 27, 9:31 P.M.

In a conference call, Jonah and Rabbi Avraham confirmed the details with their Domari contacts. The *shipment* had progressed along the appointed route with no difficulty or notice. First, there had been the leg from Pella in Jordan across the border through Beth Shean into Israel. Then it proceeded west to Beit Lechem, also known as Bethlehem, in Lower Galilee. Next, the caravan proceeded north to Tzfat, and from there, south to Magdala at the Sea of Galilee and then further south to Jericho. The Domari contact expressed high praise of the Ethiopian *House* members for their hospitality in Jericho the previous night. Finally, the caravan and its *shipment* had arrived safely Sunday morning at another Ethiopian compound in Bethany, just east of the Mount of Olives.

The rest of the *House* had accomplished their work. They were prepared. It was time for Jonah and Madeleine to prepare. They decided to leave Sara in the yeshiva dining hall with the klezmer band. Someone had actually found a French horn for Sara, and they were jamming trying to figure out how to work the new sound in. With strong hugs, Jonah and Madeleine departed the yeshiva into the night.

Through the bullet-scarred Zion Gate and into the Jewish Quarter, they quietly trekked down the road alongside the Old City wall, and soon arrived at the Kotel. Unlike the previous night, there were few people about. A few pious souls prayed in solitude at the *Wall*. Several small clusters of folk quietly strolled the plaza under the light of the Jewish Quarter above. The light refracted the *Wall's* deep amber-gold over the entire plaza, the color melding into the night some distance out from the wall. Jonah and Madeleine stepped along the edges of the darkness as they crossed the expanse. Checking the top of the *Wall*, Jonah saw no Arabs peering down from its ramparts. Everything *appeared* back to normal.

"Looks like our decoy-vigil last night paid off," stated Jonah. "Hopefully, they'll forget about us…at least a little bit."

"Uh-huh. So far…so good," agreed Madeleine.

They came to the glass entrance door of the Kotel tunnel at the north side of the plaza. A popular tourist attraction during the day, Jonah tried to imagine the site before ticket windows, turnstiles, and the gift shop. They waited in the shadows a short time. Then, on the other side of the glass, figures flickered in the dark. Keys jingled. The lock tumbled, and swiftly the door was pushed open for them.

Once in, Madeleine and Jonah hugged their friend Lazlo. And then there was the boy. Madeleine knelt down to the small dark-haired young man. Although the light was dim, she instantly recognized his Domari features—his bright almond eyes and slightly wide nose.

"Do you speak English, my dear?" whispered Madeleine, looking also up at Lazlo, who gave a finger pinch gesture to say *a little*.

"I am Nawar," the young boy stated proudly.

Jonah knelt down to shake the young man's hand. "Pleased to meet you, Nawar. I'm Jonah. You certainly look like a fine and trustworthy guide. A good firm handshake too! Thank you for helping us."

The boy nodded, and looked up at Lazlo. Silence hung in the air. They all understood they were entering a dangerous phase of the operation. Lazlo checked his watch. Jonah looked into Madeleine's eyes with a short sigh, and no words. With a very tight hug and a soft kiss, they parted….hopefully until only the next day. Lazlo stood with his charge and watched them fade into the tunnel.

When they reached the other side on the Via Dolorosa, Nawar led the way out through the Lion's Gate into the night. It would be a long journey on foot to Bethany on the other side of the Mount of Olives. They were to look for a house with a white donkey tied to a post.

Mount of Olives.
Monday, May 28. MEMORIAL DAY. 2:30 P.M.

Two trucks. A white panel and a small white flat-bed, cruised east on Highway 1. The road coursed to the northwest corner of greater Jerusalem, rounded the northern boundaries of the city, and merged into the roads just north of Mt. Scopus and the Mount of Olives. The trucks proceeded easily on the Mount of Olives Road up and across Mount Scopus. Going up the north side of the Mount of Olives, they passed the Lutheran Augusta Victoria Hospital. Menelik and Tewahido in one truck, Daniel and Gregorio in the other, scanned the hospital's bell tower. They saw a lookout who appeared not to see them. Just another warm afternoon in Jerusalem.

The trucks passed the Dome of the Ascension at the Arab village of Etur. The shrine, a micro-version of the Dome of the Rock in plain stone, supposedly marked the spot where Jesus ascended to heaven following the resurrection. It was also the visual point at which a figure disappeared from sight if one was watching him hike over the Mount of Olives to Bethany. As was typical, Arab youth manned the small dome in order to scrabble a few shekels from tourists who managed to find it. The boys paid the trucks no heed.

Going further, the small convoy passed the Pater Noster Church. Another two hundred meters, the trucks reached their terminus: The northern edge of the Jewish Cemetery. At this point there was a smaller road which ran down the Mount toward the Kidron Valley opposite the Lion's Gate of the Old City. Upon this small road, the operation's northern contingent would proceed with the Treasure of Israel.

Two trucks. A white sherut mini-van and a white flat-bed bearing a white donkey arrived on the southern flank of the Jewish Cemetery on the Mount of Olives. Other cars in tow also arrived. Maria and Marta exited the sherut cab, and likewise, dozens of Jews and Domari from the other vehicles. The people stood in the cemetery amid the stones. Maria and Marta opened

the sliding door of the sherut revealing an interior stripped of its
all its seating, and in its center: *The Shipment*.

A Hasid in *tallit* stood at their center and chanted *Kaddish:*

> *Yit-ga-dal v'yit-ka-dash sh'mei ra-ba b'al-ma di-
> v'ra chi-r'u'tei, v'yam-lich mal-chu-tei b'cha-yei-
> chon u-v'yo-mei-chon u-v'cha-yei d'chol beit Yis-
> ra-eil, ba-a-ga-la u-vi-z'man ka-riv, v'i-m' ru: A-
> mein.*
> *Y'hei sh'mei ra-ba m'va-rach l'alam u-l'al-mei
> al-ma-ya.*
> *Yit-ba-rach v'yish-ta-bach, v'yit-pa-ar v'yit-ro-
> mam v'yit-na-sei, v'yit-ha-dar v'yit-a-leh v'yit-
> ha-lal sh'mei d'kud-sha, b'rich hu,*
> *l'ei-la min kol bir-cha-ta v'shi-ra-ta, tush-b'cha-
> ta v'neh-cheh-ma-ta da-a-mi-ran b'al-ma, v'i-
> m'ru: A-mein.*
> *Y'hei sh'la-ma ra-ba min sh'ma-ya v'cha-yim, a-
> lei-nu v'al kol Yis-ra-el, v'i-m'ru: A-mein.*
> *O-seh sha-lom bi-m'ro-mav, hu ya-a-seh sha-lom
> a-lei-nu v'al kol Yis-ra-eil, v'i-m'ru: A-mein.*

The southern contingent staged their procession order. The
white donkey was set at the front. Next a line of twelve Jews.
Then, followed the white sherut bearing the *Bread of the House*.
Finally, a throng of *House people* led by Maria, Marta, and
Lazlo.

On the northern side of the cemetery, Tewahido and Menelik,
Gregorio and Daniel, and the other men unloaded the golden
Menorah, the Showbread Table and the Silver Trumpets from
the panel truck. Quickly, they transferred the Menorah to the
flat-bed truck. Also removed from the panel truck was the Treasure of Aksum, Ethiopia. The mysterious holy item, flat and
draped in purple velvet, was handed carefully to Menelik and
Tewahido. Menelik placed a richly embroidered conical hat
upon Tewahido's head and the draped flat treasure was fixed to
the top of the hat with the folds of the drapery splaying as a

shroud about his shoulders, giving him rather the appearance of a lion.

The order of the procession was set. Tewahido, with the Aksum Treasure upon his head, was positioned in front. Behind him, Menelik and three Domari men took up the *Showbread Table* with twelve fine loaves laid upon it. Then followed Daniel and Gregorio, each bearing a silver trumpet. Then, a full honor-guard of ten *House* members bearing various flags. Next, a line of twelve Ethiopians bearing drums. Finally, the white flat-bed truck with the glimmering golden Menorah standing high.

At the appointed minute, a Hasid in black suit and wide-brim hat stepped forward and faced the northern contingent. On the southern side of the cemetery, another Hasid likewise faced the contingent there. Together, their chants floated and joined each other over the Jewish Cemetery on the Mount of Olives:

Rejoice greatly, O daughter of Zion! Shout aloud, O daughter of Jerusalem! Lo, your kingdom comes to you; triumphant and victorious, humble and riding on an ass, on a colt, the foal of an ass. I will cut off the chariot from Ephraim and the war horse from Jerusalem; and the battle bow will be cut off, and the Almighty shall command peace to the nations; and the Dominion shall be from sea to sea, and from the River to the ends of the earth. Amein!

The boy Nawar departed quickly to take his post at the Lion's Gate.

All was silent over the entire Jewish Cemetery. Absolutely silent.

The *tefila* was wrapped tightly about the arm. The donkey was mounted.

The assembled contingents, north and south, erupted in shouts,

LAHMA MAHAR!!!
LAHMA MAHAR!!!
LAHMA MAHAR!!!

It was 3:00 pm. The two contingents began down their roads.

White House Situation Room, Washington D.C.
8:00 A.M. EST.

Bill Blanche glanced over the morning's intell briefings. His cell went off.

"Bill!"

"Yeah."

"*Ajax*, here..."

"Yeah, yeah...what?"

"Well. I'll tell ya buddy. I'm doin' my thing here, you know, at the bottom of the Mt. of Olives...."

"Yeah. What d'you got?"

"Well. There's some funky shit goin' down. There's a bunch of folk comin' down the hill...."

"Yeah, so what?"

"Well....you know that big golden Menorah from the Vatican?"

"Yeahhhhhh,......?"

"Well, yeah. They got it. It's comin' down the hill. And there's a bunch of people bangin' drums and blowin' horns and singin'...and then there's another group comin' down the hill on another road...with somebody ridin' a freakin' donkey...."

"Ohhhh.... shit. HOLY SHIT!...hold on. HOLD ON!...."

The Bread House, Bexley, Ohio
8:03 A.M.

The whole *House* was gathered around Rodney Fridenmaker's terminal. Next to him, Will Aaronson breathed hard watching his friend peck the keyboard, pen in mouth. At last, The Rod Man spit the pen out, and held up his left hand. His fingers ticked down what he hoped would be the last seconds of the linkage attempt. *Three, two, one...*

The room exploded into applause. Full on the monitor screen, in real-time, was the video feed from the Mount of Olives. The link with the yeshiva cameras above the Kotel was working perfectly. The room instantly hushed as the camera focused on the white donkey and its rider. *The Bread House* was in business.

The Yeshiva Above the Kotel, Jerusalem.
3:05 P.M.

The Ashkenazi and Sephardic Chief Rabbis of Israel stood at the large pane windows on the yeshiva's top floor surrounded by a bevy of rabbinical students in white shirts, black pants, and *tallit* fringes.

Mordecai, a young American student, peered through binoculars, his reddish side-locks swinging as his hands shook ecstatically.

"My son. Are they bearing all the necessary signs?" asked the Ashkenazi Rabbi in thickly accented English.

The young Hasid hopped to his feet and stumbled directly to the window, the binoculars never leaving his eye-sockets. His feet stammered spastically. "FULL METAL JACKET, REBBE!!! The Menorah! The Trumpets! The Bread Table...and Holy Moshe, it even has *bread* on it!!!"

"What shape the loaves?" the Sephardic Rabbi quickly asked, side-glancing his partner.

"Looks like twelve little boats!" answered Mordecai exuberantly holding his two hands in a V-shape as he swished them through the air, like a keeled ship navigating the sea.

"Aha! I thought so!" the Sephardic Rabbi celebrated elbowing the Ashkenazi.

Mordecai, my son...," called the Ashkenazi Rabbi. "What of the *Torah Tziyun?*"

"Ehh......" The young man squinted. "Would it be under the care of the Ethiopian guys?"

"Yes!!!" chorused the Rabbis.

"Yup! Front and center, Rebbes!"

"And, our friend, Ben Yosef?" the Sephardic Rabbi inquired.

"Yes! I think so!" Mordecai laughed. "I think they have him riding in a sherut!"

The whole circle of Jews laughed and wagged their heads in amazement.

The Bread House, Bexley, Ohio.
8:07 A.M.

Geoffrey Sinclair and Will Aaronson hovered over the The Rod Man's monitor as he quickly pecked the keys with his mouth-pen. Will called out to the rest of the *House*, "Standby for video feed export…..3, 2, 1…..BINGO!"

CNN, Atlanta. Control Room.
8:08 A.M.

All the monitors in the room jumped and flickered.

"What the fuck?!" exclaimed tech, Jim Finnerty.

"Hey, Jimbo! Are you seein' this?" yelled Sandy, another tech.

"Holy shit. WHAT is THIS?!" yelled Abby, stabbing the *escape* button on her keyboard and then *control-alt-delete.*

Several techs rocketed their chairs back from their terminals and stormed the row scanning all the monitors, finding them all the same.

Across the room, reporter John Josephs was preparing for a segment and noticed the commotion. He high-stepped to the row of confused techs, and discovered the monitors displaying an out-of-place feed. While some techs tried to run searches on the origin of the feed, Josephs squinted at the images of people moving down a hill, their forms flickered as they passed behind interspersed Cyprus trees. And then he saw it.

"ohhh…My GOD! OH MY GOD! OH GOD!!!"

"What?" yelled Jim.

"What…what? cried Sandy.

"What is it?" demanded Abby.

Joseph's face turned slowly to his colleagues looking them each in the eye. *"What is it?...What is IT?!....*You're asking me *What   is   it???...*AFTER   MY   REPORT   ON   THE MENORAH!!!!...JUST A FEW DAYS AGO???!!!!" He stab-pointed to the gold flash blinking in and out of the trees on the monitor.

"Holy Shit," blurted Jim with a stark stare into the monitor.

Josephs exploded into overdrive. "TWO MINUTES!!! We're going to breaking-news! Cue up the bites from Rome last week! LET'S ROLL!"

SPECIAL REPORT

"Good morning, I'm John Josephs with breaking news from CNN studios in Atlanta. We're looking, live, at an event in pro-gress at the Mount of Olives in Jerusalem, Israel.

We are apparently seeing a large group—actually *two groups* of people descending the Mount of Olives in Jerusalem—on two different roads. One of the groups appears to be transporting a large golden Menorah...there....we see it now. I can tell you....from my reports in Rome only several days ago, that this appears, to me anyway, to be the very same Menorah stolen from the Vatican last week. Let's roll that video....

As you see on our split screen, the images on the left, of the Menorah in Rome last week conform very well to the outlines of what we are seeing live on the right side of your screen, as we speak. The object appears to be progressing down a road behind a fair number of trees....so we have to be patient here...to see if we will get a good glimpse of the Menorah...oh, yes! There! You see the upper portion of the Menorah, apparently on a truck of some kind...And a number of people surrounding it...it is dif-ficult to estimate how many at this point....By the way, we do not know the origin of this feed we are receiving. It is being transmitted to us by an unknown source, which adds a good bit of mystery to what we are witnessing here. And this, of course, adds to the mystery over other events of the past week. As you are most probably aware, there was a shocking apparent theft at the Vatican last week...we say *apparent*, as the Vatican has thus far refused to comment on the episode…but in the wake of the alleged theft…there has been wide speculation that some subsequent major event was imminent in Jerusalem. Many rumors of the past week seemed to focus on a man named Jonah Van Meter, from the State of Ohio in the United States, said by many to be a messianic claimant of some sort. Van Meter appeared last week at a number of anti-war demonstrations throughout Europe attended by thousands. Most reports last week indicated that Van Meter intended to journey to Israel, and it was widely rumored that his exploits were connected to Israeli plans to reclaim the Temple Mount in Jerusalem. It should be understood that the Temple Mount, although in Muslim hands for many centuries, is very holy to both Muslims and Jews. And….of late…there has been a sizable interest among some ultra-orthodox Jewish groups to regain the Temple Mount in order the rebuild the Jewish Temple that was destroyed by the Romans in year 70 CE, almost two thousand years ago…….

What?.....I'm told we have CNN's own Christine Haman, live on the videophone somewhere in Jerusalem approaching the Mount of Olives. Christine?....."

"Yes, John…"

"Yes, Christine….Can you tell us what you are seeing there, and can you tell us where you are?"

"Yes. John. I am riding in a taxi, John, from my hotel in East Jerusalem. We are on the Jericho Road which runs right directly in front of the Mount of Olives, at its base….and I would say, we are approximately a half kilometer from the Mount. We are now passing below the walls of the Old City of Jerusalem across the valley from the Mount of Olives. These walls go around the entire Old City and in this particular area they border the Muslim Quarter. I am seeing many Arabs on top of those walls, John. The walls have ramparts…little walkways, which were of course made for defensive purposes centuries ago. I'm seeing, John, the whole wall topped with people in the Muslim Quarter…and I must say, they appear to be quite agitated…quite an extraordinary scene John…..

"Christine?...Are the people you are seeing on those walls…are they armed? What are they doing?"

"John. It would appear most of them are just staring and moving about. Some are shouting...I can see some fists now and again, but I am not seeing guns, but I suppose that would not preclude the possibility......

....the taxi, John, has just arrived at the base of the Mount of Olives, and so...we are going to carefully proceed with the videophone up the Jericho Road...to see what is going on....."

"Be very careful Christine....

For those who have just joined us....we have put up a split screen...on the left we have a live, anonymously transmitted, feed of an event in progress on the Mount of Olives in Israel, and on the right side of your screen, we have CNN's Christine Haman live on the videophone proceeding up the Mount of Olives from its base."

"John. We are ascending the perimeter of the Mount of Olives on the Jericho Road...We cannot as yet see the entourage descending due to the great many people on the road and lining the road, John. It is really quite noisy, as you can hear...as people are calling out slogans, over and over again. I am hearing one particular slogan, quite a bit... something like *Lama Mahar*....I am not sure. And, John. We are also hearing drums in the distance—from somewhere on the Mount of Olives...what?....Oh, I'm being told...what?...I'm being told that there is *another* group of people descending the mount from another point...quite extraordinary, if that is true....

Alright, John. We are now passing by the beautiful Russian Church of St. Mary Magdalene. It's a beautiful church which includes seven golden onion domes in its roofline....

....as we make progress up the road here, we're encountering more and more shouting people....*Lama mahar*...they seem to be shouting. Oh! John! Yes. We are starting to see a block of people approaching. Yes. We see them. All the people on the road are shouting at them. And we'll just try to settle our camera and provide a description of what we are seeing. Again, a great many people are flooding into the road....It makes it a bit difficult to separate the onlookers from the entourage.......

OH! JOHN!...This is OMINOUS! INCREDIBLE! We see a figure.....the figure is riding on a white donkey. THIS, John...THIS is clearly the JEWISH PROVOCATION that Muslims have been fearing....."

"Christine. Please explain why this is provocative."

"John. It is an ancient Jewish tradition that the Jewish Messiah would enter Jerusalem in just this fashion....from the Mount of Olives....upon a white donkey. This of course was exactly the scene that Jesus performed two thousand years ago ....

And, Oh! John! I am seeing something else that is QUITE TROUBLING indeed. The person, whoever it is, John....is upholding an *ISRAELI FLAG*. Very DANGEROUS, John. Very dangerous, indeed."

"Christine. We are able to see flashes of what you are describing, but as you say, the number of people obscures the images a bit. Can you see the person? What the person looks like?....Of course we are wondering if this person is the Jonah Van Meter so many rumors have centered around the past week."

"John. We see the figure now...clothed in white, perhaps a robe. We are just going to hurry our pace upward here, through these crowds...forgive us, if the camera seems overly shaky.............

..........MY GOD.... JOHN........

It's a WOMAN!
.... John.......
The rider on the donkey.....
is
a
WOMAN!"

Madeleine Garmu Lechem Van Meter bat Yeshua v'Miryam rode past the Church of St. Mary Magdalene out into the open vision of all Jerusalem.

The pace was steady. The donkey's breaths and steps, heedful and sure. Madeleine's gaze strong and wide. Her dress, white-shining under long crimped black hair and full breasts. Her strong right arm gripped the flag of her people, who shouted *LAHMA MAHAR!!!* from the road. Behind Madeleine slowly rolled the sherut with striding Domari, Samaritan, Ethiopian, and Jewish security. The Ethiopian drums from the northern contingent sounded in the distance. Israeli Air Force helicopters buzzed over them.

"COLORS!!!"

called Madeleine with terrible strength.

Immediately behind her, a row of flags sprung upward to the heavens, and they were the flags of the Roma, of Ethiopia, and Samaria.

Across the valley, the reaction from the wall at the Muslim quarter was automatic. A great din of noise and jeer wafted over the Kidron Valley. And they marched on.

Not far away, Tewahido made his call to the northern contingent descending on the other road.

"COLORS!!!"

Immediately, behind Tewahido, ten soldiers of *The Bread House* raised their flags.

And the flags were of:

Jamaica
Honduras
Ireland
Scotland
Brittany
Wales
Cornwall
Manipur
Mizoram

And there was a tenth flag. A small Melungeon boy carried a colonial American flag with thirteen stars in a circle, in a field of deep blue.

On the far hill of Mt. Zion...in a cemetery, Jonah Van Meter worked feverishly with his Domari men fixing poles together. A squadron of Israeli helicopters flew over the hill toward the Mount of Olives. The noise was deafening. A tremendous cloud of dust was kicked up by the chopper blades. Not to be held up, Jonah bellowed out over the chopper thunder,

"COLORS!!!"

The Domari men strained to raise a very tall makeshift flag pole, and drop it into a pre-positioned iron pipe driven into the ground. On the pole, they hoisted a string of flags that matched Madeleine's contingent: Israeli, Roma, Ethiopian, and Samaritan.

Sara stood over a gravestone and opened the Torah Scroll upon it, rolling it to *Parshu V'eschonon.*

Across the Old City in the Christian Quarter, the bell tower pinnacle of the Lutheran Church of the Redeemer was electrified with activity. Sabeel Khouri, Wal Holloway and a half-dozen lieutenants were in emergency mode and frantically sending cell phone messages, one after another, between binocular gazes at the Mount of Olives. Because nothing had occurred the day before, they were caught by surprise. At least half of their troops, if not more, had dissipated into the vapors of a moment lost. Even so, in the wake of media coverage and just word of mouth, a good many flooded back from the Muslim Quarter onto the Temple Mount. A meaningful opposition was being mounted. And in the village of Silwan too. Last minute house-to-house rousing was being somewhat successful and Sabeel Khouri was informed that a charge up the Kidron Valley could be launched in five minutes. He was also told that Palestinian residents along the Ophel Road, just south of the Temple Mount, were massing on the road and proceeding toward the Mount of Olives.

There was a tap on the Khouri's shoulder. His assistant, Munib, ushered Khouri to the south side of the platform and pointed to the flags flying above Mt. Zion. Khouri winced. Grabbing the binoculars, he took inventory. The Israeli flag was all he needed to see. He panned back to the Mount of Olives where he also saw flags advancing, and then to the Temple Mount, where he could see more Palestinians arriving to prepare a defense. Bewildered, he remembered the question that the deceased *Order* chiefs, Carion and Pierce, had rather obliquely uttered about *which Zion?*...and how knowing the answer to that question would be crucial to understanding what was at hand. Khouri, of course, knew that the Temple Mount was the first site to be called Mt. Zion. And, as a member of the *Order*, he was well steeped in its Templar lore originating on the second Mt. Zion outside of Zion Gate. But, something was amiss. The two sites were too far away from each other for them to *both* be the point of some decisive final battle with the Jews. Things would have to come down to it in one place or the other. That had to mean: *one was a decoy*, and the other not.

Khouri peered through the binoculars at the gleaming Dome of the Rock. Although he was not Muslim, he was an Arab... and....If an Arab, then a co-inheritor of all the Arab kingdoms and their glory. The *sacred geometry* of the Dome of the Rock bespoke of that Arab glory. *Jerusalem was not Jerusalem without the Dome.* He pondered deeply for long moments, and then he came to it. *Yes. Yes,* he wryly mocked himself for being so rattled to be drawn by tricks. *Of course, The Temple Mount is Mount Zion. This is where glory resides...provided one is willing to suffer some measure at first, before the glory is won.* He was sure. He was sure that Jonah Van Meter was blowing smoke on the second Mt. Zion in some vain attempt to draw attention away from the true prize so many had shed blood for over the ages: *The Temple Mount.*

"Pastor Holloway!" Khouri summoned.

"Yes, Mr. Khouri?"

"Munib will escort you to Mt. Zion outside the walls where you see the flags. Your Jonah Van Meter is trying to confuse us even as his people descend the Mount of Olives. I want you see what trickery he is trying to accomplish. And....Pastor Holloway...."

"Yes?"

"I would like to remind you. If you come before the face of Jonah Van Meter....or any of his family....I want you to make them *remember* what misfortune they have already suffered."

"Yes. You can be sure of it, Sir," responded Wal Holloway, in the tone of an obedient soldier.

And, so. Munib and Wal Holloway departed the Church of the Redeemer and set out for the flags on the second Mt Zion. And not long after their departure, another of Mr. Khouri's assistants informed him of a media report:

The rider of the white donkey descending the Mount of Olives was *not* Jonah Van Meter, *but a woman.*

"WHAT?!!! Who is she?" demanded Khouri, in complete shock.

"Some are saying, they think she is his wife."

Sabeel Khouri was immediately terror stricken and his chest felt like a sack of falling stone.

White House Situation Room.

Bill Blanche was furious.

"You're telling me you have nothing?" Blanche parroted what he hadn't wanted to hear from his agent.

"Nada," confirmed *Comet*, from his post at the Holy Sepulcher. "I've staked this church for days, and not a trace of Van Meter. Hell, there's hardly anyone here. Everyone's headed to the Temple Mount."

"Understood...out." Blanche exhaled violently. He put through the next call while checking the monitors on the wall.

CNN was split-screening flags on the Mount of Olives and the same flags somewhere else.

Blackpoint and Kundorf entered the room as his call connected.

"*Ajax*?"

"Yeah, Bill," replied his agent at the Tomb of the Virgin at the base of the Mount of Olives.

"What are you into?"

"Well…We have a Van Meter, but not the one we were expecting…I guess you're seeing that on the tube….."

"Yeah….so is there ANY connection you're seeing between this stunt and the tomb-church…whatever-the-hell-place you've been hanging out at?"

"You know Bill….to be honest…I mean it's in the same area and all…but I'm just not picking up a vibe with this church. All the people are up on the roads coming down the Mount or on the roads coming to the Mount, but nobody is paying this damn little hole in the ground any attention. My gut is telling me it's off the mark…."

"Well, *Ajax*…I'll tell you. I believe in guts. So, describe what you see. What do I need to know?"

"Well, Bill. You need to know that it looks like a shit-fight brewing up here fast. The Arabs are all pissed off over in the Muslim Quarter and there's a nasty little mob coming up the valley from Silwan. IDF choppers are buzzing 'round and 'round the Mount and I'm seeing light armor rolling up toward us on the Ophel and Jericho Roads."

"Alright, alright. I got the picture. Stand by….out."

Blanche exhaled a heavy wind again and shoved his desk chair at the conference table where Blackpoint and Kundorf stared at the monitors in complete slack-jaw silence. The split screen showed a woman riding a donkey on the right, and a man bearing a Honduran flag on the left. Blanche bombed himself in the chair opposite Kundorf.

"Things are not turning out as you predicted, Doctor. Not at all," seethed Blanche.

Kundorf was speechless.

Blanche sat there staring burn holes into both Kundorf and Blackpoint for a very long moment. But then something shuffled into place in his head. Blanche nodded to himself. He stabbed the buttons on his cell again.

"Yeah. Bill Blanche. I want you to release Eduardo Mendoza and Elaine Armstrong and have them brought down here ASAP…..Yeah….that's right…."

Mount of Olives, Jerusalem.

Madeleine's donkey reached the base of the Mount of Olives on the Jericho Road where it intersected with the Ophel Road. Violent yelling emanated from Arabs upon the Old City wall framing the Temple Mount above the Kidron Valley. IDF helicopters swarmed over the valley churning clouds of dust. Sirens wailed. The Ophel Road was blocked with soldiers and their vehicles. The air was hot and acrid, filled with eye searing tear gas, waffling of helicopter blades, and diesel fumes. Only the smell of the donkey's hide rising up from its neck was familiar to Madeleine.

The northern contingent led by Tewahido also reached the base of the mount and met Madeleine's. Tewahido stood before her.

"The way not clear Madeleine. What we do?"

The plan had been to proceed south on the Ophel Road to Zion. It was blocked. A battle was erupting.

Immediately, Madeleine pointed Tewahido toward Lion's Gate—which was only 200 meters north off the Jericho Road. She would look for signs of possible help from the Dom at the gate.

With an upward thrust of her Israeli flag, Madeleine signaled Daniel and Gregorio to sound the onward march. She slap-patted the donkey, and the combined northern and southern contingents became one and proceeded north on the Jericho Road toward Lion's Gate. But as Madeleine neared the gate, she could see the myriad of angry Arabs yelling and threatening, some running out of the gate to throw stones, scaring the donkey. Madeleine caught sight of Nawar at the portal of the gate. He made a moving cross-hand gesture and shook his head *no* signaling that the Dom were way out numbered.

Madeleine stood at a literal crossroad. She scanned over the holy train behind her: *The Shipment,* the people, and the holy relics—all in the open and subject to attack, seizure, and destruction. The whole operation was in peril. She tried calling Jonah on her cell. There was no answer. She held the cell up high to Nawar and made the same negative cross-hand gesture to him.

Wiping her stinging running eyes and nostrils, Madeleine spied the fortress of the Rockefeller Museum 400 meters up the Jericho Road. The road was clear save for some IDF vehicles. She would have to take base at the Rockefeller—the last resort—Plan *Bet.*

Again, she jabbed the flag into the air and signaled the trumpeters to call the company forward.

Nawar ran from the Lion's Gate up the Via Dolorosa to the entrance of the Kotel tunnel leading to the plaza and the Jewish Quarter. The guards automatically admitted him. He was headed for Zion with bad news.

CNN, Atlanta.

"If you've just joined us....a confusing scene developing at the bottom of the Mount of Olives in Jerusalem. An apparent religious procession, perhaps of a messianic claimant, has stalled at the base of the mount. Israeli forces are battling to contain a sudden uprising of local Muslims angered, no doubt, by the alleged messianic marchers who have come down from the top of the mount. Scattered reports suggest that many of this group came from the nearby village of Bethany. Sources close to the Israeli Army are reporting that all possible efforts to contain the disturbance with non-lethal measures are being employed. As the Israelis attempt to control the situation, it appears the procession is struggling to make its way out of the area by proceeding north on the Jericho Road….."

Catholic Cemetery, Mt. Zion.

From the gravestone, Sara watched her father work with the Domari men as they positioned video-phones at strategic places in the cemetery. One was set near the iron gate of the cemetery's side-entrance, and another near the gravestone.

Jonah checked his cell and noticed he missed a call. It was Madeleine's. Immediately, he called her. There was no answer. He was instantly worried, but had to move. Jonah tried her again, but to no avail. He had to move and keep on schedule.

Jonah called the communications floor at the Pontifical Biblical Institute. Fortunately, the call took. In short order he worked with the Communication Staff and was able to confirm a good signal path between his videophones and the Institute. The Institute would then export the feed to The Rod Man at The Bread House….and Rodney Fridenmaker would give it to the world.

Suddenly, one of the Domari guards just outside the gate hastily called Jonah. He wanted Jonah to view a television monitor in a *House* vehicle parked on the street. Jonah was almost to the gate when a huge scuffle erupted out on the sidewalk between the Domari guards and some other men trying to enter the gate. Between the profanity and flaying arms and legs, Jonah caught sight of Wal Holloway's twisted face.

"STOP!" shouted Jonah. "Let them pass!"

Jonah backed up, allowing the entry of Wal Holloway and Munib. He instructed Sara to remain behind him at the gravestone. Jonah Van Meter and Wal Holloway stood eye to eye.

"What the hell is *THIS*, Jonah? Is *THIS* the place where you have the *BODY*?" sneered Wal as he began to walk around Jonah toward Sara and the gravestone.

Jonah strong-armed Wal casting him to the dust, his ruby studded pectoral cross stabbing him in the mouth. "You go near my daughter Wal-boy…you're gonna have a new home right here."

Wal picked himself up, brushed himself off, and resumed his taunt. "Well, Jonah. I was just thinking…This just looks like such a….*mundane* setting, as it were, for such an ambitious agenda. This is just a common graveyard with common people in it. There aren't even any fancy monuments here. I would think *ending the Christian religion* would take place with a little more pizzazz…you know…*Merovingian style.*"

Jonah sneered back. "Well…Wal-boy. You never did have much respect for the common man, now did you? And how utterly fitting that you come busting in here….for what? I'll tell you what. You seek the dead among the dead. Death itself is your bloody petty little god."

"Hah. Right. Jonah. You smug moralistic son-of-a-bitch. YOU'RE the one digging up death today. Yes. This is your grand *Day of Destruction* of a 2000 year old religion. YOU are the death monger! YOU are the *anti-christ!*"

Jonah laughed. "Day of Destruction?! Oh, no Wal-boy. Today is *Memorial Day!* It's the day when the ground of memory and the seed of life transfigure each other and then…*Voila*…you get the Harvest of First Fruits!….you really should study the Bible more….*Pastor….*"

"You're full of goddamned gibberish, Jonah!" snarled Wal.

"You haven't figured it out yet, have you Wal-boy?…."

"Figured out *what?*"

"Oh. I guess I should have told you: *Today's the Day.*"

"What….*Day?*"

"Well….you know….*THE Day,*" said Jonah.

At that very moment, over the hill from the Kotel, came the staggered strident bursts of a ram's horn.

"Do you hear the shofar, Wal-boy?

Like I said:

Today's THE DAY,"

said Jonah.

Suddenly the boy Nawar burst into the cemetery. The young man was immediately taken back by the sight of the flags waving high overhead. He had never actually seen the flag of his people, the Roma, flying anywhere—out in the open, under God's blue sky.

Nawar quickly collected himself and quietly informed Jonah of Madeleine's predicament.

Jonah grimaced, but did not panic. He ordered two of his Domari men to take Wal and Munib into custody. And Jonah whispered detailed instructions to Nawar.

The boy was to return straight to the Muslim Quarter, but not through the tunnel. He was to go straight through the Cardo and into Khan ez-Zeit to the Ethiopian compound at the Holy Sepulcher. And then head straight to the Damascus Gate on the north side of the Old City.

"GO! Quickly! charged Jonah.

The boy flew out back into the Old City.

With the shofar still reverberant in his ear, Jonah focused on saving the operation. His brain searched his memory. But he knew. He knew that the past, in itself, would not provide an answer. There comes a time when a soul must extrapolate the past toward the possible...the hopeful...the needful probabilities of the future. One must do the math. Jonah closed his eyes and paced in a circular path transfixed around Sara and Lazlo at the gravestone. He thought of everything that *had* been accomplished. But also of what remained—the *yet-to-be*. He thought of all the people, the plans, the groundwork, the money and materiel......*materiel*? He remembered. Not all the supplies had been used....some of them being, rather, contingency tools...*if need be*...

"Where's the supply bag?" Jonah called.

A Domari man responded running a large duffle bag in from one of vans parked on the street.

"It have poles and flag....did we forget one....Jonah?" asked the Domari man.

"Maybe we did forget One."

"You want me to put poles together and lift up the flag, Jonah?"

"Put the poles together....give me a minute to think about the flag."

Jonah's eyes set upon Sara's, and he went to his daughter. She held out her long dark arms and held her father tightly. Picking up the Torah scroll, they sat down together on the flat gravestone. Jonah held his daughter's hand in his left hand, and the Torah scroll within his right arm. Jonah closed his eyes. His forehead broke out into a flowing sweat. His soul floated backward in time....to a man seated in a chair, a man trembling and trying to decide a matter while others circled about, dancing glorious in their own visions of grasping a world for themselves. The Question: *Do the easy thing, or the hard thing?—The way of eternal division?....or the way of Bread...the way of Peace? Even peace with those seduced by Blood?* Jonah wished the whole question would pass away into the air. He wanted to run away from the Question. Run, and run, and run—just like his nightmare always ended—running from something hard to remember, but impossible to forget. He could not run from the Question forever. The Question had a will of its own.

Sara squeezed Jonah's hand.

Jonah opened his eyes to his Domari man standing over him with the supply bag.

"You want the flag to go up Jonah?" asked the Domari man.

"I was afraid you were going to ask me that again," said Jonah taking the flag gently into his hands....thinking. He put it back into the Domari man's hands. Jonah took the supply bag and unzipped a small compartment on the end. He withdrew another smaller flag.

"This goes with the big one......
Fly 'em."

White House Situation Room

Blackpoint, Kundorf, and Blanche sat at the round table silently scanning the television monitors on the wall. The silence was broken as guards brought Elaine and Eduardo into the room.

Blanche rose. "Here at the table. Uncuff them," He directed.

"Thank you," muttered Elaine, obviously distressed, but willing to acknowledge the small courtesy.

Eduardo remained silent. His eyes were hot with fury.

Blanche addressed Elaine and Eduardo. "Even though you are un-cuffed, this *is* an interrogation. I will be honest with you two. I know that you possess crucial information concerning today's events. Regardless of what you may believe or not believe about my intentions, I wish to avoid bloodshed….here…and there. And I am concerned that what your group has set into motion will indeed result in just that: much bloodshed. Let's not do that, shall we?....So. What do we have? On one hand, we have Madeleine Van Meter attempting to initiate some sort of religious event from the Mount of Olives. But on the other hand, we do not see Jonah Van Meter. What we *do see* is a large display of flags flying over Mt. Zion. And they are the same flags Madeleine flies. So, we should logically assume that Mt. Zion is where Jonah Van Meter is operating today. Now. We need to know exactly *where* on Mt. Zion he is. We'll find him eventually, but in interest of bringing this ill-conceived event to an early close, with as little bloodshed as possible, you need to tell us where he is, *now*."

Elaine and Eduardo remained silent. They looked at each other briefly. Blanche studied their eyes thoroughly.

Blackpoint leaned toward Kundorf. "Doctor. Something is on Mt. Zion. What is it?"

Kundorf shifted uneasily in her chair and glanced at the TV monitors trying to fashion an answer. She flustered for words and with a subtle half-shrug offered, "Well, there are no Merovingian tombs on Mt. Zion. And, Jonah Van Meter has always connected his path to the tombs of his family…."

Blanche cut her off. "I am really tired of hearing your theories about Merovingian tombs, Doctor. My guys have staked out your precious tombs for days....for what?....for nothing....that's what." Blanch was exasperated. He turned to Elaine and faced her squarely. "Alright, Dr. Armstrong. So. What IS it?....on Mt. Zion that is of interest to Jonah Van Meter?"

Perhaps the modicum of respect inspired Elaine to answer. "Jews," she said.

"*Jews?*"

"Yes. Jews. You've been poking around in tombs where there are no Jews! As the saying goes, *Why do you seek the living among the dead?!*"

"What do you mean, *Jews?*" scoffed Kundorf. "Your group has been conspiring with Gypsies and Ethiopians...and *Catholics* like you!......YOU are not JEWS!"

Eduardo cracked a smile.

Elaine threw her head back and laughed.

> "Well, no....We weren't *born* Jews,
> but we're Jews *NOW!*
> Yah Fraulein!
> Welcome to Evangelical Judaism!!!"

Eduardo laughed out loud.

Blackpoint grimaced, and slammed the table violently. "WHAT IS IT? I'm not playing fucking games! WHAT IS ON MT. ZION, DOCTOR???!!!" he screamed with fire-eyes and blood-face. Blackpoint's paranoia tipped his soul into panic. His mind's eye gazed in horror into a vision of millions of parasites—almost invisible—millions of tiny ebony mites eating away at his bloody empire.

Elaine smiled coyly, unshaken. "Well, there *is* a Jewish tomb..."

"What is it?!" demanded Blackpoint.

"Oh. Does it have to be like manna come down from heaven for you? Oh, okay. I'll spoon feed you. Duh!: It's *David's Tomb*....you know?: KING DAVID'S TOMB?!!!"

"Humph. I see," said Blackpoint standing straight up and casting a look of extreme disgust upon Kundorf. He at last concluded he had invested way too much in her.

But, Kundorf's eyes bugged out and she shook her head maniacally.

"NO! THE BITCH LIES!" the gaunt woman seethed. She sprung to her feet and went around to Elaine's side and crouched down into her face. "Yah. The bitch lies. Is that not correct, my Sweetie?...Yah! There is a *place* on Mt. Zion *called* David's Tomb, but the tomb is empty, yah. It is a symbolic tomb...for Jews who have no *real* place to pray...so they make believe! Is that not correct, my Sweetie?!...Yah...Yah!"

Elaine said nothing. Her face went blank.

Eduardo took Elaine's hand under the table.

Blanche's eyes flashed. The *Postmaster* began sorting *the mail*. Between Kundorf's clumsy handling of history and Elaine's silence, *something* was there. He retrieved a document off his desk and threw it at Kundorf.

"Whatever Jonah Van Meter is doing on Mt. Zion, has something to do with his genealogy....with at least one of the names on it. Dr. Kundorf, I want you to read-off for us the surnames of the genealogy."

Blanche slowly circled the round table, his eyes closed, his mind's gears sorting and shuffling in the air. Kundorf called out the names:

Van Meter
DuBois
Brunel
Jariot
Leroy
Joire
Blancon
Wallerund
De Croix
De Coyne

Anjou
Beaufermez
Stewart
Morgan
Schenck
Grosse
Maushund
Schindler
Eysald.....

"STOP!!!" Blanche bellowed. He stopped dead in his tracks. His eyes flipped open. The silence hung, drifting like a billion flickering particles from a car's deployed air bag one second after the crash.

"SCHINDLER?" the *Postmaster* asked. "What is this? Jonah Van Meter has a *GERMAN* wing to his family????....."

Kundorf looked askance from Blanche's piercing gaze.

"Ah.....Apparently So," she answered nervously. "I had not noticed before...these smaller cadet lines in his genealogy. It would appear....ah...that...his bloodlines are not.... *pure*. He is not pure Merovingian. These cadet lines...they are, ah...actually quite *ordinary*. Perhaps...there is...ah...some *other* very secret element to Jonah Van Meter's agenda we have not yet discerned."

"Indeed. How could that be?" huffed Blanche. Looking at Blackpoint, he goaded him. "I'm sure we're paying a lot of money for this *intelligence*?!!!"

Blackpoint only glared.

"Okay, *Doctor* Kundorf," Blanch continued. "Let's see if we can *manufacture* some intelligence here, shall we? Huh? I'll tell you one thing. Something is dropping into a slot for me on this *SCHINDLER* name....Is there a *Schindler* on Mt. Zion, Dr. Kundorf?

Blackpoint stared hard at his *intelligence* source.

Elaine's face was completely blank.

Eduardo's eyes tracked each person, one face to the next.

Kundorf's eyes suddenly went wide. Her lips slid into a sick cracking smile. "Yah...There *is* a Schindler. *Oskar Schindler*.

The one from the Holocaust movie....you know? Yah! The Jew Savior! Yah! He is buried in the Catholic cemetery on Mt. Zion. The cemetery sits on the southern side of the hill overlooking the Hinnom Valley."

Blanche dropped into a chair between Kundorf and Elaine. With his hands folded behind his head he stared into the blank low ceiling. Suddenly he said, "Uhh…Kundorf?"

"Yes. Mr. Blanche?"

"Our man in question…His first name is *Jonah*. His last name is *Van Meter*. What, praytell....is his *middle* name? What middle name did his parents give to him?"

Kundorf rabidly rifled through the pages of the genealogy, and stopped. She stared at the page for a long moment. She slowly looked up at Blanche and smiled her sick smile.

"*Oskar*," she said.

"Well, there we are. *Jonah* and *Oskar*," announced Blanche. But then he turned to Elaine with a perplexed look. "*Jews*, Dr. Armstrong? Oskar Schindler was not a *Jew*, was he?"

"Depends on how you look at things, Mr. Blanche," answered Elaine. "By the petty myth of Bloodlines and such, not even King David's mother was a Jew. Maybe being a Jew is more than Blood. Do you think?"

Eduardo spoke to his boss for the first time: "Let me give you a little intelligence advice, Billy. The genealogy. It is not about the past. It is about the *future*."

Blanche just looked at him. Without a word, Blanche called up his agents on the speaker phone. "We have Van Meter's location. He's on Mt. Zion...in the Catholic Cemetery," Blanche rattled.

"Okay, Bill," confirmed *Ajax*. "*Comet* and I are on the way. We see his flags... shouldn't be too long...I'd say 'bout ten minutes...and we'll have him cleaned out of there......"

"YOU SON OF A BITCH!!!" Eduardo exploded. "AVOID BLOODSHED, MY ASS!" Eduardo leaped across the round table landing a square punch on Blackpoint's eye.

Blanche caught Eduardo throwing him back.

Eduardo lunged at Blanche, his fists flailing, half-landing and half-deflected by Blanche's stronger frame.

Blanche pulled his service revolver which failed to stop Eduardo from bellowing: "THAT SON OF A BITCH KILLED MY FATHER THE SAME WAY!!! IS JONAH VAN METER GOING TO HAVE A CAR WRECK IN A CEMETERY, *SECRETARY* BLACKPOINT?!!!"

Blackpoint sneered a laugh, wiping a trickle of blood from his eye.

Kundorf smirked like a small demon.

Elaine's strong arms wrapped around Eduardo pulling him back to her.

"HEY! What the hell is goin' on there?" called *Ajax* through the speaker.

Guards burst into the room from the hall.

"It's okay, it's okay, it's okay," sputtered Blanche. He motioned the guards back to the hall, assuring them everything was under control.

"Bill...," called *Ajax*.

"Yeah"

"Got to tell ya somethin' Bill. We're almost up to Mt. Zion...and we...uh...we see that they just put up a new flag....."

"What is it?" shot Blanche.

"Uh...not sure you're gonna believe this..."

"WHAT is it?!!!"

"Uh...well...can you believe...STARS & STRIPES?!!!........"

Blanche looked up at the monitors. He was stunned. There it was: Red, White, & Blue, with the Ohio flag directly underneath it. Reporters were all over it.

"What do we do?" called *Ajax*.

"Blanche did not answer. He moved to the monitors. They were all focused closely on an antique American Flag with thirteen stars in a circle, waving high over Mt. Zion. His eyes burned. His head spun. Blanche meandered back to his desk and gazed at the photo of his family...his *American* wife and his *American* children—with Vietnamese eyes.

Ajax called again.

"Stand by," muttered Blanche.

Elaine studied Blanche intently. There was something familiar about the drama unfolding before her—*watching a man trying to decide something.* Suddenly. She gasped to herself.

"Mr. Blanche!" Elaine called. "What was your father's name?!"

"What?" Blanche winced, shaking his head to full consciousness.

"WHAT WAS YOUR FATHER'S NAME?" demanded Elaine.

"My father's name was Matthew. Why on earth...."

"AND WHAT WAS HIS FATHER'S NAME?"

"What the hell..."

"WAS IT LEO!????"

"Yes." Blanche was stunned. "How did you know?"

Elaine snatched up the genealogy out of Kundorf's hands and stormed to the desk with it. Rifling the pages, she found the spot and read it:

Matthew Blancon, born 1600 Pas de Calais, France

Son of Leo Blancon, born 1578 Pas de Calais, France

Son of Gillaume Blancon, born 1549 Pas de Calais

Blanche just looked at her while his brain's gears raced backwards in time.

"*Guillaume* would be French for *Billy,* now wouldn't it?" Elaine interrogated. "And *Blancon* would be French for, hmmmm, oh, I don't know...maybe *BLANCHE*—do you think!!!?" Elaine poked Blanche in the chest. "Tell me Billy. Is there a *Catherine* in your family?" She looked at the photo of Blanche's family on the desk. He looked at it.

"My daughter's middle name....is *Catherine.*" he said softly.

"YAH!" exclaimed Elaine hurling the evil eye on Kundorf. "Says here: Catherine Blancon, aka Blanchen, born Mannheim, Germany, 1627. She was the mother of Sara Dubois, the granddaughter of Cretien DuBois!!! Congratulations, Mr. Blanche.

You are a certified cousin of Jonah Van Meter!!! Welcome to the *Family*!!!" Elaine ceremoniously shook Blanche's hand.

Elaine snatched up the photo of Blanche's wife and children and thrust it before his eyes. "Like Eduardo said! The Genealogy is not about the past. IT'S ABOUT THE FUTURE!!!"

Blanche gasped for air, trembled, and shook himself. "Oh, my God," was all he said. He looked upward for an eternal moment. Suddenly, he slapped his finger on the dial button.

"Yeah, Bill."

"Stand down. REPEAT. Stand down immediately. They're ours. REPEAT. They're our people."

There was a long silence...and then, "Copy......uh, Bill?"

"Yeah."

"We think you're right. These people aren't the problem. You know...We're sick of this shit. We're sick of mother fuckers in Washington making us their personal thugs. We're supposed to be *intelligence* goddammit, not the fucking Gestapo. Tell ya the truth, Bill...I think, if you wouldn't have stood us down, we just might have stood our own goddamn selves down. We're sick of this shit. Goddammit. We're not fucking Nazis. We're *Americans*!"

Blanche nodded, looking at the picture of his family. "Well. I don't know that we've been Americans...*yet*. But we can *start* being Americans from this moment. Defend the Van Meters and their associates with all prejudice. That's an order. More for me, than for you. Godspeed. Out."

The Situation Room EXPLODED into a thunderous "YESSSSS!!!!" with piercing screeches and wails of unbelievable joy punctuated by fists beating the hell out of the round table and Elaine so enveloped her body around Eduardo it was a prophecy of their wedding night.

"MR. MENDOZA!" called Bill Blanche in a loud voice, sliding a service revolver and handcuffs to Eduardo. "Take Mr. Blackpoint into custody. I am placing him under arrest..."

"WHAT!?" screamed Ashman Blackpoint, firing demonic eye-rays into Blanche. "YOU HAVE *NO IDEA* WHO YOU

ARE FUCKING WITH! *WE* RUN THIS PLANET!" he bellowed, pointing his index finger to his own chest.

Blanche kept his eyes calmly fixed on Blackpoint's. "….I am placing Mr. Blackpoint under arrest for conspiracy to commit murder….for starters. And then we'll work on *war crimes*. But for today: Let's work on:

Remembering what being American is supposed to be."

Arab Suq, Old City, Jerusalem.

The boy Nawar found Suq Khan ez-Zeit untypically quiet for mid-day. His trotting steps echoed through the ancient stone archways. Many shops were closed as most the neighborhood had headed for the Temple Mount or the Damascus Gate where word was: The Jews were approaching there.

Nawar skipped up the stairs from Khan ez-Zeit to the Ethiopian compound on the roof of the Holy Sepulcher. Entering the courtyard, he immediately found his friend Mikhail who was playing with his friend Isaac.

"Follow me!" cried Nawar urgently.

Mikhail and Isaac immediately followed Nawar down into Khan ez-Zeit. As they quickly trotted toward the Damascus Gate, Nawar explained to his friends the nature of their mission, which he had complete faith they would accept.

When the boys reached the end of Khan ez-Zeit where also Suq Al-Wad ends, they found a great throng of Arabs in the open area before the Damascus Gate. The people were clumped tightly together as they needled their way through the narrow gate to the outer courtyard. Many also were climbing up to the gate ramparts and looking out with jeers and pointing fingers toward the advancing Jews.

The boys fanned out evenly before the gate inside the wall. And they called in the loudest little-boy voices they could muster. To the ramparts they shouted in Arabic:

"THE JEWS! THE JEWS!

THE JEWS ARE ATTACKING *AL-HARAM AL-SHARIF!!!"*

They screamed the message over and over again with great histrionics native to boys who only *play* at war—who fall, and rise again, only to return home to their mothers.

It did not take long. Floods of *the angered* streamed back through the gate and down from the ramparts into the tunneled *suq*. They ran to do battle with that which they truly did not know.

Rockefeller Museum, Jerusalem.

Patting the donkey on his neck, Madeleine rounded the northeast corner of the Old City. There, the fortress-like Rockefeller Museum sat as a waiting refuge. The museum's staff was already out front beckoning Madeleine's column into the grounds.

Instantly, her heart was pierced by inner conflict. She was relieved for her people to arrive at base safely. But it was hard to leave the road.

Madeleine dismounted the donkey and stood frozen in the middle of Sultan Suleiman Road. She stared blankly at the Rockefeller staff waving her in. She gazed out at the road rising sharply before her. It appeared strangely quiet and *open*. Her hand fell gently upon her belly and she remembered Danny, not with her. She began to cry. It sunk into her that for as long as the operation seemed possible...that a Day of Peace Remembered was still possible...in some magical way, she was still pregnant. Her tears flowed bitterly and fell into the dusty hot street. She called out for Jonah, for Sara, for God,

Eloi...Eloi...Lahma sabach thani?

At that very moment Tewahido came to Madeleine. With his gentle black hand he wiped the tears from her eyes. The velvet cover of his headdress lay on the ground, the stone of the Torah exposed to the sun. As her eyes cleared, Madeleine saw the two young boys, Nawar and Mikhail, standing at Tewahido's side.

"Madeleine, these are my friends. They have come to take the Torah and hide it, so that it will not be lost. Would you give blessing?"

Madeleine nodded tearfully.

Baruch atah Adonai Elohaynu melech ha'olam hamotzi lechem min ha'aretz.

The boys lifted up the stone and covered it. In a light-glint they were gone across the street, through the Damascus Gate, and into the *suq*.

In tears Madeleine fell upon Tewahido's embrace.

"I am so sorry Tewahido. I am so sorry," she cried. Madeleine gazed back up the road toward the magnificent façade of the Damascus Gate. But, something else caught her eye. Through the staggered stones of the Old City wall ramparts, a long dark graceful hand flickered, waving and beckoning upon the joyous hops of boyish feet. Tewahido also turned his eyes upward to the small hand flowing above the ramparts like a small conductor of an unseen band.

Tewahido laughed.

And his laugh broke a smile of wonderment to Madeleine's face.

"I think we have another friend, Madeleine. And look! He is happy! See how he is laughing?!"

Madeleine laughed. "He does look happy! Such a little boy! It looks like he is waving to us!"

"I think he is saying *Follow me*," said Tewahido.

Madeleine laughed and cried at the same time. She spun herself around and looked upon the *band of Israel—The Bread of Tomorrow* behind her…waiting on her. She clutched her belly. *Maybe I AM pregnant.* Once more, she looked at the small laughing boy beckoning from the ramparts. And that was it.

Madeleine Garmu Lechem Van Meter bat Yeshua v'Miryam gritted her teeth and commanded the silver trumpets to sound. She shouted "LAHMA MAHAR!" and *Israel* shouted "LAHMA MAHAR!!!"

The column lurched forward, drums beating, banners flying—in the same air as a laughing child's hand...pointing the way.

The Bread House, Bexley, Ohio.

"Anything?" asked Geoffrey Sinclair hovering over The Rod Man and Will Aaronson. Both shook their heads "No."

Suddenly, Will hopped violently in his chair clutching his headset. "WHAT?!!!"

The Rod Man grunted an extremely loud squeal.

"What is it?!!!" cried Sinclair.

"WHOOO-HOOOO-HOOOO!...cried Will. "THEY WENT ON!!!"

"They went on?! They went on *WHERE*?!" yelled Sinclair.

"They went ON!!!—past the Rockefeller!!! They're on their way to *JAFFA GATE*!" yelled Will.

Sinclair's eyes flashed, and he laughed. "Makes sense to me! ALRIGHT PEOPLE! We're GO, GO, GO!!!!...Rod Man! Quick! I want you to get the yeshiva feed hooked up. Will. I want you to get with PBI...they'll be able to pick up Maddie and the crew as they come 'round the mountain, huh?!!! YEAH!!! LET'S GO, PEOPLE. LET'S ROLL!!!"

SPECIAL REPORT, CNN, Atlanta.

"John Josephs, live at CNN studios in Atlanta with continuing breaking news of today's events in Israel.

Reports are coming in, as I speak, of mass confusion in the area of the Temple Mount in Jerusalem. We have with us, in our studio, Rabbi Tzapperstein, a noted expert of Jewish religious and political affairs, to help us interpret some of today's events. But first, let's go live to Christine Haman, on the videophone, somewhere near the Temple Mount in Jerusalem. Christine?

"John. Indeed, a most confusing scene that we are witnessing here in Jerusalem. Much of the Muslim Quarter inhabitants had been drawn to the north side of the Old City. It was there that Jewish marchers had taken route due to their being blocked from entering the Old City because of skirmishes between local Arabs and the IDF at base of the Mount of Olives. I am hearing now, John, from many Arab people on the street, that about ten minutes ago, a report went out that JEWS, as we speak, are IN PROCESS OF ATTACKING THE TEMPLE MOUNT in order to regain Jewish control over that holy site. The anger and panic in the streets is absolutely palpable, John. As you can see, hundreds are rushing to the Mount in order to defend it. The consensus on the street seems to be that the Jewish marchers, which made such a display today coming down the Mount of Olives, was a decoy maneuver—a cover, if you will, for an unfettered Israeli assault on the Temple Mount. I, myself, am in transit to the Temple Mount. My guide, Mitri, assures me that I will be allowed entry as a journalist. We will attempt to relay more details as soon as we are able, John."

"Thank you Christine Haman. We will certainly be standing by for your further report.

Turning now to Rabbi Tzapperstein in our studio. Welcome Rabbi."

"Thank you for having me, John."

"Rabbi, what do you, as a Jewish leader, make of today's events and the possibility that Israel is mounting an attack of the Temple Mount, apparently as we speak? Are we witnessing the beginning of a cataclysmic war?....perhaps something like the famed *Armageddon* in biblical prophecy?"

"Hold on John. Hold on! I certainly cannot explain all these events today, but apparently we shall see soon enough....But frankly, John, I say to you and your listening audience: *Have a little faith.* Let me say this: Jews, in complete contrast to their current undeserved press, are not *Nazis*. And frankly, it's getting extremely tiresome, typical, and predictable that Jews are being castigated this way...."

"So Rabbi, are you saying that many are jumping to conclusions on anti-semitic grounds?"

"Yes. And ignorance. You know John, the truth is that all too often, the most that many non-Jews ever hear about Jews is in the context of bigotry with a political agenda. Jews are a very small minority in most places. When you don't know any Jews personally, too often there's the pull to accept stories—false stories about Jews. The false stories are a poor substitute for real and personal knowledge. ..."

Well Rabbi, as an African-American, I certainly can identify with that. Personally, I grew up in a neighborhood with very few minorities. So, for as little as our neighborhood had in the number of African-Americans, there would have been even fewer Jews. In truth, I cannot recall ever encountering any Jewish people in all my youth. It was not until I moved away from home and went to college that I ever met a Jewish person."

"Exactly, John. We need to talk with each other directly and not just listen to stories. That's what we've learned, hopefully, in America. In our best moments, we Americans know that *we're all Americans*. We have different ethnic and religious backgrounds, but we're all Americans. It's not rocket science for us....we understand it intellectually. But, we really, really just have to BELIEVE IN IT enough to actually DO it!!!....and just not here in America, but throughout the whole world. We, just have to get to the place where we can actually BELIEVE in a common humanity...and act on it. So, I say again John: We have to have a little faith....."

Bread House, Bexley, Ohio.

"...yeshiva Kotel video feed hook-up! Three....two....One! Export feed!"

CNN, Atlanta.

....."What?!! I have word that we are receiving another anonymous feed, live, from Jerusalem.......Okay. We have that feed."

"If you've just joined us, we are looking, live, at images from Jerusalem being anonymously submitted to us......
........Well. This is, I must say, extraordinary. Not at all what we expected. Rabbi Tzapperstein, what are we seeing here?"
".....Oh, My God.....John...Oh, My God.....THIS IS ABSOLUTELY STUNNING. I'll tell you...in terms of what I said earlier about having faith....THIS....this just pushes that concept of FAITH to the MAX!...
.....LOOK at what we are seeing in the Kotel plaza! Just LOOK at it! There is NO attack! There is NO sound of war! As you can see, John, the plaza is completely EMPTY except for three men!!!....
....let's see if we can make out who these men are...the camera seems to be focusing in...certainly Jewish, by their dress...I see *tallitot* and *kippot*.....
.....Oh, My God! UNBELIEVABLE! THAT is the Prime Minister of the State of Israel!!!...AND, he is with the Chief Ashkenazi Rabbi, AND the Chief Sephardic Rabbi of Israel!!!...My God, John!!! The Prime Minister is at the flag pole which stands over the Kotel—the pole that flies the Israeli flag over the plaza every day! John, he is taking the flag *DOWN!* He's detached it from its ropes and he kisses it....and wraps it around his body like a prayer shawl! And they are leaving the plaza John! They are climbing the steps going up into the Jewish Quarter! And look! The Israeli guards, John....at the checkpoint entrances to the plaza....they are turning...and they too, John, are leaving! *THEY ARE LEAVING!* Oh, My God. THEY ARE LEAVING! Oh, My God, John! The Israelis have not ATTACKED the Temple Mount! They have just GIVEN it to the Muslims!!!!......"

Pontifical Biblical Institute, Jerusalem.

"HO!"

"OH!"

"Here they Come! Here they Come! HERE THEY COME!"

The top floor of the Institute exploded into applause as the small white donkey rounded the northwest corner of the Old City.

At a slow and sturdy pace, the woman rode straight and up-right bearing the Israeli banner for a new world soon to be born. And behind her, the banners of the nations, the gold of the relics, and the white sherut flashed in a clear day sun. The people of the City poured out upon the road running, yelling, singing, and dancing along on the clear way to Jaffa Gate, also known as *The Gate of the Friend.*

And with great and thunderous jubilation they entered the Old City through the wide pass of the Gate, made by a kaiser who ruled only for a time.

And many sent up their shouts of *"LAHMA MAHAR!!!"* to the calls of the trumpets and the *shofar.*

An old couple hurried out of their old imperial hotel into the crowded gate plaza. In many and various ways, they had heard of old how it could be, but now in these days, they saw the glo-ries of peace passing right before them.

And Madeleine kissed the neck of the little donkey happy to trot quick.

They marched down the road of the Armenians leading to the next—and last gate: *Zion Gate.* And the people of that neighbor-hood, no strangers to tears, sent their men and boys to that *last gate.* With good directions and sharp eyes, the squad helped ease *Israel* through the turn of the *Gate.* And the bullet holes in stone, on the entry of the Gate, they left behind. For, they were on *Zion.*

Suq Khan Ez-Zeit.

Across the Old City two little boys hauled a heavy stone up the steps from the deserted *suq*. Laughing all the way, they carried the stone to the chapel of their people and there hid it under the stone floor of the altar. Covering the place with a rich rug, they shook hands with each other and laughed. Above the altar hung a curious painting depicting the ancient days when Ethiopia first received the stone. Also depicted in the painting were Hasidic Jews dressed in black, looking on. Of course, Jews did not dress that way in those days.

The Bread House, Bexley, Ohio.

Will called, "Three.….Two.….One…*ZION!!!*"

Catholic Cemetery, Mt. Zion, Jerusalem.

Madeleine rode through the archway at the west side of the cemetery with her *House* and its relics.

Jonah did not take hold of his wife, for it was not yet time.

The white sherut pulled up out on the street.

While Lazlo remained at the gravestone, Sara joined her mother at the archway.

All souls faced the sherut.

Domari men in crisp black suits came round to open the sliding side-panel door.

The late afternoon sun, though receding, was still strong over the west and glared in the eyes of all those gathered.

Out of the sherut, the Dom lifted a shrouded figure. The shroud, a black-stripe *tallit*, rustled slightly in an eastern breeze. Black umbrellas were unfolded above the figure to shield from the still strong sun. The Dom rolled the figure through the archway, stopped, and then removed the *tallit*….

Lechem

L'Chaim

"Shalom," said the old man.

His pearl-slate eyes clear, Yeshua sat squarely in the wheel chair, his gnarled hands gripping the side handles.

His skin was translucent in silverish-greys and browns revealing many vessels beneath and emanating a certain shine that only time can show forth. Dressed simply: a Jew. Black kippah, white frizzed side-locks, plain white shirt with blue sweater vest, plain black pants, sandals, and upon his forehead: the other original leather *tefila*— the mate to the one thrown into a boat two thousand years ago at Jaffa.

All was silent in the cemetery.

All was silent throughout *The Bread House*.

All was silent in the air.

CNN, Atlanta.

"Rabbi, what are we seeing here?"
"John, my son. All I can say is:

IF it were possible for a man to live two thousand years,
I think *THIS* is what it would look like."

Zion, Israel.

Madeleine stepped forward. She spoke in Hebrew. "*Shalom, Avinu Yeshua. I am Miryam.*"
Sara stepped forward."*Shalom, Avinu Yeshua. I am Sara.*"
Yeshua raised his hands and scarred forearms to them.
And they knelt to the chair to embrace their father.
Yeshua took his daughter Sara's reaching arms to his.
"Abba," she said.
And he wept.

As the western sun lowered beyond the City, its ripened radiance fell upon the stone of Jerusalem arraying all the City and the cemetery under a haze of golden light.

The prophet Jonah, standing a way off, said, "Surely this man is a son of man."

The time had come for the Aliyah to the Torah which was set on a small table above the stone of Oskar Schindler. They wheeled Yeshua to the side of the stone. And he looked at it. Raising his eyes to all those gathered, he raised also his finger to point at the stone, and he said in Hebrew,

"He Remembered,"

and nodded his head and said,

"A-mein."

Sara stood at the Torah table. To the right of the table stood Madeleine wearing her *tefila* and on the left Jonah in his *tallit*.

Sara took the blue fringe from the *tallit* of Yeshua and also from Jonah's, and in her hands she joined the fringes of their garments touching them to the scroll held open by Madeleine and Jonah.

Sara chanted: *"Barechu et Adonai hamevorach."*

The people responded: *"Baruch Adonai ha'mevorach le-olam va'ed."*

Sara chanted: *"Baruch atah Adonai elohaynu melech ha'olam asher bachar banu mikol ha'amim ve'natan lanu et torato. Baruch atah Adonai notayn ha-Torah."*

Then it was time for Sara to chant the Torah. First, she took up a rock from the ground and then she began:

"Shema Yisrael Adonai Elohaynu Adonai...."

Before chanting the last word, Sara joined her hand to Yeshua's, and they both placed the rock upon the stone of Oskar

Schindler, and they sung out together the last word, destined to become the first, the word:

"ECHAD"

which in the Hebrew tongue means

"One."

Applause broke out. Rolling slowly, and then like thunder, it billowed out over the City and overwhelmed its valleys.

Yeshua raised a finger and to him came Aaron, the friend of the prophet Jonah. Aaron brought an ancient leather bag to Yeshua. And from the bag, Yeshua took bread. He said the blessing and gave the bread to the People. In the same way, he told Aaron to take the bread from the golden table and give that also to the People. And he did so.

And then most wondrous. Yeshua ben Yosef, his arms shaking a little, held bread aloft for all to see. And in a strong voice, he spoke in the English tongue, with the sound of One who had studied and practiced in order to learn:

"Re-Member Shalom!

Re-Member Shalom!

Re-Member Shalom!"

called Yeshua.

And out over the silence of the People, a baby cried.

Yeshua's eyes went wide, and a broad smile broke out upon his shining face. And they brought to him the child to hold. Through Aaron, Yeshua asked the name of the dark skin boy and what nation he was from. And through Aaron, they answered to him that the boy's name was *Adam Oskar Romero Jacobs* from the nation of *Honduras*.

Yeshua nodded.

And while the baby yet cried, his mother Rebekah, a friend of the prophet Jonah, said that she was sorry because the baby's milk bottle was not working, and the child was hungry. This also was explained to Yeshua through Aaron.

Yeshua nodded and gave the child back to his mother. He then again asked for his bag. Out of the bag Yeshua removed a very old cup. And into the cup was poured the milk and given to the mother for the child.

And the prophet Jonah laughed greatly.

But a man who did not laugh stepped forward. Around his neck, he wore a beautiful cross with a ruby gem. His face was very troubled.

"Are you the Messiah?" called the man.

This question was translated to Yeshua by Aaron.

Yeshua smiled, but made no answer. He pointed to the man's ruby cross and held his hand open for it to be given to him.

The man gave the cross over to Yeshua. And Yeshua gave it to Aaron. Immediately, Aaron plucked the ruby gem from the cross with a small knife, and then he hurled the knife over the wall of the cemetery into the Valley of Hinnom. Aaron then returned the ruby gem to the man, and told him to sell it, and give the money to the poor.

Yeshua took again the cross with no ruby gem and laid it upon the *tziyun* stone of Oskar Schindler. With his ancient finger, he pointed upward to the flag of Israel flying above, and then told Aaron what to say:

"Yeshua say: *The cross is under the Star of Redemption.*"

"But THAT does not answer my question!" exclaimed the man. "WHO is the Messiah!?" Pointing to Madeleine he cried, "Is this woman the Messiah!?" Pointing to Jonah he cried, "Is this man the Messiah!?"

Yeshua smiled gently. He muttered "*mashiach*" lowly to himself with a small laugh. Taking a rock from the stone of Oskar Schindler, he held it for a moment looking at it.

The baby cried again. Yeshua gave another small laugh and said "*mashiach?*" Letting go of the rock, he took bread, and blessed it. He gave it to Aaron for the child, Adam.

Again the man who had worn the ruby cross called sternly,

WHO IS THE MESSIAH???

The child Adam ate the bread.

Yeshua again laughed "*mashiach*" lowly to himself. He then turned to Aaron and spoke some words with him.

And then Aaron said to the man who no longer wore the ruby cross: "Yeshua say: It is very good question: *Who Is Messiah?*

Yeshua say:

Are you?"

And many in the world who saw these things felt a strong memory come to them:

The memory of life.

The holy man of Tibet laughed.

A bishop in Rome accepted a new way.

A trader of oil in the west remained in disbelief.

And Rodney Fridenmaker stood from his wheelchair and walked.

In the cemetery, death gave way to life and the People danced in circles to the music of fiddle and flute. There were people of all nations and colors. There were Roma and Ethiopians. There were Maria, Marta, and Lazlo. There were Faith and Destiny.

The hour was becoming late and Yeshua took Madeleine and Sara into his arms to kiss them. And Yeshua noticed a strange object at the waist of Sara and he inquired of it through Aaron.

Sara laughed and said that it was a *keychain.* It bore a picture of a strange man named *Brutus Buckeye* from a large school in the land of Ohio where all the people called themselves *Buck-eyes*.

"I'm a Buckeye!" exclaimed Sara.

It took some time for Aaron to explain these things to Ye-shua, but then Yeshua laughed and tried to say the word *Buckeye*, and he spoke again to Aaron.

Then said Aaron to Sara: "Yeshua say: Of all things, you call yourself after *tree-nut*."

And they all laughed.

And Sara gave to Yeshua her *keychain*. He was most pleased as he grasped the strange object. And Yeshua again asked for the leather bag and from it, he gave Sara his cup.

Yeshua held up his hand. "Shalom, Sara *boch chai*," he said smiling grandly.

"Shalom, Avinu Yeshua!" cried Sara. And she kissed him.

[1]And in those days, Yeshua ben Yosef
showed to the chief teachers and rulers
of the synagogues the place where their
father David was laid. This was near
the City of David not far from
the second Mount of Zion. [2]In that
place they determined to build a New
Temple upon a New Zion. And they
set its reign for a time far exceeding
a thousand years. [3]And so also in
those days, the Prophet departed the
City of Peace and set his face
unto
Nineveh.

"Greycelt Man"

Greycelt man sits on the knee of a hill
Sets his face to the pearl slate sky
And marks how the ravens cry.
Greycelt man goes down to level ground
And then goes to field all day long
All day long.
When sundown comes,
Greycelt man goes his way
Greycelt man, he
Goes home.
And when he crosses his threshold,
Greycelt man, he
Fades to stone.